AN
EMPRESS
— OF —
FIRE & STEEL

by Noelle Rayne

By Noelle Rayne

First Paperback Edition September 2022
First Hardback Edition September 2022
First eBook Edition September 2022

ISBN: 978-1-9196109-3-1 (Paperback)
ISBN: 978-1-9196109-4-8 (Hardback)
ISBN: 978-1-9196109-5-5 (eBook)

www.NoelleRayne.com

A dedication

To the person who doesn't feel seen, I see you. To the person who must hide all of the elements that make them sparkle, please do not hide your magic from anyone. To the person who fears that they are different, live in your truth. Be unapologetically yourself. I think you are brave and beautiful.
With love—House Rayne.

CALEDORNA

Mountains of the [...]

The Waterfall of Uttara

[...]elmsdale City

The Fairlands

Huntswood City

Ashdale Forest

The River of Vanadey

The Temple of the Gods

The Lake of Rhiannon

SKYELIR

orth

Tolsah Bay

The Broken Sea of Thorin

lden Dimond Mine

Mossgrave

N

W   E

S

PROLOGUE
EMARA

Frost lay thick on the crisp grass that stretched out for miles as Emara made her way over to a small headstone, her black cloak attempting to warm every part of her that she couldn't feel. The grey sky overhead promised to release the gathering snow as she put one foot in front of the other, trying to move forwards. Trying to do anything but break.

Naya Blacksteel put a small hand across the middle of her back, guiding her on towards the grave, doing anything she could to suppress the emotions of Emara's heart that threatened to tear the world apart.

"Deep breaths," Naya coached, knowing what Emara was capable of should she lose control. She had witnessed first-hand how untamed her flames had been, how the element of air had aided to fuel the flames that wiped out a ballroom. "You can do this, my love."

The earth that had been disturbed by digging lay solid and lifeless atop the burial place like a small mountain top. As Emara took steps forward, she felt like she was looking down on herself from afar, like her soul was being pulled from her body; although the frosty air nipped at her skin, she wasn't numb by the cold. It was what lay in her heart that made her feel frozen. The ice of her grief had dulled every cell of her body on the inside, and she was barely holding it together on the outside.

Finally, she stood rigid above the grave, not truly looking at it. Her eyes searched the world around her to find anything to make this feel like it was a dream, like a creature or a strange being hiding in the trees of the forest surrounding them to let her know this was only a nightmare.

This wasn't real.

"My boys made sure the stone bore her name," Naya spoke from further behind, her voice sounding small and low in the clearing. "You can come here any time. It is the centre point between Mossgrave, the Fairlands, and the Huntswood Tower." She paused. "Gideon requested a beautiful meadow for her body to be laid to rest in to represent who she was. He said you would like that. You cannot see the meadow now because of Mother God's frost, but when the land warms, you will see how incredibly beautiful it is. Just like her."

"Thank you," Emara said quickly, her voice rough and almost intangible. She didn't really know if she ever wanted to come back here, but she supposed it was an option to know that she could. If she returned in the spring or summer, her best friend's grave would be surrounded by the magic of life; pink daisies and sun-yellow buttercups, spring birds in their nests, and wild mushrooms growing from the earth. The trees would be in full bloom, and the leaves would be waving in the gentle breeze.

Not like it was now, frozen and thorny.

Emara had never seen the grave of a family member, not even her grandmother or her parents before that.

So this was a first.

"I will leave you for however long you want," Naya said softly. "I promise I won't be too far. This area is known for its vibrant winter berries, and I will just be along the forest ground hunting for them." There was a silence after Naya Blacksteel spoke that made Emara's eyes water. "I think you need some time alone. Speak to her, Emara, she will hear. They always do."

Emara nodded without taking her eyes from the frozen burial ground, reading over and over the name carved into the limestone that crowned the gravestone.

Callyn Agnes Greymore.

Trying to push her mind so that it connected to the Otherside, she searched for her own abilities in spirit magic, trying to hear Cally's voice one last time. Emara waited for something to happen, for her to at least feel her presence around her. She wanted to feel her light, feel anything.

Waiting a few more moments so that she was really alone, she looked up to the sky and cursed, a sting in her nose, her throat thick. The clouds bundled together overhead, and the darkest, soul-ripping truth of her reality stabbed into her heart like a knife, carving down the middle of her chest entirely.

This was real.

Callyn—her Cally—was gone.

Emara's knees hit the ground, and as the sharp pain struck up her bones, she begged the Gods or anyone that would listen to bring her back. As her hands hit the soil where her best friend was buried, she begged them to wake her up from this terrible nightmare. She asked them to take her instead of Callyn. Instead of the light, they should take her dark. She pleaded for them to grant her strength to stand and to stop the tears from falling from her eyes. She begged for the ache in her broken heart to subside just a little.

But they ignored her.

As she lay against the iced ground, sobbing, Emara felt like the light in her life had been snuffed out. She didn't know if she would ever get it back.

CHAPTER ONE
TORIN

The flames of the cottage fire entranced Torin Blacksteel's exhausted eyes. He hadn't been getting much sleep recently. Not much at all. Lifting a green and silver chalice to his lips, he tipped his head back and let his mother's home-brewed wine slide down his throat. Normally, he liked to savour his liquor, to let the spices from his favourite rum sink into the tissues of his mouth, but he wasn't in the mood to experience that. Nor was he in a city that would sell that kind of liquor. As resourceful as he was, he couldn't pluck expensive rum out of thin air.

Torin and his brothers were still residing at his mother's cottage in the Fairlands and had been since the attack on the Uplift five days ago.

He hadn't had so much as a fireletter from his father.

Not a peep. Nothing. Zero.

A strange unease shifted in his gut.

He hadn't been called back to the tower on official duty, and neither had his brothers. Ordinarily, if he hadn't been located at the tower for more than a day, word would be sent out to any tavern in the city to find him. Someone—usually Marcus or Gideon—would call him back to his duty, finding him quickly and efficiently, but nothing had come to request their return.

Drawing in his cheeks with a breath, he rubbed a hand over his jaw. It had been *five days* of silence. Well, he wouldn't exactly call it silence. Inside his mind had been utter anarchy as he tried to fit the pieces of the Uplift together, trying to find some sensible solution to the madness that had unfolded.

Torin had yet to be successful with that mission.

He got up from the plush chair carefully, trying not to disturb Kellen dozing on the sofa opposite him, and strode to the cabinet for more home-brewed wine. He had to admit, it wasn't a *La Luna* rum and sugar spice, but it did manage to take the edge off some of the demons in his head. They were restless, sinking their teeth into every thought his mind leaked.

Regardless of how much wine he consumed, he wouldn't sleep, not while the puzzle of what happened at the Uplift lay incomplete in his mind. He couldn't relax until it made some kind of sense.

The swirling reflection of Emara's face and the darkness of her eyes that night haunted him even more when he was alone with his own thoughts. How she had sobbed. How she had raged. How she had fought and wielded not only her magic, but a weapon too.

He took another sip of wine and his thumb trailed over the stem of the chalice.

Gideon was taking his turn keeping watch over the cottage, making sure no one discovered Emara's whereabouts. Even though he'd insisted on taking the night shift, Torin hadn't argued. It would allow his brother time to clear his mind in the quiet of the forest night. And it also meant they weren't in the same room as each other.

Because you are my brother. And because I am in love with her. Because I need to know that you can lie next to her every single night for the rest of your life and give her your whole heart. Because I can. If you can, then I will walk away. But if you can't promise me to give her everything, then I will fight for her.

His throat tightened as the memory of the last conversation Torin had had with Gideon floated through his mind. He let out a sigh. Declaring Emara betrothed to him in front of the magic community—in front of his brother, who loved her—might have been a last resort to save her life, but he wouldn't take it back, even if it had hurt Gideon. Because it was the truth, and it meant that the clan would have protected her should shit have gone sideways. His clan would always protect a woman who was linked to a brethren in an alliance. Especially the second-in-command, who would one day be commander.

However, he would maybe have to handle Emara's emotions with a little more care than he had his brother's. She was vulnerable and hurting right now. She didn't need the burden of a fucking marriage alliance.

Pouring the ruby-coloured wine into his chalice, Torin stood for a moment, his muscles tense.

What annoyed him the most was that a human had

been at the forefront of the destruction caused at the Uplift.

A human.

He might have been an elite human, but he was *a human,* nonetheless. With no training in combat or magic, Taymir Solden had managed to sever the protective magical wards that surrounded any hunting or witching property to get into the Uplift. He had commanded a small army of demons to destroy everything, and he had managed to kill three of the most powerful witches in the Kingdom of Caledorna.

He'd even out-bartered the Hunters in the negotiation to take Emara.

Elite-born were often good negotiators and well-educated, but they didn't bear any magic or power that could properly influence a full room. The biggest power they held was the amount of coin they controlled, making profits off their labourers and the sales of their raw materials. They didn't tend to take centre stage in the magic world.

But Taymir Solden had.

Taymir Solden, the elite heir of the coal and diamond industry across Caledorna, had revealed that he was working on behalf of the God of Darkness. He had implied that in return for delivering Emara Clearwater to the Underworld, he would be given immortality as a reward. He had been promised by *someone* that he would be granted the power of immortality.

But by whom?

Torin wasn't convinced that that was the truth. Taymir was too insignificant to be approached by the real Dark God, Veles, or his direct disciples. So who was he actually working for?

Torin swirled the wine around the chalice, wishing it were rum in a crystal glass as he considered the pieces of evidence he *did* have.

Taymir being promised immortality meant one thing—the lore was true. Meaning, Veles had obtained the Immortality Stone and was using it to strengthen his army, using it to ensure that the darkness remained very much alive.

His next sip of wine escalated into a mouthful.

The *King* of the Underworld had at least one of the stones which could free him of his cage, unleashing him upon the world above. The world Torin had taken an oath to protect. The problem was, he didn't know how many of the ancient stones the Dark God had attained during his army's pillages over millennia.

Could the Immortality Stone be the only one that he had?

At least Torin knew one thing for sure: the God of Darkness didn't have the Resurrection Stone. Viktir Blacksteel did. And the Blacksteel Clan would be protecting it from now on. However, if Taymir was working for the Dark Army, then why had he chosen Emara over the ancient relic that could aid Veles' freedom?

Yes, she was from a witching bloodline, one that had been powerful throughout millennia, but what did she have to do with the King of the Underworld's schemes and plots to demolish a kingdom and raise the Underworld? Why her?

These types of questions had eaten Torin Blacksteel alive for days.

It didn't make sense. None of it did. There had to be another piece of the puzzle that he was missing. To whomever Taymir was working for, it seemed that Emara Clearwater was more important than a relic that would potentially see the destruction of the world as they knew it.

Interesting.

But who was the elite working for? Surely, it wasn't the Minister of Coin, Taymir's human faction leader. Although, greed and destruction did go hand in hand with the elite, so that was a possibility,

Torin tapped his finger against the chalice.

Taymir had evidently been out of his depth, a mere puppet on strings. Torin was certain someone else had been pulling the strings in his little performance at the manor. And his bets were now on the Minister of Coin. It had to be. But for what reason? What did he gain? Did the human prime member fancy living forever too? How much wealth could be obtained over several lifetimes?

He let out a sigh and drank the rest of his wine.

It was a fucking entanglement. And Torin knew he hadn't touched the surface.

Just as he placed the chalice down onto his mother's wooden table, the screaming began.

Just like it had every night since they had gotten here.

He moved faster than the wind to the spare room. Pulling the door open, it took his eyes a matter of seconds to adjust to the darkness of the room. Fractured moonlight seeped through the window, highlighting where she lay. Another scream left her throat and Torin winced at the sound. Not many sounds made him shudder, but for some reason, Emara's screams did. The sounds she had made the night of the Uplift had been the worst sounds he had ever heard. He still heard them every time he shut his eyes. He saw her face, the blood, and the chaos building around her. He saw the fire, the running, the demons attacking. The sounds of clashing steel and the dying haunted him.

She cried out again, her arms tangling in her wild inky-black hair.

Two quick strides had him across the small room, and he found himself on the edge of the bed, not getting too close.

"Emara, wake up. It's not real."

She thrashed against the fur and wool rugs that had been layered on top of her to keep out the chill of winter.

"Emara, I am here. Listen to my voice, I am here. It's not real," he said with a soft authority as he leaned over and placed his large hand to her cheek. "Emara..."

Her eyes batted open, and her body stiffened as the lucidity of her dreams turned into reality. A sob consumed her.

"Don't cry, please," he begged, almost breaking restraint. He wanted to pick her up, to hold her in his arms. Was that crossing the line? Would it knock down the wall she had built around herself? He didn't move, gripping the mattress instead. He said, "I won't let anything happen to you."

Something familiar constricted in his chest, making it harder for him to breathe. He struggled with the idea of comforting someone. He always had. He had tried several times during her recurring nightmares and through her grief to comfort her, but she had almost broken his nose as she flung out every limb she could, fighting with the pain in her heart.

And when Gideon had tried to comfort those nightmares, the whole entire cottage shook. She was clearly still not over his betrayal, so his mother had decided it would be easier to heal a nose than rebuild a full cottage, and barred Gideon from the room. Torin had told his mother to rest during the night so that she could be there for Emara at sunrise, helping her with any healing she required. That left him to make sure she got through the night.

But it was a strange thing, comfort. He hadn't always been allowed to know comfort in the process of being a warrior of Thorin. So he had always been selfish in comfort, when he could, making sure his own needs were his top priority.

This was different. She was different. It was like an urge he had never had before.

"Are you okay?" he asked, and a huskiness tickled his throat.

She didn't answer him as she lay sobbing, her full body shaking as her temperature from the trauma plummeted.

He leaned in a little. "Will you let me come closer?" he questioned, his voice not sounding like his own. When she didn't speak again, he rolled his lips hard against his teeth and ran a hand through his hair. He squared his shoulders and cracked his neck. Carefully, he pushed his large frame in beside her to give her heat. There was not enough room for both of them on the bed, but he sat for a few moments to allow her time to settle from her terrible dreams. As the minutes passed, her shaking didn't ease, and it took all of his strength to not touch her. He wanted to just pull her against him and give her all the warmth he had.

He wouldn't allow an animal to suffer this way. Could he really allow this to continue for another night? Even if he didn't normally comfort anyone, a strange pull of protection fell over him, and it almost broke his heart as she let out another sob.

For the love of Thorin, fuck it.

"Come here." His voice lay soft in the air.

Gently pulling her into his arms and onto his chest, he waited for the full impact of her elbow—or maybe it would be her fist this time—to connect with his face. But for whatever reason, tonight, she didn't kick or punch or thrash against him. She let him take her into his arms.

Her skin felt clammy against his hands, and through his hunting tunic, he could feel the cool sweat on her chest and torso. His hand felt it on her back too.

He looked down at her and something stirred in his soul at her lying in his arms. "I've got you," he said as she lay shaking against him.

The fact that one human male had done this to her made him wish he had been the one to slaughter Taymir. He wished he had been the one to ram the spear right through him—several times, of course, not just once. And he would have been sure to give him a slow, merciless death, as he wouldn't have hit any vital organs for him to quickly bleed out. Torin would have dragged it out.

Hours. Possibly days.

Emara had stabbed him with her spear before incinerating his body. The flames had come directly from the palms of her own hands, and he remembered standing in shock, watching her build a wall of fire around herself and Callyn's body on the floor. Had the terrors of that night not affected her as such, he would have congratulated her on the accuracy of her kill and the strength of her magic. He had been impressed. But her pain had been too great for her to let anyone in.

She had been so selfless and brave in those moments at the Uplift, and it was something he had admired.

He shut the thought down instantly. Admirations led to places he couldn't go.

"Same one?" was all he asked.

Emara nodded, starting to calm against him, his heat travelling to her, warming her once more.

The trauma of the Uplift and the loss of her best friend had utterly destroyed her. So much so that she couldn't even find solace in sleep. That elite bastard had destroyed that for her too.

"He can't hurt you anymore," Torin whispered, knowing it wasn't true. Although Taymir couldn't physically harm her anymore, she would never mentally get over what he had done to her. To her best friend. No one should witness someone they love having their heart ripped from their chest.

She looked up at him—without rage or anger—through lashes thick with tears. His heart almost stopped all together. Nothing but unimaginable sorrow lay within her deep black eyes, and he tensed again, not knowing how much longer he would be able to look at her like this. A dull ache in his chest reminded him of how truly helpless he felt.

Quickly, he placed the feelings of helplessness into a suppressed section in his mind and filled the void with fury. Always fury. He wanted to end anyone who gave aid to this. Anyone who played a part in this would pay for it, terribly. And Torin Blacksteel vowed that his face would be the last one they saw as they took their final breath.

He stopped his hands from scrunching into fists in front of her.

Sniffling slightly, she rolled onto her back, moving away from his arms. He instantly felt the need to pull her back in again and cradle her.

Strange.

Where she had lay on him was now cold. Empty. And he felt the first of the winter's freeze where she should have been.

Abruptly, Emara sat up fully, her nest of black hair waving and tangling down her back. Even in her hollow state, there was something agonisingly beautiful about her. Something that he had never appreciated in a woman before now.

Even if they were just friends.

His throat bobbed as he watched her. "Are you okay?"

He knew it was a stupid question, but he couldn't stop himself from speaking.

"Even though I sleep continuously, I am exhausted."

Her voice was so bleak that Torin shuddered.

Emara wrapped her arms around her legs, cradling her knees, and rested her chin on her arm. "Can you stay here until I fall asleep?"

Her voice was so tender and weak. It almost broke him. She hadn't really spoken at all since the Uplift, mostly just incoherent sobs, so to actually hear her voice again caught him off guard.

He gave himself an internal shake before answering.

"Sure," he replied, "I am not going to be falling asleep anytime soon."

She finally looked over her shoulder at him, the skin at her back exposed from the night garment his mother had dressed her in, revealing a little bruising. Even though she had fought so fearlessly, she had been hurt. Slammed across the room.

His fists tightened again, thinking of her screams, the noise she had made as she hit the marble ground as the winged demon had batted her across the room. His eyes had always been on her as he'd fought his way through the crowd to get to her.

The gown she had worn to the ball was completely destroyed, so she now wore a plain beige nightgown, borrowed from his mother. As she faced him, her eyes explored his face underneath the dim light of the moon.

But she didn't speak.

Torin swallowed, his heart rate accelerating.

When she slowly lay back down against her pillow, her hair swarming her face, he let out a long breath. Even though she *had* slept for the best part of five days, she looked depleted. The blotches on her face from crying were trying their best to settle into her skin, and she looked pale—so much paler than usual. Her glow was gone.

"Is there anything I can get for you?" Torin asked, his voice sounding croakier than before.

She shook her head against the pillow.

"There must be something." He tried to let a smile warm his face, but he knew it wasn't going to work. His face never could hide when he was angry or upset. Or feeling murderous.

"A little wine? Cheese and biscuits? I know it's late, but you can't beat a midnight snack. Especially when it involves wine."

Silence.

He tried again, this time, a little firmer. "You have barely eaten anything since you got here."

"Maybe a little water."

He turned to the nightstand beside the bed, where a glass of water sat ready. Lifting it over to her, she took it with one unsteady hand and took three tiny mouthfuls before handing him the glass.

A baby bird would have drunk more than her.

"Can you try a little more?"

She shook her head, and he didn't push her. Not today, not when she had seen Callyn's grave for the first time. The Blacksteel brothers had all dug the grave and buried the body. It had felt different to when he had done it before.

He would try again with Emara tomorrow.

Settling back into the nest of different rugs, she turned her back on him to face the wall. After putting the glass back down, Torin tipped back his head, resting it against the wooden bedframe, and folded his arms over his chest. He found himself thankful that she would even try to sleep again, knowing what she would face in her dreams. He listened to each breath she took deepening as sleep found her again. And with every breath she took, he found himself counting the promises he would make to find who was behind all of this as his eyes grew heavy and closed.

CHAPTER TWO
EMARA

Heart-warming laughter filled her ears. Her heart felt light and full as she heard the giggle of Callyn on the white sandy beach of Tolsah Bay. The rays of sun melted into Emara's face as she closed her eyes and embraced the heat. The waves of the ocean folded delicately, sending out a tranquil melody as salted air rustled at her hair, blowing it away from her cheeks. She opened her eyes to see a mass of golden hair sweeping around as Callyn frolicked on the sand in front of her. As she picked up each seashell, she danced freely, her beautiful white dress wafting out behind her. Emara let a giggle escape her as she watched her friend move like a trained ballerina. Callyn, her Cally, looked so free and blissfully at home as she twirled across the Tolsah coastline. She had always talked about coming here in the summer-time and they had finally made it. Emara let a small reviving breath filter through as she lay back, soaking in the coastal ambience, the warm sand hugging her spine in return. She was happy, comfortable, and content. At peace. And so was Callyn.

Emara jolted upright, her dark hair spilling around her shoulders and tickling down her back. She felt bile track up her throat and she pushed it down as the sting in her nose made her eyes water. Taking in a deep breath, she reminded herself it wasn't real. A crushing ache in her heart confirmed that too. The excruciating pain still lay within her chest, overwhelming her ability to even think straight.

It was just a dream.

A disillusioned nightmare.

Hearing and seeing Cally was just a cruel dream. Before she could let her emotion run its course, she pulled a hand through her hair, sweat dampening her scalp, and stilled.

Her bed felt oddly unbalanced.

Emara peered over her shoulder at the massive brute lying asleep beside her and the memories of her asking him to stay with her until she fell asleep humbled her.

And he had.

Torin Blacksteel had done as she asked. However, he had clearly allowed sleep to find him too. She felt a fleck of surprise as she took in his slumbering face. It was the first time she had ever seen peace bless his masculine features, his dark lashes lying flat against his cheekbone. The scar in between his brows that usually pulled into a scowl or added quip in his wicked grin was smoothed out, and his full lips parted, allowing her a glance at his white teeth. He would look like a painting of innocence if it weren't for the stack of muscles that rippled across his entire body. Or the hunting knife tucked into his pocket. His hulking arms lay folded, relaxed across his sculpted chest. Even in the cold of winter, his arms were bare, revealing a few tell-tale signs of his duty. Multiple scars marked their way up his biceps and down his forearm. Emara blinked a few times before taking in every inch of him.

He was beautiful.

Suddenly, the room she had spent days in alone seemed all too small.

Wriggling free from the layers that had been piled on top of her, she pushed herself to the edge of the bed, finally feeling the chill in the air. Emara looked over her shoulder again at the Blacksteel in her bed. He hadn't taken a single blanket for himself. He had let her have every single one.

Shoving them off completely, she stood, her legs shaking as her feet found the cold wooden floor. She rolled her neck, her eyes squinting at the winter sun that had started trickling through the window as it rose lazily from behind the trees.

Torin stirred somewhat in the bed in her absence, allowing his frame to spread out on the mattress a little more. His hand fell, touching where she would have been.

Distracting herself from the hunter in her bed, she thought back over the dream of Cally that had been like a dagger to her heart. They would never get to experience the Tolsah Bay beaches together. She would never get to see the happiness in Cally's smile as her toes dipped into the ocean, as she colour-coordinated an outfit to match the soft pastels of the shoreline. They would never scream happily as the cold sea waves met their waists.

Emara swallowed back her tears as she made her way out of the room and closed the door behind her. She made her way past the living area, where the embers of a delicate fire glittered, highlighting the face of another sleeping Blacksteel lying on the sofa. Padding her way through the Blacksteel cottage, she went to the large kitchenette that was cluttered with an array of jars, herbs, books, and candles. She ran her hand over the large pinewood dining table that created an island in the room. As she poured herself a glass of water, she looked out the window over the sink. Morning dew sat heavy on the branches and grass, and she took a moment to breathe.

"I can make you a hot beverage if you'd like?" a gentle but apprehensive voice sounded from behind her. She didn't have to turn around to know who it was. She knew exactly whose voice shook with the guilt of his betrayal as he spoke to her.

"Water is fine," she said calmly. Not ready to look him in the eye, she kept her gaze on the forest before her.

"You haven't had anything warm lining your stomach in days. It wouldn't be a bother for me to—"

"I said water's fine." Emara turned and gave him a sharp look that froze Gideon Blacksteel where he stood. He, too, looked like he wasn't ready to look at her fully, and perhaps her tone had shocked him. He shifted uncomfortably on his feet, and she could see the bob of angst in his throat. If she could feel anything other than unrelenting heartache, she might have felt a pang of guilt for how sharp she had been with him.

He gave her a gentle nod. "I can see that the bruising on your face is starting to heal." Gideon looked her over. The dimness in his eyes wasn't something that was familiar to her. What she had once admired in his beautiful green eyes no longer glistened, and dark undereye circles had sunk deep in his golden skin.

"When was the last time you slept?" she asked quietly, ignoring his previous statement.

"Properly?" His eyes flicked to the floor. "I can't remember."

Emara could see it all over his face. She could see the guilt of his betrayal and how stealing the Resurrection Stone from her had truly turned his heart upside down. But she wasn't ready to even speak of what Gideon had stolen from her in his mission for Viktir Blacksteel. She wasn't ready to explore that emotional plunge just yet. Her heart was in too much pain.

He opened his mouth to speak, but if she heard his explanation, his apology, or an attempt to defend himself, she might cause the whole world to shake. She could feel it bubbling like a cauldron under her skin— her magic.

So instead, she said, "Maybe I would like a hot drink."

After all, there was a nip in the air.

A glisten of hope twinkled in his eyes, but it was gone before it could fully ignite. Maybe he was also hoping to avoid the conversation that was very much needed between them. Especially when he looked like he could slip into a coma of exhaustion any minute now.

"I could make us some camomile tea? I am sure my mother has some already brewed to be served. It's warm and soothing, normally a good remedy for sleep." He walked towards her, and she moved instantly, jerking back. He froze at her recoil and put out a hand. "I am not—"

"I know," was all Emara could muster as she looked away. She knew he wasn't going to hurt her, but any quick movement sent fear through her heart. Emara placed her arms over herself as he walked past her to the pot hanging over the stove.

"Good morning," a delicate voice broke through the tension. "I thought I heard some voices." Naya Black-steel stood in the threshold of the door, folding the wrappings of a fleece night coat around her small frame. Her short curly hair was pinned atop her head, a few chocolate brown curls protruding out from the fastenings. "Emara, my love..." Her kind azure eyes that reminded her so much of Torin's glanced her over. "Take a seat at the dining table and we will get you something hot to drink." There was something about her gentle tone that could command anyone to do anything.

Emara sat quickly.

Gideon greeted his mother as she took his place at the stove. "You look exhausted, Gideon, my darling. You must head to bed after breakfast."

"I will," he reassured her as he shook a hand

through his hair. It was slightly damp from the weather outside.

"Have I missed breakfast?" Kellen Blacksteel sauntered in, a tired smile on his face. "You always said I can't miss the most important meal of the day, Mother."

"I am absolutely positive you wouldn't miss it." Naya laughed gently as the teapot came to a boil. "There is always fresh food on the table here."

As he sat at the table, a pair of stunningly unique eyes locked onto Emara's face. Unspoken words drifted between them, speaking of what she had witnessed at the Uplift. They had never fully broached what she had seen or heard.

They had never had the opportunity to.

He smiled hesitantly, but she tried not to linger too long.

What Kellen needed to know was that she would never breathe a single word of what she'd seen of him at the Uplift. She wouldn't even have told Cally if she were still here.

A sharp, sickening pain clenched tightly around her heart. As she moved her hand over her chest to stop her heart from crumbling, Kellen looked up at her as if sensing her pain, then avoided eye contact.

If only she could just reassure him that she didn't judge him for what he was hiding about himself. It made no difference to her if he preferred a male's to a female's company. Emara had always believed in love being love no matter the gender. But it was clear from what he had said at the Uplift that the hunting families weren't conditioned to see love so freely.

Suddenly, her heart hurt for him too.

"Did my invite to the morning breakfast party get lost in transit?" Torin swaggered through the kitchenette door. Emara had never thought she would see the day when she was so relieved to see the oldest Blacksteel brother.

He winked at her as he caught her gaze. All signs of how tender he had been last night were removed, and there was a wicked glint in his eye.

For a second, Emara was in awe of how he could switch his masks so easily. She wondered if he could teach her the art of it.

"All of my boys around my kitchen table so early in the morning; the Gods must have heard my endless prayers." Naya's smile brightened the room. "Bless the Mother God. I will make eggs and toast for breakfast. I may even have syrup somewhere."

"You"—Torin's hand enveloped his mother's small shoulder—"are an absolute deity of a woman. I am famished and there is nothing like your cooking." He grabbed an apple from the fruit bowl in the centre of the table. As he bit into it, he checked over Emara like he was searching for any signs of her struggling. "The men of the tower miss it deeply, Mother." He looked at her again. "They always say how the kitchen ran better when you were there."

Naya laughed and began cracking eggs into a pan on the stove. The sizzling was instant. "I do miss your charm in the morning more, my love."

He dipped his chin as a little smile graced his lips. Emara had never seen such a look on his face before.

"Where did you sleep last night?" Kellen asked Torin, also dipping into the bowl of fruit as they awaited Naya's cooking. "When I woke up, you weren't in the armchair."

"That's because I slept in Emara's bed," he said nonchalantly, ripping at the apple with his teeth.

A crash came from the sink as Gideon dropped a glass bowl against the ceramic, and Emara's head whipped around to where he stood. Naya rushed over and placed a hand on his shoulder, moving him back from the broken glass.

"Relax, brother." Torin threw a look towards Gideon's back and Emara swore it was an imaginary punch to the back of his head. "That is all we did."

Gideon whirled around and looked him in the eye. "I am glad you felt the need to clarify that."

"Oh Gods," Kellen whispered as he shrunk against his pine chair. "Here we go."

"Well, I did want to clarify that for you." Torin's gaze was unmoved from Gideon. "Just in case you had a little cry about it." Torin flashed an icy grin and chomped into his apple, unfazed. "We can't have you tearing up before breakfast."

Whatever had been going on whilst Emara gained her strength was now creeping into breakfast. Immediately, she wondered how many of Naya's meals had been ruined due to a Blacksteel brawl. Probably too many to count.

"Couldn't you have asked Kellen to stay with her?" Gideon's chin dipped, his brows matching.

"Why would I do that when I can do it myself?"

Torin's brow furrowed; they looked so alike as they battled each other. A war between fire and ice. The scar between his brows, that had been so smooth during his sleep, was now menacing.

"Because..." Gideon began, his cheeks burning with rage.

Torin put his hands in the air. "I'm sorry, did I miss the part where father died, and you were anointed commander? Does my rank fall under you now? Oh, that's right; I don't take orders from the commander's little spy."

"You're a horrible prick." Gideon gave off a terrifying glare as he bared his teeth.

"And you are a coward that lingers in Viktir's shadow."

Gideon moved forward, fist raised.

"Enough!" Naya Blacksteel's voice cracked like thunder through the room, and her hand swung up to stop Gideon from lunging at Torin. "This is not the tower. You are not in the Huntswood Markets, and this cottage will not be treated as such. This is my home. You will stop these verbal jabs at once." She eyed down her boys. "Emara is sitting right there, and how you are speaking in front of a woman is downright disrespect-ful! I am sure the last thing she wants to hear is silly bickering between boys who should be acting like men." She threw a firm warning look towards Torin and then Gideon. "Gideon, after breakfast, you will take to the spare room and try to get some sleep. I am sure Emara will not mind offering up that room for you to take some time to get your head down. Kellen, you will

wash up, and Torin, now that you have fully rested"—
her tone mocked him—"you will make sure Emara
knows the grounds of this cottage. Help her get some
fresh air."

Emara stared wide-eyed at the small woman who
bossed all three warriors without hesitation. And she
was even more shocked when the boys sheepishly
nodded back in response.

"Yes, ma'am," Kellen whispered, brows raised.

Her authority morphed into softness again as she
brought over a bubbling pot of camomile tea whilst
Gideon placed out teacups. Gideon couldn't quite hide
the frustrations on his face the same way his mother
could. With rage infused in his cheeks, Gideon placed a
bowl filled with salted eggs onto the table, and Naya
dished out warm bread on a separate plate. Torin
grabbed a few slices of bread and then piled a massive
amount of eggs onto his plate.

Emara scowled at the overloaded plate.

"What?" he said as his white teeth ripped the bread
apart.

"Nothing," she replied, taking a small piece of bread.

"Are you judging the size of my plate, Clearwater?"
Torin's brows lifted.

She looked over at everyone else's decent-sized
plates and then to him again. "Absolutely," she scoffed,
breaking up a little piece of bread and placing it into her
mouth. She tried her hardest not to show how much her
stomach was rejecting the food. She swallowed hard
and it reluctantly went down. It would be incredibly
impolite not to eat what Naya had prepared for her,

especially since she hadn't eaten anything she had brought her in days.

A corner of Torin's mouth turned up in amusement and relief spread through her. This was a far cry from the pitying looks he had given her last night, when he had taken her into his arms.

She blushed a little.

"Maybe you should try some eggs. You are going to need to gain your strength back if you want to continue training." Torin took the spoon and added a little pile of eggs to her plate. It was no match to the mountain on his.

Acknowledging that he was the only one treating her like she wasn't about to break at any moment, she couldn't help but appreciate the gesture. It was true that she might explode any minute, but she liked that Torin made her feel as normal as possible. It was a welcome change from feeling so lost, numb, and broken.

He slipped another piece of bread onto her plate with a grin, and she rolled her eyes.

Torin let out a laugh. "Oh, how I have missed that."

"What?" She choked on the swelling of her throat.

"You, rolling your eyes at me." He smiled. "It's been a while."

His stare pinned Emara to her seat and her cheeks heated as she looked down at the brewing tea in her cup. Looking up again, she realised Torin's gaze was still all over her face, and she quickly found something else to look at. Gideon chewed the inside of his cheek, his eyes down on his untouched food. Kellen seemed oblivious as he munched into a piece of warm bread slathered in butter. But it was Naya's gaze that caught her attention; her wise eyes glanced from Torin to Emara. An expression that Emara couldn't read passed across her face.

Whatever it was, she tried to ignore it as she lifted her cup to her lips and sipped her tea. It warmed her throat as the mellow sweetness soothed it. As it made its way down into her belly, she exhaled, reminding herself that she was lucky to feel the warmth. She was lucky to be alive and feel anything. It was more than a lot of people got to feel.

She just didn't feel anything else right now.

But she would.

She hoped she would feel something again, anything other than sorrow and a hollow ache in her heart. She vowed to herself as she took another sip of calming tea that she wouldn't return to the spare room in the cottage today, which was filled with the memories of her broken cries. She would try her best to not torture herself about what she had endured and had done, about who she had killed, what she had seen. Instead, she would force herself to go outside or bathe or maybe even train. Something that would take the edge off her pain.

Training.

It would take away the burn in her heart and press it into her muscles, her skin, and her lungs.

It had helped her mind process everything that had happened before. It had given her ammunition as a survivor.

This time, she would train enough to become something that left her old self behind completely. There was no one left for her to be her old self around. Emara vowed that she would train to become something that her enemies would fear. They would reveal themselves again, and this time, she would be ready for them.

CHAPTER THREE
EMARA

fter breakfast, **Emara soaked for** longer than she should have in a steaming tub of water. Naya had insisted on a similar bathing ritual to Rhea's when she had first gone to the tower, so she took the time to herself. Calming balms and scented oils had adorned her tub, and she noted them as another thing to be thankful for as they soothed her racing heart.

Feeling fresh in the new clothes provided by Naya, she found herself in front of the fire in the living area. Emara watched the flames dance together as snippets of memory from her own fire flashed through her mind. Admittedly, she was terrified of her own flames, not sure when they could soar from her hands and devour a full room. She didn't know how to control them; fire had simply consumed her in the moments of her terror.

"Captivating, aren't they?" Torin's deep voice made it known that he was behind her, and she turned to see him in full training gear. "Fire is a dangerous little creature."

Yes, it was a dangerous little creature. And clearly, she was too.

She swallowed her trepidation. "Do I need to fetch a cloak?"

"I think we will be warm enough when we get going," he said with a nod.

"Why? What are we doing?"

"Believe it or not"—he grinned—"I have missed you asking questions. I know my mother wanted me to take you on a walk through these grounds, but we are going for a run. It always helps me when I need to clear my mind."

She put up no fights, no remarks; she simply nodded and followed him outside. They made their way along a gravel path that she couldn't quite remember ever coming through. She'd been given a natural sedative after the Uplift; it had kept her from burning herself out or destroying anything else, but it had also blocked out portions of her memory.

"Okay," Torin said, clapping his hands together. He was evidently back in training mode. "Running in the woods is different from just going a normal jog around a sparring room. The Fairlands is home to all sorts of magical creatures. You need to be alert at all times. This is about keeping yourself vigilant as well as maintaining a nice pace and building your endurance." A thoughtful frown appeared across his face, and his ocean eyes narrowed in on her. "Are you ready to get back into this? If you are not, we can just walk."

"Without a shadow of a doubt, I want this," Emara

answered. She cleared her throat. "I need something else to focus on. My head is...busy."

His forehead creased. "Mine too." A moment passed between them, and she could feel frost sneaking into her bones, making her tremble. Torin rubbed his hands together. "Okay, let's warm up then."

After two days of running with Torin, Emara's legs were as heavy as concrete blocks and her lungs burned. But the ache in her chest didn't hurt like it had the first day Torin had made her run through the Fairlands. In fact, her breathing was steady; she was a little out of breath, but she continued to bound through the forest paths. She was rather shocked at how well she had kept pace with Torin. Or maybe she was shocked at how well he had kept himself at her pace. She could tell he wanted to take off, but he didn't. Her breathing had been laboured at first, but as Torin had coached her technique, her lungs had relaxed in her chest and the fire that burned in them had begun to ease. The harder and longer she ran, the easier the pain in her heart felt too, melting away memories that clouded her mind.

As they jogged lightly to the front of the cottage, she slowed to a stop. Placing her hands on her knees, she bent over, tucking her head in. "I think I have another circuit in me."

Torin laughed as he came to a stop too. "I don't think that's a good idea."

Irritation flashed through her quickly, then subsided. The rain had soaked them both, with tiny shards of ice and wind battering into their bodies, making it difficult for them to fully open their eyes. No creatures of the Fairland woods had bothered them in this kind of weather. Emara couldn't help but wonder if they had been hiding from her.

"Torin, I need to run again. Just for another lap." She left out a "please."

"You've run for hours," he said, and she watched as he moved towards her, his rain-soaked hair even darker. It slid down his forehead, and heavy droplets ran down into his thick lashes. A coldness spread over his face. "I am not just saying no to you because I want to. It's for a reason, and as your trainer, you need to listen to me. I don't think it's a good idea." His eyes trailed down her body to her legs. "I can see how tense your muscles are. You are one run away from hurting yourself. We have overworked you as it is. You're not getting an injury on my watch." He threw her a curved smirk that was as dangerous as the storm. "At least if it's not even going to be worth it."

Emara let out a small breath, knowing that all the visions of blood and burning flesh would return without the strenuous exercise. Without the endorphins of the run, she would feel that torture again. Without the rhythm of her pace and the sound of her pulse in her ears, she would hear those screams. Emara pursed her lips and crossed her arms over herself before turning back to the cottage without even looking to see if Torin Blacksteel was following her.

TORIN

"One, two," Torin coached Emara as she pounded her fists into the palm of his large hands. Magic blazed in Emara's eyes as she swung, taking aim at Torin's raised hands.

Even though the fierce wind blew in ice cold rain, Emara had asked him for something else after their run today. Apparently, she wasn't satisfied with where her head was at when they had arrived at the cottage. He had suggested combat, and with the suggestion, she had perked up a little. Something had lightened in her dark eyes.

But she was about to break.

He could feel it.

He knew of too many hunters in the Selection who had reached their physical and mental limit and snapped. But what Torin had realised after years of hunting was that there was beauty when someone crumbled. There was a magic that stirred when someone broke down. It was a test of character, and in the Selection, breakdown was where the commanders would weed out the weak. If they did not get back up and get their head straight, they did not merit the right to be a warrior of Thorin.

"Give me more," he pushed. "More. Punch harder."

And she did. She threw everything she could at him. Emara threw punches like she was battling a demon or Taymir, screams coming from deep in her throat, her wild hair whipping in the air around her.

And then there was blinding rage on her face.

"Harder. Faster," he pushed, readjusting his feet to keep up with her strength. "Come on, Emara, is that all you've got?"

A frustrated cry escaped her lips.

"Don't let that magic out. Keep it in and just punch. Punch!"

"I am punching!" she roared like a beast of the forest. A gust of wind pushed him back. As she connected with his hand for the last time, a broken sob engulfed her.

And she fell apart.

Before her legs could give out, he caught her. He lifted her into his arms where she wept and wept. She hadn't cried in days, but Torin had known that her emotions would catch up to her. It was good that this was happening now instead of when she was standing in front of the magical factions as the heir of House Air. He wanted her to get it all out now. That had been his plan. Torin said nothing as he stood with her in his arms, and they braced the icy rain together.

EMARA

"In through your nose," Torin coached.

"Out through my mouth, yeah, I've got it," she hissed.

She had been running and training for what felt like forever, days upon days. She couldn't even keep track of it anymore. Everything was starting to blur in her little Fairland bubble.

Eat, train, bathe, repeat.

Sleep was something she was working on, and with the lack of it, she was extremely irritable. In the beginning, all she had done was sleep. Now, it was hard to find it at all.

"Talking affects the breaths you need to be taking right now." Torin's brow lifted. "Try less of that."

The storming weather of winter had subsided, but it had crisped over again, freezing the water droplets to the bare branches and firming up the ground. Even with the low temperature, she found herself wiping the perspiration from her brow as she looked up at Torin, who was running alongside her.

"Why do you never show any signs that you've been running for ages?"

A lingering surprise dusted across his features for a second, like it always did when she finally spoke to him. She hadn't been very vocal recently.

"That was just a light jog to wake us up, angel." He smirked, coming to the end of their route.

"A light jog? It was hardly a light jog." She panted.

He had been increasing her pace ever since she'd recovered from her meltdown in front of him. He had pushed and pushed and pushed...and she had broken.

But just like every time they trained, she had gotten back up.

Even when she was running, her mind had told her to give up several times and rest, but Torin had coached her through it, encouraging her to stop listening to the voice in her head. He'd told her to push out the doubt, and she had.

In a test of her endurance, he had upped her training level again. When they trained for combat, he made sure they focused on lethal blows.

All day, every day was weapons, runs, circuits, and sequences.

She noticed Torin cock his head to the side with an amused grin on his face. It had been the first time she had seen it properly in a while, and it was magnificent.

Her heart stammered.

"What?" She gawked back.

"You didn't protest to the pet name." A shimmer brightened his infuriatingly stunning eyes.

He had slipped in a few pet names in the last couple of days, and she was sure it was a test to see where she was at mentality. He was always testing out the waters before they sailed.

Today, she felt a little better.

Emara pulled her arm across her chest nonchalantly, stretching off. "I have decided to take a different approach to you from now on."

His jaw tightened as he folded his arms over his broad chest, not even stretching slightly. "Do tell."

Emara inhaled sharply. "I have come to the conclusion that highlighting my annoyance for your pet names gives you some sort of thrill." She tossed her hair over her shoulder and moved on to the next arm, stretching it across her body. His glittering eyes took in every move she made, but Emara didn't let that intimidate her. Not anymore. "And I won't be aiding you in seeking any thrills."

The cold wind around them warmed slightly.

A carnal smile that she hadn't realised she needed to see revealed a dimple on either side of his cheek. His chin popped up a notch. "I don't think you realise how much you already do."

Heat made its way into her cheeks, and she released a staggered breath.

"You're so annoying." She rolled her eyes, deflecting from the fact that her skin had heated at his words. That she felt *something*.

"You can't say that to your favourite Blacksteel." He

let his arms fall and his eyes lit up like icy diamonds. "Wait. Did I just become your favourite Blacksteel?"

"Absolutely not!" Emara's eyebrows almost folded into her eyes, and she took a lunge stretch to ease the stiffening of her muscles.

"Well, we all know Gideon's out. And Kellen...well, is Kellen. So who could possibly be above me?" He still didn't move into a stretch, he stood still, like a statue of the War God himself.

"Almost anyone in your bloodline." Emara scowled playfully.

His full lips twitched. "You really are so cruel to me, Clearwater."

"Why do you say that like you enjoy it?" She finally attempted a laugh.

"Because maybe I do." He finally pulled a bulky arm behind his head into a stretch, and she noted the familiar blue vein that protruded from his biceps that always caught her attention.

"I thought you took care of your sick *afflictions* in the markets," she jabbed with a smile that warranted caution.

Walking closer to where she stretched, he released his arm and said, "I have many *afflictions*." His lashes flickered quickly like he was trying to be coy. "But I thought I would ease you back into training slowly before we talked about them." His ocean blue eyes swarmed with mischief. "I mean, if you really want to explore them now, we can, because I don't need to be in the markets. These forests are just fine."

It had been a while since she had seen that wicked

grin slash across his face, and she couldn't help but feel a little relief in her chest.

She was as sick as him.

"No, thank you." She was thankful again when she saw his grin widen and then when he closed his lips to contain it. "I think our training will be adequate. I don't need to be delving into Torin Blacksteel's secret hobbies."

A low chuckle escaped his throat. "None of them are a secret, angel."

She sighed. "Are we really back to pet names?"

"Absolutely." A subtle smile graced his lips in exchange for his devilish grin. "Why would we not be? Training has resumed."

Secretly, she was thankful for that too. She didn't want to be fussed over. She didn't want anyone to act differently around her because they knew of her pain or what blood ran through her veins. She needed something that was normal enough for her to clutch onto, something that was familiar.

"Come on, then, let's get this fresh hell over with," she said as she stalked towards the door of the cottage. Torin was not only coaching her practically, but theoretically too. Apparently, there were thousands of books on how to train in combat and weaponry that Torin insisted she must read.

"Always the enthusiast about reading with your favourite mentor."

"*Favourite* is a far cry."

"I stand by my statement," he said confidently as he

walked in front of her to open the door to his mother's cottage. "After you."

Emara stopped in her tracks.

"Why are you so cheerful?" she asked. "It's getting on my nerves already."

He let out a barking laugh. "Because it seems the vow of silence you took has come to an end. This session is going to be enjoyable." His gaze met hers. "I can feel it already."

Emara tore her eyes from him as she crossed the threshold of the room, feeling a little less tightness around her heart. It wasn't much, but the exercise had really helped. And maybe having an actual conversation that wasn't in her own head was good too.

As she walked into the cottage, she noticed the other Blacksteels were sitting around the fire.

Before Emara could read any expression or the solemn air that was heavy in the room, Torin's husky voice broke through the silence.

"What's wrong?"

Naya Blacksteel looked up, concern warping her features as her lovely eyes darkened with sorrow. "Word has come from the tower."

Emara felt Torin stiffen beside her.

Gideon stood and Kellen's eyes were also now on Torin. But it was Gideon who spoke, "The Empress of House Earth was found murdered this morning." He walked forward with a letter in his hand. "The prime has called an emergency hearing, and Father has agreed for it to be held at the tower. The attacks are happening again."

Fury crossed Torin's face, but he didn't say anything. Goosebumps laced Emara's skin from head to toe like a fine gown. She watched Naya Blacksteel try to fight back a mixture of both sadness and frustration as Kellen rested one arm around her and lay his head against hers.

Gideon finally reached where they stood, and as he looked Torin in the eye, he said, "It's time to go home, brother. We leave now."

CHAPTER FOUR
EMARA

Emara had travelled back to the Blacksteel Tower by a portal Naya had created, her magic so strong that she could still feel it tingling on her skin, the static energy dancing in her hair. Her stomach felt queasy as she climbed the stone steps to the foyer, cursing that she would never get used to the way witches preferred to travel.

Before she could think about emptying the contents of her stomach, Marcus Coldwell's familiar face appeared at the doors, and he greeted them all with a warm smile that lit up the dimness of the foyer.

"Commanding Wife Blacksteel, what a pleasure it is to have you here." Marcus took her hand and kissed the top. "I wasn't expecting you."

Naya's name amongst the Hunters' threw Emara off guard.

Commanding Wife.

"Marcus, it is lovely to see you, regardless of how unsettling the occasion." She walked through the door first, followed by Emara, then her boys. "It's been some

time since I saw you last. We didn't even manage to reac-
quaint ourselves at the Uplift."

"I am sure there will be time for catching up,"
Marcus said.

"There always is with old friends," Naya confirmed
with a smile.

"Miss Clearwater, the Tower welcomes you back."
Marcus put out his hand, and she placed her hand into
his before he kissed it formally. Emara smiled at
Marcus, wondering if he bought her fake grin, and said
nothing in return. In all honesty, she didn't know how
she was feeling as she entered the tower. The last time
she'd been brought here, she was with Cally to recover
from the attack on her old home—a home now lost to
her old life. They had experienced this entire journey
into a new world together, a new world of demons and
magic.

And now, it was only Emara.

"Torin, Gideon," Marcus welcomed the brothers in a
masculine embrace. "Baby Blacksteel." He ruffled a
hand through Kellen's hair.

Kellen smoothed it out again. "I despise that
nickname."

"Gods, Marcus, you're acting like we have been gone
for years." Gideon chuckled.

"The tower isn't the same place without you."
Marcus's brown eyes tightened, forming creases in his
dark skin, the only sign that gave away his age.

"No *father* to greet us back from our travels?" Torin's
voice rang off the foyer walls and Emara wondered if he
wanted everyone in the tower to hear his sarcasm.

"No, Commander Blacksteel is rather pressed for time at the moment. He has some heavy paperwork in regard to the investigations of the Uplift, and it needs to be completed before the hearing for the prime."

"That will have him in a splendid mood," Naya stated before she rolled her eyes.

"Isn't he always in a splendid mood?" Torin remarked as he swaggered up towards the direction of the dining hall and disappeared. His voice was still audible as he greeted the other hunters.

Marcus nodded politely and glanced between Emara and Naya. "I am guessing you would like to be escorted to your rooms?"

"No need; I know exactly where my quarters are, Marcus." Naya lifted a hand. "I did live here."

Emara had noticed the difference in her tone and body language since stepping back through the tower doors. It was colder, a mask to cover her true warmth, and she wore it like a second skin.

The wife of the commander.

"Of course, Commanding Wife Blacksteel." His lips thinned into a line on his face.

Warrior or not, he clearly respected the tiny woman.

"I will head to my quarters, but not before I see my sister." Her eyes twinkled.

"Your sister?" The words left Emara's mouth before she could swallow them back.

Naya smiled, adding that warmth back into her cold mask. "Yes, my sister. I think you may know her." She slipped a little look towards Marcus. "She goes by the name of Rhea."

"Rhea is your sister?" Emara couldn't stop her mouth from opening in shock.

"She is, indeed." She smiled again. "Although I am not present in the tower, I still need my eyes, ears, and blood within these walls to make sure my boys are looked after." A fierceness coated her face. "Marcus, please make sure Emara is settled into her new room."

His brows furrowed as his lips parted. "New room? I thought she would like to return to her old one in the infirmary?"

Naya pouted before she spoke again, her mask reinstating itself firmly on her face. "I know your intentions weren't to insult me, Marcus, but I hate to inform you that you have."

Marcus straightened, his hands immediately going behind his back, his face drained of colour.

"In case you have forgotten yourself, Emara Clearwater is the elemental heir of House Air. She is about to lay claim to the House as their empress." She lifted her chin, and although she was more than a foot shorter than Marcus, she somehow managed to look down at him. "A pokey room in an infirmary—where warriors take their final breath—will not do. She is to be escorted to new accommodation. Something fit for an empress of this kingdom."

Marcus nodded, trying to recover from his dressing down. "Of course, ma'am. I wasn't thinking."

Emara's jaw almost hit the floor for a second time. In all her grief, she had almost forgotten about her bloodline and what it would mean for her as an *empress* of a witching coven. Her stomach flipped and a sickening sensation watered in her mouth.

"See to it that she has one of the rooms in my quarter in the west of the tower, one with her own bathing chamber." Her emerald cape swept the floor as she walked forward before looking over her shoulder at Emara and winking.

Marcus nodded and bowed, stepping into line behind her. "Right away, Commanding Wife Blacksteel."

"Oh, and Marcus." She stopped in her tracks and threw another look over her shoulder. "Could you please inform your commander that his wife has returned to the tower? I think it's best that he should know that I intend to stay for a while."

"Right away, ma'am." Marcus leapt into motion at her command.

Emara couldn't help but feel a little twitch at the corner of her lips as she watched the emerald cape disappear down the corridor in a flood of authority.

CHAPTER FIVE
EMARA

Marcus directed Emara through never-seen-before corridors of the tower. They were more decorated than the ones she had seen previously; it was clear that this wing was actually inhabited and not just for training hunters. They stopped outside a large set of gilded double doors that were much larger than the ones that hung in the infirmary.

"This will be your new room." He pushed the doors open to reveal a large open space with a full view of Huntswood city just below the window.

For the third time since stepping through the foyer doors this morning, her jaw dropped. Emara glanced at the double bed with a chrome frame that spiked into tiara-like-points.

Champagne-coloured sheets lay below several plush pillows that were displayed stylishly, dressing the bed. A padded comforter draped over the bottom of the bed, spilling onto the floor like melted gold, touching woven rugs designed with ancient runes in deep golds, purples, and burgundies. The warmth of the colours contrasted beautifully with the light that poured into the room, making it fresh, yet cosy. A vanity area sat against a panelled wall to the right, with a stunning mirror framed with metals and mosaic tiles that looked like it had been crafted by Rhiannon, Goddess of the Moon and Dreams. A deep windowsill lined with rosy cushions bordered the windows, and Emara could already see herself lying there. Reading, dreaming, wishing...

Emara looked over her shoulder at Marcus. "I am going to be sleeping in here?"

He smiled. "Yes. It's fit for an empress, don't you think?" His eyes were kind, but they revealed a slight sadness as he looked at her. "The bathing chamber is to your left." He gestured to a door that she hadn't yet explored.

"I didn't know the tower had rooms this...pretty." Emara could feel her eyes bulging, but she didn't care; she just loved that she had her very own bathing chamber.

He chuckled. "Naya will be just along the corridor from you. She liked this wing of the tower enough to decorate it in her own style, and we haven't changed anything since her departure." He looked at Emara, and his chin dipped. "I will see to it that all your things are brought from your old room."

Oh Gods, she hadn't even thought about everything that would still be in there; her books, her clothes, and her keepsake box had all been abandoned. It was such a *human* oversight in this magical hurricane of madness.

"Thank you for offering, Marcus, but I am sure I can collect my items. I don't want to burden you."

"No, I insist." He held his hand out as if to stop her. "An empress of the magical world gets these things done for her."

She lowered her head. "I would hardly call myself that."

He let out a small, huffed laugh. "You will get used to it."

Pressing her lips together lightly, Emara formed a tiny smile.

Will I?

Turning, she cast her eyes over to the windows, really taking in the city view from this room. Before she knew it, her feet had travelled over to the deep windowsill.

It was stunning.

She could see the architecture of the city from here; the buildings, the workplaces, and the homes built around the old temples. Everything about it was combining the old with the new, making it seem vibrant and magical. However, she recognised that she hadn't really seen Huntswood fully, just the markets, and excitement managed to flicker in her heart at the prospects of being down there, exploring and taking in the culture of the city. Quickly, she added this view to her list of things to be thankful for. She was thankful that she was alive to see this, to experience this view, and imagine all the possibilities that were submerged in Huntswood. All the life...

Her chest ached.

Cally would have loved this room and the wonders of looking down onto the city. Gods, she would have only taken one look out this window before she fled into the city to seek out a seamstress or a tavern. Emara placed a hand over her mouth to stop a cry escaping as she choked back tears.

"Emara," Marcus' voice croaked.

She turned to face him again, pulling back the emotional wave that pushed into the shore of her eyes. She had cried in front of the hunting clan enough. If she was to earn an inch of their respect as a member of a magical faction, then she would have to clamp down on her emotions. She would have to be like Naya, like her grandmother.

"I am truly sorry about the loss of your friend." The unexpected words knocked the air from her lungs. He continued, "She was pure sunshine, a light in the tower that made us all smile." He lowered his gaze. "Even in those ridiculous outfits and sinful shoes, she gave us all hope that things are changing. It doesn't matter how long she was here with us, she still made an impact." He looked at her again, catching her gaze. "I hope she gets the justice she deserves."

If Emara was going to consider being an empress of a coven, an influential witch in the kingdom, then maybe she could instil justice herself. Her words stuck in her throat, but she strangled them out. "Justice will prevail, Marcus. I have faith in the Gods."

"It's all we can hope for in a world where evil attempts to poison everything good," Marcus said before walking over and placing a hand on her shoulder. His dark brown skin seemed flawless in the open light, and his brown eyes gleamed with a promise that was both bold and wise. "You are still under the protection of the Blacksteel Hunting Clan, and no one makes a move against us without paying the price."

The words from Marcus should have shocked her. He had always seemed friendly and generous. But his words marked a pledge of something darker. Something that she felt in the veins of her own heart. Something violent.

Whoever was an enemy of hers was now an enemy of his. They were an enemy of the Blacksteel Clan, and she was sure they would know it.

She nodded in confirmation that she understood him.

"Settle in," he said, shifting on his feet before heading towards the door. "If you need anything at all, just call on us."

"Thank you, Marcus." This time, her words couldn't hide the emotion lining her tongue. "That means more than you know."

He smiled and shut the doors behind him before she slumped against the window to stare out at the Kingdom of Caledorna, a kingdom that she could represent as an empress.

CHAPTER SIX
TORIN

The briefing room in the tower was packed full of hunters old and young. It was obvious to Torin that word had been sent to bring even the oldest of hunters to the tower. Gods, it looked like a few of them had come out of retirement for this.

However, the one hunter he hadn't seen was his father, and he didn't know if that made him relieved or on edge.

Probably the latter.

Marcus and Gideon flanked either side of him as they sat at a desk much too small for warriors of Thorin, waiting on Viktir's arrival. Kellen claimed the chair in front, running a small throwing knife over his fingers, aloof as always. And as more and more hunters arrived, squeezing into any spare space that they could find, the more it royally pissed him off.

Didn't they have training rooms they could use, rooms more suitable for men of their size?

Maybe his father's punishment had already commenced.

Torin didn't like waiting. Patience wasn't a quality at the top of his best attributes—unless he was coaching a certain witch.

Dale Wellprose, a hunter who stayed within the tower walls as a member of the clan, walked past, scuffing the table with his leg and bumping into Torin's torso. A flash of rage went through him, and he wanted to floor the young man with one punch. This amount of testosterone in one room was a perfect recipe for *disaster,* especially when tensions were so high.

This kind of environment reminded him of the first stages of the Selection, crowded and too loud. He much preferred it when the weak had been whittled out or had gotten themselves injured, leaving only the strongest.

A buzzing hush fell over the room and Torin's eyes darted to the door, finally witnessing his father walking through in fully kitted hunter regalia, weapon belt gleaming as he moved. He hadn't seen his commander for some time now, had not even received a single communication. The violet circles under his eyes told Torin all the information he needed to know. He, too, hadn't been sleeping, and if Torin knew his father like he thought he did, he would have been racking his brains for days, mulling over all the events of the Uplift. Thinking through strategies, looking over possibilities, and meeting with influential members of society, who he could manipulate into seeing the Uplift the way wanted them to. *The hunters saved the event, and everything was under control.*

Viktir Blacksteel drew in a breath as he stood at the

front of the briefing room, a familiar coldness in his eyes.

Torin had never seen his father–the commander–as an older man, but today he looked his age, with the grey-speckled hair and the creases on his face.

"Hunting Clans, thank you for joining us at the tower." His bottle-green eyes flicked around the room, taking in who from his brethren had come. "Even in retirement, you are loyal to your oath, and the Gods will not forget that."

A few of the elders nodded in agreement.

There was no retirement in hunting, and this was the reminder.

Torin took a long breath and crossed his arms over his chest, ready to hear the first communication from his leader. He felt Gideon do the same.

"Our world has known dark times before, as you all know, and we were created and put on the soil of Caledorna to make sure that the catastrophic events that happened to our Gods' good people did not happen again. To prevent history from repeating itself."

Torin did all he could not to shift in his chair and draw attention to himself, especially when his father was still to deliver his punishment for not giving him the intel on the Resurrection Stone.

He had betrayed his father's trust; a punishment would certainly be delivered.

"I am afraid to inform you that the darkness of the Underworld is rising up like never before. The Dark Army has struck again since the Uplift, and they have struck deep, right into the heart of the community. The magic world has not witnessed calculated violence like this since our great war, centuries ago." He shifted, moving forward gracefully. "I am sure word of the Uplift has spread to you all by now, and rumours of scandals will be circling." His stoic face hardened, and the silver in his hair glistened under the light. "But I am here to tell you first-hand that what happened at the annual Uplift was not an accident. It was a premeditated attack on this community by *one* elite member of society who had been conspiring with the Dark God."

Evidently, it wasn't just Torin who felt the intensity in the room; a few hunters shifted in their seats, letting out a heavy breath. Creaks and groans of the wooden chairs broke the silence left by the commander's stern voice, and it gave Torin room to exhale.

"We do not have all the answers of why he meddled in such darkness, but what we can tell you is that he managed to trade his soul for immortality."

Torin's eyebrows pulled together as he realised Viktir had willingly skimmed over why Taymir Solden had even shown up to the Uplift in the first place, to trade Emara to the Dark God for immortality. Why did he leave out a vital piece of information?

Torin's foot began to shake under the desk.

"The King of the Underworld is moving in different ways than we are used to. He is purposefully targeting the human faction—the weaker and uneducated—who are unaware of what he really is. He's tempting them to join him with bargains they do not truly comprehend. What this elite did"— he took a breath—"was a bold move. He knew of the Underworld and how wrong it is, yet he put his faction at great risk." His jaw tightened and he found Torin's gaze. "Since the Uplift, every empress of the Rhiannon's covens have been murdered. Just this morning, more news came by fireletter that the only empress who remained alive—the Empress of Spirit—has now been slaughtered in her own home."

House Spirit had lost their empress too. Now there were none.

A spine-breaking wave of gravity weighed on Torin's body, and a low whistle came from a hunter behind him.

Fuck.

"Was it a demon or a member of the elite who killed the Empress of Spirit?" A hunter with an astute tone asked.

"The Dark Army," the commander answered. "You may know this already, but I will make it clear again that the elite male responsible for the brutality at the Uplift was taken care of that night. And we don't suspect any more of the elite humans to be involved in anything to do with the darkened."

A few curses flew across the room, and Torin raised an eyebrow, trying to remain calm.

He wasn't convinced that more of the elite weren't involved.

Every single empress was dead—killed, murdered.

But why? Did the elite want something they had?

What was more interesting to him right now was how much of the event his father was skimming over. It had been Emara who killed Taymir Solden. Although he had been *'taken care of,'* his father seemed to intentionally leave out by *whom*. The hunters who had been there would have seen Emara take out the Solden heir like she had been conjuring her flames for years, but no one seemed to question it. No one dared to.

His father *had* been busy influencing the factions, indeed, and his approach—Torin assumed—was that he was protecting Emara. But for what reason? Was it because of their marital agreement?

Torin bit into his lip.

However, the information to absorb from this briefing was that empresses of earth and spirit had been killed after the Uplift, not by the same elite member, but by the Dark Army.

The magic in his blood thrummed to fight at the thought of them.

Viktir's voice brought him back to the present conversation. "Five of the most powerful witches in this kingdom have been murdered, and we haven't seen something so detrimental to the magic community since the Great War. With the loss of the empresses, every magical ward they had put in place to protect our lands has been severed, leaving us wide open for an attack. Anything of this magnitude would draw the attention of the prime, and because it took place in our territory, there will be an emergency summit requested here. The prime will want the next elemental heirs to ascend with immediate effect." Viktir walked off to the side, looking over his men. "And we are going to help reinstate order to help with the damage that has been caused to the covens, but more guidance on this will be highlighted at the summit." Viktir changed his direction, his boots heavy on the floor. "Now, we are all aware that the prime is made up of Hunters, Fae, Shifters and Witches. However, they also have an elite faction, so I am going to say this now: do not, and I repeat"—Viktir's icy gaze found Torin's once again—"do *not* do anything to provoke the elite or endanger their community in any way. They are part of the prime just as much as we are, though they aren't part of the magical community, and they are protected. We cannot hold them all responsible for one man's actions, regardless of the effects. We do not need a civil war on our hands, not as we battle the Dark Army every day."

Torin could feel himself snarling but stopped himself and swallowed. He wasn't convinced it was just *one* man's actions.

"You all fall under my jurisdiction, and you must remain professional at all times. Do you understand my order?"

A collective *"Yes, Commander Blacksteel."* vibrated through the room, but Torin just dipped his head in acknowledgement.

Torin wasn't going to make any verbal promises that the Gods could hear, especially not promises that he knew were near impossible to keep. Viktir expected him to sit at the summit like a good little dog and not bite the hand that attacked him?

Not likely.

Torin liked to bite, and if he got to the bottom of who was responsible for leading the Solden heir down the route of darkness, he wouldn't be on his best behaviour, that's for sure.

"The other clans from around the kingdom will start to arrive tomorrow." Viktir allowed a taut smile to pull at his lip, his tone a little lighter. "Some of you might not have crossed paths in years, some might have caught up at the Uplift. However long it has been, we all have a duty, and we are *all* on high alert." He pointed a finger and scanned the room, making Torin want to reach out and snap it. "Behave! I know how you *boys* can get when you all come together; it would be in your best interest to remember this is not a family reunion." Viktir moved from the centre of the room with a crooked smile on his face. "It is a professional summit that will be scrutinised by the eyes of the magic world. We must get to work making the tower fit for such a purpose. Have your affairs in order. I shall see you tomorrow, bright-eyed and pristine."

No matter how light-hearted Viktir tried to be in front of his audience, Torin could see his stone-cold mask lying just underneath.

When the commander left the room, the hunters burst into a warm chatter, filling the space full of baritone and bass tones.

Marcus leaned forward in his chair and ruffled Kellen's hair again. "Do you know what that means? The Stryker's will be in the city tomorrow. Didn't you meet their youngest at the Selection?"

Kellen didn't turn, nor did he fix his messy hair, he just kept spinning the knife in his hand.

Marcus sat back, raising his eyebrows at Torin and Gideon, who both shrugged. Although Torin was the wild card of the family, he didn't rule out Kellen for unpredictability. His youngest brother was very unique, a law unto his own.

"Well,"—Marcus grinned again—"you know that means Artem is going to be here too."

Torin smiled. Artem Stryker was his closest companion from the Selection. They were like brothers, forming a bond amidst the harsh conditions in the process to become a warrior of Thorin. Artem had been healthy competition for Torin, and they always attempted to best each other even now. But he liked that about him. They could spar and combat, similar in height and almost identical builds, and they never knew who would win. They could have been twins, but Artem was fairer-haired with golden eyes and inked from head to toe.

Gideon let out a hearty laugh. "By the Gods, Huntswood won't know what hit it with both Torin and Artem roaming around. Lock the tavern doors now."

The boys chuckled.

"Well, it looks like Huntswood is about to find out. It's been a while." Torin winked at his brethren.

CHAPTER SEVEN
EMARA

A knock on the double doors startled Emara's dreamy gaze from the city view. She must have sat there looking out over the city all day, hunched against the frame of her window. The sky had changed to a darker colour of grey and she knew it was past lunch, or maybe even dinner. Stars had started to sparkle and peek through the clouds.

"Come in," she called, wondering who could be at her door.

Naya Blacksteel's sapphire eyes peered around the doorframe and found Emara. Her honey-brown hair curled naturally, resting above her shoulders, and a delicate smile highlighted her elegant face. She walked towards Emara holding a dish wrapped in a cloth.

"When you weren't at lunch or dinner in the dining hall, I thought I would bring it to you." She smiled, her tiny shoulders coming up to meet her ears in a charming gesture. "It's chicken with roasted vegetables in a sticky wine sauce." Her eyes lit up, trying to entice

Emara into eating. "It's delightfully tasty, even if I didn't cook it myself."

"I got lost inside my own head for a while." Emara moved off of the window ledge and took the dish from her hands. "Thank you so much, you didn't have to do that."

"No, I did, my love." Naya placed a delicate hand onto her arm. "You need to eat."

Emara looked down at her toes scrunched into the woven rug. "I just don't feel hungry," she replied, her voice small and croaky.

"I know, but you must start eating properly if you are training like one of my boys and learning magic. You can't run yourself into the ground."

Taking the dish over to the windowsill, she felt the warmth from the plate heat her hands. It did smell wonderful.

"You love the view, huh?" Naya tipped her head to the side, displaying her graceful neck.

"I do," Emara said as she took a roasted carrot from underneath the cloth and munched down on it. The buttery vegetable melted in her mouth, and her stomach rumbled. "I didn't grow up in the city, so this view can sometimes catch my breath."

"It can still do that for me too," Naya said softly. "I used to sometimes find myself up on the roof just taking in its beauty with the wind on my face."

Emara's eyebrows struggled not to reveal her surprise as she also thought of Torin on top of the tower. "You didn't grow up in the city?"

"I didn't." Naya took a gentle seat beside her. "I

grew up north of the Fairlands, in a smaller village than Mossgrave. It was beautiful, all green hills and fresh air. I stayed in a humble cottage with my mother, my father, and Rhea. She's delighted to have you back here." She smiled, her lip curling up at the side in a way that reminded her of the Blacksteel boys. "My mother was a healer for a hunting clan close to Helmsbrook city. She was very talented, so she travelled wherever they needed her. That earned us a lot of coin." Naya's eyes shone brighter as she spoke of her mother. "My father was human and worked as a woodsman for neighbouring villages, so we knew hard work too. But I loved it in the Fairlands. It was my home. And it wasn't as complicated as the cities we travelled to."

The fact that Naya's father was a human surprised her. However, from the minute she had met Naya, Emara knew she had come from humble beginnings. She was kind and thoughtful, and her own cottage in the Fairlands had been sentimental and homely.

"Why did you leave the Fairlands?" Emara asked as she took a little piece of chicken and forced it down.

"I got married."

"Oh." Emara stilled.

"Well, as you can probably speculate, my marriage wasn't for love." Naya looked out to the city below her as lamps started to twinkle in the distance.

Emara shook her head, trying to be polite.

"It's okay, my love, it's common knowledge in the tower. We have lived separate lives since Kellen was just a babe." She smiled again, but this time it didn't reach her eyes. "After I raised my boys, it was time for me to leave this environment, as much as it saddened me."

Emara wondered how many of those smiles she had shown to her children to hide the pain behind her glittering eyes. The pain of being married to the commander couldn't have been easy.

"I am sorry for sounding intrusive, but how did you end up married to the commander?" Emara asked.

They were complete opposites, so it was a wonder to her how they had been matched together. Naya was soft and warm, and Viktir was hard and cold.

Naya laughed softly. "Being my mother's daughter, I developed many of her healing skills. I was one of the best healers in the kingdom, just like her. But I wasn't born into the bloodline that held any titles. I just happened to be highly regarded within the earth coven, and due to my mother's social connections, hunting clans started to notice me. The Empress of Earth had already been promised to another clan, one a little larger than the Blacksteels. However, my mother did all she could to see that I married into a *worthy* bloodline. My mother considered herself a social climber, but I, for one, was never interested in the hierarchy of the magic world. I was happy where I was. I was content with the simple things in life—my garden, my vegetables, and healing anyone who needed aid." She ran a hand over the hem of her olive-coloured skirt. "But I can see that my mother was coming from a place of good will. We all want the best for our children." Her voice shook as she spoke, but she quickly gathered her strength. "Just before my alliance with Clan Blacksteel, our little village was raided, and my father was killed in battle. Out of fear, I agreed to my mother's terms with Viktir's father. I did it to provide wealth and power for my family and my coven."

Naya let out a small sigh, her delicate lashes fluttering quickly.

"I knew she wanted protection and strength, and I couldn't stand my family not having that after my father's death, so the alliance was set between myself and Viktir. I accepted his proposal. In exchange for my healing and skills, I would gain protection and a family." She laughed gently. "I say that like I didn't want those things. Of course, I did, but I didn't realise how hard it would be to become a mother to warriors." She rubbed her thumb into the palm of her hand. "And, of course, Viktir Blacksteel's sons had to be the best Gods-damned warriors known to the kingdom. It's safe to say that I was naive of how difficult it would be to become a commander's wife."

Emara swallowed down fear and gave her a small smile. Hearing Naya talk about Viktir that way somehow made him seem less scary and daunting.

"It wasn't all bad," Naya added. "I have three handsome sons. I don't regret my marriage to Viktir." She beamed as she spoke of her boys. "I count myself lucky every day that they live, and that I have lived to see them grow and dream and become men. I will be thankful to my dying breath for the happiness they have brought me."

Her grey-blue eyes looked into the distance once more.

Emara swallowed, guessing where Naya's thoughts had trailed off to. "I can't imagine living in fear of my husband or child dying in the hunt. Every time that alarm rings, it sends a shudder down my bones. I don't think I will ever get used to it."

"I am afraid you must, my darling." Her gaze caught Emara's. "Because that is going to become your fate." The sparkle left Naya's eyes, and it caused Emara's stomach to flip. "As the empress of a coven, you will be aligned with a hunter with a respectable status. It is how it has been since the beginning of time; witches marry hunters, Faerie marry into other worthy Fae families, and Shifters mate. Humans sometimes get caught in the crossfire of magical love," Naya added. "And as the treaty between House Air and Clan Blacksteel stands, it is my first-born son who is promised to the Empress of Air."

So many thoughts crashed into Emara's skull.

She almost stumbled over her words. "Surely, it would have been the girl who died that night who was promised to the first-born Blacksteel son. Should it not be Maradia that was promised to Torin?" She looked up at Naya to see that her face had straightened out. "Does that not mean that the alliance died with her?"

Naya shuffled closer, her heavy skirt falling around her legs, and placed a hand over Emara's. "No, my love. That alliance does not die with her. What Torin said at the Uplift was correct. It still lies with whoever is in line for the crown of Air after her. Maradia was never really the heir of the coven, she did not have the blood of the

Clearwaters. She only stood in because you were believed to be gone."

Emara's heart jumped into her throat, and her stomach churned like a raging sea.

"As it stands, the magic in your blood ensures that you are destined to be the next Empress of Air. You are the rightful heir to that title." Naya squeezed her hand.

Emara nodded her head quickly, her mouth drying more with every second. "I know what element lies in my blood."

The realisation of saying it out loud smacked into her, making every single piece of food she had just consumed travel back up her throat. She was the grand-daughter of Theodora Clearwater, Theodora of House Air, the previous Supreme of all witches.

Her head buzzed and her heart scrunched again. Waves swirled like a riptide in her stomach.

Naya must have noticed, because suddenly, Emara felt a calm pour over her body before the earth witch spoke. "I am not really sure if this will help soothe your fears, but with all of the empresses who have lost their lives, it won't just be you who will ascend on the next full moon. Every coven will have a new empress. You are not alone."

Something about that did make Emara feel a little lighter, even though it shouldn't. Perhaps the other witches felt the same way she did.

"I won't be the only one?"

"No, my love, all the new empresses must ascend." Naya took her hand and squeezed it again. "Most of them will have been primed in witchcraft from birth, but that doesn't matter. I saw what raw talent you have, the burning power that soared from you and the unyielding winds that whipped around you. You have magic, girl, strong magic. You must talk to it, *your air,* and tell it what you want. That is the key."

She could feel it now, stirring and urging for release, but that scared her more than it comforted her.

"I don't know how to control it properly, or even summon it." Emara let out an exhale that was almost followed by tears.

Ascend.

Witches had to ascend to become the empress of their House. Emara had read about the ascension of a witch from all the resources in the library. But all she really knew about it was that it was a ritual to connect the witch to the crown and title of the House. She had sought out that information after learning who her grandmother had been.

Naya leaned in further. "I am here for you. I will guide you. We have some time before the Cold Moon reaches its full potential; I'll teach you the basics. We can't possibly cover everything with the time we have, but I won't let you go in blind. I know for certain that my boys won't either." She smiled and rubbed her thumb along Emara's hand. "I have a feeling they are rather fond of you."

Emara looked back to Naya. A burning rose in her chest that caused a hot flush to cascade down her back and neck. Another dreaded, almost suffocating question arose. "What will happen to me if I don't want to marry Torin?"

Naya looked down at her hand but didn't let go. "It can be seen as a betrayal to the clan, a rejection." She caught Emara's gaze. "The coven might also see it as a betrayal to them. After all, you are doing it to strengthen and unify the magic community, to ensure that your coven will always have an alliance should they feel attacked or need protection." She swallowed. "Like now."

"Oh Gods." Emara pulled her hand from Naya's and stood. The air in the room felt sparse in her lungs and they tightened. "Oh Gods." Her heart rate doubled, pounding in her ears. She could feel the vomit rising again.

Naya stood too. "Listen, sweetheart, don't worry about your alliance to the clan or any sort of marriage proposal. Not yet." Emara studied Naya as she spoke again. "With everything that is going on, Viktir won't push it just yet. He's too busy. What you need to do now is much more important. You need to search your heart for an answer on what you want."

Emara stood still, her lips parted, unsure of what to say.

Naya swept a loose curl back from her face. "Do you want to be the Empress of Air? Do you want to be in the magic community? Because if not, I can arrange right now for you to hide when the time comes."

Like her grandmother had hidden.

But what kind of life would she have?

Emara bit into her lip a little too hard as she thought over the question. "Do I have a choice?"

"Everyone has a choice, Emara."

A smoky silence fell into the air.

After a few moments of thought, she admitted, "It doesn't feel like I have a choice. I am inexperienced. I am new to this. I don't know what I am doing." Emara's breath left her sharp and quick. "I mean, I am damned if I do marry Torin, and I am damned if I don't. If I don't become the Empress of Air, the Gods that oversee this world would shun me just as much as the magic community would. And if I do, I am promised to marry someone who doesn't even love me, who will probably never love me. But because of an ancient alliance that was probably carved in stone by the first hunter and witch, I have to."

Her heart punched against her ribs and she blew out a breath.

Naya's face was surprisingly distressed, and she was quiet for a while. "I think you would be surprised with how things could change for you."

"What do you mean?"

Naya paused before her authority crept into her posture. "Torin is not who you think he is. He isn't like his father, not on the inside."

"I know he is not," Emara agreed.

Naya took a step forward. "Then if you are scared to let him in because you think he is incapable of love, then you are wrong." Naya lifted her chin. "He is more than capable. He has loved me fiercely since he was born, and he has protected me from his father in every part of his life. A child shouldn't need to protect his mother."

Emara flinched, and a vision of a young Torin

standing in front of his mother, protecting her from a violent commander, inched itself into her mind. She did all she could to hold back the emotion that travelled up her throat and into her eyes, but the tears fell. They fell for Torin and Naya; they fell for Kellen and Gideon too. They fell for how much protection and unconditional love was there from Naya, and she wondered if her own mother had felt the same.

"He just needs the right person to love," Naya continued. "He needs someone to keep him on his toes and be his equal in the life that was given to him by the Gods." She wiped away her own tears. "He took the marriage treaty hard because he was never going to settle for anything less than extraordinary love, and he was convinced he had to."

Naya's words hit Emara like a punch to the face. It was something she had vowed to herself long before she was even old enough to understand love. It was something she was unwilling to compromise on. Her heart.

And Torin had clearly vowed the same.

Something shifted within her, causing a wave of untouched emotion to course into her chest and dust off a few snowflakes that surrounded her grieving heart.

For a second, something like remorse and sympathy struck her.

Torin Blacksteel was a warrior with unmatchable swagger and a mouth that spoke profanity like a first language, but he was more vulnerable than she had once thought. She had seen him on the rooftop of this very tower, looking like a broken man. She had seen the concern in his eyes for her as he thought Eli Baxgroll's blood was her own. And she had even seen the soft, genuine smile when she had made him laugh as they danced at the Uplift together. She knew Torin had a mask. She knew there was a depth to him that she hadn't explored.

But she was unsure if she could marry a man who didn't love her, even for her coven.

"Are you in love with Gideon?" Naya asked outright.

Another invisible punch struck her across the face and gut.

Am I in love with Gideon?

Oh Gods, she didn't know how she felt about the middle Blacksteel brother. She had shared moments with him that she had never shared with anyone. Her feelings for him had been real, raw, and honest.

And then he had betrayed her.

"I don't know. I..." Words failed her.

"If you were in love, *true love*, then you would know. It would consume every part of your soul, and you would know." Naya paused, something like unease wrinkling her brow. "What he did..." She pushed her tongue to the roof of her mouth for a moment and then let it relax. "What he did for his father doesn't change your feelings for him, does it?"

Emara looked out into the city for an answer that she wasn't going to receive.

Naya whispered, "It hasn't changed your feelings for Gideon, but what has changed are your feelings for Torin."

They both stood in silence as she let Emara soak in the truth of her words.

Emara couldn't help but let the emotions she'd held back since this morning pour from her eyes. Salty tears found their way onto her cheeks and lips. She'd promised herself she wasn't going to cry here. She crossed her arms over her torso, biting into her cheek.

She had failed.

"I don't want you to feel guilty for how you *feel*," Naya said softly, but with intent. "But you must admit to yourself how you feel, my love, before it's too late. Holding in your emotions isn't going to get you anywhere."

Emara wiped the wetness from her face. "It sounds like you know a thing or two about that."

"More than you will ever know." Her sapphire eyes glittered once more from under her lashes.

Emara wondered what great stories lingered behind her words, what sacrifices she had made for her family, for her heart, for her sons. What pain had made her so wise.

"All I know is that any of my sons would be lucky to have someone like you, Emara Clearwater. A Blacksteel needs a fierce woman, someone who will stand her ground and fight for what she believes in. Whether that be at Gideon's side or at Torin's, I feel in the stars that it's you." She exhaled. "And if it is not, then so be it. Fate will tell us in time."

CHAPTER EIGHT
EMARA

A strange noise pulled Emara from the hell of her dreams. Dreams of dark wings and screams, of glass smashing and roaring fires, of destruction and obliteration. Nightmares of her own magic. Sitting up quickly, she swept the hair from her face, feeling a clammy sweat thick on her brow, and she tried to slow her breathing.

A booming knock penetrated her door again and she squinted at the window that exposed the city below. The twinkling lights of the city dulled by nightfall told her that she had certainly not slept in for breakfast—or training.

Another impatient knock broke through her heavy breathing.

She hopped out of bed, wondering who it would be at this hour of the morning. She slipped a silk, floor-length robe over her night gown and padded to the door as another boom sounded.

"I am coming," she almost shouted, tiredness and impatience crawling up her throat.

As she opened the door carefully, a waft of liquor hit her face before she could see who it was. Her immediate instincts had proved her wrong to think it was Torin, as emerald eyes met her stare.

"Gideon," she breathed, pulling the cord on her dressing gown tighter around her waist.

"Did I wake you?" He staggered forward and then back.

"Did you wake me? Yes, you woke me," she hissed. "It's the early hours of the morning. Are you drunk?"

Gideon nodded with a hiccup as he sauntered into her room, uninvited.

Emara stood with her mouth open, bewildered at the sight of him. He wasn't just drunk, he was *intoxicated*. She had never witnessed Gideon being remotely close to intoxication.

"You're welcome to come in." Her nose wrinkled and the sarcasm dripped from her lips.

"Thank you," he said, oblivious of her tone, as he leaned against the wall close to the bathing chamber door. His face was flushed with the amount of alcohol he had consumed, and his chocolate hair was wild atop his head, more untamed than usual. His dark tunic was tight around his chest and a few of the buttons were unfastened at the top, exposing his neck. He was unarmed. No weapons.

Strange.

"What are you doing here?" she asked as she folded her arms around her.

"I wanted to see you," he replied, his stunning eyes travelling the length of her face.

She tucked a strand of dark hair behind her ear. "Couldn't it have waited until a decent hour?"

He took a moment before his lips parted. "I fear I have waited too long already."

And there it was...

"Oh Gods, Gideon." She shook her head. "We are not having this conversation, not now."

"If not now, when?" His face was flat with uncertainty, causing the darkness of the room to invade all the angles of his handsome face.

"Maybe when you are sober?" Her jaw hardened and set into place.

"Drunken hearts allow us the courage to speak our sober minds," he replied as he stood up from the wall and swayed slightly. He moved forward, and as he reached for her, she placed up her hand for him to stop.

And he did.

With her hand against his chest, she swallowed. "I don't think this is a good idea," Emara spoke up, looking at the ground, his boots, his laces—anything but those glittering green eyes.

"Please just look at me." His voice was weak with desperation.

She did as he asked, her lips still set hard around her teeth.

He let out a small breath. "You won't even look at me properly."

"I am looking at you now, Gideon, or are you just too drunk to see out of your own eyes?"

He rocked back on one foot, his brows pulling down in a way that made his cheeks narrow and his eyes sharp with hurt. "You may be looking at me, but not in the way you used to." Something in his voice broke, something she feared also broke in her heart.

He walked into her hand, allowing it to push against his chest, and she could feel the solid beat of his heart under her fingertips. She wanted so badly to hold him, but she couldn't. Her heart wasn't ready.

He finally spoke. "I am still the same person you felt something for before I took your stone. Nothing has changed." His lips parted and her heartbeat picked up to the same speed as Gideon's. "I did you wrong, I know that, but I am still the same person you thought I was before. Things don't need to be different between us." Optimism flared in his eyes, and she was regretful that she ever looked up in the first place. "We can work through this."

"Gideon," she breathed as he placed his forehead onto hers. The act stopped her from saying anything more.

"I did what I had to do because it is my duty to be loyal to my commander. I will always need to be loyal to him. You know that," he whispered, and she could still smell the sweet alcohol on his breath.

"I understand that, Gideon—I do—but that doesn't make what you did okay." She pulled her hand from his.

"I know it doesn't, but we can come back from this. I am still the same person."

"Well, I am not!" She pulled back fully. "In case you have forgotten, there are two people in this relationship, not just you. Your actions have caused this...this rift between us." Shadows and regret lingered in his eyes as she spoke, turning them a shade of dark jade. She lifted her chin and continued, "I was happy. I was so happy to let you in. But you broke something that I value most." She wasn't about to say her heart, so she opted for the second best. "You broke my trust, Gideon, and you can't take that back. What's done is done."

"If I had known that the stone meant that much to you, I would never have gone through with it." He drew a hand down his face.

Heat, boiling heat, bubbled through her blood, and something under her skin started to prickle. "The fact that you stand there and stay that you would have defied your commander is a downright lie, Gideon Blacksteel, and you know it. You would never defy him, even if he ordered you to give me over to Taymir."

A flash of rage made itself known on his face. "Don't you dare say that."

She had never seen him flare his anger towards her; it took her a few seconds to steady herself.

"I would have done anything to protect you from Taymir, even if it meant exposing myself and what I had done to you. I did what I did to protect you." He took a step closer, filling her space with muscle and the smell of liquor. "I should never have taken the stone from you. I didn't know what it meant to you. I should have found another way."

Emara took a long breath. "Tell me something, Gideon, did your father take the stone to protect me or to keep it for himself?"

Silence filled her room, and Gideon took longer to respond than she thought he would.

"I only knew my father wanted it. I didn't know his agenda. I promise you, I would never have taken it had I known he would have kept it."

"Will you stop saying that?" She flung out her hands in frustration and created some space between them. "Do not promise me anything. Your promises are void. It doesn't matter what the stone meant to me. The fact is that it belonged to me, it belonged to my grandmother, and whilst I was thinking about giving myself to you"— she trembled at the thought—"you were thinking about your mission. About getting close to me, to use me."

He closed his eyes and spoke on an outbreath. "You are getting it all wrong."

"Really, Gideon? Am I getting it all wrong? Which part?" A dry wind fluttered past her hair.

"The part where you think I wanted to actively betray you." His nostrils flared. "I never wanted you to feel like that. What I felt for you was real." He paused, not taking his eyes from her face. "What I *still* feel for you is real." He looked her over, his face hopeful. "I thought I could have told you after—"

"But you didn't tell me!" she nearly screamed, and even in her rage, she noticed a breeze blow through Gideon's hair. "You seduced me, *almost* to the point of no return, for a mission that your father ordered you to do." She paused, seeing the hurt on his face. "You knew it was wrong. You knew I wouldn't have given myself to just anyone, and even though we didn't sleep together, you still worked behind my back."

"I had no choice," he exclaimed.

"Everyone has a choice," she echoed his mother's

words from earlier. "You could have chosen to be my partner and see me as an equal, but you didn't. You saw me as an object in a game of '*who can find the ancient relic first.*'" He flinched at her words again. "You could have asked me about it and I would have told you. Gods above, I probably would have given it to you had you included me in your *mission,* because I trusted you. But you didn't see my worth, only the stone in my possession."

Gideon's face paled and as he struggled to find his words, emotion darkened his eyes even more.

"I know you care for me, Gideon. And I do for you, *greatly.*" She closed the space between them. "My feelings for you haven't just disappeared. What I felt for you was real too." She swallowed her admittance. "I just think—"

"It's too late." Gideon's face scrunched in hurt.

"You didn't even let me finish what I had to say."

"You don't need to." His eyes narrowed. "You are promised to my brother. It is best if you lay your focus there."

Anger spiked like a spear through her chest, and she stilled. "How dare you tell me where I should lay my focus. How *dare* you?" She seethed, and the half-awake beast that lay under her skin erupted. "Where I lay my focus is my choice and it always will be. And right now, that focus is going to be on myself. *Me.* Emara Clearwater." She pointed so hard into her chest that she flinched, and a gust of wind blew around the room, causing the chiffon curtains to sway. It swirled and gathered like smoke. "I will *not* be putting my focus into a bloody *Blacksteel,* that's for certain. I have learned my lesson there."

"Calm down, Emara." His eyes darted around the room, and then back to her.

"Don't tell me to calm down!" she roared, pinning him with a stare. Air whirled around the room, and she was sure that something fell over and broke, but she was too angry to rip her eyes from his face. Her hands felt warm, dangerously warm. And—

A husky voice broke through the turmoil in her head. A voice that was not Gideon's.

"Lesson number one, brother." Torin Blacksteel had somehow opened the door without her hearing or noticing and there he was, striding over to them, his hair blowing in the wind. "Never tell a woman to calm down; it will only make things worse." He threw a look at Gideon and his brow fell. "Much worse."

"Great." Emara threw her hands up. "Now I have *two* extremely insufferable Blacksteels in my room before dawn."

"Lucky you." Torin raised a dark eyebrow as a corner of his mouth turned up. She focused on it long enough to hear the rustle of the wind around her room, and panic broke through her as she acknowledged that the wind was her own element. Torin gave her a wink that suggested that he knew she had it under control.

Talk to it, Naya had said.

Her hands only tightened into fists.

"Come on, brother, let's go before you are the root cause of the destruction of this tower." Torin clapped a hand on Gideon's shoulder, but no one moved.

The enchanted wind lashed at them all as they stood in a potent silence, glaring at each other.

"I was just leaving." Gideon dragged his eyes from Emara's face, slurring his words.

"Good," Emara spat.

"Wait. Is he drunk?" Torin's eyes squinted as he looked from Gideon to Emara and then back to Gideon. "Did you seriously go to a tavern without me?"

Gideon staggered and scowled, mumbling something incoherent under his breath.

"The betrayal." Torin placed his hand over his heart. "Since when did you become so edgy and sneak off to a tavern to drink yourself into a sulk? That's my thing," he jested.

"Sometimes you just need to be alone," Gideon grumbled.

Torin couldn't hide his sly smile. "Have you even been to bed yet?"

"No." Gideon side-eyed his brother. "I haven't."

Torin let out a barking laugh. "Well, you better get at least an hour in, today is going to be a long day."

Gideon frowned and ran a hand over his face, looking sleepy.

"As much as I'd love to watch this brother bonding time, I would really appreciate it if you could take it elsewhere." Emara flashed a false smile towards Torin. "I was busy sleeping, like a normal person at this hour."

"Didn't sound like sleep from my room." Torin laughed as he put a hand around Gideon's shoulder and steered him towards the door.

"What do you mean 'your room?'" Emara's brows pinched together as she followed them.

"Oh, didn't my mother tell you? My room is just down the corridor." His wicked lips twitched upwards and Emara let an angry exhale through her teeth. Torin chuckled. "I will see to it that my brother gets to his room. See you at breakfast"—Torin gave a lazy wave and a smug smile—"neighbour."

Emara slammed the door shut behind them. She felt the vibrations rattle up the stone walls and through her bones.

She didn't know what was worse, the fact that Gideon had come to her room drunk, pleading his innocence, or the fact that Torin Blacksteel's room was down the corridor, mere metres away from her room. She marched to her bed, threw herself onto the mattress, and pulled the sheets over her body, letting out a groan. Maybe no Blacksteels would find her under the sheets for a few days.

CHAPTER NINE
EMARA

The dining hall was full of new faces come breakfast time. Well, faces that Emara had never laid eyes on before in the tower. They were certainly hunters, but they didn't belong to the Blacksteel Clan. The tables were stacked full of brute like warriors of all ages from all around the kingdom, clothed in different versions of combat gear.

She grabbed a block of butter as she stood, waiting for her bread to warm, scanning the room. Some were eating, others catching up with men who sat next to them, but Emara didn't want to stare for too long. They were all rather...well, rather alarming with their scars, their weapons, and their booming voices.

Removing the bread from the stove, she spread the butter across its surface, and it melted immediately. She took a bite, and the salty butter dissolved on her tongue; it was mouth-watering. She moaned.

A loud masculine greeting snapped Emara's attention to the threshold of the dining hall door. A few of the hunters had gotten up from their seats to make their way towards the new faces that had entered.

She noted Torin Blacksteel stride over to them before being bear-hugged by a heavily inked male, who was roughly the same height as him. The male pretended to throw a few slow punches and Torin ducked them.

Emara had to admit the hunter Torin was greeting looked rather frightening as his solid frame stood in the threshold of the door. He was built like a machine of violence, but he did have a rugged handsomeness about him, a charm in his eyes. Although he was extremely handsome, Torin was even more beautiful than his friend. The genuine smile on his face lit up the whole room.

She choked on her toast and swallowed.

Praise the Gods, no one could hear her thoughts. She took another bite of her breakfast.

Another male with the same russet-coloured hair, only longer, embraced Torin too. His face was a little familiar, but she couldn't think where from. Perhaps she had met him at the Uplift and just couldn't place him. His features were less mature than the first hunter, but he, too, had the frame of a highly trained warrior. She noticed Kellen move over to greet him; their gazes lingered for the longest second, and then Kellen disappeared from the dining hall like he had performed a magic trick.

Emara put her breakfast down on the table in front of her. She no longer felt in any way capable of eating, even if she had promised Rhea and Naya that she would keep trying.

Just then, she felt a warm presence at her back. Turning, she almost wished she hadn't. Gideon stood there with a shameful frown carved into his mouth.

He held out his hands. "Before you punch me in the face," he began, "can we take a walk in the gardens?" He looked her over. "Please."

There was a longing in his words, a dishonourable glint in his eyes that she knew made him suffer. Even though she was mad at him, she didn't want anyone that she cared about to feel pain. She took a deep breath and then nodded, making her way out of the crowded dining hall to the gardens where she had once kissed Gideon Blacksteel without question.

The wind was bitter on her skin, and the crunching snow under her boots made her shiver even more with each step that she took. Even the winter roses were hiding from the cold, sad and crumpled against one another. They walked in silence for a few moments, making Emara squirm under her fleece cloak, which was doing all it could to warm her. Gideon guided her to a small wooden bench that had a memorial plaque on it, brushed by gold paint, and they took a seat. She had seen a few of these benches on her travels around the gardens, in memory of the fallen. It didn't feel right to sit on them, but she took Gideon's lead. She had witnessed a few hunters sit by them and pray, asking the Gods to protect their brethren on the Otherside.

Gideon's eyes found hers immediately. "I just want to start by saying I am incredibly sorry for this morning." His gaze didn't falter, and she knew he meant his apology. "I should never have come to your room in that state." He lowered his eyes shamefully. "I don't know what I was thinking. I don't expect you to forgive me for any of it, but I had to apologise to you again, even if you don't want to talk to me. I am truly sorry."

Emara looked up at him through her dark lashes, and she could have sworn he flinched.

"I was in no state to have *that* kind of conversation last night." His jaw slanted as he pondered over a thought. "I think we desperately needed a conversation, maybe just not like that."

"No, not like that," she whispered, feeling the full sadness of her heart for what they once had. It had been quick and fast, like falling in love at first sight.

"I am sorry for taking the Resurrection Stone from your room. It had been in your family's possession, and it was wrong of me to take it from you," he declared. "You were right in what you said last night; if my father told me to steal the Fae king's crown, I would do it. Because I swore an oath to obey. No matter how wrong it may feel, it is how I am conditioned—to obey him." His shoulders shrunk and vulnerability coasted on his face. "That is not something I am proud of, believe me." He looked away from her eyes, casting his gaze out to the storm of snow that looked to be headed in their direction. "I just wish things were different."

"Me too," she whispered again. "But they are not."

"I know." His gaze found hers and a sorrow like the loss of a loved one pushed its way into his features. "Can you find it in your heart to forgive me?"

She let out a long breath. "Gideon, I have forgiven you for taking the stone. It seems small amongst everything else going on."

He seemed surprised to hear it. "Thank you." A smile warmed his lips only to disappear within seconds. "I would love to pick up where we left off, walking the gardens together, reading together, training together. But only if you want to."

She shook her head, her heart disagreeing with her thoughts and what she was about to say. "I can't do that, Gideon."

Hurt spilled into his eyes, but he controlled it like the warrior he was. His lips parted and then closed.

"If I let myself do that, then I believe my heart will disobey my head and I will fall in love with you." She found herself instantly wishing she had never said the words out loud.

"Then why can't you stop listening to your head and follow your heart?" His dark brows pulled over his pine eyes. He looked so agonisingly beautiful.

She sucked in a breath.

"Because I will be an empress who must use her head instead of her heart." She swallowed, allowing the silence to last long enough for her to shift uncomfortably. It was the first time she had really acknowledged her blood proudly, and it terrified her. "Because I am not the girl you once walked these gardens with, I am not the same girl who accepted your white rose, and I am not the girl who waited for you to come back from the hunt. I am not that girl, and I realise now that fate was always going to promise me a different path. As much as I would like to be the girl you want, I am not."

"You are that girl to me." He shifted closer to her, trying to reach out to her. "Elemental heir or not, you are that girl."

Shaking her head, she took in his face. "I have changed, Gideon. In such a short time, I have changed. I now have a darkness inside me and I fear it will never leave. The girl who you fell for was as pure as the rose you gave to her. But I can't pretend. I am not her anymore. I have a hollowness that makes me feel vengeance. I am scared of myself, and I am petrified that my magic could make me something unrecognisable."

"That's not true." His voice shook with disbelief. "Your magic won't do that to you. You are good through and through. You are full of the light."

Recently, with the thoughts she was having, she wasn't sure of that anymore. Would the old Emara want revenge so roasting hot that she wasn't scared to burn a whole kingdom to the ground to find who was responsible for the Uplift?

The old Emara wouldn't have wanted the destruction. She would have found justice another way. But now? The flames of her untamed magic licked the inside of her bones, waiting to devour.

"I cannot go back to how we once were Gideon. I am sorry."

Gideon looked like he was fighting with a demon inside of his mind before he spoke. "Emara, we have options. Time. I will go to my father and beg him not to push for the alliance to be with Torin but with me."

That struck a chord.

Emara let out a harsh laugh. "If you think that will solve anything, you will be bitterly disappointed. Even the thought of an arranged marriage makes my blood boil."

He took some time before saying, "I won't give up on you."

Her nose stung as she tried to hold back the emotion crawling up her throat. "Perhaps you should."

"I believe fate brought us together, Emara. I know it did. That first night I saw you, standing in your demolished bathroom, I knew I was supposed to find you. I feel it every time I look at the moon because she has the same magic you do, the same magic we have. Don't give up on us," he begged.

Emara let the monster that lived deep down in her darkness and sorrow speak. She let the friend who was grieving, the granddaughter who had not mourned properly, and the person who was broken, speak. "Sometimes fate brings two people together only to rip them apart."

CHAPTER TEN
EMARA

Emara's heart skipped a beat every time a faction of the prime entered the large sparring room. The floors were polished, and the training equipment had been put away, out of sight. She had been in this room many times before to learn of the Dark God or for combat. But she had never been in this room to attend a summit meeting with the hierarchy of the magic community.

Dark wooden chairs mapped out rows down the long sides of the room, creating a rectangle in the middle of the space that had been designed to allow the prime to sit at the top of the room, in large throne-like chairs.

Emara took her seat beside Naya Blacksteel, who had some healers who worked for the clan sitting beside her. Moments later, Gideon and Marcus took the seats beside them, looking focused and wearing hunting attire, their weapon belts secured against their waists.

A few days had passed since her conversation with Gideon in the garden, and she hadn't really seen him around the tower, not even at mealtimes, and she worried that he was avoiding her.

She couldn't blame him, of course. She would be avoiding her too if he had said the same things to her.

Naya, however, had practically joined herself to Emara's hip, informing her of who each clan member was as they arrived and what their importance was. Not to mention, she had Emara's head swarming with knowledge about witchcraft, and she had also been instructing her in practice. Just soft magic, like lighting a candle and shutting the door with her predominant element. But it was a start to helping her control and summon the elements that she had.

Naya leaned in and said, "We will take the hearing one step at a time, my love. I am sure you won't have to do anything, with Viktir having already informed the prime about the Uplift. But if one of the faction leaders speaks to you, acknowledge who you are by using your full title, and always bow before and after they are finished talking."

Emara swallowed down some sickening trepidation at the thought of being asked anything, but she nodded.

"Looks like the Baxgroll wolves have arrived," Gideon said to Marcus, looking over his shoulder as the Alpha strolled into the room. "It looks like most of the factions are starting to arrive."

Emara watched as the Baxgroll pack filtered into the room, the Alpha standing tall, with his eldest son at his side. Murk gave his pack a nod before he took his seat at the head of the room. The king of wolves' dark gaze found where the Blacksteel Clan was sitting, and he acknowledged them with one prolonged nod of his head—no smile—and Gideon mirrored the gesture, showing respect.

One elegant-looking male glided through the entrance, wearing a cerulean robe, and Emara noticed he had guards on either side of him, dressed similarly but in a lighter blue. The crown perched on his head was topped with stars that swirled like they were in a galaxy of their own. The shimmering diamonds glistened as he gracefully stood at the front of the room. His pointed ears protruded through his winter-white hair, and his features were sharp and proud, with an ancient regalness. His shoulders squared, revealing his royal tunic, which was the same colour as his cape, but with grand gold and silver details embroidered through the fabric.

There was no denying who that was.

The King of the Fae.

Faeries were a species that Emara had read about in stories since she was a little girl. As she looked around the room, she realised that she could have said that about everyone here.

A few of the elite representatives in one of the front rows were looking rather uninterested, representing the human faction. Nothing about them looked like a normal villager or city worker, with their expensive shoes and warm furs slung around their necks.

Viktir Blacksteel appeared with an older man who wore his full battle attire—a dark tunic and leathers with a metal crest pinned to his shoulder, with the initials *CC.*

Chief Commander.

Viktir looked to be engaging in polite conversation as he guided *his* commander to sit at the top of the room, in one of five chairs that crowned the seating arrangement.

As the minutes passed, the last of the magical factions filtered into the room and nested into their seats.

A head of inky-black hair finally strolled through the room towards her, and her lungs squeezed.

"You saved me a seat." Torin Blacksteel plunked himself down into the chair beside Emara with a cheeky grin. "How nice of you," he said as he scanned the room, his eyes narrowing in on who were present.

"I certainly did nothing of the sort." Emara looked around the room too, holding her hands together tightly, trying not to show her nervous shaking to the warrior beside her.

"Don't worry." Torin turned to face her. "I won't tell anyone that you are being nice to me." She found it hard to breathe as she watched a sinful smile devour his face. "I promise."

"I think it would be *nice* if you found a seat elsewhere." She turned her head to look at anything else but his eyes. His ocean-blue eyes.

"There's no other seat I would rather sit in." He nudged her with his shoulder, and she rolled her eyes. "Plus, I will keep you right should they need to speak with you."

"I don't think *you* would be the first person I would

choose to keep me *right* in a formal meeting like this. You can't even be here on time."

He laughed, a gentle chuckle that was husky and hearty. "I am the best kind of person to have on your side in a meeting like this. Maybe you should re-evaluate your thoughts." He clasped his hands together and she watched his movement through the side of her eye.

"Maybe you should *re-evaluate* your seat," she nipped.

A deep voice came from beside Torin; it reminded her of silk and honey. "Do you both realise that your conversation is full of flirtatious undertones?"

Emara looked over at the male sitting two seats down. She hadn't even noticed anyone else around her since Torin had taken his seat. He always had a way of doing that. Sitting beside Torin was the heavily inked male from the dining room, a smirk on his face.

Torin chuckled, his eyes sparkling. "She can't help herself."

Emara shot Torin a look of disgust and then looked right into the inked warrior's eyes. "The last thing in the world I would want to do is *flirt* with Torin Blacksteel."

She sat back in her seat, her arms tucked in at her chest and a scowl on her brow.

"I like her already," said the male as he eyed Torin, amusement thick on his features. "I am Artem, of Clan Stryker." He held out his hand, knocking his elbow into Torin's chest.

Emara grinned as Torin took the intentional blow and she held out her own hand. "I am Emara Clearwater," she said. He gave two professional shakes and let her hand drop, narrowly missing Torin's lap.

"Oh, I know who you are," Artem said, and his eyes smiled in a way that let his boisterous streak shine through. His jawline was almost square, and it bulked out the frame of his face. Emara noticed that the hunter had a tiny sliver ring curled in his left nostril. "It's a pleasure to finally meet the witch that everyone is talking about."

Emara took in a breath, finding it hard to breathe, and blinked a few times.

"Now look who's flirting." Torin drew his eyes from Artem's face and Emara questioned if she saw a flicker of annoyance in Torin's eyes.

She had to be imagining it.

"I can't help myself," Artem said in jest, mocking Torin.

"Well, you had better help yourself, Stryker," Torin warned with a low smile that dropped his brows.

Her breathing hitched.

A knocking sounded three times, and it had everyone straightening in their seats, turning their attention to the front of the room. The five seats were now full.

From left to right, Emara could identify most of the factions. Murk Baxgroll sat as the leader of the Shifters, probably outweighing them all in mass. The Fae king sat elegantly next to him, contrasting completely in every way possible. The chief commander who represented the hunters sat in the next chair, and a stunning woman, with dark brown hair and even darker eyes, took the second-to-last seat, clad in crimson. Being the only woman on the panel, Emara knew she was the representative of the witches.

The Supreme.

She hadn't noticed her coming through the door, but as she took in her presence now, a knot of nervousness balled in her stomach. The Supreme was the one who governed the witches, the most powerful of them all. She was the one who was viewed as closest to a deity as modern times would get; the Gods had gifted her the power of all elements.

At the end of the row sat a representative of the human elite faction, or as Emara knew him, the Minister of Coin. She didn't have to think about what monster slithered beneath his skin.

The monster of gold, slavery, diamonds, and greed, one of the ugliest monsters in the kingdom.

She recalled a memory of when he had visited the village of Mossgrave, when he would come to oversee his minions recruit workers for the gold mines he owned. He would entice poor families into signing up their sons or daughters to work the longest and harshest of hours by giving them a little profit, and they would treat him like a king. The workers would probably die in the bleak conditions of the mines before their families ever saw the benefit of their work. That's one thing her grandmother had disclosed to her—the horrors of the elite mines.

Emara's blood boiled at the sight of him, sitting there in an emerald-coloured tunic only mass riches could buy, covering his fat, overfed stomach. He dripped pretentiousness. Even the pocket watch, dangling on a chain from his tunic, was probably worth more than her entire village had earned in one year.

The chief commander stood swiftly, walking forward into the centre of the room, and it took every ounce of strength for Emara to keep her thoughts from going to that dark place where notions of Taymir Solden often lingered. He had been cut from the same cloth as the Minister of Coin.

Elite.

High-bred.

Pigs.

Emara felt Torin's arm muscles tighten beside her as his faction leader spoke.

"We gather all factions of the kingdom together today in a state of emergency." He lifted his chin and let the brassy tones of his voice echo through the hall. He placed his hands behind his back and Emara couldn't help but wonder if all hunters had the same habit. "We are not going to waste time going over old tales of Gods and monsters." He spun, now directly facing where Emara sat. "We are here today to formulate a plan for our community to endure these dark times and rebuild our faith." He looked further down the line. "As it stands, we have lost an empress of each witching coven, resulting in us being in the weakest position the magic community has been in for a long time."

Emara couldn't help but tighten her muscles. Her lungs almost caved in. The back of Torin's finger flicked against her leg, prompting her to breathe. She did. And it was a gentle reminder that he was there, her coach.

"Many lives have been lost, not only in the covens, but in our Shifter community." He gave a grave nod to Murk Baxgroll who didn't move an inch, his feral face stony. "In our Fae community and also in our human community." He acknowledged every faction without a mention of the hunters. "We must take action against the evil of the Underworld, and we must pull together to combat our greatest enemy. A summit has not been called upon to recite the talks of previous wars. We are at war. We know another great war is inevitable. It is not a question of *if*, but of when."

Murmurs of agreeance spread through the room, and with it came a stale, eerie atmosphere that lingered like a thick mist.

Emara shifted on her seat, and Naya Blacksteel's calming hand rested on her forearm, draining the thoughts of battles and carnage out of her mind.

"Until we are in the position to engage in a full-scale war against the dark one, we must protect our communities where we can. The five members of the prime have decided to act on this immediately." He gestured to a hunter, who took quick strides across the room and handed over a scroll. "We have decided on these actions in regards to the most recent events and all must be followed by oath, in all factions."

He pulled the scroll open. "Witches of title or importance will have guards assigned to them from now until it is safe to remove them, and the guards will be made up by a cluster of hunting clans." He looked over to where the Supreme sat as she glowered at him, power radiating from her gaze. She gave him a small smile.

"Dedicating three hunters to each newly rising empress will protect the ascension that will take place at the Cold Moon, fourteen nights from now."

Apprehension sunk deep into Emara's stomach.

Fourteen nights!

Naya gripped her hand even more.

"The witching covens cannot afford for any of the promised empresses *not* to ascend, and with the murders becoming increasingly high among the witches, we must do everything we can to ensure the empress' safety. Our kingdom depends on it." The words rang through the hall, lying heavy on Emara's chest. The kingdom depended on her ascension.

Once shown how, she would be the most valuable asset to the coven and anyone who aligned with them. She would be the one that her coven turned to.

Sick promised itself to her mouth. Her heart almost stopped. But a calming, ancient voice spoke lightly, *"We will be right behind you every step of the way."*

She swallowed back the heaviness of her new duty.

The chief commander continued, "Between the prime leaders, we have arranged a list of names who will be required to be guarded at all times, not only in the magic-wielding factions, but with the elite humans too." The chief looked over at the leader of the humans. "We have not forgotten how vulnerable the human faction is to the Dark Army."

A pang of anger curled in Emara's chest. It was the humans without coin who needed protection, not the elite who already had private guards. Did they need to swallow up the resources of the warriors of Thorin too?

As the chief commander began reading through the names on the list, Emara tried to make sense of who everyone was, trying to pinpoint where they sat in the crowd.

She let out an exhale.

"Something wrong?" Torin's raspy voice reached her ears in a whisper.

"I'm not sure I am following everything." She hated to admit it to him.

"The chief commander is running through the rankings of who will be protected. It will be down to how well a hunter performed in the Selection and how highly regarded they are that will determine the pairing of the guards with the witch. Of course, they will have taken into consideration how highly regarded the witch is too."

"Aren't the witches and the elite capable of protecting themselves?" Emara whispered, thinking of the poor humans who were unaware of what was pending.

"Of course they are, but there is only so much magic a witch can project before her body tires, and she burns herself out. A hunter's body is built from birth not to tire in battle. We have the strength of conflict and destruction in our bones. We have war in our veins."

The blood of Thorin.

"What I don't understand is why witches haven't been trained in combat."

"Some will have, if they have asked for it, but it's frowned upon," Torin whispered back. "Witches are female. The prime agreed centuries ago that females didn't belong in the affair of war unless it was for healing purposes, so they were never allowed to train. And they very rarely ever challenged it. Until you walked through the door, a female had never been trained in the Blacksteel Tower. But again, that is kind of our little secret. You can't tell the prime we have been extending our training hours for you to practise with weapons and advanced combat."

"I won't," she promised, feeling gratitude in her heart.

He smiled back at her.

"Emara Clearwater." Her name reverberated off every wall. "The promised elemental heir of House Air."

Her head snapped 'round so fast, she almost broke her neck, as did Torin. Naya nodded in her direction, and Emara took in a deep breath. She stood before bowing and then straightened, her gaze on the chief commander's focused stare.

"Do you swear upon the God of Rhiannon that the blood that runs in your veins is the same bloodline to the heirship of House Air?"

"I do," she choked out, the inside of her mind whirling. "Chief Commander," she remembered to add the appropriate etiquette.

The chief nodded. "From this point on, indefinitely, you will be placed under the protection of following hunters: Magin, of Clan Oxhound, Artem, of Clan Stryker."

Both warriors stood to attention, but she didn't dare look, not as the whole room watched her with curious glances of their own. She could see the inked warrior out of the corner of her eye, and the other hunter stood at the back of the hall.

"And Torin, of Clan Blacksteel."

"Well, what do you know?" Torin shot a glance her way as he stood beside her, towering above. She let out a discreet exhale that she had been holding in and kept her vision on the chief, but she couldn't hear a single word he was saying as she processed her pairing. Her heartbeat drummed in her ears.

Torin leaned in. "To be paired with three of the best hunters in the kingdom..." He nudged her a little with his elbow. "They clearly think you are special, Clearwater." He nudged her again with his shoulder.

Her cheeks bloomed red. "I swear, if you nudge me one more time, I will stab you in your sleep," she hissed quietly at him, low enough for no one else to hear.

As her trio of hunters bowed and took their seats again, the chief commander moved on to the next pairing. Torin lowered himself back into his chair as Emara did too. "Are you threatening to come to my room, Miss Clearwater of *House Air?*" A wicked grin tugged on his lips. "At least you won't have to travel far from your own. That could come in handy."

"In your dreams." She balled her hands into fists, trying to keep focus on what the prime members were saying.

She failed.

He chuckled beside her and tapped a finger on his knee as his voice turned dark and alluring. "You don't want to know what goes on with you and I in my dreams, angel."

She swallowed as a heat started to gather low in her core.

How could he be so brazen in front of *so* many people? How did he have the confidence that no one would hear him?

He probably liked the thought of that.

She scowled, wishing that she had the same level of nonchalance that he did.

"No, but seriously, you have been given great protection, Emara," he added with no quip or jest lining his tone. "I am happy with your guards."

Before she could open her mouth to speak, the chief commander's voice cut through the muffled voices in the room. "Sybil Lockhart, promised heir of House Earth, you have already made claim to your bloodline, and will be placed under the protection of following Hunters: Marcus, of Clan Coldwell, Arlo, of Clan Stryker, and Gideon, of Clan Blacksteel."

Emara allowed herself a glance at Gideon as he stood. His face gave nothing away. And as he accepted his newest mission, Emara wondered why her heart felt heavy. As the lists went on and on, going through every witch of importance and every hunter that would protect them, Emara tried her hardest to focus, but her mind was racing, spinning.

"It's almost over," Naya Blacksteel whispered as she placed a hand over Emara's twitching thumbs.

The Fae King spoke gracefully, drawing her attention. "We also would like to give permission to extend our Fae guards to the human faction." His violet eyes blinked once, convincing Emara that he was not, in fact, a stone statue. "It has been an era since we guarded human life, but we feel now, more than ever, it is necessary."

The chief commander glanced at the other members of the prime, then nodded at the King of Fae. "Your permit is granted. The hunters thank you for your generosity. It will allow us to not stretch our clans so thinly across Caledorna. The Gods will not forget it." He looked over at the sole woman on the panel. "The Supreme's guards will be as they stand now. You will keep the hunters who reside at the amethyst palace."

A smile expanded across her creamy-skinned face, and she nodded in acceptance.

"Do you have any requests for guards, Alpha Baxgroll?" The chief asked his prime leader for the Shifters.

The alpha smiled, keeping his dangerous fangs hidden under his lips. "We have no requirement for guards. I have many Shifters in a position to be placed where they need to be."

"I have one request, Chief Commander." The Supreme finally sat forward in her chair, and everyone seemed to be caught off guard. "I would like to ban all portaling by a witch's hand." She gave off a coy look, but Emara had the feeling she liked all eyes to be on her. "It is not safe for my witches to be using portals. We need to save all of our strength; portaling significantly depletes our magic, and I think it would be sensible to stop them at once. Therefore, until I lift the pause, I would see them banned."

The chief commander drew his eyes from her and

rolled the long scroll into a cylinder. He looked up to see if the other prime members had any objections to her wish, and as the silence grew heavy in the room, he nodded. "Granted. Please send your communications out as soon as possible to establish your newest legislation." Turning back to the crowd, he said, "These protection orders fall in place at the light of dawn, tomorrow. The promised empresses must get ready to leave for Amethyst Palace, where the ascension will take place."

Her ascension was taking place.

At the amethyst palace.

In fourteen days.

"These witches are the future of our kingdom." The chief commander's voice echoed through the room as he looked over his crowd once more. "Protect them with your life."

Emara's shoulders tensed, and a flurry of nervous emotions curled in her stomach.

Naya placed a delicate hand on Emara's arm. "Don't worry, my love, I will see to it that you have everything you need."

Emara allowed a small smile to shape her face before the factions began moving.

CHAPTER ELEVEN
EMARA

The summit was less painful than Emara had thought it would be. Not that it wasn't intense, because it was—at times she had fought with the sickness in her stomach to stay down—but she hadn't been asked any questions about the Uplift, and the reprieve that engulfed her heart once it had finished was overwhelming.

She wasn't ready to talk about the Uplift.

The summit had gone pretty much like Naya had said it would, although she hadn't predicted the new rules for the witches.

She thought about what it would feel like to have a person (or *three*) at the back of her heels, everywhere she went. Everything she would do, their eyes would be on her. Torin Blacksteel's eyes would be on her.

Her heart squeezed tightly.

Torin Blacksteel was her personal guard.

Her lungs pinched, her muscles tightened, and her stomach flipped. Granted, there were another two of them in her trio, but did the Gods really want to punish her so much that they would assign Torin to her? Weren't there another thousand hunters that could have been put in his place?

Or had they aligned Torin to her as an acknowledgement to their treaty?

No, no, no. She couldn't think about that right now. She couldn't think of marriage again, not when there were several things that took precedent first—like ascending!

"They clearly think you are special, Clearwater. To be paired with three of the best hunters in the kingdom."

Torin's words drifted through her mind and caused a spasm of nervous energy in her belly. Did she even want to be classified as *special?* Emara wasn't sure that would ever sit well with her. In her old life, she was a small village girl, a nobody. Now, in this new world, she had one of the most important bloodlines in history. She was the granddaughter of the late Supreme. And now she was going to ascend to be an empress of her coven.

She exhaled and fiddled with the sleeve of her shirt as she walked behind Naya and Kellen. They were discussing how he had been assigned to a powerful witch who belonged to House Fire. She wasn't destined to be an empress, but she was a well-regarded witch in the coven. Apparently, that was more than Kellen had hoped for.

Quickly, her thoughts turned to Gideon.

He had been placed as a guard for the House of Earth empress, which meant he would leave with her.

A twisting feeling stirred in her gut. She would see Gideon again, that she knew. He would be at the ascension; she just didn't know where to place the disappointment of not being able to see that he was okay before he made it there. But then again, it was selfish of her to want him as her guard. She knew that too. It would just have been nice to have someone she was already comfortable with.

Maybe this time apart would do them good, clearing both their hearts and heads of the mess they had caused. Possibly this time would allow her to let him go and he could let go of her too.

It would be better that way.

They made their way along to the second largest sparring room, by the order of Viktir Blacksteel, and as she entered, witches were being acquainted with their guards. A humming of chatter sounded over the room. Oversized maps of Caledorna were being pushed out onto the floor. Fae guards were being assigned by their king as he liaised with the Shifters to see what territory they covered, taking pressure off their faction too. And the elite were negotiating with the chief commander about who would be their protection, evidently unhappy with what was provided.

It felt like the buzz of the tower had turned up its intensity levels by a million.

Naya Blacksteel looked over her dainty shoulder and encouraged Emara to stand beside her as she stopped. "There is no need to have that worried look on your face, my darling." She smiled gently. Emara released the frown she had been wearing. "You will be just fine. Plus, you have my boy to look after you." Emara tried to smile, but Naya choked back a laugh. "You are going to have to get better at hiding how you really feel underneath that face of yours. It will get you into trouble as a female of power in this kingdom."

"Ah, there you are." Torin Blacksteel's voice drifted across the space and found her. She turned on her heels, as did Naya. "Emara, I would like to introduce you to Magin Oxhound. He is going to be the third guard in your cluster." Emara's eyes drifted from Torin's to Magin's. The male was just shorter than Torin and more like Gideon in his build. However, she couldn't pull her stare from the scar that ran from his lip across to his ear. It was still raw, and it looked like a healer had done everything she could to bring his skin together. She wondered what kind of demon he had been fighting to receive a scar like that. "He was the personal guard to the late Empress of Air." A change in Torin's tone caught her attention and she flashed her eyes over his face quickly before returning her attention to Magin. He stood stoic, but there was sorrow in his eyes.

"It's lovely to meet you." She bowed her head and let a warm smile grace her lips.

He nodded back, keeping his lips shut.

"I wish that was the response I received," Torin said as he raised his eyebrows. "Do you just save those pretty scowls for me?"

"I don't scowl," she argued, her cheeks flushing pink.

"You are doing it now," he teased.

A cough interrupted them and Artem Stryker made his presence known, standing beside Torin before he moved into position, forming her trio.

"Miss Clearwater." He bowed. "We have already

been acquainted. It is an honour to be your guard." A mischievous grin pulled on his mouth, and he danced his eyes between Emara and Torin. "I can't believe we have fallen into the same cluster, Blacksteel." His grin widened. "It will be like old times."

That comment pulled Naya's attention off of fixing Kellen's tunic. "I hope not," she said light-heartedly. "I would like to believe you will both behave and not lead each other astray," she scolded them with a grin. *"Like old times."*

"No ma'am." Artem placed his hands behind his back and raised his chin in respect for her. "You have my word." As his charming grin lay sincerely on his face, a few of his inked markings peeked out from underneath his tunic, the detail covering his throat.

"Good. All of your focus must be on high alert. You have someone very precious you need to protect."

It took a moment for Emara to realise that Naya was referring to her. She felt all four males direct their attention to her face, and she blushed.

Again.

"I don't know if 'precious' is the correct word choice for *our* empress." A flare of amusement lit Torin's eyes.

"And what words would you use?" Emara snapped, unable to control her tongue, her eyes narrowing.

He couldn't hide the bedevilment on this face as he answered her. "Defiant, feisty, stubborn, reluctant to take orders, to name only a few."

The nerve of him. "I could name a few more than that for you."

Artem's wide smile lit up his face as he looked between Torin and Emara. "This is going to be great."

"I am glad we entertain you so much." Torin threw a look over at Artem. "You should focus on prepping your weapons for the trip to the palace."

"You will be damned if you think I'm going to focus on that before I enjoy tonight," Artem batted back. "I can prepare them on the journey."

Naya inhaled and exhaled a slow, steadying breath. "Dare I ask what is happening tonight?"

"What happens after every prime summit." Torin's wicked smile almost put Emara's heart into her mouth.

"The factions don't travel all this way to the city to not tear up the markets for a night or two." Artem flung a wink in Torin's direction. "It has been ages, even years, since some of us were last here. The clans are going to take advantage of every second in those taverns."

"You are right about that," Magin jumped in, finally including himself in the conversation. Emara got the feeling that he was more of the silent type in comparison to her other two guards.

He might be her favourite already.

"You boys are a whole lot of trouble." Naya laughed. "You better be careful." She looked at all of them individually and they nodded. "Your duty starts at dawn."

"We understand, Commanding Wife Blacksteel," Artem assured her. "But every hunter needs a blowout before the start of a big mission."

"You have been surrounded by hunters for decades." Torin placed a hand on Naya's shoulder. "Surely, you don't forget what comes before a big mission, Mother."

"Oh, I don't forget. That is exactly my point." She tightened her grip around Torin's hand on her shoulder and challenged him with a wicked smile of her own. Emara wondered if there was a story or two, rich in tales of the markets, that lingered in Naya's mind. "Please excuse me," she said, interrupting Emara's train of thought. "I must go and see that my other son is settling with his cluster." She paused and spoke to the boys. "Behave, all of you." She placed a hand on Torin's face and rubbed her thumb on his cheek, having to stand on her tiptoes to reach him.

"Always." He flashed her a charming grin that made Emara's heart tingle.

All three warriors bowed their heads to the commander's wife as she took her leave with Kellen.

Artem focused on Emara. "Will you be joining us tonight?"

"That depends on your plans." Emara placed one arm over the other across her torso. "Will I be guarded all night?"

"Absolutely," Torin replied quickly.

"Then it's a no from me." She refocused on Artem.

"Don't be hasty." Artem put his hands out to stop the conversation from turning sour. "Why don't you just come, it will be like we are not even there. Your last night of *freedom*." He smiled at Emara; it was a captivating smile that would have made Cally combust where she stood, but Emara knew immediately that he was just being friendly towards her. Her heart broke thinking of Cally, and she tried to push down the darkness that ate away at her soul.

"Besides, our duty doesn't technically start until sunrise tomorrow."

"I'm sure the markets would love to see your wild side one last time before the eyes of the magic community learn who you fully are." Torin's words were laced with something that had Emara's heart lodged in her throat, and she wasn't sure if it was because of the way he looked at her or if it had been the truth in his words. The eyes of the magic community would certainly be on her, a girl who had claimed an empress' crown without being trained in magic at all.

The lost Empress of Air.

She shuddered at the thought.

"I think that ship has sailed." Artem snorted and Emara's eyes darted to his face.

"What is that supposed to mean?" she asked.

"Anyone who is going to be an empress of a magic coven will be talked about," he said. "Particularly when she is betrothed to one of the most talked about and fiercest hunters to have graced the kingdom in a long time. It's a power pairing." Artem shot a wink towards Torin, but his face had paled, not reciprocating the banter. He blinked and looked down. Emara's full spine recoiled.

"Did I say something I shouldn't have?" Artem's voice trailed off. "Okay, I have absolutely talked enough.'" He put his hands up in surrender. "I think myself and Oxhound will leave you two to talk, but you should come tonight."

Emara let her protruding scowl fully form.

"Or not," Artem added with a grin. "We are leaving now."

Artem and Magin bowed out quickly, leaving them alone. It had been the elephant in the room since he had declared it at the Uplift, since he had announced his ties with her as a bargaining tool to save her. But that didn't change the fact that it was true. She was promised to him by some ridiculous, out of date treaty. Even if she was a little grateful that he had never broached the topic, that didn't mean she wasn't going to make how she felt about the situation clear. She had been avoiding it, but now, as he stood in front of her, she couldn't.

"Listen,—" Torin started.

"No, you listen to me," Emara interrupted him, feeling fire in her stomach. "I am not going to discuss *this* with you right now, here." She blinked as Torin bit back a response. No one ever really interrupted Torin when he spoke. "We haven't discussed the alliance and I want to make myself clear. There is no marriage or wedding or discussion of it in the cards yet," she said through her teeth. "I have agreed to nothing."

"Did you just say *yet?*" Taunting amusement washed over his face.

She gritted her teeth. "I said I have agreed to nothing and I will not be discussing this with you now."

"I didn't bring it up." He held his hands out innocently.

True.

She shook her head, flustered. "Well maybe it was a good thing that Artem did. Because...well...well, because now you know where I stand on it."

Torin moved closer to her, his gaze not faltering. "And where do you stand?"

"Alone," she reiterated. "I stand alone. Not betrothed, not engaged. *Alone.*"

Something smouldered in his eyes; it wasn't amusement or wicked flirtations. It was something deeper, much deeper.

"We can talk this through another time." He paused, a muscle in his jaw tightening. "But I agree, it won't be now."

She lifted one brow. "Good, I am glad we agree on something."

"I would bet that we probably agree on more things than you think." He leaned in closer. "But only time will tell."

"I wouldn't be so sure about that," she sassed him.

He laughed, looking down at her through his dark lashes. "Anything I say, you disagree with." He laughed again. "I have never had that before. I find it...*thrilling.*"

Her heart quickened. "Well, you better start getting used to *that* kind of thrill, because it's the only one you will be getting from me."

"Oh, I intend on getting many of those delicious little thrills from you." His ocean-blue eyes pinned her where she stood, sparkling like polished sapphires, zoning out everything else in the world.

"You are the most infuriating person I have ever met." Emara's heartbeat pounded against her ribcage.

Why in the sweet kingdom of Caledorna did her heart react like this to him?

And then it dulled, an unwanted thought hitting home.

He would certainly be having *thrills* tonight, probably as many as he wanted, and the mere thought of him entertaining different *thrills* made her stomach swish in a way she didn't understand.

She shouldn't feel like that. Not when she had no right to, no ties. They didn't mean anything to each other. He was just a guard and she, an empress. Eventually, maybe an alliance for each other. But that's all it was.

This time, it was her heart that swished.

She couldn't stand here much longer. She needed to see the view of the city from the calming windowsill of her new bedroom. The four safe walls of her room. A bath. She needed to breathe.

"Have a good night, Torin." She panted from her accelerated heart rate. "Enjoy your last blowout before your duties commence."

"I intend to." He smirked. "But I should know, as your newly appointed guard, if your face will be making an appearance tonight."

"With you? Absolutely not."

"Oh, that's right, I forget myself, you have a fear of enjoying yourself."

She moved closer to him. "I know exactly how to enjoy myself, and under no circumstances does that ever involve you." She almost growled like a Shifter. "Like you seem to *think* most things do."

"You do wound me." One of his little dimples appeared and she had to shut her mouth before she said something that wasn't an insult. "When you say things with such venom, you break down my self-esteem." He placed a hand over his heart. "You break my heart."

She scoffed. "Even if you had one, that's not the only thing I would like to break right now."

A husky laugh broke from his throat, and the loudness reminded her that there were other people around. A lot of other people. And they were now staring.

He stepped in, now so close to her that she could feel the heat from his body. "Violence is the way to my heart, angel. By all means, go ahead and try me."

She looked around herself, glowering, "You are—"

"Devilishly handsome? Diabolically sexy? A god amongst men?"

"A lunatic," she hissed. "You are a deranged lunatic! And I would be damned if I went out with you tonight."

His brow danced up. "Your loss, angel."

"No, *angel,*" she mocked, "that's your loss."

She stormed off, heading for the door before he could open that annoyingly perfect mouth again.

"Angel is *my* pet name," he shouted from behind. She could hear the swaggering smirk in his words, but she didn't turn around. "You can't steal it."

It took Emara all of her strength not to swing around the door and throw him a rude gesture. Knowing Torin, it would only incentivise him to keep going. And when the room was full of so many people who would soon be looking to her for council, she needed to act accordingly. So she marched to her room instead.

CHAPTER TWELVE

EMARA

S team rose from the warm water that soaked Emara's skin. Rosebuds, lily petals, and jasmine floated all around her body on top of the water. She wasn't sure how long she had been in the bathing chamber, but she had been there long enough to have topped up the water a few times as it turned cold. Her damp hair now smelling of roses and honey, she decided it was time to get out of the water. Her skin was as wrinkled as the old bark off the ancient tree of life.

Placing a soft cotton towel around her body, she padded out of her bathing chamber and into her main room, taking a seat at the vanity table. Her hair was slicked back from her face as she brushed out the knots, and the inky mass lay heavy on her back, soaking into the robe she had crossed over herself.

She lowered the brush and stared at her appearance.

The dark eyes of the girl looking back seemed broken. Her cheeks were hollower than ever before. Her skin was paler and didn't seem to be glowing like it always had. Her lips were still hers, but the smile behind them struggled to come through.

She barely recognised herself through the sadness that threatened to consume her.

Emara slammed the brush down onto the vanity unit, swallowing the lump in her throat.

She didn't want to be an empress of brokenness. She wanted to be a strong Empress of Air. The last time she had looked in the mirror, she had been going to the Uplift; she had been full of confidence, finally beginning to find herself. Her hair had been wonderfully wavy, her face had been painted to perfection, and her dress...

Her dress has been made for a goddess. Callyn Greymore had made sure of it. A deep ache plunged from her heart to the pits of her stomach.

She didn't want to feel like this anymore.

She couldn't stand it, feeling empty and alone.

She had felt it after her grandmother had died, but it was nothing in comparison to how she felt now. She was truly alone. Emara felt darkness crawl into her heart and wedge itself into her hollow cavity. She had no hand to hold through tears that she cried.

Everyone has a choice.

Naya Blacksteels soft voice whispered from the back of her mind as Emara remembered how the Earth Witch had held her hand.

She didn't have to be alone. She could still validate her feelings, but she didn't *need* to be alone. She didn't have to let the darkness win. If she was a warrior, like she wanted to be, if she was training to fight...she would fight.

She couldn't let the mindset she was in now break her down even further.

Emara wasn't going to. This was her last night of freedom before everyone in the magic community looked at her like she was divine. This was the last night where she could roam freely, *anywhere.* This was the last night she would be without guards and protection for Gods knew how long, and it was probably the last time she could say what she wanted, wear what she wanted, and be who she was now. Gods, it was probably the last time she could do anything she wished before the ascension. Drink what she wanted, eat what she wanted, kiss whom she wanted.

Tomorrow, all of that was gone.

She wasn't sure what her life was going to look like after the ascension, after tonight. She was about to have at least two guards with her at all times, in fear of someone trying to kill her or take her. Or sell her to the Underworld for Thorin knows what reason.

But she had one more night just for her.

A thought struck her like a lightning bolt from the sky, starting her heart again. A little air blew around the room and the palms of her hands began to warm.

This is not how Callyn Greymore would be spending her last night of freedom. She wouldn't be alone, wallowing in her own grief. She wouldn't let the darkness win. She was the light. She would have her magic box of tricks ready, and a daring dress already laid out on the bed with accessories to match. Emara wasn't really sure what being the empress of a coven meant, but she sure knew it wouldn't mean freedom, not all of the time. Not in the way Cally would demand.

The weight of her new title sat heavy on her chest.

Tonight, she could forget all of it, forget about the destruction and devastation that had been caused by her attempted abduction. She could pretend like it didn't exist. Tonight, she could be whoever she wanted to be without having to answer to anyone. She wasn't an empress yet, she wasn't betrothed, she hadn't ascended. She was no one.

She was *anyone*.

She stood, the vanity chair scraping along the floor. She could be whoever she wanted to be. She could enjoy it, despite what Torin *bloody* Blacksteel said about her, despite what she had lost, despite how she felt. She owed it to Callyn.

Her light.

She absolutely could have a good time instead of sitting opposite a mirror with tears tracking down her swollen face. She was made of stronger stuff, and she was about to prove it.

She took off through the doors of her new room and headed in the direction of her old one where it all began.

CHAPTER THIRTEEN
TORIN

The bar of La Luna was heaving, filled with all kinds of magical creatures. The flashing lights from the enchanted beacons made it hard to tell what species roamed among them, but he knew hunters were a dominant presence. After all, the majority of them didn't know the next time they could get a night like this again, a night with endless drinks and limitless female attention.

Some of them would never see another night like this. The Gods would claim them, or maybe the Dark Army would.

Typically, Torin Blacksteel would have at least three females hanging around his neck by now, but any advances they had made towards him tonight he had declined. Normally, he would have sunk a full bottle of his favourite rum, but he didn't feel in the mood for that either. Usually, he would feel the thrumming music pump through his veins.

But not tonight.

What in the Underworld was wrong with him?

He took a small sip of his rum on ice. It tasted the same as usual, so nothing was wrong with the liquor. It was clearly him. Something was *wrong* with him. He had been in a funny mood as of late, a mood that he couldn't place or decipher.

Artem Stryker sat beside him with a gorgeous blonde on either side, Marcus was chatting to a redhead in the corner, and even Gideon was chatting to a small brunette by the bar. She was attractive, but the majority of the females in here were. He just didn't fancy the chase tonight. To make himself feel better, he had concluded it was because of all the questions that had been eating at his mind recently.

Yeah, that was it. He was tired.

It was all the mystery of the recent events that had taken over his mind, and he was exhausted.

"Are you going to sit there all night or are you going to get yourself involved?" Artem shouted to him over the pounding of the enchanted music.

"I am involved," he shouted back before he swallowed the remaining liquor in his glass. He slammed it down on the table and before he could sit back on his seat, a girl swanned over with another drink for him. She sat down next to Torin, her blue chiffon dress riding up her thigh as she took a seat. She crossed her legs and leaned in.

"I have been waiting all night for you to finish that drink so I could bring you a new one," she purred into his ear.

Honestly, he hadn't even noticed her, and he normally would have noticed anyone watching him, especially a beautiful girl. He nodded in thanks, but didn't lift the drink or even look at her. He watched the dancefloor as the bodies intertwined with each other in the rhythm of the music. The atmosphere in La Luna was one of a kind, but tonight, it all felt flat to him.

The girl placed a hand on his thigh. "You are Torin Blacksteel, aren't you?" She smiled seductively with rose-pink lips.

"I think you already know the answer to that," he answered, not hiding his increasing irritation. "Playing dumb isn't attractive."

He sat back, looking over at his brethren as the eyes of the female drank him in. He didn't take in the details of her face or hair or even what she was wearing. The warmth of her hand on this thigh did nothing.

Something was off.

Majorly off.

Whilst his brethren were taking full advantage of this night, kissing, laughing, getting blinding drunk and probably working their way to spending the night with someone, Torin felt alone.

Torin's pulse quickened at how irritated he felt.

Suddenly, Gideon sat down at the table, and a little relief swept over him that he would no longer be left with his thoughts that were turning darker by the second. The girl removed her hand from his leg at his dismissal of her. And he was even happier when the girl got up and left.

"Brother." Gideon nodded and handed him a drink that he trustingly took. It was his special, a sugar spiced rum and ice, which brightened his mood a little.

"Why are you over here when you could be speaking to that pretty brunette at the bar?" Torin eyed Gideon whilst taking a drink.

"Meeting girls in a tavern is not my style."

But this was no normal tavern, this was La Luna.

He managed a small laugh. "Lighten up, Gideon; we have a huge mission to complete and only the Gods know when it will end. You should enjoy tonight while you can."

"Maybe you should take your own advice, brother." Gideon relaxed into his chair.

Maybe he should.

Just then, out of the corner of his eye, a female with silky dark hair strutted past in a burgundy dress that was cut low enough from behind to expose her tanned back.

Torin sat forward in his seat.

He didn't have to see her face to know who it was as she moved through the crowd. He would have known that body anywhere, that hair anywhere. Her long legs were bare against the twinkling lights of the tavern, and she walked with confidence through the crowd—confidence that sometimes only came out in anger or in training.

A twitch in his pants reminded him to breathe.

He took the glass in his hand and drank the contents, not taking his eyes from where she walked as the crowd parted for her. Stealing a quick glance at Gideon, he noted that he had seen her too.

Their little argument this afternoon had led him to believe that she would be staying well within the tower walls tonight, but again, she surprised him. How had she gotten here? Did she come alone? If she came here alone, he would scold her for that later, but she had finally sparked his interest tonight.

As she walked up to the bar, she flicked her beautiful midnight hair over her shoulder and looked around, searching the crowd. *Was she looking for him?* He almost begged the Gods for it to be the case. He rolled his tongue against the roof of his mouth and then onto his teeth before taking a breath. By the time she had ordered a drink, his pulse was practically jumping out of his neck. He noticed a few males checking her out, their eyes roaming over her, appreciating her beauty, and his drink glass almost shattered under his grip.

If any of them were brave enough to go over there and speak to her he would—One started walking.

He stood abruptly, nearly taking the table with him. His heart thundered in his chest, harder than when he trained. She politely smiled at the man who had gotten a little too close for his liking. He wanted to tear the guy's head off his shoulders.

"Easy," Gideon warned subtly, putting out his hand. But it was enough to catch the attention of Artem. He always was a hyper-observant bastard. He looked from Torin to Emara and shuffled himself out from the grip of the females on his side.

"What's going on, my man?" Artem stood directly in front of his view.

"Nothing. Get out of my way."

Artem placed a firm hand against Torin's shoulder. "You can't go over there like a crazed lunatic. She won't take that well. I saw you two together today." He almost laughed. "You need to soften your approach if you don't want her to swing a fist towards your face."

"Or melt it with her flames," Gideon reminded him of her little trick, and Torin could have sworn he saw a little piece of protectiveness etched into his eyes. But Gideon did not move. He wasn't prepared to go over to Emara and intervene in her little conversation with her *new* friend.

He tried to smile, and he was sure it failed. "Thank you both for your marvellous advice, but you will have to excuse me. I have a spleen to rip out."

He pushed past Artem Stryker, knowing he wouldn't stop him. None of them could. Maybe all of them at once, but they weren't about to get their asses kicked out of La Luna, not tonight.

Walking closer, he took in every breath-taking detail of her. She was stunning. Magnetic.

As she laughed, he could see the shimmer that dusted a line down her cheekbone like a cosmic strip of stars, highlighting the bold structure of her face. As she tucked a strand of glossy black hair behind her ear, he could see that she had studded them with diamonds. He took in the thin straps of that torturously low burgundy dress; it had him thinking of how much he would like to take them off her shoulders, one by one, with his teeth. The material of the dress hugged her curves deliciously, shaping around her ass, and he felt like he might need to crawl the rest of the way towards her.

Get yourself together, he barked inwardly. *You are a warrior, a fucking warrior.*

A warrior who wasn't ashamed to admit that he was about to drop to his knees and beg Emara Clearwater never to flirt with another male again.

But he wouldn't do that to her. He couldn't.

She had every right to do what she pleased. However, he did enjoy toying with the thought of hunting every one of them down and killing them for even thinking for one second that they could seduce her.

Or maybe he could stick with torture. He didn't need to go as far as murder.

No, he couldn't do that either.

She wasn't his. She didn't even like him. But why did that encourage his wicked heart to want her even more?

He almost laughed out loud at the thought.

As he neared, he noted that she had painted her lips a deep red, making them look full and plump as they sat against her white teeth in a coy smile.

His personal favourite.

The man who had approached must have said something that entertained her and she laughed again, loudly, a delicate heat spread to her cheeks.

Okay, torture was off the cards, and it was back on again for straight up murder. Bloodshed.

I will not kill him. I will not kill him, he promised weakly.

Torin pushed his thoughts to the back of his mind and sauntered up beside her, allowing all of his insecurities to disappear into the crowd behind him. He straightened his face, bringing out that cocky mask he

used so much, too much, and said, "Hello, angel." He gave her a full, gleaming smile that he
knew exposed both dimples. "Miss me?"

EMARA

Emara's chest tightened as she took in the devastating sight of Torin Blacksteel in his tight black tunic and leathers. The dimples of his smile made it hard for her to breathe, but she held his gaze and pushed up her chin. She wasn't going to let him affect her. She hadn't gotten all dressed up just to come here and have her night ruined by him. Well, not ruined, but he did like to take up a lot of her attention.

She had slipped on this burgundy dress that Cally had left lying in her room and flung on a pair of fashionable shoes that were certainly not hunting boots, making her feel semi-attractive. As long as she *strutted* in them, Cally would be proud of her for even turning up here.

"Torin," she said on an inhaled breath. "This is Doriel Vettoman."

Doriel placed out his hand apprehensively to shake Torin's, but the warrior didn't move.

Emara blinked.

"Doriel." Torin seemed to be thinking something over as he finally shook the other man's hand. His grip tightened and she could see the colour in Doriel's face drain. "I am Torin Blacksteel. Emara's betrothed."

Emara spit out her drink. There was no way that drink would have stayed down even if her life depended on it.

Betrothed?

Who introduces themselves like that? What in Rhiannon's name...

Before she could rectify the situation by reassuring Doriel that she was absolutely *not* engaged to Torin, he spoke. "I didn't realise she was spoken for." The man shook his head, his ice-white hair brushing against his chin. "I don't want to cause any trouble."

"I am not betrothed," Emara exclaimed. "I am not spoken for, you are not causing any trouble. We were actually just getting to know each other." She snapped her head towards Torin before giving him a dangerous glare. "And you were just about to leave."

Torin's nostrils flared. "Oh really? Is that what he was looking to do? Get to know you?"

Mother God, give me strength.

A little fear crept deeper into Doriel's almost black eyes. "Yes, brother, I promise I only wanted to know her name."

"Brother?" Torin spat. "You are certainly not a member of my brethren," he said dangerously. "If you were really getting to know him, did he tell you that he's a vampire?" he asked Emara.

She stilled.

"I take that as a no. Do you know how strong the scent of your blood is to a creature like him?" he asked her. When she didn't respond, he turned to the man. "I suggest you leave before I defang you and make you walk in the sunlight."

The vampire's face turned motionless. "I wasn't going to feed on her, I swear."

"No, because feeding on her would be the last move you ever made." Torin's threat struck hard and he removed a hand from his pocket. "Now leave."

Doriel waited a few seconds before taking a risk by glancing at Emara again. "It was nice to meet you. Enjoy your night." The vampire bowed his head.

He left and Torin snarled at his departure.

"Are you serious?" Heat rushed all over Emara's body as the male took his leave. Torin's stare didn't meet hers for a few seconds as he watched for the vampire and his friends to make an exit. "Torin, what in the Underworld was that? Are you crazy?"

His gaze snapped to her face. "That," his mouth nipped out the word, "was me saving your ass from being someone's meal. Did you know vampires favour *pure* blood over anything else?"

Virginal blood.

Emara's cheeks swam with heat before she saw flashes of red in her vision. "I can handle myself, so don't you dare bring your macho bullshit over here and ruin my last night of freedom. You are not my guard yet. I am still free of you."

He leaned against the black limestone bar nonchalantly and glowered at her. "You can handle yourself, can you?"

"Yes," she hissed.

"I don't think coming out alone, unarmed, is handling yourself particularly well. We spoke about this in training."

"Just because I am not wearing a weapon belt does not mean I am not armed," she battled back. "You should know that." Surprised flashed onto his face and she felt a smug grin form on her own. "See, you don't know everything." She pulled up the hem of her dress ever so slightly to reveal a small dagger strapped to her thigh. His face changed instantly, and he brought his gaze up to hers.

"You are really trying to kill me, aren't you?" he said as his masculine jaw sharpened at a lethal angle.

"Excuse me?"

His intense gaze was back on her once more. "You cannot waltz in here, wearing *that* dress and have a dagger strapped to your thigh and not expect me to fall in love with you."

Even though she felt the jest in his words, they slammed into her heart, making it race at an unthinkable rate. "You have probably fallen in love with every girl in La Luna tonight."

"I don't fall in love with anyone." His words were lined with something more meaningful, something that made her avert her eyes from his face.

"I have made the mistake of going out unarmed before, I won't make that same mistake twice."

A muscle ticked in the side of his jaw and flashed his eyebrows up. "Again, you surprise me."

"Have a little faith in me for once and you wouldn't be surprised." She took a little sip of her drink, wishing it was a gulp.

"Oh, I do have faith." His gaze lingered on her face.

"Besides, I know I can protect myself with my magic. But until such times that I know how to actually harness it without killing people, I will stick to weapons. I have had some training with them, at least."

"You really are on track to make me fall in love with you if you keep talking like that." He smiled, but it wasn't wicked or flirtatious. It was real.

She laughed, her heart picking up pace again. "You are an idiot."

He watched her face whilst ordering a drink with one hand. The barmaid placed two drinks down and Torin handed one to her. "Pop it on my tab," he said without looking away from her.

She lowered her lashes. "How did you know what I wanted?"

"Because I know you," he said and her heart thundered like a brewing storm. "You like something that's sweet but has a kick to it, something that burns going down to let you know that you are consuming alcohol. You wouldn't want to be deceived," He smiled, and her stomach flipped. "Or maybe that was just a lucky guess."

"It seems you are very observant when it comes to what I like." She angled her shoulders back.

"It's a good thing I want to be observant with you,

since it's going to be all I am doing for the foreseeable future."

Her breathing hitched. She took the drink from the bar and sipped it. "Gods, that's strong."

"But do you like it?"

"I do." She was surprised at her honesty.

"It's an elder whisky with a peach syrup." He threw her a smile. "I thought you'd like something with a little dark kick."

Her heart stammered. She did like it. She loved it. She took another sip without breaking his gaze. The dark smoky tones worked with the fruity notes to splash taste all around her tongue.

She swallowed. "More to the point, what you did there with Doriel was out of line, Torin."

He relaxed, putting his free hand into the pocket of his leathers. "I only told the poor little vamp to scram."

"Scram?" A laugh burst from her mouth. "I am sorry, did you just say scram?"

"Why is that entertaining to you?" His eyes lit up.

The laugh finally reached her belly, and she couldn't believe it. A laugh hadn't reached her belly in so long. "Scram is a word my grandmother would have used to shoo away birds that pecked at her flowerbeds, not a word I would expect the notorious Torin Blacksteel to use."

"I am glad my unpredictability made you giggle," he said as he sipped his drink.

And he did make her laugh. Which made her scowl at him again.

"Torin Blacksteel?" Breighly Baxgroll came out of

the crowd, breaking the tension between them. "How are you?"

"Hey, little wolf," he said, turning his gaze back to Emara. Breighly noticed.

"Emara Clearwater, right?"

"Yes." She cleared her throat. "Hi." Emara held out her hand. Ignoring the gesture, Breighly stepped straight in and embraced her in a hug. Shock hit Emara at first, but then she returned the gesture.

"It's so nice to finally meet the girl who sat with my brother in his final moments." Breighly's lips turned into a thin line as she pulled back from the embrace. "Torin told me about what you did for him, so thank you."

Unexpected sentiment choked in Emara's throat as she looked at the wolf. "It was an honour."

Emara meant what she said. She had never experienced anything like what she did with Eli Baxgroll, it had truly changed her.

"A spirit witch told my father that you took away his pain in his final moment and he crossed over to the Otherworld painlessly." She lowered her eyes and Emara's lips parted in disbelief.

She took his pain?

She blinked.

"The pack will always remember what you did for him." Breighly's eyes filled with emotion, but the strength of her features stopped it from pouring through. "If you ever need anything, and I mean anything, call on me and I will return the favour." She swallowed down any remaining sentiment. Emara nodded graciously. Breighly's painted dark lips pulled into a smile. "What can I get you to drink?" she said, lightening the mood. "It's on the house."

"A large rum on the rocks. Extra sugar spice."

"Not you." She snickered, dragging her eyes from Torin. "Emara, the drinks are on me tonight. You can have whatever you like."

"The alpha will not be happy if the wolf that runs the bar is running around giving everyone free alcohol," Torin joked. "Then again, he did put you—the market's party girl—in charge of his tavern. So more fool him."

"While the big wolf is away, the cubs can play." Breighly flashed a smile in Emara's direction. "Plus, I run this tavern the way I want. You saw the sticker on the front door, *do not enter if you are bothered by questionable morals.*"

"Oh, I am not questioning anything about *morals.*" Torin took a sip of his drink. "I'm known for many things, but hypocrisy is not one of them."

The wolf snickered at Torin. "Emara." Breighly's deep brown eyes found Emara again. "This is a place where you can let your gorgeous hair down. Plus, you look like you could have a fun night out."

"I have been trying to tell her." Torin rolled his eyes mockingly. He must have inherited Naya's playful traits, because she couldn't imagine Viktir being so spirited, not in a million moons.

"You can tell me all you want, but I am not going to listen to you." Emara raised one brow at Torin and sipped from her drink. "I have told you before, I don't fall under you."

Breighly tipped her head back and laughed loudly.

"You are fierce." She nodded in appreciation. "And you hold your own. I love that."

"Tell me about it. She's threatened to stab me on multiple occasions, thieved my dagger from my belt, burst my lip..."

"Poor little hunter," Emara mocked.

"You are my hero." Breighly snorted as she clinked her drink against Emara's. "The witches need more women like you."

In a way, Emara had never felt more like she had received a better compliment in her life, but she was quite sure it wasn't true. "I don't know about that."

"I am." The blonde grabbed the drinks and placed another one in Emara's hand. "Let's go and see what talent is out on the dance floor." She grabbed Emara with her free hand. "You don't need to be stuck with the hunters all night. Wolves have more fun." Her brown eyes swirled with excitement, and they reminded her of how Cally would have looked at her. Breighly winked. "Come on, let me show you how the wolves party."

CHAPTER FOURTEEN
TORIN

"**W**ho was your little blonde friend at the bar?" Artem asked as Torin fell back into his seat beside him.

"Breighly Baxgroll." He laughed.

"The alpha's daughter?" Artem's eyebrow lifted and Torin could already see the bad ideas running through his mind.

"Yes, the alpha's daughter," he confirmed. "So don't get any ideas."

"I have nothing but ideas now." Artem's gaze wandered all over the bar.

"Well, don't, he would have your balls for breakfast." Torin sipped his rum, finally savouring the sweet and spiced taste.

He sighed. Ah, that was better.

"Did you ever go there?" his friend asked.

"Absolutely not." Torin choked out a laugh. "We are friends. She's like family. In case you haven't noticed over the years, I tend not to form attachments to anyone."

"I know." Artem grinned. "You don't tend to have a soft spot for anyone." He glanced ahead. "Until now." He sipped his drink too.

Another thing they had in common—the love for a fine rum.

Torin pulled his eyes from Emara on the dancefloor delightfully swinging her hips as she laughed at Breighly doing the same. It had been a while since he saw her truly laugh, and a little movement in his chest signalled it was time to shut it down.

"I don't know what you mean," he said, taking another sip. This time the rum was a mixture of fruit and wood as it lay on his tongue before smoothly gliding down his throat.

"Torin, my man." Artem placed an arm around Torin's shoulders. "I have grown up with you, fought with you, went through the Selection with you, seduced women with you, and I have never seen you look at a girl the way you look at Emara."

"That's ridiculous." He threw the rest of the liquor to the back of his throat and slammed the glass down. "You're being ridiculous." He fought hard to keep his cool demeanour intact.

"Does she know?" Artem nodded at Emara.

"What?"

His golden eyes lit with a flame of enjoyment. "Does she know that you love her?"

He tensed. "If you don't want a broken jaw, you will shut up right now."

"I am serious, brother," Artem said, finally resting back into his chair. "Have you told her how you feel?"

His throat bobbed. "Gideon's heart lies with her. He is the one who loves her."

"Oh shit." Artem sat, now watching her on the dancefloor too. Freedom dazzled in her eyes as the lights flashed down on her smiling face, her hair wild as Breighly encouraged her to spin and spin.

"But what about you? Where does your heart lie?" Artem's question caught him off guard. "You have the alliance, right? You and Emara are promised to each other?" Artem sounded like he had found a loophole, a way to encourage him to talk.

He ran his teeth over his lip. Torin shook his head. "I will not marry her without her willing consent. I will refuse it."

"What?" Artem snapped his head towards Torin. "You can't do that. They will exile you for being disloyal to your clan. Your oath will be stripped, and your title removed."

"I will not push her into something that she doesn't want." He met Artem's gaze.

"I respect that, man, I really do. But you can't be disloyal to your clan. It's an oath we took as children." Artem's brow tightened.

"Exactly. We were children." Torin's sharp tone cut its way through the music that seemed to disappear as the depths of his conversation unfolded. "We didn't know what love meant as children. We didn't fully understand what taking the oath meant either, not really."

"Now you are the one being ridiculous." Artem sat forward, leaning in with a pointed finger. "You are Torin *fucking* Blacksteel. You are the definition of what a hunter is and what it means to take the oath. You are the first-born son of Viktir Blacksteel. You were always destined for the fate of the oath." When Torin didn't respond to his pep talk, Artem ran a hand over his face. "Look, you have plenty of time to work that out between you both. Just be open to the idea."

"That's if she doesn't kill me first." Torin smirked.

A raspy laugh left Artem's throat. "True, but you will have me there to get in between you if it comes to that."' He patted Torin on the shoulder. "Man, Blacksteel..." He couldn't hide his smile. "We don't bat an eyelid at demons trying to rip into our flesh, but we shit our pants at the thought of falling in love." Artem looked ahead again. "We don't let ourselves dream of that kind of fate. Fairy tales don't happen to men like us, and it's easier if we don't get attached to the idea that it could be possible."

Only once in a blue moon did men like them get that chance.

Torin remembered that Artem would play the same part for his clan; he, too, would marry for an alliance, being the first-born son of the chief commander, and second-in-command of Clan Stryker. It was clear that he had the same concerns about settling for a marriage proposal that meant an unhappy life and nothing but your sword and the next battle to look forward to.

"No sign of who you are being aligned with?" Torin asked.

"Nope." Artem took a drink before raising his glass into the air. "So I am going to enjoy what I can whilst I can. Fuck, I might even be brave enough to ask the pretty wolf for a dance."

"Knock yourself out. But don't come crying to me when she breaks your heart or the alpha breaks your neck. I did warn you."

"I look forward to it." He grinned from ear to ear and propelled himself out of the chair.

Torin watched as Artem moved onto the dancefloor beside Emara and Breighly, manoeuvring around the crowd they had attracted.

About an hour later, Breighly had proven that the alpha was well and truly nowhere near this tavern as she writhed on top of the bar, dancing. She had paid everyone in the tavern attention—except Artem. Torin laughed as jealousy filled his friend's eyes. She knew what she was doing, and Torin appreciated the social politics of it; he had once used the same tactics to win over his interest for the night. Kiss someone else, someone that wasn't the one you wanted to kiss, and see how they reacted. He watched as Emara danced with anyone who clung to the beat of the music, and it seemed everyone flocked to her naturally, interested in Breighly's new friend.

Either that, or they already knew who she was.

He had promised himself that he wasn't going to interfere with the rest of Emara's night, but as she swayed on her heels, almost falling, Torin was at her side in a flash. "Woah. Are you okay?" He steadied her.

"Are you okay?" she slurred back.

Thorin, give him strength. Was he the only person as of late who wasn't getting rat-assed drunk? Gideon, and now Emara? Did that mean he had turned into the sensible one? Fuck, no! He would need to find a way to rectify that immediately, but he would tend to Emara first.

"Do you need to go home?" he asked her.

"To the tower, you mean?" She slapped his shoulder and laughed.

"Yes, to the tower." She swayed again, and he placed a hand on her hip to steady her properly. "What have you been drinking?"

"Not your rum, so you"—she bopped his nose with her index finger— "don't need to worry about that."

Torin blinked in disbelief. Did she just bop his nose?

He stopped himself from laughing before he plastered on his mask of *responsible guard.* "I am taking you home, let's go."

"No, I think I will stay right here." Her head still moved to the music, and her arms were floating like a butterfly in spring. "I like it here."

"Oh yeah? Well, you are drunk, and I would prefer to get you home in one piece. And this is top secret"— he leaned in—"but those shoes are extremely high, and I am scared for your ankles."

"My ankles are just fine," she mouthed to him, but all he could think about was biting into her bottom lip and dragging it through his teeth as she smiled at him. He thought about what she would taste like, what she would feel like. "The more you tell me to go home, the more I don't want to." Her voice brought him back from his wayward thoughts.

He tried to compose his face, but a laugh snuck

through. "Oh, I know, you do everything you can just to defy me," Torin declared. She smiled back at him, and his pulse quickened. "But that is besides the point. As of a few hours ago, I officially became your guard, and I believe it is in your best interest to get you home safely."

"I believe it is in my guards' best interest to be *less* bossy." She circled him, strutting in those dangerous, sensual heels. "After all, you are talking to the soon-to-be Empress of Air, you know," she reminded him with drunken confidence. He could hear the joke in her tone, but it was true.

He shoved one hand into his leather pocket and leaned in closer. "Empress of Air or not, I will put you over my shoulder if I have to and take you home. We have a big day ahead of us tomorrow."

Her cheeks hid a blush under the lights of the tavern well, but he could still see it. "When did you become so responsible?"

"The minute I was put in a position to protect your life," he said without even thinking. She stared at him, and he could have sworn her eyes changed colour at his words. He didn't know what in the Underworld that meant, but she didn't cower away from what he said. Torin swallowed. "So you can either walk out of here with me holding your hand, or I can put you over my shoulder and go. Your choice."

She didn't ponder his proposal long. "I think, as the Empress of Air, I should get a choice on how I walk out."

He smiled back at her, exercising control. She would need that. That was a good trait to have. "Of course, you do. I have given you the options."

"I will walk out with you," Emara said.

"Damn, I was really looking forward to you putting up a fight and getting to put you over my shoulder."

She rolled her eyes as a little smile tugged at her fake frown. "I will walk out. But I am not holding your hand."

"Not even to make our way through the crowd?" he said jokingly. "As your guard, it would keep you close to me."

"Nope." She smirked, and it almost stopped his heart. "If my guard is skilled enough, he should be able to do that without touching me." Her eyes changed again as if she were thinking about something naughty. He thought about offering up his right arm to the Gods to get an insight to what was running through that pretty little head of hers.

"Fine," he said, removing his hand from where it had been tucked away. "This time, I will take my losses. But next time, I won't be such a pushover. I might require you to hold my hand."

"Never, Blacksteel." She beamed. "Now are you going to take me home or stand there with your poor negotiation skills?"

He cut out a dry laugh at her insult. Why did he love it when she tried her best to insult him? "I never thought you'd ask, angel."

She punched him on the bicep playfully as she led their way towards the exit, his hand firmly placed on the small of her back.

EMARA

By the time Emara had gotten back to the tower, the burning sensation on the balls of her feet had worn off the buzz of her head. Yawning, she hid a wince as she placed one foot in front of the other.

Damn fashionable shoes!

How did Cally waltz about in these like they were her winter boots?

She winced again, the nippy ache returning not only in her feet, but in her heart too, sobering her thoughts and body.

"I could carry you to your room, you know," Torin said as he walked beside her.

"I think I can manage," she jeered.

"You don't have to be so stubbornly independent; I can see that you are literally about to scream with pain any second." He looked her over from head to toe with those sinful eyes. "I mean, I am not complaining about how you look in them, but they are not exactly practical for walking."

"I think I can make it to my room," she huffed, bringing her eyebrows down into a scowl. She hoped she looked annoyed, but it was really because of the pain. "I don't need your big, strong muscles to get me up all those flights of stairs," she mocked. "I have my own."

Looking forward, he removed his hands from his pockets and fixed the black tunic that cuffed his wrists. "I am just saying, I think you would enjoy it."

Emara wondered how many girls Torin Blacksteel had carried up the stairs of the tower and her heart stiffened. "And I am just saying absolutely not."

"So stubborn." He let out a small chuckle and placed his hands back into his pockets.

They walked for a few flights of stairs before she spoke again.

"I am surprised you even offered to take me back to the tower." She thought over her last minutes in La Luna. "Well, I didn't exactly have a choice in the matter, but still." She threw him a glance full of sass as they walked up to her door.

The scar in between his brows closed in. "What do you mean by that?"

"Well, let's see, maybe we could start with the whole *flinging me over your shoulder* thing?"

He stifled a laugh that didn't reach his eyes. "That's not what I mean. Why are you surprised I offered to take you home?"

Emara's lips parted as she hesitated. "I just thought that, given this being your last night of freedom, you would have wanted to enjoy the *company* of someone or be with the clan."

"I am *enjoying* myself now."

"You know what I mean." She rolled her eyes, feeling the embarrassment rise on her cheeks.

He let his hip lean against the side of her doorway and his toned arms crossed over his chest. "You mean you expected me to be out fucking anything that caught my eye?"

His profanity stopped her breathing, but yes, she had meant that. "That's not exactly how I would put it."

"But that's what you meant," he said quickly as a dark cloud rolled over his eyes.

She rolled her lips, wondering if she had crossed the line.

"Emara." Her name on his lips snapped her head towards him. "I am going to make this very clear...I don't know what you have heard of me." He dipped his head closer to where she stood, rigid. "The majority of it might be true. I have a reputation as a single man in Huntswood. But"—he paused, his eyes seaming smaller than before—"that doesn't define me. I am a young man with a duty that could wipe my life away in a second, and if *that* doesn't, I am to be in a loveless, forced marriage." He paused again, and Emara swore she could hear both of their hearts beating. Fast. "So you are absolutely right, I would have been out there tonight doing whatever I wanted, because when I wake up from my next sleep, I am not promised to see the sunset that night."

Her heart stopped, and guilt ate at her stomach. "I am sorry, I shouldn't have made a comment—"

"It's not your fault," he cut in. "That is the life I have lived for a long time, but it's not what I want to do any longer." Her heart quickened as she wondered what he meant by that. "I haven't wanted any of that nonsense for some time." He looked towards the ground. "I have been selfish and reckless and downright disrespectful at times, that I know." Dark emotion sparked in his eyes. "I have gone days where I have regretted every night of *fun* I ever had, every woman I led on. I have gone months in darkness, not ever seeing a way out of the toxic cycle I created for myself." He swallowed and lowered his voice. "But that's not who I want to be anymore, not when I look at you."

She fought hard to keep her face from revealing how hard her heart was pounding. "I have a feeling that you will be whoever you want to be, you just need to find your own way of doing it."

"You're right about that." Torin let out a small but genuine laugh. "I will always be myself and I will not apologise for that. I will not apologise for who I have been in the past either." He lifted his chin but kept his ocean blue eyes fixed on her face.

Emara knew that the meaning of his words went deeper than what he showed on the surface.

"I wouldn't expect you to," she whispered, unable to detach herself from his piercing gaze.

He paused for a moment as he looked over at her. "For the record, I asked to take you home tonight because I *wanted* to. I wanted to be the one to walk you to your door." His thick brows moved down and a vulnerable expression passed over his face. "I didn't want to spend my night with anyone else, even if that meant just walking you here." He let time breathe, allowing every word to echo through her ears. "And when you walked into La Luna tonight, you almost killed me wearing that little dress, by the way." He bit down on his lip and she pictured him doing it to hers. "But when I saw those vampires checking you out, looking you over like they wanted to taste you"—his chest started to rise and fall sharper than before—"I felt murderous. And you need to know that I am not sorry for that."

"I didn't intend on making you feel like that," she choked out. "Murderous, that is."

"Oh, angel, I know." Finally, a Torin-like smile appeared, and he removed his weight from the wall. "None of this is on you. It's me. I am just used to getting what I want, and you..." He laughed, his wickedly full lips revealing his perfectly white teeth. "You don't make it easy."

She swallowed, staring up into his gaze. "Is that what you would want? For me to make it easy?"

Because that was never going to happen.

His mouth shut before opening again. "I want you to be *you,* always. Because whatever you are doing..." He trailed off and looked away from her for a moment before meeting her gaze again. "It's driving me fucking wild." His eyes glittered with an untamed intensity. "And you know how I love *wild.*"

Emara's heart stopped beating entirely. "I have a feeling I might not be wild enough for you," she admitted. Something she had thought about many times, even though she shouldn't have.

Damn it, she shouldn't have said that.

"Emara," the rasp of his voice almost sounded like a

plea, "you are enough. You will always be enough. Don't you dare ever think that you aren't."

"And how do you know that for certain?" The depth of what she had asked was so much more than just a question, and the air around them charged, fuelling the intensity.

"Because I have always known what I wanted, what I wanted to feel when I looked at someone." He moved closer to her, his face only an inch from hers now. "And when I know what I want, I will do everything I can to make sure I get it."

Flushed, she looked over his stunning face as a tingle ran down her spine. "And what would that be?"

Slowly, he glided a hand over her collar bone and curled his fingers behind her neck, his features sincere on his striking face, and she was pretty sure she stopped breathing all together.

Her head dizzied with the rush of desire at just one touch.

"Right now?" he said coarsely.

"Yes," she breathed.

His other hand brushed over her hip and rested there, making her feel so much closer to him, like the walls of the tower had vanished and it was just their souls intertwined in a universe of stars.

"Right now, I would like nothing more than to carry you through the threshold of that door and take my time undressing you out of that tempting little dress."

Yes, she was sure she had stopped breathing.

She inhaled, causing the burning in her lungs to disappear. But he didn't stop.

"I would start by kissing you from that gorgeous mouth, down to here..." He tightened his grip on her hips. "And before you'd beg me for more, I would trail my tongue to all sorts of desirable places." His eyes had melted into a sensual pool of lust, and it was so, so dangerous to see him like this.

"And then?" she asked before she could stop herself.

Why could she not stop herself from wanting more? Hearing more?

"I don't know how much longer I would be able to hold myself back after that." His voice was husky from the restraint, like he was about to take her right here and wrap his mouth over hers, claiming hers.

Her lips parted. "Then maybe I wouldn't want you to stop yourself."

Again, she'd shocked herself at how confident she was around him, at how fluid her reactions were. She shouldn't be, she didn't have a single clue of how this worked. She had very little experience in the bedroom activities and, well, Torin had a lot.

That thought should have intimidated her more.

The shots of glittering stardust in La Luna had a lot to answer for. But now, she was sober, and the only buzz she had was from the thrill of Torin Blacksteel's words.

All the dangerous little thrills.

His gaze smouldered with a red-hot desire that intoxicated her, but he didn't lower his head to kiss her. Instead, he spoke. "I made a promise to myself, and I also made the same promise to you. I told you that when you are ready and want to explore the deepest, darkest desires that you have, I would be waiting." The promise in his voice practically stripped her bare. "And I am still waiting. And I will wait for as long as you need. What I promised myself is that I would wait until you told me that you wanted it. Because you said that you would never want to kiss me, but here we are, an inch away from exploring that."

"Here we are," she repeated, inches from his face, so close that she could smell the familiar scent of frozen berries and pine. So close, she could lean in and brush her lips over his.

"Are you admitting that you are ready to explore that?"

"I am not admitting anything," she breathed, unsure she would be able to claw back any of her self-control.

His eyes locked with hers again, this time with intense security. "Well, I am telling you now, I want all of it, every last part of you. When you are ready for that, you are going to ask me to kiss you." A lascivious smile pressed against his lips. "And when you do, we can go exploring that desire I know you have burning inside you."

A spiralling cord of sensations made their way to her core. She swallowed. "And if I never ask you to kiss me?"

"You will," he smirked.

"Your self-assurance makes me want to punch you in the face."

A sensual snicker rasped through his throat. "I wouldn't expect this conversation to head in any other direction, would you?"

"No." Emara couldn't help but feel a grin turn up the corners of her mouth. "I should head inside," she said without moving, her body still inches from his, aching for his touch. His mouth was still inches from hers, and she was desperate to feel what his lips were like.

His dark lashes swept down and a dimple appeared on the left side of his cheek. "All you need to do is say *two little words* and I will come through that door with you."

Torin Blacksteel knew what he was doing. He knew how to turn on that sensual charm of his, a charm that had probably never been challenged. But he had never seen Emara activate her own. He thought she was putty in his hands, and she was ready to test what kind of power she really had.

"Would you like me to say those two little words right now?" she purred.

"Undeniably." Sparks lit up his eyes.

She batted her eyelids. "Okay, are you ready?"

"I was born ready," he said, looking from her lips to her eyes.

"Here they are..." She let a sensual smile of her own slash across her face.

"Say them," the small impatient plea escaped him as his chest hit hers. Every part of his warmth swept in and almost took her feet from underneath her.

But she would win this, especially tonight.

She ran her teeth over her lip and he watched every moment of it before she said slowly, "Good. Night."

Smiling, she turned her back on him and shut the doors behind her. Out of the sight of his ocean blue eyes, she slid down the panels of the door to the floor and she ran a hand over her face before placing it over her heart.

It was still beating. It was beating so fast that it might grow wings and fly from her chest.

Surely, she couldn't do this, toy with dangerous desires and escape with her heart still intact?

One thing was for sure, with Torin being her guard, she was about to find out.

CHAPTER FIFTEEN
BREIGHLY

A beam of light cascaded through the window to Breighly Baxgroll's bed, her eyes aching as she awoke from the night before. Blinking her lids open, her eye sockets felt like they had been gouged out with a hot spoon.

Damned liquor! The shots she had been drinking off the belly of a Fae last night always gave her the worst hangover in the kingdom, and she never seemed to learn her lesson.

That was the untamed wolf in her.

She groaned, moving a hand to her face, sweeping her wild blonde hair from her forehead that seemed to be glazed with sweat. Come to think of it, she was roasting hot. She felt clammy, like something was sticking to her, a scent that was not her own.

Oh, no.

Suddenly, a thousand memories of last night in La Luna filtered through her mind. Her on the bar top, dancing as the crowd took in every shake of her hips. It wasn't the first performance she had ever done. Other glimmers of her memories peeked through; taking shots of hard liquor, taking off her top as the whole bar roared in delight, kissing a nameless Fae, kissing someone else, and a whole lot of ink.

Another groan escaped her. Why did she have to take it too damned far every *damned* time? Why couldn't she have just a normal night in the markets? Well, she supposed *normal* and the Huntswood markets didn't really go hand in hand, but, recently, it seemed like it was her mission to get as fucked up as possible.

She rubbed one foot on top of the other and the tingling pain from wearing heels ran along the pads of her feet. A wolf's pain threshold was higher than a human's, possibly higher than a hunter's—

Oh, fuck. *A hunter!*

She turned her head slowly, hoping to find an empty bed, but she knew by the heat under the blankets that she was not alone.

"Good morning, sunshine," a silky deep voice said softly.

Breighly snapped her head in that direction, sending a wave of dizziness with her. Lying beside her on the bed was the butt-naked, inked male from last night. His cheeky smile glittered into his chocolate brown eyes that had golden flecks glittering through them, and his wide jaw expanded.

"Round five?" he suggested. "Before I need to go."

"Round five?" her voice came out rougher than expected. And higher. She coughed down the surprise that grazed against her throat.

"Things did get *very* hot last night." He raised one

eyebrow, which already annoyed her with its perfectness. No guy's eyebrows should be that perfect. "You suggested round five last night before falling asleep, leaving me all alone."

She wriggled slightly against the mattress to find that she had no underwear on either.

Great! This wasn't going to be dignified by any means, but she may as well get it over with.

"Okay." She sat up quickly—too quickly—flinging her legs out of the bed and pulling all the sheets with her as she stood, draping them over her nakedness. "You need to leave and leave quietly." Her legs felt like they were walking through water as she took a few steps back, putting space between them. Swallowing a wave of nausea, she ordered, "Now."

The man in her bed lay sprawled out idly, his head propped on his hand, amusement coating his face. He was still naked, and he didn't seem to give two shits. She noticed the tattoo that trailed its way onto his square jaw —thorns and vines of the ancient world—and quickly, a vision of how much she had kissed into it last night, how much she had licked at his throat, came to the forefront of her mind.

She blinked the thoughts away, her gaze meeting his again. "Are you fucking deaf? You need to leave, now."

Something consumed his eyes, but it was not hurt. Delight, maybe? Did he find this funny?

He bounced from the bed immediately and stood in front of her, everything on show, bold as brass. He was not shy, and with what he had going on downstairs and across his body, he didn't need to be. He was racked with muscle and built like a machine of war. She wanted to pull her eyes from his form, but she couldn't, and her wolfish instinct kicked into play, hangover or not.

A heat clenched deep into her core, and an alluring attraction made her body ready for him again.

She shut it down quickly. She was not having sex with him again, no matter how fucking handsome he was.

"Are you sure round five is off the table?" he said confidently. "Last night, you couldn't get enough." His smile dazzled her so much that she rocked on her feet.

She managed to recover quickly. "In this short space of time, I have concluded that you are not deaf, just intellectually challenged." She managed a smile lined with more attitude than he could handle. "Do I look like I am up for round five?"

She praised Vanadey that he was not a wolf, because if he was, he would be able to tell that she was attracted to him.

Her *scent* would give her away.

A small laugh left his throat in a way she found endearing, but she didn't let her face change from the growling wolf that she was. He picked up his white shirt from the floor and wrangled it over his body in one quick movement. He caught her gaze as he stepped into his trousers which gave away instantly who he was. Leathers. He was *definitely* a fucking hunter. Every other faction in the kingdom had moved on from leather, but she supposed warriors of Thorin needed attire that protected them better than what she would wear. If her eyes didn't feel like they may fall out at any moment, she would have eye-rolled herself into next week.

For the love of Vanadey.

She'd promised herself that she wouldn't sleep with hunters anymore. Wolves were supposed to stick to their own. *Mate.* She couldn't do that if she was constantly linked to hunters. Why was she always attracted to something she couldn't have? It was like her heart rebelled against the idea of finding a mate, so she continued to fuck with warriors of Thorin who would never find anything more in her than a good time. It was easier that way.

"Will you hurry up?" she hissed quietly. "I thought that hunters had been blessed with the ability of speed. Or was yours lost at birth?"

He slowly buttoned his leathers around his defined hips. "If you keep being mean to me, I might fall in love with you." He laughed temptingly and gave his short reddish-brown hair a shake. "Hunters are twisted like that."

"Then you really are as stupid as I thought," she said, her heartbeat starting to slam against her ribs. "Fucking hunters and their egos." She wrapped her hands around the sheets a little tighter, looking away. "You are all ridiculously deluded."

"You are a mean little wolf, aren't you?" he said, his golden-brown eyes dazzling with rampant energy. "But you are funny, I will give you that." A tattooed hand ran across his jaw as he laughed again. "I must say, I have never been kicked out of bed before."

"Well, now you have. And you better be quick to add

it to your list of 'Never have I evers' before you get your ass kicked by a handful of people." Her jaw locked in.

"A handful of people?" he questioned like it had piqued his interest.

"My father, my brothers, my *boyfriend*," she trailed into a lie. Breighly always told men she had a boyfriend to get out of a second *meeting*. It normally made her seem untrustworthy and put them off instantly.

He laughed again, this time running two tattooed hands down his face. She noticed one hand had a beautiful black rose inked across his skin and the other a skull. Her throat tightened. It was kind of...badass.

Why was she always a sucker for a bad boy?

"You are something else." He stalked closer towards her, closing the distance between them. This was not good for her alcohol-lined stomach. "You have a boyfriend? After what we did last night?"

His voice was low and curt, and it did something to her heart. Now that he was closer, she could see a petite silver nose ring in his left nostril. A flashback confirmed that she had absolutely tried to bite the nose ring whilst they—

"Yes." She swallowed, the lie feeling strange on her tongue. "Not that it is any of your business."

His eyes darkened, his eyebrows pulling down. "I think that you will find that it is my business, little wolf."

"Don't call me that." She tried to stand a little taller, lifting her chin as she looked at him. "You have no idea what I am capable of, and all of those things don't take my height into consideration."

It was true, wolves tended to be deadly on demand.

"I think I got a feel for some of those things last night." His smile was remindful of the wild time they had had as he shoved his feet into boots. He straightened and his gaze was back on her. "Can I have my fighting knives back now?"

"I have your fighting knives?" She couldn't remember why she would have taken his knives. She was more than capable of handling herself against a hunter. She certainly wasn't scared of a few weapons.

"You wanted them as props for a little role play," he said, his eyes swarming with liquid gold that made her feel a way she hadn't felt in a long time.

Before she could speak, she was moving to hide the blush on her cheeks, pushing his brute strength towards the door. He let her command the way as he laughed.

"It's time for you to go, big boy," she said, yanking him by the shirt.

"Big boy?" His laugh bounced off the walls of her room. "That's the first compliment you have given me all night."

"And now it's day, and that will be the last." She dragged him through the hall. "Get out!"

He laughed again, a deep rumbling in his chest, a laugh that made her feel both sides of her mouth turn up slightly in awe and in rage.

She spun to face him, and Breighly had to look up at him as she glowered. "What is it exactly that you find so funny?"

"You," he said, clamping his lovely lips together. "You make me laugh." He held her stare with his beautiful eyes and his shoulders squared.

He didn't back down.

She swallowed down any feeling of adoration for that and pushed her face into a scowl. "I do have a great personality, one that almost everyone finds charming." She pushed him out the threshold of the door to her cottage. "Too bad you won't see it again." She cocked her head to the side. With a passive aggressive smile, she said, "Have a nice life."

"Wait," he yelled, flinging out a hand. She stood, holding the door open. "My knives, my weapons. I need them for today. And I am guessing that you don't since you have those sharp claws that you liked to dig into my back."

Narrowing her eyes, she dragged herself to her room to find his weapons. Looking around, she noticed them gathered in a heap on her floor, next to a weapon belt. She scooped them up, ran down the corridor, and threw them onto the grass outside. She held onto one, the biggest weapon on the belt: a fighting axe.

He ran his tongue over his lips. "Was that so hard?"

"Fuck you," she sneered.

He laughed and pointed at the axe in her hand. "I am going to need that one too. She's my favourite."

A shiver ran down Breighly's spine as his smile taunted her. She brought her arm back and launched the axe. As it flew past the hunter's head, he ducked, and then his eyes were on her once more.

He flashed her a smile as his eyes filled with lust. "Can I see you again?"

This time she was the one to let out a laugh, a little louder than she should have, and said, "Absolutely not."

Slamming the door behind her, she trailed back into her bedroom, dumping her body onto the mattress. Dawn looked like it was already light in the sky, but she wasn't ready to get up. She wasn't ready to face the world. She had just had sex with a hunter in her own home. All she could smell was his scent. It was all over her bed.

If her pack caught wind of this... She groaned.

That's the last thing she needed. There would be murders. The princess of the wolves was not allowed relations with a hunter.

The alpha forbade it.

CHAPTER SIXTEEN
EMARA

Gentle snowflakes cascaded down her bedroom window, making it hard to see the city against the white backdrop of the sky. A few had pressed themselves against the glass, sparkling subtly. Emara ran one finger over them, feeling the chill of the window countering the heat of her hands. She had awoken before dawn, finding the nerves of leaving for the ascension building in her gut, and had decided to practise some magic. She had only started to settle into this room and now she would have to leave it for Gods only know how long. She was about to journey through parts of the kingdom she had never been to before, and both excitement and apprehension swelled in her heart at the thought.

Today marked a change for her, even more change than she had already gone through.

She had lived a very sheltered life before finding this new world. It was clear to Emara that her grandmother had constructed her old life in a way that hid her magic.

It had hidden the fact that the magic world existed all together.

Why had she done that?

She could feel her magic now. She could feel it like she could feel her chest rise and fall with every breath she took. It was thriving and it was alive.

A knock at the door had her on her feet. As she opened the big double doors at the entrance to her room, Magin Oxhound stood before her. He bowed his head once, and she tried not to look at the healing scar that pulled across his face.

This was it.

This was the beginning of being a guarded member of magical society. With everything that had been going on against the witches, part of her was grateful to have the protection. The other half of her, the darker half, wanted to rebel against it, rejecting the idea that *she* wasn't enough to keep herself safe. But she wouldn't make a spectacle of herself, not when so many people would have their eyes on her. Would her coven be scrutinising her every move, wishing Maradia hadn't crossed over to the Otherside?

"It's time to leave," Magin announced, dressed in full guard regalia. It was something she had witnessed hunters wear at the Uplift, but she had never expected her guards to be wearing it to escort her to the Amethyst Palace. He wore his family crest on his chest. It had an array of weapons with the initial *O,* but above that was a pin the symbol of House Air.

The triangle was formed in a silver metal with a line of gold through the point. It was the symbol of her house, her blood, a symbol that her grandmother would have had marked on her skin.

She swallowed, wondering if she would ever get the same mark inked on herself.

"We must make our way to the foyer." Magin stood with a stony expression, his large arms behind his back and a weapon belt low on his waist.

"I will get my cloak," she said as she turned. Emara glanced at the door as she walked away, half expecting Magin to have left. But he stood like a limestone statue. "Are you waiting for me?"

"If you don't mind, Miss Clearwater—"

"Emara," she said quickly. "Please, call me Emara. We don't need that type of formality."

He smiled faintly in acknowledgement, his scar only allowing a taut grin.

Her lips thinned. "If you would like to head down, I won't mind. I have a few things to gather."

"With all due respect, Miss—I mean, Emara—I can't. I haven't been given the order."

She stilled for a moment, the sack that she had been putting things into swaying on her wrist.

The order. Who was the order coming from?

"And who commands you?" she asked, expecting him to be in charge of the cluster. After all, he had been an empress' guard before.

He shifted on his feet. "For this cluster, it has been decided that it will be Torin who will command."

"For the love of Rhiannon," she said out loud before she could think. "And who decided that? Were you not a guard to the late empress before? Shouldn't you be in command?"

Magin flinched.

She stopped speaking and clamped her mouth shut.

His gaze met hers. "I was her guard, yes. But Blacksteel has the highest-ranking score from the Selection. And with my failure to protect her"—he cleared his throat—"it was decided that Torin would be our lead."

A sharp pain shot through her heart. "I am sorry, I—"

Words failed her.

She had been so caught up in having Torin's name mentioned that she had forgotten herself. Magin had been guarding the Empress of Air the night she was murdered. He probably blamed himself for her death. He would blame himself.

She was a bloody fool.

Her throat closed in as she spoke. "I didn't mean to offend you. If I have, I am deeply sorry. I shouldn't just assume."

"You have not offended me," he reassured her, posture relaxing a little. "I am just deeply remorseful that I did not save her that night. Maradia was a good and honest person, and she loved her craft and coven."

Darkness flashed across his face, and Emara saw every bit of shame that Magin had endured since the Uplift.

"I am positive that you did everything you could to save her." Emara made sure she sounded confident, but her voice was small.

"And it wasn't enough." Heart-shattering guilt scattered on his face, pulling at his scar.

She inhaled sharply. "Maybe the Gods have given you a second chance," she said lightly. "Because they can see how worthy you are and want you to feel validated in your duty. We cannot win every battle. We must know loss before we can find the strength to win the war."

A thankful smile tugged on one corner of his mouth. "Spoken like a true empress, Miss Clearwater. I will take this opportunity to put everything right, I promise you that."

And she knew he meant it.

Standing in the foyer, Emara was glad that she had borrowed the heaviest cloak possible from Naya Blacksteel. The cold air from the ever-opening door as the hunters made their way out nipped at her hands, nose, and cheeks. She watched as, one by one, the hunters prepared themselves for leave, either with their empress or to journey to their protected person.

"Ready to leave?" a deep voice tickled the back of her ear. She spun to see Torin Blacksteel standing behind her. Her mouth parted to speak, but she halted as she took in what she saw. He, like Magin, was dressed in full guard regalia. He wore a light grey tunic that fitted him like it was made for him, and the high collar, reaching his chiselled jawline, brushed his skin. The light colour complimented his complexion more than she would ever have imagined, invigorating his azure eyes, bright and sparkling. His dark hair lay neatly on his head like a sheen of soft ink, and his skin looked darker against the pale colour of uniform, glowing like the sun. Her gaze travelling down his chest, she could see the crest of House Air pinned against his heart, and something moved in her chest. Silver metal formed two arrows that split through a sword, and it sat behind a dark banner that read, *Blacksteel*. His crest, pinned beside hers, looked...*good*.

Her heart fought against her rib cage to escape.

Torin gave a half smirk as he prompted her again, "Well?"

"I am not sure if I am ready," the honesty fell from her mouth.

"Don't worry." He examined her face thoroughly, a note of concern tying at his brows. "Everything will be fine."

Just as she opened her mouth to speak, Gideon appeared from the dining hall. Her heart stopped. She had forgotten he would be wearing the same guard regalia. His eyes met hers, and something punched into her chest as she saw the pin of House Earth upon his chest beside his clan's crest.

"I will give you two time alone," was all Torin said before vanishing quickly. She heard him bark orders before he slowly disappeared into the fuss of departing.

Gideon strode up, positioning his feet shoulder-width apart as he settled in front of her.

"Did you enjoy yourself last night?" he said, dipping his gaze before bringing it back to meet her face.

He was beautiful. His emerald eyes contrasted against the grey of his uniform perfectly, and his hair sat messy and wild atop his head. And his lips, lips that she had once kissed, relaxed into a lovely, polite smile. Always the gentleman.

"I did," she said back. "A little too much fun, perhaps. The wolves led me astray." She allowed a small laugh to break free.

"I don't think anyone could lead you astray, Emara Clearwater," he said, smiling back at her.

"True." She chuckled, raising one eyebrow. "I take full responsibility for my behaviour."

Gideon's laugh was small this time. "It was good to see you having fun. You needed that." He nodded, and Emara held in a gasp at his observations. "With that being said"—he shifted the weight of his body from one foot to the other—"make sure my big brother doesn't get himself into any trouble."

"I don't think the Gods themselves could stop that from happening." She looked over to where Torin stood. His face was unreadable as he observed the hunters' preparations.

"Well, maybe not the Gods," he said, "but funnily enough, he listens to you."

The comment snapped her attention back to Gideon.

"I highly doubt that."

"You would be surprised at how much he has changed in the short span of time since you have been here." Her face must have shown either shock or disbelief, as Gideon said, "It's true. Somehow, you make him a better person."

Her heart lodged into her throat.

It was so strange to hear those words come from Gideon's mouth, especially when, before the Uplift, she would have wished it were him she made a better man. Not that she had to, because he was already a good man, a man loyal to his oath and duty. But it felt like so much time had passed since he had kissed her in the gardens, since their eyes had locked together to create something special that first time in her infirmary room. Even when it had been no time at all...

Emara had to admit that something had changed deep from within her, a shift she couldn't explain. Maybe she would never be able to explain it.

Instead of trying to fathom her surreal feelings, she simply said, "I hope you have safe travels, Gideon." She placed a hand on his arm, and he watched it touch his tunic. He looked up. "Don't get yourself hurt; I am counting on seeing you well at the ascension ceremony." She managed to smile through an emotion that sunk her heart into her stomach.

"I count on making it there safe and well." His mouth parted, and he took a heavier exhale than normal. "I know my brother will protect you with his life."

She nodded, a swell of anguish catching her throat. "So, this is a goodbye?"

It felt like that in more ways than one.

"I hope not." He smiled down at her. "I look forward to seeing you again. Stay safe." He rubbed a hand over her shoulder and took his leave.

For a moment, she could hear nothing but his voice drifting through her head. She closed her eyes and took a second to normalise her breathing as she made peace with her heart.

CHAPTER SEVENTEEN
EMARA

Emara followed Torin as he led them out to a small holding behind the tower to a large stable. Horses stood there, eating a pile of thick, golden straw. She had never been in the stables before, and as she looked over her shoulder, she could see the menacing tower looking down on her. From the outside, it looked like an ancient place of worship, long in its stature with railing on the top that looked like a jagged crown. The rusty-coloured brick looked weather-beaten, with square windows barred with old iron. Many of the city folk probably thought the building was used for medicine or healing practices, but Emara could see the magic in its structure.

As the flakes of dusty snow drifted slowly to the ground, in no hurry to meet their end, she waited for Torin to instruct them to leave.

Magin had been at her heels the whole time as she walked through the gardens, and she wondered how long it would be before she had to advise him that she needed more space than what he was giving her.

Emara reckoned a day, at most.

She just needed time to get used to this level of...protection.

It dawned on her suddenly, as she watched all other hunters scattering like working ants, readying their travel kits onto their horses, that someone was missing.

Where was the tattooed part of her cluster?

Emara hadn't had so much as had a glimpse of him since last night at La Luna. He had been showing interest in Breighly Baxgroll, but as free and wild as Breighly was, she had been kissing someone else before Emara left, so she doubted he would have waited around.

Emara considered how liberating it must be to carry yourself in a way that wasn't deemed acceptable by society yet owning every part of it. That was who Breighly was—who Cally had been. They were free, unapologetic, and strong.

And that was who Emara longed to be—needed to be.

Closing her eyes, she took in the pain that she felt in her heart and turned it into something worthwhile. She turned into a hardness. She turned the anguish into strength, pain into steel. Taking a deep breath, she uttered a prayer of self-confidence to any God who would listen, that the courage she had now would stay with her on this journey. She was going to need it.

Before her dark flames could melt away the newfound, liberating steel in her heart, Artem Stryker marched into the stables, looking a little dishevelled.

His cloak was askew, and his russet hair wasn't neat like it had been yesterday.

He had guilt plastered all over his face, and Emara could see his panting breath swirl up into the morning. Magin turned and nodded, but Emara noticed that Torin stood statuesque, his eyes narrowing.

Artem was the first to speak. "I haven't missed anything, have I?"

"You haven't." Torin's words were forceful, yet calm. Calm in the way the sea rolled back and forth before the storm breached the shore. "Had you been any later, we would have had a real problem, Stryker." Torin's jaw hardened and the crease in his brow dragged together, causing a menacing glaze to film in his eyes. "Ready your horse."

Artem glanced over in Emara's direction, and a plea of forgiveness took up residence in his eyes. Heart beating fast at how serious Torin was, Emara lowered her lashes and chin in a subtle nod of forgiveness towards the latecomer.

"It won't happen again," he told her as shame crept into his stare and hardened his jaw. "You have my word."

"It's quite alright, Artem," Emara reassured him. "We were only setting up the horses for travel." She looked over them, pondering a thought. "Come to think of it, there are only *three* left for us. We are missing one."

All of the hunters had taken their horses and were on their way, leaving only three horses for her cluster in the stables. They all stood in silence as Emara's point lingered like frost in the air.

Torin dragged a murderous stare from Artem's face

and looked her over. The danger that had lingered just a few seconds ago was replaced with a slight smile, and his features softened. And so did the tension that surrounded them. "That's because we only need three horses."

"But there are four of us," she pointed out, glancing around them like her calculations had deceived her. Surely, one of the clan hadn't taken her horse. Torin had mentioned this journey would have been a lot easier by portal, however, it was now forbidden. So they were going by horseback, as the challenging terrain wasn't suitable for wagons.

"I know there are four of us," he said, and his eyes sparkled with delight. Emara knew she wasn't going to like what he was thinking.

She flicked her eyes over to Artem and then Magin; they both looked like they could burst into laughter any moment. She had to give it to Magin, though, he at least was trying his hardest to remain neutral, unlike Artem, who was now sniggering.

Was there some sort of inside joke that she wasn't party to?

She looked back to Torin, who also had a smug grin.

"If you think for one second," she began, "that I am riding on a horse with you this whole journey, you have another thing coming."

Artem let out a full-blown laugh and then straightened, pinning his lips together like a child that was about to be reprimanded. Emara shot him a glare so sharp she wished it could have pierced him (just a little).

Torin pulled his gaze from his brethren and his icy

glare pinned her where she stood. "That's exactly what I am thinking." His head tilted slightly. "An empress requires to be close to her guards at all times."

She wanted to kick him into next week. She couldn't ride the full way to the Amethyst Palace on a horse with Torin. She had too many strange feelings after their encounter last night, and she would like to forget all about them. She had almost lost control of herself, her good mind, at his words, his touch.

She lifted her chin to match his. "I would rather walk the full way than be sat on a horse the entire time with you."

Torin turned to his audience. "Do you see the way she treats her lead guard?" His wicked smile appeared, showcasing both dimples, and her heart stammered. Artem's eyes widened and Magin looked sideways at Emara, telling her he wanted to be kept out of this. Torin turned his attention back to her, bringing down his dark eyebrows theatrically. "Why can't you be nice to me? I thought we made a truce last night."

Heat burned in her cheeks. "I have no idea what you are talking about."

He winked at her, knowing she knew exactly what he was referring to.

"I am telling you now, I want all of it, every last part of you. When you are ready for that, you are going to ask me to kiss you. And when you do, we can go exploring that desire I know you have burning inside you."

Emara had entered a game even more dangerous than the hunt, a game that she knew she shouldn't play, a game she had never played before but already felt addicted to.

"I can ride alone." She looked between the hunters. "I have a dagger strapped to my leg, and I am feeling rather confident in using it these days." She shot the warning to Torin alone.

"I bet you do, angel," his husky voice purred. "As much as I would love to engage in a one-to-one combat session with you right now, we must be on our way." He leaned against a wooden fence, dripping with confidence. "I need to get you to the Amethyst Palace on time, regardless of how you feel about sharing a horse. And as lead guard, you need to ride with me."

Emara went to open her mouth, but she closed it again quickly. As much as she hated to admit it, he was right. She was delaying the inevitable. The plan was that Artem would carry the food and water, and Magin would be carrying the extra weapons and shelter. She just hadn't realised that Torin's horse would be carrying her. If she put up a fight, it would only eat into their travelling time.

She groaned.

She picked a horse and approached it. He was a stunning destrier, a horse that was sturdy enough to carry a heavy load and quick enough to escape any unwanted company.

She put out her hand, allowing the horse to familiarise itself with her scent.

"Hi," she whispered to the ebony beauty.

Blinking at her, the horse allowed her to make

contact. She ran her palm down the length of its face and then scratched under his chin.

"He's called Ledi." Torin stood behind her as the other's readied their supplies. "He's mine. I named him after a mountain in the north."

She looked over her shoulder. "You never told me you had a horse."

"We don't use them often, only for missions like this." He patted Ledi's side. "My mother gave him to me when I completed my Selection."

Emara watched as Torin tended to his horse, brushing him down, dusting off any hay that clung to his coat. He checked his legs and then his hooves before turning back to Emara. "Do you need a hand with the mount?"

Her grandmother had gifted her riding lessons from a local farmer for her eighth birthday, so she knew how to mount a horse. She laughed, sticking her foot into the stirrup and placing her hands on the saddle. To her surprise, Emara hoisted herself up more elegantly than she expected, like it had been no time at all since she had done it last. Swinging her leg over, she sat proudly on top of Ledi, a horse of war.

She had to admit that she was a little apprehensive given the size of the horse, but she wasn't going to let Torin think she feared anything.

"There are many things you won't need to help me with, Torin Blacksteel." She took hold of the reins and patted between Ledi's ears. "And one of them is mounting a horse."

He pursed his lips, an impressed expression overtaking his amused one. "Well, we can add that to the list of things that I have learned about you."

"I told you a long time ago not to underestimate me." She smiled, feeling a little smug.

He put his foot in the stirrup, and with one swift movement, he was sitting directly behind her on the horse. Even through her cloak, she could feel the warmth of his chest travelling from his body to hers.

"I am realising I still have a lot to learn about you," he said, his warm breath caressing her ear. His voice was so low, she was sure she was the only one who could hear it. "And I plan on learning everything you will allow me to know."

The air was no longer chilled between them, but hot and thick.

She took in a sharp breath. "You should learn immediately that I can be quick tempered around males who think they can make demands of me." She squared her shoulders, and as her muscles moved, she could feel him move too, adjusting to her new position like they were two parts of a puzzle.

"I think that was the first thing I learned about you." He chuckled behind her, and the tone sent her heart into a frenzy. "Are you boys ready?" He cast his voice behind him, cutting their secret conversation short. Emara peeked around, her cheekbone almost grazing Torin's chin, to see if the other men had mounted their horses.

Torin let Artem pull out in front and then steered Ledi into the middle of the formation. Magin followed at the rear, and the horses' hooves could be heard on the frozen ground as her trio of guards made haste to the mountains in the north.

The journey to the northernmost point in the kingdom had begun, a journey which would lead Emara to the grounds of her ascension.

CHAPTER EIGHTEEN
EMARA

The frosty air scratched into Emara's cheeks, making her face feel frozen. Her hands were numb too, as were her legs and feet. They had been riding for hours now with only a few exchanges from the hunters on which route to take breaking the silence. She knew they were headed north, but she had no idea how to navigate her way there, making her feel like a spare part. Torin had said that they should reach the palace a few days before the ceremony, weather permitting. Right now, it wasn't exactly the best weather to travel in, but at least it had stopped snowing.

However, looking at the thick white clouds overhead, she was certain it could flurry down any moment, making everything damp and even more drenched. She moved her hips to relieve the pressure off the bones that had sat in the leather saddle in the same position. Groaning, she moved again, not wanting to wriggle too far down the saddle into Torin.

"Are you okay?" Torin asked.

"Apart from basically being a block of ice, I am just stiff from riding for so long."

She hadn't ridden in years; she had stopped around fifteen after suffering a break in her arm and had never gotten back to it. She had loved being at the Mossgrave stables, so not returning had been a decision she deeply regretted now that she was older.

"It takes some getting used to," he agreed. "You will be sorer tonight than when you had your first training session with the clan."

She giggled, fighting back the chittering of her teeth. "I don't think that is possible."

"Here," he said, taking the reins from her hands. "It's my turn again." His arm muscles made her feel like she had a wall around her to keep out the chill of the wind. She quickly put her hands into her cloak and cringed at how cold they were. After a few moments of wrapping her hands in the cloak, they began to tingle back to life, and she let herself relax further into the saddle, easing the ache on the base of her straightened spine.

"You don't have to take the reins for long," she said, her breath swirling out of her mouth like smoke. "I can take them when my fingers feel alive again."

"And if I protest against that, will you listen to me?"

"Absolutely not."

"I didn't think so." He laughed. It was nice to feel something warm against her neck, even if it was only for a second. "Tell me, why are you so stubborn?"

"Why are *you* so stubborn?" she countered. They had a history of repeating the question the other had just asked to see who caved and answered first. "I have a feeling you always get your own way, but I don't understand why people give in to you."

"I never get my own way with you," he said bluntly, and she wondered what he actually thought of her.

She *had* to disagree with him out loud, even if, internally, she did agree. Emara didn't know why she felt the dying need to always challenge him, but she did.

His voice broke through the silence between them. "I am stubborn because I don't like having my decisions made for me. I have never really had a choice in anything I have done. Being born a hunter, my training, my childhood—even as an adult, my decisions are made for me daily. When I work, what I do, when I train, what I eat, who I will spend the rest of my life with..." She tried her hardest not to stiffen at the thing he said last. He was right. He didn't have a lot of choices. A little burn in her chest made itself known.

"So I am stubborn in the choices I can make because *I* can make them," he continued. "I don't need to compromise with them the way I do with everything else. Am I selfish to want *something* my own way?" She could hear in the build up of his voice that it was more of a statement than a question, but she answered it anyway.

"No, you're not," she said softly, thinking over all the decisions that had been made for her in her life. They had one more thing in common. "I think you must be brave, every day, to allow people to make life choices for you," she admitted, and he tensed behind her, his muscled arms locking her in. She looked ahead at the trees of the forest, ignoring them. "It is something I struggle with a lot, and I didn't realise that until I came here. I haven't really had the opportunity to make my own choices in life, and I am not really sure if I will get to make any of my own decisions from now on."

The only tell-tale sign that he was still on the horse was the feeling of his heartbeat against her back.

"You will get to make more decisions than you think." He shifted, gripping the reins a little tighter.

"But what if none of what I am being offered is what I want?" Her voice sounded higher than usual. "What if the things I am to decide between are not what I truly want at all?" Her heartbeat quickened at the thought of it all, the thought of the truth. "What if I don't like being a leader who needs to make important decisions to best my people?" she whispered.

Torin took a moment before he answered. "You are the kind of woman who will not stop until she has what she wants, Emara. What you need to remember is that you are the one in control of the decisions you make, even if what is being presented in front of you is not fully what you wanted. You can still decide. You have the power to alter things now." His words swirled past her ear, and she looked down at his hands on the reins. They were full of marks and scars that proved that he had spent a lot of time with weapons and training. And she thought about how one hand had rested on her hip last night, heavy and tempting.

She deliberated in her head about what to say back, but the words died on her tongue.

"Emara." Something in his voice pulled her spine together, tightening every muscle connected to it.

Mother God, what is he going to say?

"I will not go through with the alliance if that is something you want to reject. I would"—he paused and Emara felt dizzy—"I would rather suffer the consequences of my commander than make you feel like that was your only option. I won't do it."

If Torin's arms had not been a strong wall around her body, Emara would have fallen from the horse. Her mouth dried and emotion swelled in her throat. He would defy his commander just so that she would have a choice.

Was Torin Blacksteel selfless?

"I will not put that pressure on you. I want to give you back that choice," he added.

Her heart felt like it was being pulled from side to side, up and down. She had not been prepared for that, not in a million moons. Her mind whirled endlessly.

"Torin," Emara breathed, not meaning for her emotion to mirror his, but it did. She couldn't hide it.

She would be entirely grateful to the Gods that she could not see his face as this conversation took place; if she could see his ocean blue eyes, she was sure it would be the end of her.

"I would never let you suffer the consequences of that." She bowed her head, looking at the wiry wool of her cloak. "Not after everything you have done for me. I wouldn't let you pull away from an alliance that your clan has offered my coven. I know what that means for you, for your family."

It meant exile from the clan or punishment that inevitably led to death. Naya had told her all about it.

She would never allow for that to happen, and she didn't want to give Viktir the opportunity to hurt Torin more than he already did.

A feeling that she didn't quite understand punched into her stomach.

She had accepted her bloodline and the responsibility that came with it.

Emara cleared her throat. "I am not ready to *fully* commit to the alliance or even think about it right now." She had to be honest with him. "But that is not me shutting it down entirely. I would not dishonour you."

The longest moment of her entire life passed, and he still didn't speak. Was he thinking about her words? How had he taken them? Maybe it would be better if she could see his face.

A gentle lilt in his tone clarified that he was done with the seriousness of the conversation. "Are you saying you are warming to the idea of being my wife?"

"No!" she barked, louder than expected, and Artem turned to look at them with a cheesy grin.

"That is not what I am saying" she hissed sharply, only to Torin.

"Has she stabbed you yet?" Artem called from the front.

"Not yet," Torin confirmed, and Emara could hear the terrible delight on his face without having to see it.

"Not even a swinging elbow?" Artem snorted. "I heard you are rather fond of them, Emara."

Emara turned as much as she could on the saddle to face Torin. "Do you keep anything to yourself?"

Torin's ice-blue stare penetrated through her, and it

was the first time she had seen it in hours. With the backdrop of snowy-white trees, he was a striking contrast. His glowing, tanned skin, his sharp jaw, and his dark brows, his warmth.

Her heart stopped. Emara quickly turned around again before he could speak.

Yep, he definitely had that infuriating smirk splashed all over his stupid face.

"I keep a lot of things to myself." He chuckled, and that deep laugh warmed her broken heart a little. "But there are some things I struggle to keep to myself."

"Really?" A cynical laugh escaped her.

"Shall I let you in on a little secret? We do like to keep a few of those between us."

"I hardly think we have a *few,* but carry on."

The pulse was back in her neck.

"I really struggled last night."

"With what?" She swallowed, knowing directly where this conversation was about to lead.

Her stomach flipped.

"I struggled to keep my thoughts of you...pure."

"Mhmmm," she hummed, feeling that familiar heat working its way back down her spine and into her core.

He leaned in and whispered against her neck, "I struggled keeping my hands to myself with you in that wine-coloured dress. It took my mind to unthinkable places."

Oh. "It wasn't *that* sensual," she tutted, trying not to think about what his thoughts had conjured.

"Trust me," he fired out quickly, "it was a very

mischievous little garment. And I dare say it has been my favourite yet."

The whispers of what he'd promised to her last night, the sounds of his want, his eyes stripping her bare, all came flooding back. She pushed her knees into the side of the saddle, praying it would help take the edge off.

He chuckled as if knowing exactly how her memories had affected her.

Maddened by his self-confidence, she decided to play a little game of her own. "If we are both going to be revealing our secrets on this ride," she said, her voice low, "maybe I have a little one of my own."

"Go on." His tone was overly encouraging, and she bit back a smile.

"I will only reveal it if you promise never to speak of it again," she said firmly.

"The suspense is killing me, so I am going to agree with anything you want."

She turned around to find his intense gaze. "I am only saying this because we are hours into this ride and I am growing tired of your small talk."

A flash of white teeth bit into his lower lip as he raised his strong chin. "You don't like my small talk?"

She groaned, turning back around and facing a blanket of frost. "I don't like small talk at all."

"What about pillow talk?"

"I am not answering that." She shook her head.

He chuckled again, and this time she could feel it come from his stomach.

"You have three seconds to spill, or I am going to make you ride with Artem," he threatened lightly.

She rolled her neck and took a deep breath. "I really struggled last night too."

"I have never been more interested in my life to understand why." He sat forward, his broad chest pressing into her back. "Please continue."

"Maybe if you stopped talking for a moment, I would have the chance to," Emara snapped.

"Consider this my last sentence until you are fully finished."

She shushed him and let a small giggle drift between them. "I struggled with not saying those two little words."

He sat back on the saddle, the heat from his body leaving her and the cold invading the space between them. She missed it instantaneously.

"Well, well, well," he said with tremendous satisfaction, and she already wanted to punch him. "Did I just fall into another realm, or are my wildest dreams coming true?" She promised herself that she wouldn't look back to see the grin she knew was on his face. "In fact, I know it's not my wildest dreams, because in my wildest dreams, you would have said those exact words, last night, wearing that little wine dress."

"Shut up." She laughed, flinging her elbow back into his stomach.

"I've been elbowed," Torin yelled to his brethren.

"Yes!" Artem chanted a few times as he twisted his body around in the saddle to look. "Pay up, Magin," he shouted past them.

A curse came from the guard on the horse behind her and Torin snickered.

Emara whipped her head around. "Why does he need to pay up?" she demanded.

Artem let out a laugh. "I bet Magin that we wouldn't make it to our base camp before you did something violent to Blacksteel."

Her mouth fell open. "Something violent?"

"You said she would have punched him, it doesn't count," Magin huffed from behind.

"Punched him?" Her eyes popped from her head.

"I didn't specify what direct infliction she would cause." Artem grinned. "I just specified the timescale. Pay up, Oxhound."

"Damn it," he grumbled from behind.

Emara's jaw almost unhinged as it fell open further. "You were all really betting on me to have inflicted pain on Torin before the night was out?"

"Absolutely," All three males said in unison. She turned and scowled at Torin.

"You make me sound like I am a tyrant."

"From what I have gathered, you seem sweet and lovely," Artem said, smirking from ear to ear. "But sometimes you can look at Torin like you are about to stab him in the neck." He bellowed a laugh. "I mean, if I am honest with myself, I am here for it."

"Thanks, brother." Torin's sarcastic tone made Emara stifle a laugh.

"I can't lie to you, Blacksteel"—he looked past Emara at Torin—"that girl has a way of putting you in your place that even my father couldn't do in the Selection."

Torin chuckled behind her.

And she let out one breathy laugh, unsure of how that was possible.

He let go of the reins and wrapped one arm around her waist, pulling her against him. An instant heat swelled in her stomach and spread all over her body, causing the hairs on her skin to rise. Her heart rate doubled in seconds.

"I don't mind if it's you who puts me in my place," he whispered. "But only you."

CHAPTER NINETEEN
EMARA

As the grey sky turned a soft shade of navy, they finally found a clearing suitable to rest and get shelter for the night. Her trio had set up camp within minutes; they had probably lived like this many times during the Selection. Artem and Torin had erected small tents and Magin was working on teaching Emara how to build a fire from dried wood he had brought from the tower. Knowing the weather was working against them, it had been a clever move. She thought about trying to light the wood by her own flames, but if something went wrong, she could take out the whole camp, so she opted for a survival-without-magic kind of night.

By the time Emara had watched Magin create the fire, Torin and Artem had unpackaged the salted meat, and for the first time in what felt like forever, she felt a little hungry.

Once they had tucked into the meats and cubed cheese that they had brought from the kitchens, Magin announced that he would take the first watch, allowing the sleepy Artem to get some rest. Emara had a sneaking suspicion that a certain wolf had kept him up all night, and if he was going to make it through tomorrow, he needed to rest.

Emara had been surprisingly grateful for Breighly's company in La Luna. Her energy had made it easy to forget about her troubles for at least one night, and that's all she had wanted. She also reminded her of another blonde-haired, unapologetic rebel; even though thinking of Cally tore her heart to shreds, Breighly had filled that dark void, even if it had been for a short time.

A wave of emotion hit her as she sat watching the flames of the fire. Emara wasn't sure if it was sadness, tiredness, or bleak nothingness that overtook her, but she stood, ignoring the idle chit-chat of the hunters, hoping to slip away into the tents without being noticed. She didn't want to be around anyone, not if she was going to have one of her...moments. Suddenly, all three hunters stood to attention, and Emara's skin leapt from her bones.

"What the—" She jumped.

She looked over them, a hand on her heart, and they stared back.

They were her guards, she remembered.

How fast they had reacted to her movement was a reminder that they were not just boys, idly strolling to the palace—they were warriors, men bound by oath to protect the kingdom. And her.

"Which tent is mine?" she asked, feeling the eyes of them all on her, too intense. She looked over the clearing, seeing that they had only erected two. "Are there only going to be two tents?" she shot a glare towards the three of them.

"We couldn't bring four, that's not how this works. We had to pack light. You are lucky we haven't only got one," Torin announced.

"That would be an interesting night," Artem said lowly, putting an axe back into his weapon belt. She hadn't even realised he had unsheathed one until now. "No, but seriously, did you expect four tents?"

"I..." She clamped her mouth shut as she looked around their makeshift campsite. "I actually don't know; I have never done this before."

"We are not close enough to the nearest village to find an inn tonight—maybe tomorrow or the next day. But you can have your own space and the hunters will share. We will be on shifts, anyway." Torin picked up a large stone that sat close to the fire, the size of a small cat, and walked towards her. "Follow me."

She followed him without any hesitation. She had been riding for hours and the thought of finding sleep was all she could think about. Torin pushed aside the entrance to the tent and ducked inside, followed by Emara. He placed the rock at the bottom of the fur sack that was designed for a warrior in the winter, and there was a small oil lamp glowing in the corner.

"Where will you be sleeping?" she dared to ask, looking up from the rolled-out mats on the floor.

"In the other tent with Artem." He nodded towards the opening, his back still hunched over a little, the tent restricting him to stand his true height. "Why? Did you want me to stay here with you?"

Emara's heart twitched at how sincere he was, and she had to bite back any snide response she would have normally jabbed his way. "I will be okay. Thank you."

Torin nodded. "The stone from the fire should give you heat for some time. Keep it at the bottom of the sack, it will warm your feet." He looked her over. "Should you need more warmth, just call on me."

"I will not be needing more warmth—"

"I was referring to how one of us would bring you another stone from the fire."

She fought to hide her smile. "Sure you were."

A lazy smile warmed his face. "Your mind is getting filthier by the minute, Clearwater." He chuckled. "Try and get as much sleep as you can." He turned to take his leave, but Emara's hand shot out and caught his thick forearm. He turned, not hiding the shock that burst across his face.

"I like when you laugh sincerely," she said at the speed of her beating heart. "I just thought I should tell you that."

A mist of emotion dispersed within his eyes, reaching nowhere else on his face. His lips parted, but he said nothing.

"I didn't want you to see another day without knowing that," she said, the words catching in her throat. He looked stunned. Torin Blacksteel looked utterly stunned. "And now I can go to sleep knowing that I have finally silenced Torin Blacksteel."

Was he blushing? No! Not in a million moons.

Is he? She strained her eyes to see in the darkness of

the tent. If he had, he had made sure it was brief enough for her to almost miss it.

He moved over to her, close enough to touch her. "And I am going to sleep tonight, thinking of your words." He pushed his hand into hers, and both warm and cool tingles scattered across her palm. She looked up at him as he pressed their hands tighter together. He elevated their intertwined hands, and for a moment, she expected him to kiss her flesh, but he didn't.

He placed her hand over his heart.

Choking down a swallow, she looked at him in bewilderment. It was a gesture that felt more intimate than she had ever expected it to.

"Can you feel that?" he said, his husky voice broken with a dash of vulnerability.

She nodded, referring to the heartbeat that now slammed into the palm of her hand. She could feel it travelling all the way through her arm and she imagined it moving from her own arm and into her heart.

"Yes," she finally managed to whisper.

"I wanted you to go to sleep tonight knowing that no one has ever made my heart beat as fast as you do." He squeezed her hand, pushing it closer into his strong chest.

Her head dizzied, fuelling a rush of warmth that spread through her skin. The hairs on the back of her neck stood. Even though they could see the air from their breath swirl around them, she was boiling hot. She had no idea why, but somehow, those words wormed their way through her chest and wrapped around her heart like a blanket.

"Sleep well," he said before releasing her fingers from his grip. Emara's hand lay on his chest for a few seconds before she slid it slowly down, the drum of his heart fading as it travelled further from the beat. She wasn't ready to let her touch drop, but she did.

"Good night," she whispered, really wanting another two words to break free from her lips. Two little words that she was certain Torin wanted to hear too.

He smiled a heart-crushingly beautiful smile and gave her one long nod before leaving the tent.

A rush of cold air slapped her face, reminding her that it would be inappropriate of her to act on her deepest desires right this second. She ran a hand through her hair, pushing it back off her face as a feeling coiled around her stomach and pushed itself south.

She knew the feeling. It ached in all the most feminine parts of her.

She cursed out loud as she removed her cloak for bed, wishing it was Torin who had taken it off.

TORIN

PRAISING the Gods for the cold air that practically punched him in the face, Torin stalked over to the tent he would be staying in. Magin crossed paths with him, nodding as he took up his stance outside Emara's tent. He would be there until Artem changed with him halfway through the night. Torin shot him a look over his shoulder, warning him to protect her with his life.

Taking one of the stones that enclosed the fire for himself, he entered the tent. Artem was already in his sleeping sack, awaiting his return.

"Did she give you a black eye?" Artem asked. Torin noticed his face was way more enthusiastic than it should have been to ask that question.

"Not this time." He laughed, removing his boots and weapon belt. Torin quickly put the stone at the bottom of his bedroll and leapt into the furs. It had been a while since he had a mission where he had to camp out, but the memories of his training and the Selection process were rooted permanently into his mind.

"She matches you well, Blacksteel," Artem said as he lay on his back, staring at the tip of the small tent.

Changing the subject before he ran over to Emara's tent barefoot and broke all the promises of not kissing her until she asked, he replied, "What about *your* little love match from last night?"

Artem laughed out loud at Torin's words, and it reminded him of sharing a station with him in the Selection. Artem always got into trouble for laughing, but they would lie awake at night and talk through everything from family, to weapons, to the Gods. It had been a comfort for them both, something only a member of a hunting clan would understand. Something only a second-in-command would understand.

"Brother, I have never met anyone like her." Artem's stomach heaved in his laughter. "Firstly, she kicked me out of bed like she was ashamed of me. Secondly, she didn't ask when I would return, and thirdly, she didn't even ask my name, which I am sure she didn't know." He shot a glance over at Torin.

He smiled at the thought of Breighly Baxgroll pushing a six-foot-five warrior out into the forest.

"Then she threw my fighting knives at me, almost stabbing my feet, before launching an axe at my head."

To Torin, the biggest shock of all was that the wolf had missed. He knew she was capable of hitting her target, which meant she *wanted* to miss. A smirk pulled at the left side of Torin's mouth.

"Oh, and to top it all off, after our *night of passions,* she informed me as she was shoving me out the door that she has a boyfriend."

"Well, that's a lie," Torin informed him as a little chuckle escaped. "Breighly Baxgroll doesn't have *boyfriends.*"

Artem's head cranked around. "What? Are you kidding me? She told me she had a boyfriend."

"Do you think if she had a *wolf* boyfriend, she would have let you sleep in her sheets? Her man would have been able to smell you from miles away. She's played you, brother."

There was a moment of silence. "She has, indeed," Artem admitted in a higher pitch. "I feel used." He laughed, putting an arm behind his head.

"Well, I did warn you." Torin lay his hands over his chest, where moments before, Emara's hand had been. All day she had been so close to him, skin-to-skin as they rode together. It had teased every mischievous thought possible from his mind and tortured every wicked part of him too. He turned around, facing the opposite direction from Artem. It was a precaution in case his thoughts of her took a turn for the *darker* side, as they always did.

What was a guy to do?

"I think I am into her, Blacksteel."

Unable to believe what he was hearing, Torin hauled himself around to see Artem. "What?"

Had his brother lost his mind in the Huntswood markets? He wouldn't be the first.

"She was different," Artem said, his eyes still on the ceiling like he could see the stars through the fabric.

"Of course, she's different; she is a wolf," he reminded him. "Wolves *mate*. There is no point in getting dragged into that."

"I know." Artem pushed his jaw out to the side.

"You are just not used to a girl who isn't stumbling over themselves to be with you." Torin laughed hoarsely. "You will get over it."

"Didn't your mother ever tell you not to throw stones at glass houses?" Artem laughed.

True.

They both sat in silence for a while, letting the chuckles die in the chill of the night's air.

Sleep must have found him because when he woke, the morning light from outside glowed around the foundations, lighting the inside of the tent. Instantly, he shot up, thinking of her. The flame in his chest burned as he thought of her face, and the fire roared through his veins. Torin had to make sure she was okay, he had to see her.

Fuck.

He took a breath.

In that moment, he knew that he would give up his own life for hers. And it was not because of his oath to the clan, but because of the indisputable feeling in his heart.

CHAPTER TWENTY
EMARA

T he next few days were much of the same. They would ride until nightfall and then find a safe place to camp. Torin had kept himself quiet and Emara wondered if what she had said the other night in the tent had been too much.

Was it too real?

I wanted you to go to sleep tonight knowing that no one has ever made my heart beat as fast as you do.

She couldn't possibly count how many times she had played that moment over and over in her head. How she had replayed the beating of his heart under her palm, how he had looked at her. How she had felt. It was an *odd* feeling, a feeling that made her blood warm, but she also realised how up to her neck in terror she felt when she pondered how deep her feelings could go.

Magin's horse stopped quickly, snapping her attention back to her surroundings. Torin tugged on the reins, slowing them to a stop, and Emara imagined that Artem had pulled to an abrupt halt behind them too as she heard his horse complain. Magin put up a gloved hand and Torin let out a sharp exhale.

"Stay on the horse," he commanded, not a single compromise ringing through.

An unsettling whirl played around in her stomach as Torin dismounted Ledi. The horse let out an uneasy whine that curled the fear even further into Emara's bones. Distracting herself, she patted his giant neck.

The moon was the only light above them now; the forest trees were unforgiving, letting little to no light through the thick branches. Normally, they would have been setting up camp by now, but Artem knew of a small village nearby where they could turn in for the night. The idea of sleeping in real beds instead of on the frozen ground was too appealing, so they'd kept riding. Her body would never forgive her after this journey. It ached from the discomfort of the forest floor, and she had practically begged the Gods every night to hurry this journey along.

She heard metal scratching against a case and knew Torin had withdrawn fighting knives.

Oh Gods, something was out there.

Could he hear or see something that she couldn't?

In that moment, a crashing realisation sunk into her bones. However powerful witches were, they didn't have the same instincts and senses as the hunters. Warriors of Thorin were born to detect danger, and even if witches could feel something bad in their gut, hunters could detect the danger quicker.

Magin dismounted too.

Another sound of boots hitting the ground came

from behind her, letting it be known that Artem had dismounted his horse.

Deep in her gut, she knew this wasn't good.

Her pulse quickened. Her magic tingled.

A branch snapped to her left, causing her head to swing in the same direction. Ledi shifted underneath her, trotting to the side and she pulled on the reins to calm him, still trying to pat between his ears.

"Do you still have that dagger strapped to your thigh?" Torin asked, his stance changing. She knew the stance well. It had been one of the first things she had learned in combat.

"Yes," she answered him. Pulling aside her cloak, Emara ran a hand over the fastening. The lethal blade was cool on her fingertips as she unstrapped it from where it clung to her combat leggings. The blade glinted under the moonlight, and she gripped the thickness of the hilt.

Out of nowhere, a rush of movement came from the trees. Ledi jolted to one side, and she had to clutch onto his mane to stay mounted. Torin jumped into action, hurling a knife through the air and landing it between two crimson eyes. Emara's full body shuddered as she watched the black blood pour down the creature's face. As the animal crumpled and died, the smell of sulphur hit the back of her throat.

It wasn't an animal.

It was a demon. They were being attacked by demons.

Fear was a strange thing. You could either let it take over, paralysing everything from your mind down to your toes, or you could let it build into adrenaline, channelling it into every movement, every decision, every breath you took. Fear could become bravery.

Emara decided on the latter.

She wasn't going to let fear ruin her life, not when the people who surrounded her fought so valiantly to protect her.

It happened so fast, after Torin threw the first knife.

Blood-red eyes broke from the trees and darkness, caging them in. Her guards burst into action. Magin unsheathed a double-edged spear, similar to the one she had trained with before, and began stabbing through flesh. Artem had jumped out in front, a knife in one hand and an axe in the other. And, of course, Torin had pulled his double swords from his back after running out of throwing knives.

He was unfalteringly violent as he halved through torsos, leaving them like dead leaves on the forest floor. He spun with grace from one slaughter to the next, ensuring their utter demise.

The demons were different from what she had witnessed before. They were not like the one that had been in her home the night her grandmother was killed —a high demon—nor were they like the winged beasts that had attacked the Uplift, trained for battle.

They were smaller, looking more like feral hounds walking on their hind legs, but with faces that looked like burned, human skin. They had rows and rows of teeth, and they looked rabid with the desire to taste and feed.

But their awful crimson eyes were the same.

Magin let out a roar that caught Emara's attention. One had climbed onto his back and had sunk teeth into his shoulder. Before she could think anything through, she flung herself off the horse. What felt like tiny needles pierced up through the pads of her feet, reminding her of how human she truly was as shooting pains jolted up her ankles to her shins.

She was a witch, though, not a human, and she had learned some basic training. It was time to put it to the test. Powering momentum into a sprint, she gripped her fighting knife hard. As she approached Magin, he was still struggling, one demon on his back, another in the clutches of one hand. She pulled her arm back and drove her dagger forward, straight into a spine of rotten flesh. The demon bucked and let go of Magin's neck and he spun, spearing it through the heart quicker than she could follow. That was all he'd needed, a split second of reprieve, and she had given him that.

"Thank you, Emara."

She blinked only to find that he was already on to the next kill.

"Emara!" Torin's rough roar was like a warning call sent from the Underworld.

She whirled around to see a demon hurl itself against her. Its body collided with hers and they tumbled to the ground, her skull smacking against the root of a tree. A screech of pain escaped her as the demon slammed on top of her, its claws finding her shoulders, and it hit her body into the ground again, knocking the air from her lungs.

All she could see was a sparkling blur of mad eyes and ferocious teeth.

Screaming, she struggled to swing her arm around, plunging the dagger into the side of its neck. Out of instinct, she closed her eyes to avoid the blood hitting her eyes, but warm gunge sprayed down on her face, narrowly missing her mouth.

The creature shrieked in pain, and the smell of its rotten breath had her stomach jumping. Emara managed to keep her weapon out at arm's length, the blade still embedded deep within the demon's neck, but unfortunately for her, it wasn't dead.

Not yet. She hadn't hit the brain, the heart, or taken its head completely off.

Damn it. Why did she go for the neck? In pure panic, she had missed her opponent's weakness.

She was stuck under this beast as its vile teeth still gnashed at her. The demon clawed at her, snapping and snipping at her with its putrid teeth.

The weight of the demon's body lay on her legs, disabling her from moving them, and she wondered how much longer her arms could hold before her strength would give way and its teeth devoured her.

A sharp blade pierced through the chest of the demon, stopping an inch before her heart. She let out a scream as the demon did and the blade withdrew itself before the demon was flung aside like a phantom wind had propelled it into the air. Torin stood above her, covered in dark blood.

"You almost stabbed me!" she yelled, her hand

clutching her cloak where his blade had almost penetrated.

"Do you seriously have that little faith in my precision?" He smirked, holding out his hand for her to take. "My sword would never have touched you, angel."

She didn't take his hand. "You were one freaking inch away from my heart," she complained as she stood.

"Don't be dramatic." He smiled carnally. Without warning, he spun and severed a demon's head from its neck as it approached from behind. Turning back to her like he *hadn't* just decapitated a demon's head from its shoulders, he said, "I have impeccable accuracy. And you should know that you can't kill a demon by stabbing into its neck. You need to decapitate it or pierce its brain or heart."

Heat flushed her cheeks at her mistake. "Well, thank the Gods for your *accuracy*," she snapped. "Or my heart would have been on the other end of your bloody sword."

"Like I said before, you need to have more faith in me." Even though it was cold, a little sweat had formed on his brow, and he wiped it away, still clutching both swords. "Have I ever let you down yet?" he asked.

Although she knew they were in the middle of one of those conversations that had utterly ridiculous timing, the question rang through her.

He had never let her down, not once.

He turned again as another demon came towards his back. He stabbed from behind, skewering the demon like he was making lunch, and pulled the creature over his head. The demon's body hit the ground in front of

Emara, and she couldn't help but flinch at the sound it made. He pulled his second sword up and ended its existence with one sharp stab to the heart.

She didn't fear what she had just witnessed, how Torin didn't so much as flinch as he killed them. She didn't fear that he looked her in the eye after it like nothing had happened. She wasn't afraid when she was with him.

She was safe with him.

"It's clear from my end," Artem shouted, pulling her gaze from Torin.

"A small legion of lesser demons." Magin panted, holding his shoulder. "Why they would be out here, I have no idea. It's not a usual gathering spot."

"They have probably gotten themselves lost in the hunt for human flesh," Torin added.

"Trust it be us that comes across them." Emara fixed the cloak around her neck that had gathered funny from her fight.

She started walking back to where Ledi was still waiting, untouched, but Torin caught her elbow.

He searched her over, probably looking for any injuries. The thought of his eyes trailing over her under the moonlight sent her heart racing.

"I am okay." She held up her hands when she realised what he was doing. She noticed that her right hand was covered in blackish red gore and assumed her face was too. Torin moved into the space between them, clearly taking a better look at her.

"It's not mine," she said, holding out her hand to

him. He took her hand in his own and looked it over. "I promise."

Torin exhaled and looked over her hand a second time before wiping it down his tunic. The blood smeared over his grey uniform, and she could feel the hardness of his muscles underneath the material.

"Better on me than on you," he said, his eyes dimming with shadows that could only be found in the darkest parts of the ocean.

"I think you have enough on you," Emara replied.

"I have nowhere near enough on me if it keeps you safe." His lashes lowered, causing her stomach to roll and flip. "We need to get out of here," he commanded his brethren.

"I think we are an hour out from the closest village," Artem said, readjusting his weapons on his belt.

"Come on." Torin took Emara's hand, dwarfing hers in size. "Let's get you to the inn." He tugged her along, threading his fingers through hers as they walked back to their horses.

Looking down at her hand in his, she prayed to the Gods he wouldn't let go of it until they were out of the forest.

CHAPTER
TWENTY-ONE
EMARA

And he didn't.

Even when they entered the humble inn, which was cosied into the front of a small village, he still held on to her hand. The front room of the inn was small, and it smelled like the smoke from an old fire had burnt out hours ago. A rustic bar sat in the corner, with a few bottles of liquor to choose from all displayed on polished oak barrows. The tiles of the floor lay cracked under Emara's boots as she walked in a little further whilst her guards sorted the arrangements for the night. It wasn't the freshest place she had ever stayed, but it sure did beat lying on the cold ground.

The innkeeper, who was a small but well-rounded woman, must have decided that the blood all over Emara's face and body was unacceptable. Quickly, she was directed to her room, leaving the boys downstairs to enjoy a whisky that Artem had ordered to take the edge off the cold and the pain in Magin's shoulder.

It was clear that the human innkeeper knew about the world of magic, and it made Emara wonder how many humans actually knew about the monsters that roamed outside.

"Everything you need should already be in the room for you. There are fresh towels and hot water," the innkeeper said.

Before Emara could say thank you, she had turned on her heels, making her way down the flight of makeshift stairs that looked centuries old.

Turning the rather large key in the sticky lock, she pushed the door open and entered her room. It reminded her of a horse's barn with wooden panels on the walls and more wooden beams in the centre of the room, dividing where the bed and bathing areas were. No walls broke the two rooms apart, but Emara was just glad to be in something other than a tent. A humble fire warmed the room to a cosy temperature that had her skin tingling.

She shrugged her cloak off and let it fall to the ground.

She knew where her priorities lay.

Gliding across the room, she made it to the bathtub in a few seconds. She turned the water faucet that looked a little worse for wear and ran the water until it turned scalding hot. A delighted sigh escaped her mouth as steam evaporated and rose into the air. It had been days since she had bathed, or even washed, and she did a tiny happy dance on the tip of her toes in anticipation of what the warmth would feel like against her skin, what it would feel like for her body to be hugged by the purity of the water.

Stripping herself of her clothes fully, she dipped

her toe in, and the rising steam came to greet the back of her leg. At first, it burned and niggled uncomfortably at her skin, but she persevered and lowered the rest of her body down into the tub. It wasn't quite one of the baths that she had at the tower or in Naya's cottage, where she could perform a tantalising bathing ritual, but she sure as heck wouldn't be taking any sort of warm bath for granted again. Reaching for the basic soap that smelled like grapefruit and lilac, she ran it over her dirt-covered hands and face. She scrubbed everywhere she could, paying close attention to her hair, as it was filthy from where demons' blood had dried.

Not knowing how long she had lay in the tub, sifting through everything in her chaotic mind, she finally looked at her wrinkled hands. Maybe it had been an hour? Or maybe it was longer. Her eyes closed as she floated in the bathtub. It was enough to ease the strain on her back from riding and to steam the dirt and demon blood from her skin.

But she was also grateful just to be in this moment, centring herself, like Naya had taught her.

Three quick knocks pounded the door and the round door handle turned quickly.

She let out a muffled squeal, her eyes flying open as she tried to cover herself with her arms and hands. Given the fact that the bathtub lay a few metres from the bed, in an open space, she didn't exactly have anywhere to go or hide.

"Excuse me, this room is taken."

Dark, perfectly placed hair and broad shoulders

strode through the door and halted, taking in the sight of her bathing.

"Are you serious?" she hissed ferally. "Get out!"

One eyebrow sprung up. "Well, hello to you too," Torin said as he closed the door behind him.

"No, I am serious, don't close the door." Her face flushed cerise as her arms tugged her femininity tighter. "What are you doing?"

"I am coming into my room," he said casually, carrying a few bags and dumping them close to the old drawers that sat tall in the corner. Clearly, he was unfazed by a naked girl.

A knot tied tighter in her stomach.

"No, no, no!" she protested. "This is not your room. Can you not see it is currently occupied?" She pulled her legs closer to her chest. She was sure everything was hidden. Thank Gods the lathering of the soap had caused a lot of bubbles.

"I can see the tub is occupied." His eyes danced dangerously, pebbled in mischief. Moving closer to lean against the large beam in the middle of the room, he let a dry smirk appear, revealing one of his dimples. "Had I known I could have been up here, being party to this, I would have drunk my night cap quicker."

"You were not invited to this party!" Her voice almost split the beam of wood that his massive weight leaned against. Wincing, Emara regretted how loud she had been, but she did imagine the beam falling, taking Torin's smug smile along with it.

"That's a shame." He pouted. "I also planned to bathe, you know." His grin travelled all the way to his eyes. "Maybe we could be in there together." He nodded in the direction of the tub.

"Over my dead body," she jeered, wanting to flick water in his direction.

"What have I told you about being mean? We are rooming together tonight. People who share rooms together should never be aggressive towards one another. It's impolite."

"And barging into an occupied room isn't?" She pulled a towel from the railing bolted through a wooden panel beside her. "Please, turn around," she said. She stood and placed the towel out, blocking Torin's view of her. She jumped out the tub and wrapped the fluffy towel around her body, all flushed.

And as she looked up, to her surprise, Torin had turned around, giving her some privacy. However, her pounding steps in his direction gave him the heads up that she was directly in front of him, and he turned to face her again.

"We are not sharing the same room." She was unfaltering in her words.

He laughed, looking at the drips from her wet hair running down her arms and face. "I think you will find that we are. We shared a horse, and a few snacks on the way here. What's sharing a bed with your favourite guard?"

"This is not a joke, Torin." Her eyes widened. "We can't share a room." Her voice was small but stern.

"Why? What's the matter?" A twitch flickered under his eye. "Are you scared you are going to want to say my *favourite two words?"* His smug smile relaxed his features, making him look younger.

Yes.

"No," she croaked. "I am not scared of that. I know I won't say them."

He pushed himself off of the beam. "I think that *is* what you are scared of." He closed the gap between them. "Besides, it was either me or one of the other two. We could only get two rooms. The third is for the innkeeper and her husband, unless you want to sleep with them?"

Why was there a shortage of everything around here?

"So I don't need to share with you." Her chin lifted. "I choose...Magin."

"Really?" His thick neck bobbed as he swallowed. "Because I can go and get him for you now if you'd like."

She knew he was calling her bluff. There was no way he would let anyone else sleep in the same room as her. And Torin was the only one she really knew. She at least felt comfortable enough around him to be herself. She let out a sharp exhale. "You drive me insane."

"I think you like it, angel." He rolled his lip between his teeth.

"There is only one bed," she acknowledged, completely ignoring his pet name for her. "That's ridiculous."

"I will make room for you on it." His infuriatingly cute dimple appeared on his right cheek this time.

She wrinkled her nose in irritation. "Turn around," she said, sulking. "I need to get dressed."

He let out a lazy laugh, but he did as he was told for once.

Heading to the bed, she pulled the longest nightgown that she had from her satchel. It was the only nightgown of suitable length that she had packed from the tower, knowing that when sleeping rough in the forest, she would be wearing her travelling clothes to keep her warm.

She paused.

But that was not the only nightgown that she had brought for the Amethyst Palace. She had packed much more fashionable pieces, knowing she would be at the capital of witches. She had been in Huntswood, after all.

And if Torin wanted to keep on playing this dangerous game—this enticing little game—maybe she should play along for a little while.

"Did you bring the burgundy dress?" Torin asked, dripping in sensual tones as he faced the wall. "You can change into that if you like."

As she glanced over her shoulder at him, he had strapped his hands over his chest; the muscles of his back threatened to burst his tunic.

Her eyes burned into his back like her flames were licking him. "If you mention that bloody dress one more time, I will strangle you with it," she promised.

"I always knew you had a kink," he purred.

She ignored him and pulled out another nightgown, one that was cut from expensive emerald satin with thick lace straps that travelled into the plunged neckline. With her chest heaving, she placed it over her arms and it slid into place on her body. The material hugged the curve of her breasts and then hung loose around her hips. The hem came down to her mid-thigh, and she was sure it was bought from the *daring* section of the Huntswood markets.

Oh Gods, how did she think packing *this* was a good idea? She had thought she would be alone in these situations, not sharing a small room with Torin Blacksteel. He, however, had strolled in here so confidently, with the audacity to say that *she* couldn't handle sharing a room with him because *she* was scared to admit that she wanted to kiss him.

Like she wouldn't have the restraint.

Smug bastard!

He really did overestimate his effect on women. Or maybe he just underestimated *her*.

Since he was so sure that it would be *her* who caved into her desires and not him, maybe she should test that.

She swallowed hard as she made her way around the bed.

Maybe she could just test those desires to see how she felt too.

Torin's back remained facing her and she second-guessed what she was about to do.

A flutter in her stomach reminded her of innocent nerves, but the pounding in her heart reminded her that she was alive, she was in control, and she certainly wouldn't be underestimated by any man. Ever.

She wouldn't kiss him. But she could play with him for being a self-assured, egotistical, self-righteous man.

He thought she wanted to kiss *him* more than he wanted to kiss *her.*

Her breath caught.

Maybe it was true. The Gods themselves only knew, but she would be damned if she was about to show him that.

She perched herself against the railing of the bed, the curve of her bottom, resting against the wood, lifting the emerald fabric slightly higher up her thigh. She lifted one bare leg over the other and dragged a hand through the top of her wet hair before flipping it over her shoulder, making it untamed. Rolling her lips between her teeth, she looked down. She slowly dragged one finger down the cleavage of her night gown, hooking her finger into the fabric and adjusting it lower, exposing more of her skin. Her hand shook, but only a little, as she placed it back down against her thigh.

She was getting better at controlling her fear. But this was an addictive kind of fear, the kind of fear that thrilled every part of her, that gave her heart something to feel other than cold nothingness.

She ingested every last piece of confidence that she could before she said, "I am done."

He turned, his wicked tongue tucked into the side of his cheek. At first his eyes were lazy with satisfaction and his arms were still crossed over his chest. But that all changed the minute he saw her, the second he took her in. His eyes became wild with hunger. His shoulders tensed as he dropped his hands down by his sides. A muscle ticked in his jaw, but there were no signs of his devilish smile.

No, it was gone.

What had replaced it was something more gratifying.

Shock.

"What's the matter?" She played with an innocent expression. "Are you not a fan of the emerald nightgown?" Her tone was satisfyingly light. She was getting better at this game too. He dipped his chin, and his lips parted to say something, but no words came. He swallowed hard. She was sure she could see the pulse in his neck, or maybe that was just the pulse from hers beating through every single part of who she was. His eyes explored her again, as if the shock had worn off and he could finally take in the details.

Well then, she thought to herself, *let the games begin.*

CHAPTER TWENTY-TWO
TORIN

It was official. She was trying to fucking kill him.

She was trying to kill him, and she knew it. That naughty little angel knew it.

Torin tried his best to hide a smile that warranted her so much respect, but he wasn't going to offer up his cards just yet. She was playing him at his own game and it kickstarted a burning desire to stride across the room and just take her there and then.

But he would fight back.

Even if he wanted every fucking perfect inch of her underneath him, even if he wanted his mouth on her—everywhere—he would fight back.

He trailed his eyes down her sleek wet hair that slid down her back and he imagined holding onto it whilst sucking the most delicate parts of her neck.

A strain against his leathers confirmed that he was well and truly solid from one look over her.

One fucking look.

He was in trouble.

Maybe he should have sent in Magin. Then he

wouldn't be close to breaking any promises. However, that meant someone else seeing her like this.

No, absolutely not. Then he would be closer to breaking necks. Just the thought of another male seeing her like this sent a fire through him so fierce that he didn't know if he could control it. Torin exhaled, taking in the curve of her breasts in that delicious jade nightgown. He'd thought he liked the burgundy gown, but this...this was the kind of garment you left on whilst devouring her.

She sat sensually against the bed like the Gods themselves had hand-delivered her as a test. His pulse pounded against the veins in his neck, his temperature rising with every second that he drank her in. Emara's tempting nightdress exposed more skin on her thighs than he thought he could handle. She had the kind of curves that intimidated a boy and sent a real man wild. He wasn't intimidated by any of it. He was entranced.

Her eyes were on him too, analysing his reaction. He didn't care how he looked as he ran a hand over his jaw, unable to hide the expression on his face.

"That...is...a very dangerous game you are playing, angel." He kept his eyes on her face as her lips parted a second before she spoke.

"I know," she responded, the lyrical lull of her tone light, keeping their eye contact unbroken.

He hadn't expected her to admit that she was playing him, but she had said it so confidently that she even had him fooled.

"Are you sure you want to play this game?" He took his time as he walked over to where she sat. "I have been known to be the winner," He leaned down, so close to her face, and placed a hand on either side of the wood, barricading her in. "Every time."

"Not this time," she said, not even a stain of colour flushing her cheeks.

She was getting good at this—very fucking good, indeed.

Emara lifted a hand to his face and ran a thumb over his jaw and then down to his chin.

His heart pounded.

Why did the Gods send her? *Why? Thorin, why?*

He was about to crumble to his knees, but he managed to keep his front for a little bit longer.

"We shall see about that." He straightened. With one hand, he reached up to his collar, unbuttoning the fabric of his grey tunic. Lifting it from the back of his neck, he pulled, taking it over his head. He threw it onto the ground and watched as her beautiful, cosmic eyes explored his body, changing colour from a light grey to a fiery darkness. The longer she lingered, the deeper the lust grew on her face.

That's the reaction he had been looking for.

She wanted this just as much as he did.

Squaring her shoulders, she stood, taking Torin by surprise, and he moved back with her, giving her space. She was much smaller than him, and if he really wanted to, he could pick her up and throw her onto the bed. But he refrained, awaiting her next move in their dangerous little game.

To be fair to Emara, this was the best game of '*who was going to crack first*' he had ever played, without a single doubt. Every other time, it had only taken him looking at someone a certain way and it was game over. So he delivered his *game over* smile.

But she didn't flinch.

Not Emara. Not his angel.

Instead, she moved her hand from her thigh, up to her navel, travelling up her waist, circling in sensual little swirls as it reached her breast. She tugged at the lace of her nightgown strap, and it fell off of her shoulder, sliding gently down her golden skin. She threw him a sensual smile, knowing exactly what she was doing.

And that's all it took.

One fucking lacey strap and Torin Blacksteel, second-in-command of the Blacksteel Hunting Clan, was undone. He moved towards her, his legs unwilling to stop. And she fired up her hand, halting him in his tracks.

Evidently, he would stop if she commanded it. He would rack his brains later for the answers to why he took orders from her and barely from his own commander. Not now, not when she looked so beautifully distracting.

A dominant, smug smile pulled her lips into the most beautiful thing he had ever seen.

How the fuck is she about to win this? Torin didn't care. He would let her win, even if it meant she would give him nothing but a small kiss. One. Just one. Just enough.

Who was he kidding? It would never be enough.

"Say them," he begged, his nostrils flaring. Those two little words he had promised not to cross the line for until he heard them from her mouth.

Kiss me.

"Say them," he pleaded again.

"Do you not want to play anymore?" she said mockingly, pulling at the other strap on her nightwear. He watched it fall down her other shoulder and he envisioned himself licking where it lay.

To the mother of all Gods, what was this cruel torture? She was going to be the ruin of him.

"I think it is pretty clear that all I want to do is play." He let a charming smile cross his face as he looked down at the massive erection bulging from his leathers. Her gaze followed. Her eyes flashed to his. The most endearing blush finally flared in her cheeks, and he had to stop himself from saying something ridiculously crude. "I think it's pretty clear that I have never wanted to *play* so much in my entire existence."

She swallowed, and he watched it track in her throat. "Would it not be foolish of me to say those two little words?"

Kiss me.

He severed the distance between them in one final stride. "Then let's be foolish."

Only their uneven breathing could be heard before she spoke again.

"I don't know if I would be enough for you." Something in her voice broke, sending his heart into a frantic rhythm.

His jaw clenched. "Then you are blind not to see what I do."

Emara looked up at him with magic swirling in her eyes, brilliant and bright. She put a hand onto his bare skin, on his sternum. She hadn't even touched him below the waist and he felt like he could explode.

"Would it be only me?" she asked with a shy glint in her eye.

Her question rocked him. Was she actually considering it? Did she think there were others?

"Yes." *Of course.* "It would be only you."

The truth rocked him even more.

"Are we still playing?" she asked as her hand pressed into his skin.

In a way, her question was completely innocent enough to break him, but he saw the dark desire in her eyes, and he knew that if she wasn't ready, he wouldn't take this any further. But she wouldn't be doing this...

"I was never playing," he answered her.

She looked up at him through beautiful lashes that accentuated her eyes.

Was she ready to say the words?

His heart pummelled into his ribcage like he pounded into a punching bag. He ran a hand over her skin and curled his hand behind her neck. She shuddered under his touch.

She came back fighting and ran her hand down to the trail of hair that lingered just above his leather waistband.

It was maddening torture.

She was winning.

She turned, her back brushing his torso, and pushed her backside into him. Grazing his hardness with her ass, she tipped her head back and arched into him.

Fuck it. She had won.

"You win," he breathed, still not laying a hand on her. "You win, just let me kiss you before I lose my fucking mind."

She threw a look over her shoulder, her hair tickling his bare chest, and her lips parted.

There was a knock on the door, and the sound of Artem Stryker's voice broke through the thick, charged atmosphere. "Torin?" He knocked again. "My man, are you in there?"

"Disappear, Stryker," he roared without taking his eyes from hers. Her shoulders stiffened as she looked at the door, but she didn't move her body from where it pushed into his.

"Magin has used all the water in our room. Can I use yours? Emara wouldn't mind, would she?"

Torin was going to kill Stryker for this. He was going to peel the skin from his bones. "You better leave now if you want to keep your heart in your chest."

He could visualise it with every second he spent speaking through a door and not parting Emara's lips with his own.

"You need to let him in." She chuckled, pulling away from him.

"I don't need to do anything," he assured her, his hands finally finding her hips to hold her where she stood. "With the exception of finding myself on that pretty mouth of yours."

She gulped. "What does it matter? I won anyway. You caved first."

He loosened his hands from her hips. A game. He had cracked first. He swallowed his own pride. "You're right. I did lose. And I always will if I am playing with you."

A moment passed between them, and she turned her body around to face him. Her gaze searched his face, probably looking for mockery, but she wouldn't find any because he wasn't playing any longer. He wanted her. And he wanted her now.

"Guys, I am freezing my dick off out here," Artem called. "Let me in."

Emara let out a giggle. "He is not going to leave."

Torin took a deep breath, letting his chest puff out as he marched through the remainder of the room and almost ripped the door from its hinges.

"Be nice," Emara squealed from behind him.

The door opened to reveal a naked Artem Stryker with a tiny towel draped around his hips. He pictured himself flaying off every last tattoo with his hunting knife before he spoke. "What?"

Artem swaggered into the room casually, clearly unaware of what he had just ruined, what he had interrupted.

Torin's fist twitched.

"Magin used every single drop of hot wat—" Artem paused, his golden eyes moving from Emara to Torin and back to Emara.

"You better keep your fucking eyes on me, brother," Torin demanded, knowing full well how enticing she looked in that little emerald nightgown. Was it wrong of him to only want his eyes to see that?

Yes, it probably was, but he didn't care.

"Did I interrupt something?" An obnoxious grin

spread across his friend's face. "Did you two finally give into your sweetest temptations and begin making beautiful, violent babies together?"

"I will knock you clean out, Stryker," Torin growled.

"You didn't interrupt anything," Emara cut in, placing her arms around her waistline.

Her body language told Torin that she didn't want Artem to see her like he just had—confidently seductive. It was just for him. He liked that.

He loved that.

Somewhere deep and dark, a possessive flame ignited, only intensifying his want of her. Fuck.

"We were just talking...playing a game." She finally smirked back at Torin.

"Which is it?" Artem's eyebrow arched, and amusement lingered on his face. "Talking or playing a game? They are two very different things."

"You can play a game and talk at the same time." Emara glanced at Torin again, her eyes glittering.

She was showing signs of empress-like confidence, and the warrior magic in his blood thrummed through his veins to match it.

"Can I join your *game?*" Artem grinned like a feral wolf from ear to ear.

"Absolutely fucking not!" Torin dragged his eyes from Emara's unwillingly and looked over Artem. "You have ten minutes to bathe and get out."

He strode over to a beam in the far corner of the room and stood against it. At least the situation in his pants had cooled off. Only Artem fucking Stryker could ruin this moment for him. Emara sat on a side of the bed, riffling through her bag, and he wondered if she would have said those two words he desperately wanted to hear. She pulled out a book that looked like it had been bound by Mother God herself and began reading.

"This is nice, isn't it?" Artem broadcasted his voice across the room as he lowered himself into the bath. The warm water gushed from the faucet. "Us, spending time together. We don't really get quality time when we are riding."

Torin dragged his eyes from Emara's concentrating face. "It's fantastic," he mumbled.

"You see, we used to be inseparable, Emara," Artem announced as he brushed soap up and down his arms. "In the Selection, our Tori-boy used to get really homesick and long for his mother."

Emara shut the book and lowered it to her thigh with an enigmatic grin.

Torin invaded the conversation before it could go any further. "You have five minutes to finish what you are doing and leave, Stryker. I would use my time wisely if I were you."

But Artem continued without batting an eyelid. "But he powered through to become the best of the best, didn't you, mama's boy?"

"Four minutes." Torin's fist twitched again. It had been a long time since he had punched Artem's face, but he was happy to end the dry spell of fists right now.

"I am happy he has found you, Emara," Artem stated as he trailed soap all over his ink.

She choked.

"Three," Torin growled.

"He has this tough exterior." Artem looked over at Emara with a wink, and Torin had a maddening urge to blind him.

"Two." Torin's chest puffed out.

"But our favourite Blacksteel just loves to brood," Artem counselled. "When we all know that, really, he is a big softie on the inside."

"One." Torin choked out as he bounded towards the bathtub.

Artem's hand went up. "That was seconds, brother, you said I had minutes."

"I changed my mind. Get your ass out of my room and get to your own. Emara doesn't need to hear about our lives in the Selection."

"Yes, I do."

He turned to see her grinning.

Artem raised himself from the bathtub, naked as the day he was born. Emara probably wasn't used to the brashness of hunting life and the way they were all conditioned in the Selection, so Torin quickly grabbed a towel from the floor for Artem and herded him out of the room like unwanted cattle.

"Towel, please." Artem smiled as he crossed over the doorway.

Torin balled the towel up tightly and hurled it at him. Before he even witnessed the towel smack into Artem's face, he slammed the door shut.

He sighed, standing at the door in case Artem had a second wind of bravery to interrupt again.

Emara laughed, flinging the book onto the bed. "Do

you not like it when people find out you are not a big, bad warrior?"

"First of all, I am big, and second of all, I am bad," he said, crossing the room to the tub. He pulled out the plug to drain Artem's bath.

"I can confirm that you are big—"

He turned to face her. "Are you talking about what you saw earlier?" Torin lifted an eyebrow.

She pinned her lips shut as a blush tickled her cheeks pink. "Shut up and let me finish what I was going to say."

The pent-up frustration on her face gave him more satisfaction than it should have.

"Carry on." He smiled and turned the hot water on again to fill his own bath.

"What I was going to say"—her eyes dragged from his to his body as he began to unbutton his leathers—"is that it's obvious that you are *large,* physically. In... person. And you are obviously a warrior. But I don't think you are bad at all."

It was so endearing when she was flustered.

"And how do you know that?" he asked as he removed his boots.

She watched him kick them off. "Because my grandmother once told me that if you can look a person in the eye, you can see who they truly are, you can see their soul. And when I look at you, I don't find anything bad." Her words caused a conflict in his chest and he stood still. "Misunderstood, maybe, but not bad. Not after everything you have done for me."

Torin waited a moment before he stripped off his leathers, just leaving him in his underwear. Emara's pupils dilated and her cheeks turned red. Her full, beautiful lips parted, telling Torin she liked what she saw. Good. But he took a few seconds to ponder over what she had said as he turned around and dropped his underwear. He got in the tub, and the roasting water warmed his feet.

"Misunderstood, maybe, but not bad. Not after everything you have done for me."

He finally looked over at her. "If you are talking about me protecting your life, protecting you, then do not think that for one second I would choose otherwise." His tone changed as he sat down. "But that doesn't make me a good person. It makes me good at what I do."

He wiped a hand down his face, and with it came blood and dirt from the fight.

"No." She shook her head, as she sat watching him from the bed. "What makes you a good person is how you have helped me. How, at times, you have given me the truth I deserved to hear, even when I didn't want it. And how you have pushed me to own who I am. You are a good person because you have integrity. I know you are good because I feel it when I am with you."

His mouth dried, and he scrubbed the soap over his body. "You don't know what I am capable of, what I have been trained to become from a young age."

She hadn't seen first-hand what he had done, not completely. Hunting wasn't always dealing with just demons and the underworld.

He rose from the tub, grabbing a towel and placing it

over his hips. Emara pretended to politely fiddle with the pages in her book, but Torin knew there was no way she was reading anything, especially with that pink blush spreading her cheeks.

After a few moments of silence and Torin getting ready for sleep, he sat on the edge of the bed. He hung his head and looked down at his hands. "I appreciate the fact that you think I am good, Emara. But I just don't want to disappoint you when you see me do something that isn't."

Because that would come. It was inevitable with him. He had the worst temper, and an undeniable rebellion that burned his heart dark. That combination was always a recipe for disappointment. His father had told him that countless times.

When Emara didn't speak, Torin leaned back with a sigh and rested his head against a pillow.

To his surprise, Emara turned to face him. "I maybe can't see what goes on in your head," she said, "but I think I understand what conflicts you." She reached out, running a hand along his arm before it settled there. His eyes followed it, in disbelief. "You question if your duty is worth it—if it is *all* worth it. You are unsure if your reason to be born is what you truly want to be. Maybe I am wrong, but I think you want more than that."

He turned onto his side, his massive frame, taking up a lot of the bed, but his eyes rested on her. His heart rate increased. "Like you do? You want more from life too."

She looked down at her hand on his arm. "That's

where I have to admit that we do have *some* similarities, Torin Blacksteel. We don't like to settle."

He wasn't sure he was even in control of his own limbs as she ran her fingers down his arm and grabbed his hand. She squeezed it, and he lay still, waiting for her next command. She said nothing else.

As they looked at one another, Torin realised it was the kind of exposure he wasn't used to.

He felt seen. And that wasn't normal.

But she wasn't normal. She was a paradox, a beautiful, intelligent, terribly stubborn, surprisingly sensual, paradox. And he had never wanted to protect something, someone, so much in his entire life. As her eyes closed and her breathing turned heavy, he realised he would take anything he could get from her, no matter how trivial. A glance, a brush of their hands, a deep talk, a laugh, a kiss. *A game of who would cave first.* He would cave again and again, and he would play her game forever, even if it meant he never won at all. Because even with her just letting him close, like they were now, he had won an entirely different game altogether.

CHAPTER TWENTY-THREE
EMARA

Torin had made the decision the following morning that they weren't leaving the inn. The snow had fallen thick, and the wind had picked up, making travel impossible. He also pointed out that it would allow them all time to rest, especially time for Magin to heal. So Emara had read through some books on magic that Naya had gifted her, and she even snuck in a chapter or two of Torin's book on weaponry. He had made himself almost invisible except at night, when he had come through her door soaking wet from his patrol around the forest near the inn. He had taken a quick bath, sighing in relief at the warmth, and Emara had tried her hardest to keep her eyes on the pages of her book like she had done the night before.

Falling asleep was easy when it was next to a warrior who could fight off any of your demons, and the beating of his heart had been a soft lullaby in the night as he lay next to her, sending her body into a calming sleep. No crimson eyes or razor-sharp claws revealed themselves in her dreams that night, not lying beside Torin Blacksteel.

Although her eyes were not open and she was somewhere in between this realm and the one of rest, she felt light flash past her. Heat warmed her face, but it felt unnatural, not like the fire that still crackled lowly across from the bathing tub.

Emara felt a presence in the room.

Half-concerned, she blinked one eye open, scanning the room for anyone who had come in. Her head still lay against the pillow, but during the night, her hand had found Torin's, and it seemed to still be intertwined with his. She opened both eyes, her heart picking up speed from its lazy slumber.

It couldn't be morning.

Torin didn't stir, his breathing deep and wandering, his brow smooth and unbothered by his thoughts.

Her heart ceased as she glanced from Torin to a large orb that hovered close to the door. Radiant light poured from the colourful sphere that dangled like a small Faerie in the middle of the room. She removed her hand from Torin's, fixated on the bobbing globe, and blinked again, convinced she was seeing things.

Dreaming.

She had to be.

She blinked again, but the oddity remained at the door, reminding her of the way a jellyfish would swim in the ocean. She couldn't pull her eyes from it. Through the most bizarre level of trust, like she knew it, Emara felt instantly connected. She had felt its energy before and wasn't afraid. Any concerns she had when she had woken up vanished.

The orb moved slowly towards the door, and a cool breeze entered the room, fluttering the loose strands of her hair. Emara felt an instant urge to touch the energy, like she wanted to put her hand through the centre of it. She moved with cat-like grace so as not to wake Torin as she slinked herself out from underneath the blankets.

She was terrified that if he awoke, the orb would disappear.

He would probably take a swing at it before she could find out what it was.

The door opened on its own behind the orb, inviting her to take steps forward, and Emara's lips parted.

"What are you?" she whispered to the magic that pulsed all around her.

The orb floated like a cloud from her sight and into the corridor. A tugging feeling in her muscles had her walking to find it, to keep up with it. She did her best to control her breathing whilst the orb led her down the stairs to the deserted front of the inn.

What in Rhiannon's name is this thing?

The lock on the inn door slid quickly to the side with no signs of struggle. A chill ran up Emara's spine, but again, she wasn't afraid. The door of the inn creaked open, and the orb disappeared out into the darkness of the surrounding forest.

"Do you want me to follow you?" she whispered. The orb appeared again in the doorway, a bright light of mystical colours that lit up the room and disappeared again.

She followed it out into the forest.

THE FOREST FLOOR was frozen under her bare feet as she followed the ball of light into the ancient woods. The Cold Moon had made an appearance for the first time, a thick horseshoe glowing above her, bright, wonderful, and wise.

She didn't know how long she had been walking, but it felt like the orb parted the trees for her, moving vines and thorns from her path. It even warmed the ground, where she stepped felt like the summer sun was in the sky instead of the Cold Moon. She did find it odd that she couldn't feel the chill of the wind against her skin; the only sign of it being there was the constant wisps of hair that floated against her face. Every part of her gave into the orbs' demands and she followed it blindly through the forest.

Before long, the sound of gushing water drifted from between the trees. She followed the glowing ball of starlight until it stopped just at the entrance of a high clearing. Emara stood still as she glanced out at the relentless water that poured from the top of a rock face into a darkness she could not see the bottom of.

It was a waterfall.

Although she had heard the sounds of its magic long before she had really seen it, she hadn't been aware of its beauty, not until now. She had seen streams that led to decent-sized waterfalls in Mossgrave, but this one was different. This one seemed to feel...well, it felt magical. The very sound of its waters charmed her ears, and the strength of its current pulled her in. It wasn't over-whelmingly large, but it was a good drop into the pool below. The water sprayed a glittering dust of light mist up into the night air, and the winter wind blew it across to where she stood.

She didn't know how far she had walked, but as she felt the magic tingle on her skin, she wondered if this could be the Waterfall of Uttara, God of Stars and Dawn?

Emara took a breath that chilled down into her chest, and she felt the magic dance on her lips.

It had to be the Waterfall of Uttara.

Its magnificence was just as remarkable as the stars that twinkled above it.

The light flashed in front of her vision, and she took a step back, her feet finding their way across the damp cliff top, away from the drop.

"Why have you led me here?" Emara whispered. She shook her head and looked over to the waterfall again. Had she gone so insane that she expected an orb of light to speak back to her?

She was truly losing it. Emara pinched herself, expecting to awake back in the bed of the inn.

She didn't.

Unexpectedly, the sphere expanded, elongated, and

flashed brightly. Emara fell back in disbelief, flinging her arm over her face to shield her eyes from the blinding light that stole her vision.

After a few seconds of blinking gold stars, she looked up. A glowing figure stood where the orb had been, and if Emara hadn't already fallen to the ground, her legs would have been swept out from under her.

Beautiful blonde hair bounced atop petite shoulders. High cheekbones and a warm smile shone at her.

It was Callyn. It was her Cally. Callyn Agnes Greymore.

She stood speedily; it made her dizzy, and she blinked again. Her throat swelled, as did the emotion in her eyes.

No, this wasn't real. She was dreaming. She pinched herself again, harder.

"You are not dreaming," the figure confirmed as if replying to her thoughts. Something solid punched into her gut and she felt like she couldn't breathe.

It sounded like Cally.

"I am," Emara croaked. "Please let me wake up," she begged. "This is cruel. Please, let me wake up."

"You are not dreaming, Emara." The glowing figure laughed, and it sounded just like her laugh too. Emara's mouth opened wider as her heart cracked open entirely, but no words or air came out or in.

"It's me, silly," the figure said. "I promise."

Emara let out a laugh that turned into a sob. "It's not," she managed to say. "It's not you. You are gone. You are gone." Her legs shook, but she managed to lock her knees to keep standing.

"I am not truly gone. My spirit still watches over you." Cally smiled, her beautiful face glowing in colours of soft gold. She was like a sparkling yellow diamond, and her features shimmered and glowed with each movement. Her eyes, her stunning eyes, were still blue, and she wore the same silky slip-gown she had dressed in the night of the Uplift, but it wasn't stained with her blood.

It was pure white.

"H-how?" Emara tried to speak, but nothing really came out.

"I do not have long," Cally advised, her shoulders squaring. "I have only gathered enough strength to come back into this world and visit you for a short time. I have some pretty strong witches who are anchoring me from the Otherside." A Cally-like grin tugged her lips up at the corners.

"My grandmother is with you?" Emara swallowed a cry.

Cally nodded. "The witches have so much power over here. They are helping me connect to you through spirit. You can't touch me, but I am here, I promise you that. My spirit will always be with you."

"Oh Gods, Cally." Emara's voice broke, and so did the tears that welled in her eyes. "I can't do this without you. I—"

The golden figure stepped forward a little. "You can," she assured her. "And you will. You will ascend soon to become empress of your coven, and you must."

"Why?" Emara's tears streamed from her eyes, but she still managed to search Cally's face for answers.

"Because the kingdom needs you to. You are the only thing that can stop the darkness. The world as we know it now depends on your ascension." Cally spoke with an assertive tone, and Emara found herself wondering if she had ever left. It was like they were having a normal conversation, alive. But she wasn't. A sharp pain blistered through her heart as Cally spoke again. "You are the key. You always have been."

"What does that even mean?" Emara shook her head violently, her whole body trembling.

"I don't have time for philosophical breakdowns." Callyn gave an eye roll, and she placed a hand on her hip. "You are a smart girl, you will figure it out. I can't give you *all* the answers." She smiled, and Emara burst with sadness at how real this encounter felt. Only Callyn could make her laugh and cry at once. "I haven't come here to talk about your future or what the Gods have in store for you. I have come here to speak to you about the present."

Emara wiped her face, trying to understand. She didn't want to talk about the present. She wanted to be in the past, with Cally.

"I felt the need to remind you that you must let yourself feel. You need to let your heart take over and stop condemning yourself with grief." Callyn shut her eyes for a small second. "I don't want you to feel the sadness you feel over my death. That wasn't your fault. That sorrow is not only for you to bear. You must let it go."

"How can you even say that?" Emara cried, her throat thick with relentless torment. "Of course, it was my fault. I got you into this…this mess because of who I am—"

"But you didn't. I was in this life before you knew me."

"What?" Emara's face tightened, and a bitter shiver lodged itself into her spine.

"You hid a secret from me about who *you* were." She shot her a look. "Even though who you were was never really a secret to me."

Emara stilled. Every muscle strangled her bones.

"Let me go. I know who you are. I know what you are. I love you."

Emara shook in disbelief.

Callyn had known Emara had witching blood.

How could she have known?

Her blue eyes twinkled with a secret of her own. "But I hid a little part of me too, so don't feel guilty."

Emara's heart stopped.

"I wasn't human, Emara." Cally looked at her through her lashes that glittered like the moon had sprinkled stardust all over her face. "I was born a witch —to the House of Water, to be precise."

Emara didn't breathe for the longest of seconds. "You—"

She nodded. "So do not feel guilty about my death. I was in this even before you were. That was how the Gods had written my path."

"You are a witch?" Emara made a gurgling sound like she was being strangled. Maybe she was. Maybe her magic was betraying her and sucking the air from her lungs. That's what it felt like. "No," she managed. "No, that's not true."

"It's true. I had to come back and let you know that your guilt isn't properly placed, and to tell you who I am."

Emara stumbled back a few steps, ears buzzing. "You were from the magic world?"

Callyn paused, her eyes glazing over. "When I was born, my mother believed a prophecy that a Spirit Witch had spoken of that claimed that I would never gain any magic." A sadness filled her eyes, and it was so unlike her to show her soul the way she did now. She had always protected her soul. "And my family saw that as a sign from the Gods that I wasn't worthy of being in the coven. They believed that I was undeserving of being inducted into The House of Water from birth." Cally's head tilted downwards, and Emara felt a new set of tears track down her face. "The woman who called herself my mother didn't know if she should turn her back on the coven and face a lifetime of ruin or stay within the coven and face a lifetime of shame for giving birth to a muted witchling. So instead of my mother aborting me from her womb, she gave birth to me and dumped me in a random village outside a temple of worship. I was sent to an orphanage, where I lived until I met you." Their eyes met. "Until I met your grandmother."

Emara wanted to go to her, to hug her and comfort her, but in fear that her spirit would disappear, she rooted her feet into the ground.

"She knew what you were," Emara breathed. "Didn't she?"

Cally nodded. "She did. No matter how small my magic flickered, your grandmother would have sniffed it out the minute she saw me. She may have given up her life in the magic world, but she was still powerful and wise." She giggled softly, and the laugh warmed the brokenness inside Emara's chest. "That's why she took me in. She knew where I had come from and wanted to give me a second chance. She knew that my magic was extremely faint, and there was little she could do about it. Still, she didn't want to give up on me. I have a feeling that she had learned from past mistakes, and this was her chance to put things right in the eyes of the Gods. She could give me—us—a normal life."

Emara stood for a few moments in silence, letting the astonishment dissolve in her mind as she looked at her best friend. An orphan of the covens. Her grandmother had known about Callyn the entire time.

"Was it real?" Emara looked over her best friend's face, her chin revealing a shake. "What we had, the friendship, was it real?"

Cally moved properly for the first time in her new form. She had always been ladylike in how she walked, but now she glided like a goddess. She stopped just a touch away from Emara. "Of course, it was real. Don't you dare for one second question that. Everything about us—every laugh, every tear, every fight, every night we stayed awake talking for hours—it was *all* real. Your grandmother wanted me to make you feel as normal, as human, as possible. She didn't want you to find out who you were. And, ashamed of my magical background, I was happy to play human too. After all, who wants to be a witch who has no more magic than a mere village girl?"

Emara bit back her sobs. "Why? Why didn't she want me to know who I really am? I need the truth, Callyn."

"Because it was dangerous, Emara." Cally's tone turned more sinister, and Emara's spine curled at the sound. "It still is. Look what is happening to powerful witches across the kingdom. And do not think you are being overlooked because you are new to this world, because you are not."

A potent silence stiffened in the air.

Emara took a deep breath and asked, "Am I powerful enough to protect myself?" Gods, she had so many questions to ask.

"I don't think you need me to answer that." A small smile pulled at Cally's lips.

"I need you to answer it." Emara's throat threatened to close as she spoke. "I can't"—she looked down at her trembling hands—"I don't think I can do this."

Cally walked a little closer again. "What you need to do is let go of everything that holds you back from being who you truly are. You need to live in the moment, live in your light. You need to follow your gut and trust your instinct." A glint of emotion flickered in her eyes. "I think we have both learned that life is so desperately short and utterly fragile, and you must make sure you live, Emara. Not just exist, *live.*"

"I am trying, but I—"

"I know you miss me." Her glowing hand reached up, hovering over Emara's arm. But she couldn't feel her touch even when it rested atop her skin. "And I miss you more than you will ever know. I gathered enough strength to come to you tonight to let you know two things. You have the most powerful witches that ever graced the kingdom on the Otherside, backing every step you take. It is time for you to be powerful too, just like them. Feel your magic, awaken it properly. It is time for you to be everything that an empress is, fierce and strong and bold." She looked over at her, her face changing. "And the second was that it is time for you to give into your heart, because with the wall you have built around it, you won't ever unleash that force, that superpower, that is brewing beneath your surface."

Emara knew exactly what she meant by that. If she had been with her every step of the way, then she would have seen everything. She was referring to how much she suppressed her feelings for a particular Blacksteel brother.

"But you and him—"

"Don't," Callyn cut her off again in that best friend kind of way. "We were nothing to each other. But you are something to him. You don't need to be on the Otherside to see how he feels about you. The witches up here can't believe how much he has softened." She let out a small giggle. "He has a few fans up here, believe it or not. He's infamous, even in the spirit realm."

Emara snorted through her tears and rolled her eyes, wishing she could hug her best friend and not let her go.

Cally rolled her lips before saying, "I love you, and I promise that when you are finding it hard to breathe, I will be there, keeping the air in your lungs." Cally's voice broke, but she pulled back the sadness that had weaved onto her face. "I will be there, holding your hand. And I will have your back. Always." A tear ran from Cally's eye. "We all will. Your ancestors have waited a long time to see you wear your moonlight like a crown." She smiled, her face gleaming with pride. "The road you are about to take will not be easy, but when you walk it, just know that you are not alone."

Emara's sob heaved in her chest, and every inch of her body left like it could have crumbled. "I will never be alone. Not when you will always be in my heart. I will never forget you, Callyn Greymore."

"You better not!" She grinned like a summer morning as tears also dripped down her cheeks. "Make me proud, Emara Clearwater. I don't doubt for one second that you will. This was always your destiny." Cally's figure flickered in and out, her face still smiling. "It's time for me to go back."

Emara took a step forward as if to stop her, her heart bursting into her throat.

"Believe in who you are. Let go and feel the magic, feel it around you. I'm here. Always." Cally's voice rang around the trees and disappeared along with her figure. The light folded in on itself, spiralling around, and then vanished like a puff of smoke. Like she had never been there at all.

A whimper left Emara's throat as she looked out at nothing but the forest, the midnight-coloured water still flowing heavily from the waterfall into the pool below. The moon beams made their way down to earth just to glow upon the tears that sat on Emara's face.

For once, she didn't feel empty. She felt whole.

She felt a purpose bloom in her heart. A hope.

"Emara." A raspy voice pulled her from the surreal bubble that had formalised in her mind. She spun, facing the direction in which it came.

Torin Blacksteel stood against the backdrop of the trees, his tunic twisted like he had shoved it on quickly and his breathing laboured. Holding a sword in his hand, his eyebrows pulled down. "What are you doing?" he asked, a note of concern in his voice.

"I..." She trailed off, not quite sure what to say. Her emotion was still bubbling in her heart.

"Why are you out here? How did you even get to the Waterfall of Uttara?" His voice was soft, even for him.

She looked around herself again, finally taking in everything. Come to think of it, she wasn't sure if she even remembered. The thin veil of magic that had been swept over her was now gone, and she wasn't sure she could remember the way here at all.

"I don't remember," she muttered.

"You don't remember getting out of bed beside me and walking almost half a mile—in your bare feet, may I add?" His eyebrows crunched tightly together and his jaw sharpened.

To someone else, he would look menacing in the eerie light of the Cold Moon, but to her, he was devastatingly beautiful. Soul-crushingly handsome, even if he was currently trying his hardest to scold her. His hair fluffed over his forehead drowsily and his tight tunic hugged his extraordinary frame, revealing his rock-hard torso that was heaving with his panting breaths. His arms bulged out from the side, so powerful that she could only imagine how destructive they were in full battle, but they had only ever cradled her, kept her safe, and fought for her.

"Emara, can you speak? You are scaring me." His tone was short, and his eyes darkened in a way she had never seen before.

Torin Blacksteel felt fear?

"Please speak," he begged her.

So she told him. She told him what she could, how she had witnessed an orb, and how she had felt as it floated in their room. She tried to explain the feeling of how she knew that she had to follow it, but his expression of concern had only deepened. She explained to him about Cally and how she had appeared in spirit to let her know who she truly was. She left out that he had fans on the Otherside; his ego didn't need that kind of boost.

"And you didn't think of waking me up as you saw a massive orb floating in the room?"

She huffed. "No, Torin. I didn't." The frustration crept into her forehead, creasing it.

She had, and she had chosen not to involve him.

"It could have been anything. I am your guard!" He threw a hand out in exasperation. "You need to inform me of these things. It could have—" He stopped himself and placed a hand up to his temple. "It could have hurt you."

"It wouldn't have harmed me. I trusted it."

A dry laugh slipped through his lips. "How can you possibly know that?"

"Because I did," she bit out. "I did. I knew it in my heart. I knew it wouldn't harm me. I don't know how, but I did." She looked him over, her eyes narrowing. "As my guard, you should trust me."

"I do, but you should have awoken me. Sometimes magic can trick you into thinking something that's not real."

"No," she said sternly. "I have instincts just as much as you do, just as powerful," she reminded him. "And I trusted that I would be okay."

Callyn had told her to trust her gut, and she would.

He walked towards her, his brows slowly pulling down again. "I don't want to row with you over this."

"We are not rowing." She crossed her arms over herself.

"Well, there is a first time for everything." He smirked sharply before his jaw locked back in. "All I ask is that you please tell me the next time a random orb visits you whilst we sleep." His fierce cheekbones were highlighted by the glow of the moon, and it hollowed out the structure of his face to present a wildly hand-some profile.

"I can't make any promises," she said, turning to face the waterfall. Something about the way the water fell into the pool reminded her of the wild magic that she so eagerly longed for. She walked forward, the grass damp under her feet from the melted snow and halted after a few steps. Its enchantment echoed to her through the air, pulling her towards its torrent. The mist of the water was still hitting the rawest of the earth's rocks, spraying up into the wind and finding her face.

It was glacial and heart stopping, but it was thriving.

"Emara?" Torin's voice was more like a warning for her to stop.

She turned to face him. "Cally said I needed to live, not just exist." She turned back to see the cascading water that tumbled towards the ground speedily. "She said I needed to let go of...everything."

"I don't like the direction this is going." She heard him step forward. "Angel, come away from the vertical drop, please." His tone was full of sarcasm, but it was lined with a little fear. She would never have heard it before if she didn't know him like she did now, but it was there.

"You have also told me that." She paused. "To live." She turned back to face him and her hair was now untamed silk around her. "Haven't you told me to live on the wild side once or twice?" She felt the cold wind brush her back from the raw energy of the waterfall, casting her dark hair around her shoulders and face.

"If you are thinking of jumping into that waterfall to prove that you can be wild or that you are alive, you have another thing coming." He took another step forward. "I have plenty of things in mind that we could do that would make you feel alive, and let me tell you something, jumping off the edge of a waterfall is not one of them."

Her heart hammered in her chest.

"That's exactly what I thought you would say." She took a step backwards.

His face hardened and his spine tensed. "You are not going in that waterfall, Emara."

"You don't tell me what I can and can't do, Torin."

His eyes narrowed. "Are you crazy?"

"Maybe." She smiled, feeling an overwhelming emotion that she couldn't pinpoint. The magic in her veins screamed and danced as her heartbeat battered against her ribs.

"Emara, over my dead corpse are you jumping into the Waterfall of Uttara." He let out an exasperated breath.

"I am pretty sure you are not the boss."

His teeth clashed together, and she watched as he deliberated over some options in his mind.

"I am pretty sure that I am much faster than you and that I could stop you before you jumped," he said.

She raised one eyebrow and pretended to move, then stilled herself quickly. Torin reacted in the same way, shaking his head, his eyes narrowing to make him look menacing.

Emara let out a cackle. "I thought you had a wild side, Blacksteel. Where is it now?"

"I am not jumping into the Waterfall of Uttara," he said again, his tone a little sharper.

"What are you scared of?" She cocked her head to the side, and he sniggered, looking away from her. "Are you scared of water?"

His lips pursed.

"If it's not the water you are scared of, then what?" she asked.

He ran his tongue over his full lips. "The Waterfall of Uttara is not just a normal waterfall. The legends say that the waters of the Goddess have been said to wash and strip away the links to your subconscious mind, revealing layers and layers of how you truly feel. It's an enchanted landmark of the Gods, Emara."

"Surely, that is just a myth," she fired back with one eyebrow raised.

"And so were witches and demons to you just a few moons ago." He lifted his dark lashes, revealing how wild his eyes could truly look under the stars. Unruly, and full of sin.

Layers and layers of true feelings. Layers and layers of pretend masks washed to the bottom of the sacred pool.

Emara swallowed. "And that scares you, to have revealed what truly lies in your heart?"

"Does it not scare you?" Torin replied.

It is time for you to give in to your heart.

It was time for her to find out the truth, even if she knew it all along. The Waterfall of Uttara would strip her bare, right down to her heart.

She looked directly at him, and in a split second, she turned, bolting towards the edge of the rock. She could hear her name screaming from Torin's mouth, but it was too late as she leapt from safety into the unknown water below.

CHAPTER
TWENTY-FOUR
EMARA

Falling wasn't what she expected. Her stomach flipped, and her heart was in her mouth, but a thrill ran through her bones, a thrill that almost took the edge off her thundering pulse. Even though the air ceased in her lungs, making it hard to take a breath, she felt free.

She wasn't afraid anymore.

She hit the water, plunging into the dark, ice-cold pool. Her joints stiffened as her heart fought to keep her alive, hammering in her chest at the instant shock of cold that smacked her body. A thousand needles pierced into her skin and her hair branched out like seaweed, strands weaving and linking with each other. The water fought like a plague to enter her mouth and nose, and she kicked her legs, trying to find the surface.

However, the silence of being under the water, under the magic of it, felt secure despite knowing how quickly she would run out of air. But for just one moment, she stole a second to listen to her magic—to her heart—and she wondered if she bore the element of water too.

Would it show itself to her now if she stayed underwater?

A heavy smash bombed down past her in the pool, creating currents that rippled towards her. They knocked her off course, but the burning in her lungs reminded her to fight, to kick and swim. She couldn't stay here in the peace of the tranquil water, and now wasn't the time to explore if she bore the element of water.

Emara kicked harder than before and finally broke the surface.

Inhaling the sweet, frosty air into her lungs with a gasp, she reminded herself she was lucky to be alive. The rush of exhilaration reminded Emara that her heart was still beating hard and fast in her chest, and that magic thrummed in her blood, warming her.

It was a promise that she would *live,* not just exist.

Live.

A hearty laugh broke from her throat as she pushed her hair back, treading the water that came up to her neck. She had never felt anything like the power of the Goddess' waterfall. Feeling the magic soaking into her skin, she laughed again. Dark hair broke the surface of the water a few paddles away from her before strong shoulders protruded up from the pool and his eyes finally caught hers.

Torin ran a hand over his face to take the water from his eyes, and then he pushed his hair back.

He blew out a breath. "Are you fucking serious?" he exclaimed. "Are you insane? You could have killed yourself."

She kicked her legs softly, feeling every inch of her skin prickle not from the cold, but from the stare that lingered across the pool. Both soft and hard sentiment crashed over her; she was alive, but there were so many times recently that she had come so close to death, yet cheated it.

Her heart pinned still in her chest.

All at once, every moment, every touch, every unsaid word crashed into her mind, and all she could see were ocean-blue eyes that consumed her heart. All she could see was a mouth that bore her favourite grin, and a face that she couldn't stop thinking about. Even though he hadn't uttered a word, she could hear him breathe heavily, and the raspy moan of the word *angel* always sent her heart into a beat so violent that it vibrated through her chest. The waterfall behind him fell away, and the stars that looked over them aligned.

She was powerful. She was liberated. She was a woman, a woman who had deep feelings. She was a woman who had feelings that desired to be explored, uncontrollable and undeniable desires that beckoned across to the man a few feet from her. She wasn't going to waste any more time pretending those desires weren't there.

Her pulse thickened.

She was a woman who was going to take what she wanted—be who she wanted. She was a woman who was going to be brave and fearless, not just when she was training, but always. She was a woman whose desires burned right through to her soul for Torin Blacksteel.

"Kiss me," she whispered, her lips wet from the water that coated them.

Torin's face stilled, and she could see his chest heaving under the blanket of dark water. His expression changed from a raging warrior to a man in utter disbelief in a short second.

A vulnerability flashed in his icy eyes.

"Kiss me," she said again, her voice croaky but unyielding. "I want you to kiss me, Torin Blacksteel."

It was a demand this time, not a request.

His lips parted like he was about to ask if she was sure, but instead, he cut across the water towards her. In a flash, he had his body pressed against hers. "I never thought I would hear those words," he said, pushing one large hand to the side of her face, grabbing under her chin with his thumb.

"I said them," she whispered, almost too close to his lips. His familiar scent of frozen berries and pine surrounded her, infused with rainwater. It was intoxicating.

"Say them again." His husky voice teased her, his eyes darting between her lips and her eyes.

"Kiss me."

His eyes fluttered closed, a low moan ripping from his chest before he smashed his lips against hers. The kiss was not soft, nor was it innocent. It was wild. It was pure and animalistic as he held her against him with one strong arm, securing her body against him. The other clutched the back of her head, moving it to where he wanted her, demanding where she should be. His lips moved against hers, and Emara took the chance to deepen the kiss, feeling a rush of unfamiliar adrenaline. Her lips parted for him, and he brushed his tongue against hers. An explosion of fire and desire burst in her stomach; it rushed through her, tingling deep in her spine, blocking out the cold. She plunged her hands into his hair, pulling at him, desperately needing him closer.

More. She needed more. She couldn't think of anything else. She clawed at his neck, silently begging for more.

He gave in to her demands, parting her lips further with his own. The kiss was scorching hot against her lips, and as he breathed into her, moving her head with his large hand, he ran his fingers through her wet hair. He moved slowly, gliding them through the water until he found a place to stand, but he didn't stop kissing her, as if stopping would be tantamount to death. She grabbed frantically at his tunic, as if she could get her body any closer to his. Her lips entwined with his so exquisitely, melded against his so perfectly, she wasn't sure she had taken a breath that wasn't Torin's too.

It was fiery need and want, desire untouched until now. She had never been kissed like this; the burning feeling in her core tensed, ready to explode at any moment. Pounding water splashed over her head, crashing against her shoulders. Torin sheltered her from the hard weight of the waterfall, taking the brunt of it. He had pushed them into a small cavern behind the curtain of water, allowing them to continue unseen.

He grabbed the curve of her ass with one hand, urging her to wrap her legs around his hips with the other. She obeyed him for once, linking her ankles behind his back as he walked them to the pool's edge, still kissing her like his life depended on it. The water level fell around them, letting her know that they were no longer submerged in the pool, but she hadn't opened her eyes to check. She was more concerned about slamming her lips against his, her nails digging into his massive biceps as she held onto him.

He walked quickly, now on solid ground, but he didn't put her down.

Not yet.

He angled her head to the side to intensify the burning kiss and, suddenly, her back was against cold stone. She gasped at the intense difference between her heated skin and the cool rock, and he took the opportunity to drag his teeth down her lip.

The dual pleasure and pain sparked an all-consuming fire in her core.

Torin let her slip down him, lowering her legs to the floor, her toes reaching sand. He claimed her lips again with his own and pleasure exploded from her mouth, dripping like molten lava down her spine. She tipped her head back, their height difference never more obvious than in this moment, as her hips moved towards his of their own accord. He lowered his head, panting against her neck, and whispered, "I never thought you would say those fucking words."

She ignored him, seeking out his lips again. She gave him one desperately long kiss, willing him to shut up and take what she was giving him. Changing the pace, he caressed his hands down her arms, sending torturous shivers over her body. Slowly, she felt him guide her backwards until her back touched the cool rock of the cavern wall.

She let out a breath at the sensation and he stole a kiss behind her ear.

Her mouth ached for him, her hands longed to search him, her core wanted him against her—*in her*. Giving in to her desires, she pulled him in again by the shoulders, silently begging him to keep going. A sensual chuckle escaped his lips and Emara could feel his warm breath brush her face. She so desperately wanted to feel his lips on her again, anywhere. She drove her hips against his, encouraging him closer.

He let out a breathy moan when her core brushed the bulge tenting his leathers. "You are going to be my end, Emara Clearwater," he declared.

"Somehow, I doubt that," she panted.

"Now you are the one underestimating yourself."

Her lips were consumed by his before she could respond, fast and sharp, until he pulled away again. He was doing this on purpose, teasing her, leaving her wanting more. She knew full well what wicked smile graced his lips without opening her eyes. Her feet dug into the sand, her toes curling in sweet frustration.

"Now that I have finally kissed your pretty little mouth." He trailed a finger over her upper thigh, distracting her as he spoke. "I want to keep exploring you. You have no idea how many times I've dreamed about this," he whispered as his lips tickled her ear. "I don't want it to be over."

Her spine arched, pressing her breasts against his

chest. "Then shut up and do it," she demanded, her heart jumping against her chest. "Kiss me."

"Do you want to keep exploring, angel?"

She could feel the sinful smile on his lips.

"Yes. Just kiss me."

"So bossy." He laughed quietly as he placed a hand on her face. He scattered kisses down her jawline and onto her neck. His kisses turned deeper and more passionate as he worked his way down her neck, licking and sucking at a maddening pace. He drew circles on her thigh with the tips of his fingers as he kissed into the apex of her collarbone. She threw her back against the coldness of the rock, struggling against every instinct not to pull his lips back to hers. She wanted to feel everything he wanted to do to her, no distractions.

He kissed down the front of her night garment, biting against the wet satin. *Gods,* how she wished it were her bare skin. He lowered himself to his knees, and Emara's breath caught in her throat. "Look at me," he commanded. She brought her head from against the stone to look at him through hooded eyes. The light was dim, but she could still see him. "I want you to look at me as I kiss you," his honeyed, deep voice commanded, sending shockwaves straight to her core.

Her stomach flipped and her head buzzed with the melody of her heartbeat.

A warrior, on his knees before her.

He didn't move his eyes from hers until he leaned over and pressed his lips against her inner thigh.

She shuddered.

A tingling sensation worked its way up from her

toes, spreading across her thigh into the most intimate part of her. He kissed up her skin, almost like he was chasing the thrill with his mouth. Her head flew back against the soft rock and a harsh breath escaped her, her hips arching into his touch.

A small moan broke free from her lips, and he smiled into her thigh. "Are you disobeying me already? I want you to look at me."

"I will always disobey you." She laughed as her eyes met his again, gleaming with a mischief that should be frowned upon by the Gods.

"And why does that make me want you even more?" he rasped.

His chest rose and fell as their gazes interlocked, and something took root in her soul.

This is fated.

He moved quickly, giving in to the intensity of their stares. This time, he wrapped his arms under her thighs and pulled her down to fall into his lap, straddling his hips. He ran both hands up her thighs and past her ass to press into the centre of her back. He rocked her against him and she felt a *very* solid part of him press into her core.

"You are unbelievable." His voice sounded hoarse, almost strained with hunger. His lips found hers in a desperate tangle of moans. Emara rolled her hips against him, grabbing on to his strong back. His hands ran through her hair wildly as he lifted his hips to meet hers, finding an intense rhythm. He moved his warm lips back to her neck, nipping and teasing with his teeth, encouraging her to move against him harder.

She was *aching.*

"More exploring?" he said, his voice so husky she barely recognized it.

She nodded, a slave to whatever this was between them.

He lifted the hem of her nightgown with one hand and splayed his fingers underneath it, settling a palm on her hip. His fingers quickly found the edge of her underwear, playing with one of the few barriers between them, teasing her, sending her heart into a frantic hammering. As if he could hear her blood pumping fast through her veins, he hooked one finger around the edge before Emara heard a soft rip.

Well, that was one way to remove them.

He moved his lips from her neck down to her collarbone, trailing his tongue down until he asked against the skin of her breast, "Do you trust me?"

"Yes," she breathed, unwilling to open her eyes lest it ruin the moment.

He pushed her back, balancing her with one open palm, and softly laid her on the floor of the cavern. In an instant, he was on top of her, and she finally ran her hands over his back, dragging him down against her. She explored his body, running her palms down his chest, feeling the layered muscle tense beneath her touch. It instilled confidence in her that she didn't know she needed.

Even through ultimate desire, he was patient with her.

He allowed her to drag a hand down to the top of his leathers and she rimmed the soaking waist band with one finger. He moved so quickly, she didn't have time to register the breaking of his control as he pinned her hands above her head. All she could hear was his ragged breathing and the pounding sounds of the enchanted water hitting stone. He dipped his head to her shoulder, pulling at the straps of her nightgown with his teeth. Emara could barely hear the noise from the waterfall anymore, her pulse drumming in her ears from the scratching of his teeth against her soft skin. He tore the garment down, revealing her feminine curves. The only part of her body not exposed to him was beneath the dress that now lay loose across her midriff.

"You are so beautiful," he whispered as he looked down at her, a dark craving in his eyes.

Ducking down, he took one breast into his mouth, circling his tongue over her nipple and sucking hard. Her spine arched, bucking her hips against his solid centre. She rasped out a pleasured gasp, and a gratifying groan escaped him as he licked and sucked again, grinding against her bare core. Not stopping his assault of her delicate flesh with his tongue, his hands traced down her navel, ghosting over the line where her underwear used to be. The thought of him inside her both thrilled and terrified her. Was she ready for this big step? Could her body handle something so soul-changing? Emara chuckled inwardly; her body knew what it was ready for. She rolled her hips against him, wanting more.

Always more.

"Are you sure?" he asked, his voice lower than she had ever heard it before.

"Yes," she breathed, still rocking against his touch. "I am sure."

She had never been surer.

Wasting no time, his finger found her centre.

"Fucking Underworld, Emara," he hissed, her wetness coating his hand. He coasted one finger through her as his mouth found her skin again. The world around her sparkled, teasing her into a realm of sheer pleasure. Throwing her head back, she moaned, calling his name. She was sure the enchantment of the cavern echoed it back.

Encouraged, his lips were soft but fierce against hers, claiming her mouth as he worked his fingers just above where she wanted them most in small circles, teasing her most sensitive nerves. Her hips arched against him again, and he pushed one finger inside of her.

She almost crashed there and then.

She gasped again.

He moved them expertly, flexing his fingers in time with her hips as she rode them. Each stroke had Emara's nerves on fire, goosebumps exploding across her skin.

By the Gods, is this what it felt like?

As he worked her closer and closer to climax, he flicked his wrist, and the sweet tension of pleasure boiling in her blood, swirling over every cell of her being, snapped. Her hands clutched onto his back, gripping at his bare, wet skin. His muscles tensed under her hold as she tightened around him.

She was so close.

He introduced a second finger, and with two thrusts, she became undone. Her body felt like it wasn't hers, her hips rising up of their own accord as she cried out, stars bursting across her vision.

He pressed a thumb into her bundle of nerves and drove his fingers in one last time. The tension exploded and tingled through her body, causing her to shake in ecstasy. A whimper escaped her mouth as her knees pulled together, her thighs shutting around Torin's hand, and she coiled against him. For a moment, she listened to Torin's harsh breathing before her muscles finally relaxed. His heart, too, slammed against her chest before his muscles gave in to the tension and he softened. He dropped himself to the ground next to her and she felt herself go limp against the cold floor. It was chillier than it had been before, and she could see little sparkles in the dark of the cavern that she knew weren't really there.

Torin ran his nose up the side of her cheek and kissed delicately into her temple as he withdrew his fingers from inside her. His lips demanded hers a second later, but this was softer, sweeter than before. These kisses were different, sweet and tentative, and they made her stomach dip. He pulled her against him as they took a moment to breathe, lying together in a profound silence. Just like the tension in her core, her heart exploded at the gesture.

She looked over at the waterfall pouring into the pool, noticing that the sky was brighter outside, sending glittering blue and lilac shadows into the cavern as the light broke through the cascade.

She had no words, nothing, her mind emptied of everything that had ever troubled her. Her heart was steady and warm. Her body relaxed against the sand and the warrior who held her in his arms.

Torin was the first to speak. "Are you okay?"

"I'm...wonderful." She almost laughed. "Are you?" she asked him back, knowing small talk was a buffer to the magical tension.

"You can't ask me that question and expect any answer other than yes," he said, tracing a pattern on the lacy fabric of her nightgown that now lay on her stomach. "Not after that."

Emara smiled; she wasn't even sure he saw it as they lay for a few more moments, taking in the sounds of the awakening nature around them.

He let out a small sigh before he spoke again. "The sun will be up soon, and what kind of guard would I be if I didn't get you home before that happened?"

"A very bad one," Emara teased, finally looking at him. His features were softer than before, more relaxed, and one of his wicked dimples appeared just in time for her heart to explode for a second time.

"Come on," he said, rising to his feet. He put out his hands, and Emara took both before he hoisted her up from the cavern ground, where she wished she could stay for a few more minutes, maybe hours.

Torin pulled up the straps to her nightwear and gently placed them back on her shoulders before kissing the lace. Emara gave him a gentle smile and turned. Before she could walk, he swung her into his chest and their bodies collided, now familiar with each other in a way they weren't before. He held her in his arms, looking into her eyes.

"Were you really going to leave here without kissing me?" he jested, lifting his eyebrows.

"I guess I was," she battled back, sticking out her chin. "What are you going to do about that, Torin Blacksteel?"

His dark lashes fluttered up to reveal his icy glare. "There are a lot of things that I would love to teach you." He leaned in and brushed his lips over hers as he smiled. He pushed her mouth open just enough for him to claim it. But all too quickly, he pulled back. "But that will have to do for now."

His wicked grin was outrageous.

She fought back a smile. "I am okay with *that*."

His eyes flashed open and looked her over. The desperate hunger was gone. Maybe the starvation was satiated for now, but his appetite for her still gleamed in his eyes. He broke their gaze as he moved his hand to find hers. "Come on, let's get you back." He smiled a smile that fully thawed every icy part of himself.

Her breath caught in her chest, and she wondered if Torin Blacksteel had ever smiled at anyone like that before.

CHAPTER TWENTY-FIVE
EMARA

I t had taken longer to get back to the inn than what Emara had thought it would. She couldn't remember walking so far and she certainly hadn't felt the temperature outside when stepping out of the inn in her bare feet. But now, with her soaking wet hair hanging down her back icing her bones with every swish, she was freezing. Emara used her fire to heat her hands, keeping frostbite away from her fingers. The rest of her was still painfully cold, but she didn't want to push herself and accidentally destroy the forest.

Torin had persuaded her to let him carry her before her toes became victim to the frost. He stole a kiss or two before he picked up the pace to get them back to shelter. This time, his lips were soft against hers, not in the animalistic way like he had kissed her before, but in a delicate and gentle way. It was the only thing keeping her mind from the numbing cold that etched itself into her bones.

Approaching the inn, he still didn't drop her. He pulled her closer to him, like he was savouring every last drop of their time alone. He kicked the door open with ease and made his way up the rickety stairs. It was a wonder they supported the weight of him alone, never mind her on top. He let her slide down his body as he reached the top of the stairs, and needles pinched in her toes as they touched the ground. Turning her head to the door of the room, she noticed it had been left open wide enough to see that Torin had left in a hurry—and open enough to see that someone lay sprawled across the bed.

Torin cursed under his breath and Artem Stryker lifted his head from the pillow.

"Oh, good," he said, a grin threatening to rip his face apart. "The wanderers have returned."

"In case you haven't picked up on it yet, I am in no mood for your mindless antics, Stryker." Torin walked in front of Emara, shielding her wet body from his brother. The emerald nightgown that she had worn the night before was slick against her body, leaving nothing to the imagination.

"I bet you're not." Artem winked at Torin and pulled himself up fully from his laxed position. "You had your leathers in a twist leaving here."

Emara wanted so badly to see Torin's face fill with rage or embarrassment at Artem's words, but he had positioned himself so that she could only see his back.

She stepped out, knowing eventually Artem would see her anyway.

"So you managed to find her, our Empress of Travels and Wander." Artem looked over Emara quickly, his gaze not lingering long. She had a sneaking suspicion it had everything to do with Torin and the glare that threatened to burn a hole in his face. "I thought you were about to burst a blood vessel when you realised she was missing."

Emara didn't dare look at the warrior who stood beside her.

"Did you forget you are under the protection of the hunters, Miss Clearwater?" Artem smiled, but there was a cutting jest in his tone that made her think about her actions.

She had been extremely reckless. She was under the protection of the hunters and it had been silly of her not to inform them of what she had done.

But she had loved every minute of it, breathing in the air of liberation.

"I have already given her *the talk,*" Torin said, pulling off his wet clothes. His tunic hit the ground with a slap. "You need to leave for her to change." Torin stood with his hands on his hips in nothing but his leathers.

Artem glanced through the small window that sat above the bed and then to the clothing on the floor. "That's funny." His brow pulled down. "The last time I checked outside, it wasn't raining or snowing." His chin lifted into the air. "So that raises the question as to why the both of you are absolutely drenched."

Emara tried to hide the red-hot beam in her cheeks. She peeked over at Torin. He straightened, pushing back his shoulders. His neck—a neck that she had kissed and moaned into just a short while ago —bobbed.

Running his tongue along the inside of his check and a hand through his wet hair, he said, "We fell."

Artem failed to hide the amusement that spread across his face. "You fell?"

"We did," Emara confirmed, not looking at the inked warrior but at the water on the floor that puddled around them both. Torin walked over to the railings and pulled down a fresh towel before draping it over her shoulders. The heat from the material instantly warmed her.

"Into a waterfall, to be exact," Torin said as he ran a towel over his hair. "Emara decided to go exploring. And we fell."

Emara nearly choked on her own breath and threw a dangerous look his way, but his eyes burned with that same fire as when he had licked her, sucked on her flesh, and stolen her mouth with his own.

She swallowed.

His appetite didn't stay sated for long. And, apparently, neither did hers, as her toes curled into the wooden floor.

Artem barked out a laugh. "All right. If that's what you want me to believe, I will play along. But if you expect me to really believe that Torin Blacksteel fell helplessly into a waterfall, you must mistake me for a fool."

"Why just Torin?" Emara asked, slightly offended. "Why is it believable for me to have fallen into a waterfall and not him?"

Artem got up from the bed and walked closer. "Because I have trained with him." He slid his eyes to

Emara's. "I have seen him dodge five demons whilst eating a turkey leg."

"That's a true story." Torin's eyes met hers, and a buoyant excitement danced there.

"So there is no way he *fell* into a waterfall by accident," Artem said as he crossed his arms. "He either jumped in after you, or you pushed him."

Emara let out a loud hoot. "Pushed him?"

"She did," Torin confirmed. "She pushed me."

He turned, giving her a subtle wink that made her stomach flutter. If Emara hadn't known what he was capable of with that wicked mouth as he pulled it into a grin, she would have described his smile as innocent.

But she couldn't now. Or ever.

"All right, all right." Artem snorted. "I am just glad you are both back in one piece. I will retreat for now in the hopes that, someday, I will learn the truth." He held out his tattooed hands in surrender. "But only if you swear to make me part of the wedding party."

"Artem, don't go there," Emara warned as she shivered into her towel.

"I could do a speech—"

"Don't go there, I said."

"I also look good in a dress jacket. Maybe you could appoint me *best man of the union*."

"Right, that's it." Emara dove towards him.

Before she could reach Artem, something strong grabbed her around the waist, pulling her back. She kicked and punched as a gust of air brushed through the room, but all she could hear was a chuckle. Somehow, it had become her favourite sound.

"As much as I would love to see you attempt to kick his ass," Torin purred into her ear, sending her into a different kind of frenzy altogether. "I don't want you to summon a wind that could literally tear this inn apart." She stopped thrashing against him and stilled in his grip. "I know how talented you can be in that area. Let's leave this inn standing, shall we?" He smoothed a hand down her arm, calming her.

Torin was right. She could summon air, and it would only take a small gust to blow this inn apart. Then there was her fire that burned so horribly when she was enraged; she dreaded to think of how quickly this pokey little inn would go up in flames.

Instead of punching Artem, she made a rude gesture at him.

Artem's laugh shook through the inn. "Fell in the waterfall..." He wiped away tears of laughter. "Yeah, right," he muttered as he left the room. "Fell."

Emara's air swooped in and slammed the door shut, and the whole room shuddered around them.

Was it that obvious, what had happened between them? Maybe they would never be able to hide the broken barrier again. Was she ready for that? Did she want to hide it?

Torin's arms relaxed around her and his hands slid to her hips, manoeuvring her around to face him. "Has anyone ever told you how captivating you are when you get all worked up?"

She let out a huffy laugh. "I am pretty sure it has only been you."

"I like the sound of that," he whispered before his

lips met hers. His bottom lip grazed over her own, teasing her into submission.

She couldn't stop it, this *pull* towards him. How she felt around him was indescribable. She felt safe yet unpredictable. She felt like she couldn't breathe when she looked at him, yet her body had never felt more alive when he kissed her, like her lungs were deprived of oxygen until his lips were on hers. The consuming desire she had for Torin Blacksteel was wild, surreal, and profound. It was like nothing she had ever felt before. There were times when she wanted to kill him, and in the same minute, she wanted to slam her lips against his and let him devour her. He was the most strikingly attractive man she had ever laid eyes on. And yet, he seemed to want *her.*

She pulled back from his lips. His closed eyes fluttered open and he stared at her for a long second.

"Are you okay?" He did not front his mocking tone, nor did his insanely beautiful smile appear. This was Torin in his most genuine light.

"Yes," she said, pulling back even further.

Was she okay?

Her heart quickened and she lifted a hand to rub her temple.

"You don't seem to be." His eyes worked over every inch of her face.

"I just—"

"Is it about what Artem said about the union?" His jaw tightened and a flash of violent rage slammed out any concern. And then it was gone, replaced with a gentle emotion. "You know there is no pressure from my side about that."

"It's not that." She sighed, unable to get through the buzzing sound in her head and the wave of insecurity that threatened to appear any moment.

"Is it because I lied about you pushing me into the waterfall?" he teased, one eyebrow lifting.

She dragged her teeth along the bottom of her lip and turned away.

He shifted his weight onto both feet. "Talk to me, Emara."

The second he spoke her name, a warm, rolling feeling coiled in her stomach. She looked at him. "I just..." She paused, placing a hand on her navel to steady the nerves. "What I did...with you. I have never done that with anyone before."

Concern lit his eyes, his brow pulling down enough to show that something about what she had said troubled him. He took a small step towards her. "I don't want you to feel embarrassed about what we did." His hand came up to her face and brushed her cheek.

"I don't feel embarrassed," Emara declared, shaking her head. "I just want you to understand how much that kind of thing means to me." Lowering her lashes, she found the floor. "What I gave to you was...trust."

What she really wanted to say lingered thick in the air.

Please don't break my trust.

He ran the back of his hand down her jaw, and with one finger, he tilted her head back up to meet his gaze. "I want you to understand how much that meant to me too." His words were more sincere than she could have ever imagined him capable of. "What we shared together..." He cupped another hand on her face and his nostrils flared. "It means you trusted *me* enough to be intimate with you." The sharpness of azure in his eyes turned soft, and her heart melted. "I will never take the trust you graced me with for granted, I promise you that." He lowered a hand to capture hers and brought it up to his lips. He kissed her forehand and then her temple. "You have seen parts of me that I truly despise and yet you still kiss me like you haven't seen them at all." His voice trembled a little, and it sent a wrenching feeling into Emara's heart and gut. "If you think for one second that I will hurt you"—he let out a breath—"I will not."

"You can't promise me that," she whispered as his thumb rubbed into her cheek.

His jaw clenched. "I can promise you anything I want to as long as I mean it."

Emara let out a small laugh, and it banished a few of her insecurities. He had told her that she was enough. But was she? Could she be enough for Torin Blacksteel?

She hated feeling so insecure. It wasn't something she was used to, but her trust had been broken before.

"Is that because you are a cocky bastard?" She tried to hide a smile as she pushed down her vulnerability enough for it to choke and die out.

A dark eyebrow rose in challenge to her. "Would you expect anything else?"

"I do now." Emara lifted her chin, relaxing her shoulders. "Now that I know there is so much more to

Torin Blacksteel than bloodshed, liquor, and an over-inflated ego."

He chuckled. "You see, I always knew there was more to you. I just didn't know if I would ever be the one to see it."

Would he be the one to see every part of her?

"I don't have any problems letting you learn more about me." She allowed herself a confident smirk, even if she wavered saying it. "As long as you keep showing me all the different sides of you too."

He let a sly grin form on his lips. "We might have a deal on our hands, Clearwater."

CHAPTER TWENTY-SIX
EMARA

G littering white snow covered the tips and crevasses of the mountains ahead. They had made it to the north, and the sky was a silver backdrop behind the jagged highland. Riding through the forest clearings close to the mountains was breathtaking, the grandness of all of the sister mountains a colossal presence. Branches hung heavy with snow, and they passed too many to count as they began their ascent up the foot hill. It was a different kind of air that filled Emara's lungs. It was a kind that turned her breath to frost inside her lungs, but also filled them with the purest air that she had ever taken in.

They had been riding for over an hour on a steep incline, and not much conversation had flowed between anyone. Artem looked to be staring vacantly at the view, lost in his own thoughts. Magin had been eating a handful of nuts, and Torin, well, she could still feel the rising of his chest touching her spine. But everyone was silent, except for the two voices inside her head. They were the same voices that assisted her in every thought, one with the purest intentions and the other a little darker. The quiet had allowed Emara to mull over everything that had taken place over the last few days.

The swell of her heart increased and so did her pulse.

Drawing in a breath that sliced through her lungs, she allowed herself to think about what had happened at the Waterfall of Uttara. It was the first time she properly had the time to think about it, and it was overwhelming. Everything about it had been consuming and fervent. Every part of her had burned for more of him, for his hands, for his mouth, for that relentless passion he offered.

For all of him.

Torin Blacksteel's kiss had been claiming and so blunt with desire, thinking about it made her question everything she had ever known. It underlined how plain and simple things had been before in comparison to his kiss. A brief tensing in her core reminded her that she was, in fact, sitting in such short proximity to him on the horse that she could turn around and her body would be touching his within seconds. Her lips could be on his in that wild, craving way. The darkness in her mind nudged her forward to wrap her legs around him and run her hands through his dark, silken hair, whilst pulling her teeth over his lip—

"Why are you tensing?" the huskiness of Torin's low voice startled her back to reality. She sent a quick prayer up to the Gods that he could not witness how red her cheeks were, or he'd know instantly exactly why she was tensing.

"Um, I am just a little sore from riding" she lied.

"Uh-huh." The smoothness of his non-belief slid past her ear.

The heat from her embarrassment cast from her cheeks right through her body and into her heart.

It was strange, she had always reserved her heart for someone who she thought would be sensible and honest, someone who would colour within the lines and do the right thing. She had imagined giving her heart to someone who would challenge who she was but not fully rock the foundations of her soul. Emara had envisioned being with someone who wouldn't make her question, morally, who she was or make her reconsider the bubble that she had lived in for so long. From what she had fabricated in her mind of what she had wanted, it certainly wasn't Torin Blacksteel.

But from the moment she had kissed him, she knew it was different. For the love of Rhiannon, from the moment she had met him, she knew he was magnetic. Now, something in her had completely shifted, changing the shape of her heart entirely. She couldn't explain why or how, she could only go by the truth that lay in her own heart. She had always wanted someone to set her soul on fire, but she had always been searching in damp ground before. Now, she was the match and Torin Blacksteel was the flame.

"When we get to the palace, will your room be close to mine?" she asked, breaking free from her deepest reflections.

"Where are your naughty little thoughts wandering to?" He chuckled from behind her, gripping the reins on the horse tighter. The horse mounted a large stone that was heavily set into the foundation of the mountain, causing her to slide back in the saddle. Her weight pressed into Torin's chest.

"Clearly, not where yours are headed." She rolled her eyes, hoping he could hear the roll from the sound of her voice. "I just mean will you be close to me because you are my guard?"

"Essentially, yes. But I don't know how many people will stay for the ascension and what rooms will be available. I have only been there twice before. The Amethyst Palace is a sacred fortress, dating back to the ancient world, to the Gods. And it's home to the supreme and her subjects. She runs it like she owns the place, but a lot of the witches will stay a while, probably until after the ascension or winter solstice."

"You celebrate the winter solstice?" She couldn't find the energy to hide the shock in her voice.

"Yes," he breathed. "I don't know why you sound so surprised. All of the magic factions do."

"I'm sorry, I didn't think hunters would conform to human celebrations."

He huffed a laugh. "I think you will find that the winter solstice, like most events, are festivals of the Gods, not the humans. The Gods celebrated these festivities long before humans even walked this world." Torin paused. "And since we descended from a bloodline of the Gods, we celebrate them too—especially winter solstice. It has been said that Thorin was the first to exchange a gift with a human woman, giving to her a weapon to protect herself from the darkened. And that is how the tradition of gift giving on the shortest day of the year evolved."

Emara chewed the inside of her cheek for a second. "I find it strange that Thorin would gift a human *woman* a weapon to defend herself, yet your faction doesn't allow women to be hunters."

"Don't shoot the messenger, I don't make up the rules."

"But if you could decide the rules, would you let women fight?" She angled her head, awaiting his answer.

He sighed. "This question is impossible to answer."

Emara's lips thinned. "Is it? I don't think it is."

"Of course, you don't. You are not a hunter."

Emara raised her chin, tucking her hands back into her cloak. "I think you are being a coward not to answer it, regardless of your position on it."

After a few moments of nothing but horses' hooves on rock, Torin spoke. "You're right, I was being a coward not to answer your question." She allowed shock to settle between them at the fact that Torin had admitted that she was right. It was astounding. "The reason I found it impossible to answer that question right away was because my mind went straight to you." An intense silence filled the air around them before he spoke again. "And the thought of you fighting something so vile disturbs me. Having you endure long training hours, and then if you were subjected to battle conditions..." He sat up straight behind her, her body curving against his. "I don't think any man would want to see a woman suffer things he could take the burden of. But then I realised that I would; I would let women fight because they have just as much to fight for as men, if not more." The gravity of his words hit her heart unexpectedly. "And if all women are as feisty as you and my mother, then I would be happy to have you on the battlefield beside me." She could hear the smile on his face and a lump formed in her throat. "I can't lie, though, everything in my instincts, in the make-up of who I am, would be screaming at me for you not to fight. I am a protector, I can't turn that off. But I would always let you fight, should that be your choice."

Her voice was quiet when she said, "I wouldn't expect you to turn off everything you are to allow me that grace."

"Being a hunter is not everything I am." Torin's lips brushed over her ear, sending her heart leaping in her chest. "But more to your point, have I not already proved that I would let you fight when I handed you my sword in the tower's gardens?"

He had. Good Gods, he had. And then with Taymir, and then with the lesser demons in the forest.

She let the silence soak in as she drifted her mind over what he had said, wondering if Viktir Blacksteel had ever done the same for Naya. Her guess would be that there would be no chance in the underworld that Viktir Blacksteel would be proud to fight beside a woman.

But Torin would be.

"I hope that answers your question," he said finally, breaking through the quiet.

"It does," she whispered back.

"I have a question for you," he said, with a little more reluctance than she was used to. It sent a pang of worry into her stomach. "When you think of your magic, when you feel it, do you feel air being summoned, or do your fingers start to tingle with fire first?"

The question almost knocked her from the horse and the breath whooshed from her lungs.

It was the question she had locked down in the pits of her soul, not wanting to explore any of it.

So the simple answer was that she didn't know.

She didn't know if she was more dominant in fire or air. She hadn't had enough time to explore it. Did that make her claims to the Air title a deception?

Her skin pimpled.

Through a vision gifted by a spirit witch, she had seen how poorly her mother had been treated for being a fire bearer and belonging to House Air. Emara had witnessed what her own grandmother had done to her mother for it. Her thoughts also turned to Callyn. Her best friend, born of the House of Water only to have been abandoned because of a prophecy.

Why were the witches so scared to step outside their own House and thrive with different elemental magic? Why were they doomed to dismissal or neglect should their fate choose a different element? Is that not what the Gods had paved for them?

Emara swallowed. "I am not sure what I feel first," she choked out. "I cannot say for certain. Sometimes I feel air quickly build around me, and other times I feel fire stirring in my veins."

Torin hummed behind her.

She plucked up enough courage to ask, "What would happen to me if I admitted that my Fire element is just as strong as the element of Air?"

Torin let out a large puff of breath, and she wondered how long he had been holding it in. "It depends. If you wanted to make a claim to the Fire crown, they would make you do a trial against the current Empress of Fire to test if you were stronger. And the trial is not pretty. The witches are ultimately entering into a tribunal that will result in one of them dying."

A whimper escaped Emara's lips. "And House Air would reject me for claiming another element as my dominant power?"

"Correct. Unless you have all five elemental powers, and they are all as strong as each other, in which case you could be the next supreme. You would be in the running to rise as the crown witch."

Emara inhaled slowly, controlling her frigid breathing. "I haven't shown any signs of bearing the element of Water yet. And my strengths in Spirit and Earth are questionable."

"Give it time," Torin said. "You have barely scratched the surface with what you can do. You are untrained, and you have shown signs of true power. You have no idea what could be unearthed at any moment. Magic is a funny thing. You know as well as I do that it surprises you at every turn. But if you are showing signs of every element, and they are all feeling strong in your arsenal, keep it to yourself until the right moment. No one else needs to know what weapons you hold. You don't need any more targets on your back, not until we suss out all the other empresses' ambitions and why they are being killed off."

Her breathing hitched at his words, the thrumming of her sorcery making her heart pound faster.

"No one else needs to know what weapons you hold."

"Do witches really endanger each other for power?" she asked Torin.

He must have heard the concern in her tone. "The supreme wouldn't allow that; she needs a united front. She needs a strong union between the covens. However, that doesn't stop the catty politics between Houses, or the jealousy, should one be more favoured. But don't worry, I will protect you from that."

"I will protect you from that."

Her stomach dipped.

"Blacksteel," Artem shouted from out front. "We are about two hours away. Do you want to pick up speed?"

"Sounds like a plan, Stryker."

"Two hours?" Emara exclaimed, breaking the intentions of where her conversation was about to go.

Torin chuckled, and she could feel the vibrations from his chest through her cloak. "Relax," he said. "You are tense again." He wrapped an arm around her stomach and pulled her into him. "You could maybe get some sleep, since you were up *early* this morning," his tone danced suggestively in the air.

But she didn't fire a snide return his way, she simply leaned back against him and let out a small sigh. There was so much yet to be answered about who she was and her purpose, but she couldn't dive into that dark cave just yet, not when she was so close to ascending.

Because the kingdom needs you to. You are the only thing that can stop the darkness. The world as we know it now depends on your ascension.

She let her head fall back against Torin's chest and listened to the beating of his heart. It had become a sound that spoke to her in a way she never thought possible, a song that gave meaning to her journey.

The steady beating of his heart and the constant clicking of hooves must have sent her off into a slumber, because she awoke to the sound of her name.

Torin whispered again, "Emara."

She blinked open her eyes and her gaze instantly found why he had awoken her. They were high into the mountain range now, and a thick cloud lay below where they rode, cascading down into the valley.

A gasp escaped her, and she sat up further.

The sky had cleared up and the winter sun burned a glowing yellow above them, casting a light onto the layer of fluffy cloud. The peaks of the mountain could no longer be seen; she was so close to the top, but not quite there yet. She swung her legs over the saddle and hit the uneven ground, bending her knees. Walking towards the cliff's edge, she could see for miles into the distance, and through little waves of smoky cloud, she could see the kingdom below her.

Looking over to her left, she placed a hand up to shield her eyes.

A glittering fortress sat on the edge of the mountain, sending out sparkles of violet, lilac, and lavender. Its ancient magic sung out to her, grasping her attention. Something inside of her acknowledged the olden magic, like her blood knew its melody, and she inhaled sharply.

The fortress had been carved from the mountain itself, and its remarkable structure seemed to be floating like one of the shimmering clouds. The pointed tops of the fortress were solid crystal, and the windows were all stained glass from what she could see, swirling in all different colours and shapes.

Her eyes couldn't quite believe that something like this could exist.

She turned back to where the men sat atop their horses. "The Amethyst Palace!" she breathed, looking directly at Torin.

"There is nothing quite like it in the whole of the kingdom." Artem mirrored her tone of admiration.

If the scenery wasn't so sublime it could blind her, the palace was wholly spectacular on its own. But the two of them together, where the landscape met the palace, was outrageously beautiful. It sat like one gigantic, ancient crystal at the side of the mountain, magic thrumming from its infrastructure, and it was as if the mountains themselves bowed to it.

"All the great witches have ascended here." Torin

looked her over and a dipping sensation rolled in her stomach before she felt her heart lurch into her mouth. She wasn't sure if it was because of his words or the way he looked at her like she was more beautiful than the crystal fortress.

But she could feel the magic in her blood calling to the ascension place, like it craved for her to get there in a heartbeat and unite with a fate she was destined for.

Emara looked back to it, its glittering edges winking at her, inviting her towards it.

"Come on." Torin gestured for her to get back onto the horse. "We are almost there."

Pulling herself back onto the horse, she mounted gracefully and fixed her cloak back around her. Torin sat with one hand around her waist as they made their way towards their destination.

The Amethyst Palace.

CHAPTER
TWENTY-SEVEN
BREIGHLY

The Ashdale forest was strangely calm, most of it a glittering glaze of frost. Breighly had always preferred summer solstice as opposed to winter. It meant she could wear less clothes when shifting between her wolven form, which she was currently in as she watched over her woods. Summer also meant the singing of birds could be heard, the shuffling of grass parting for other animals like the gentle deer or the curious fox that liked to graze in heat. Breighly particularly liked the buzzing of the humble worker bee as she searched flowers to collect nectar from. It was a summer melody, and she would pretend to hear it as she stalked through the desolate trees, ignoring the crunching of the solid ground. Summer also meant that she could have more time under the sun, rather than the moon, which had sent her into a batch of craziness lately.

Well, not just lately.

Always.

Her father and brothers always scorned her for

blaming the moon for her bad behaviour, but her "bad behaviour" had become more frequent recently, and she didn't need to be under the moon for it to occur. So maybe it wasn't just the moon. But she would blame it anyway.

Her bad behaviour took many forms too. The constant urge to disobey any order from her alpha, sneaking out after hours, offering specials in La Luna that were not agreed with the pack, getting blindingly drunk and kissing everything in sight.

It was getting ridiculous.

A pang of guilt struck through her. She knew she shouldn't act the way she did, but it was the only thing that subsided the pain for a little while.

She ignored that ache in her chest as her powerful wolf form prowled back through the forest to the family cottage, where she could already see Roman waiting for her. She sighed before quickly shifting back into her human form. Stretching out her muscles that always seemed a lot smaller and tighter after she transformed, she stalked up the wooden stairs to her home.

"I can see you went patrolling without me." Roman's dark eyes narrowed in on her face. They were exactly the same shape and colour as hers, as were his cheekbones and chin. But he was stretches taller than her, and she tried not to look at him as he spoke.

"Again." He crossed his arms over his chest and his dark blonde hair rustled in the icy breeze.

"Yeah, well, I had to clear my mind and I couldn't listen to you whining the full patrol." Her feet sounded harsh on the wood as she stomped up the last few steps.

Roman took the loose shirt from his own back and handed her it, looking away. She quickly shrugged it over her almost naked body and folded her hands around her waist. Even though she had the heated blood of a wolf, the winter chill ran through her human skin and dug into her bones. It wasn't like this when she was under the protection of her wolfy fur. Sometimes she wondered if she should just stay in wolf form and run and run until she ended up somewhere else entirely.

Roman turned to her. "You never used to patrol without me."

Pain lingered on his features for a second before his chest puffed out, just like Waylen's did when he was angry, and just like Eli's had too. A stabbing pain cut through her heart at the thought of her fallen brother. But since her heart had turned to stone just after his death, she decided she was going to push it down until she could breathe again.

"Yeah, well now I like to patrol alone," she spoke so sharply that she had to hide her own flinching at the sound of her voice. She pushed past her brother who had only entered this world two minutes before her. Since that moment, they had never been apart... until recently.

"You weren't alone a few nights ago," Roman shot his words at her back, and it almost hit like a dart, right on the vital killing spot on the spine. She halted as he continued, "So, I am guessing that you're just picking and choosing when you want to be alone."

She turned, facing him, as irritation grew thick in

her veins. Normally, Roman was the only one in the world who didn't annoy her. Tonight, the Gods were making an exception for him.

"What did you just say?" She pulled her lip back over her sharp teeth.

His eyes narrowed in on her face again, making him look more wolf than human. "You heard me. I am not going to repeat myself."

In her mind, she had already thrown a punch in his direction, but somehow, her body wasn't in the mood for a fight, which was irregular. When you grew up with three older brothers and your father was the alpha of the pack, you had to learn how to kick ass from a pretty young age.

"If you are going to make any more spiteful remarks towards me, I would suggest you be brave enough to say them to my face." She opened the door to the large cottage that had been in her family generations, swinging it so hard that her elbow cracked. "In case you haven't picked up on my mood through our *twin telepathy,* I am severely irritated."

"Is that because you keep fucking hunters?" He cut deep.

She flinched.

"Shut your Godsdamned mouth and stay out of my business," she roared, slamming the cottage door behind her.

She heard the door reopen and stomping feet came in behind her, hard and fast. "It's pretty difficult to stay out of your business when I have the room next door to you," he growled, catching up to her in a snappy second.

"You hear *everything*. Vanadey didn't grant me powerful hearing so that I could listen to what you did the other night."

She hadn't seen her twin since she had thrown that inked hunter out in the morning dew, and Roman had been so angry with her when he had awoken that he hadn't spoken to her at all at dinner. So she had shifted, and hadn't been in human form since. She had just lived in the woods, running, hunting, and star gazing, when the weather allowed it. She'd been doing anything she could to not face her brother, her cottage, her room.

She swung to face him now. "Maybe you should get a fucking life, Roman, then you'd stay out of mine." She powered through the short hallway to her room, hoping he would split off to his.

He didn't.

"I have a life," he snapped, walking after her. "And you used to be in it."

She turned to see him standing in the threshold of her room, almost reaching the wooden beams overhead.

"You are shutting me out, Bry." His tone changed, causing her throat to dry up as he looked at her. "You... you can't just shut everyone out because Eli is gone." He looked at the floor and then back to her. "We are all hurting, but how we get through this is together, like we always have. You know the law of the pack."

The lone wolf is never really alone, for all wolves howl at the same full moon.

The pack. Her pack. Her father's pack.

"I am not shutting everyone out." She pulled her shoulders back. "That's not what I am doing."

It had been different since Eli had been murdered under the Blood Moon; she couldn't deny it, and neither could Roman. A part of their family was broken, and it would never heal. A part of their pack was gone and would never howl at the same moon as them again, not from this world.

Roman finally came through the threshold of her door, his long arms hanging loosely by his side. His sandy hair looked darker in the dim light of her room, and he took a deep breath. "I know that's what you are doing because I want to do it too." A muscle under his eye twitched. "I want to shut everyone out too, Bry. But I won't."

She didn't know if the lump in her throat was due to their twin connection or because the wolf instincts picked up on how each other felt, but she could feel it low in his heart—that deep sorrow, unnerving and rattling.

Loss.

"Stop thinking you know everything that goes on in my head." Breighly squinted her eyes at him.

He huffed a laugh. "Praise fucking Vanadey that I don't know everything that is going on inside that mess." Roman let a small, wolfish grin appear as he pointed to her temple.

Her mouth twitched up identically to his.

His strong throat bobbed with emotion. "But seriously, don't shut me out. I need you."

"I won't," she said, the lie thick in her throat. "I am not shutting you out. I just need to be alone sometimes, and that's something the pack doesn't get."

Breighly knew she had shut down the very minute Eli's body set sail down the River of Vanadey. It had felt like part of her had gone with him, out into the broken sea of Thorin that swallowed his body whole. Breighly knew she needed to be strong, just like her brothers would be, as the eyes of the Shifter community were on them. Just like she needed to be to earn the respect of her faction as the only female of the Baxgroll family.

But she was well and truly fucking that up, unable to tame her conduct.

So she suppressed every feeling—no matter how big or small—that she could sense creeping into her heart.

"Waylen is worried about you too," Roman said. "You are even more *feral* than normal."

She let out a half laugh as she kicked her way through the mess in her room. "I am not feral."

Her father had always joked about how he had three sons, but the most feral of his children was his daughter —his princess.

"You are wildly feral at the moment." Roman walked in and closed her door. "And can I just say, I was about three seconds away from coming in here the other night and slitting your throat."

She combed her golden hair behind an ear as the mortification of her drunken antics with her hunter "friend" surfaced. "I am sorry about that." She tried to sound as sincere as possible, but her sassy attitude won the battle—as usual. She cringed again, thinking how she would feel if it had been reversed, and tried again, "I am sorry. Truly, Roman, I am."

If she had heard Roman doing what she had...

Ugh, the sick almost travelled up at the thought of it.

"You should be sorry." He glared at her. She knew how much it would have taken for him not to charge into her room and end the Warrior of Thorin there and then. "You are lucky you don't have the room adjacent to Waylen. And even luckier that he is out on business with Father."

A shudder crawled up her spine as she thought about how much of a blood bath that would have been.

It could have resulted in one of them dying.

She sighed and flung herself onto her bed, which was, of course, an untidy mess.

Her head was a mess. Her room was a mess. Her life was a mess. Everything was a mess.

A snigger came from across the room and suddenly Roman flung himself onto her bed too, and they lay there like they had when they were kids.

"I think you kissed about twelve different people in La Luna the other night." Roman stifled a laugh. "It's a good thing you are running the place and not Waylen. He would have killed all the creatures hanging around you."

"Fuck," she hissed.

"And a few of them were female." Roman laughed. "You stole one of them from me." He leaned over and flicked her face with his middle finger, pinging her cheek. "Weren't you supposed to be working behind the bar? Not drinking it dry and dancing on top of it. If Paps finds out..."

"Oh Gods," Breighly wailed, draping an arm over her face. She had tried to block out every memory of that night, especially the morning after, but every time she thought of him, something stirred in her chest.

She slammed down on her thoughts quickly.

She turned to face her favourite brother. "Roman, please tell me that I didn't try and kiss the new Empress of Air."

"No, Bry, you didn't." Roman's eyebrow arched the same way that hers did.

She let out a sigh of relief.

"But you did try and drink a shot of whisky out of her cleavage."

"Fuck, fuck, fuck," she hissed again. "Why am I like this?" She threw her hands up.

"I did manage to stop you before that happened," Roman reassured her.

Breighly looked over to the brother she had shared their mother's womb with and whispered, "Thank you." She swallowed down more guilt than she could chew. "You didn't have to do that."

"Of course, I did." He looked back at her, his brown eyes a little warmer than before. "It's what we do for each other. We stop one another from making a complete and utter cock of ourselves. I suppose it's a bit of a harder job for me these days." He pinged her face again. "But Vanadey knows I try so that I will pass over to the Otherside gracefully when the time comes."

Breighly finally laughed a little.

It was true, she had never known them not to cover for one another. They always stuck together. Roman would have her back—even if she was wrong—and she, his.

She linked her arm under his, like they did when they were children, and they lay there for a few minutes of silence, comfortable just being.

"Don't go patrolling without me, okay?" he said, his voice deeper than usual. "It's not safe out there right now. It's not just witches that are falling, but wolves too."

Something dark lay in his eyes, and Breighly's feral impulses flexed under her muscles. She would eliminate anything that would harm him.

A wave of understanding drifted unspoken between them, and she nodded. "I won't go patrolling without you."

As Breighly looked out at the moon that was trying her hardest to give off a blue shine, she wondered how long it would take before she would break that promise to him.

CHAPTER
TWENTY-EIGHT
EMARA

Torin had met with the fortress' guards at the largest iron-grey doors Emara had ever laid eyes on just moments ago, confirming who they were. Now, the guards, in similar uniforms to her trio, were escorting them through the corridors of the Amethyst Palace, a place so divine that she could feel the magic of the Gods within the walls. Quartz traced lines in the carved-out mountain, even on the inside of the palace, and the passageways were spacious enough to line up an army. For the sheer size of it, it felt warm, warmer than she expected, and chrome beacons were lit with balls of fire all down the corridors.

Emara tried to control the tightening knots that had developed in her stomach as her boots clicked along the polished floors, but her nerves were so tangled that she couldn't unravel them.

She was here.

In the place she would ascend. In a place that would forever change who she was.

As if sensing her nervous tension, Torin placed a

hand at the small of her back as he walked beside her. Giving a nod down at her, he let her know she was safe. The swords that were always strapped to him peeked up from behind his solid shoulders as a reminder of that.

Magin was in front, chatting about their journey to a guard he was acquainted with, and Artem was two steps behind Torin, sauntering casually like he had seen the palace a million times. She peered around at him and he lifted his eyebrows in a taunting fashion, eyes flicking to the hand at the base of her spine. Emara stuck out her tongue, her mind fighting against her body to supress what she wanted to do—flip him off.

Artem stifled a laugh that drew Torin's attention, and he looked from Emara to over his shoulder.

"I would be careful if I were you," Torin told Artem, his head turning back in the direction they were walking. "She is around her own kind now. She is more powerful than ever in the energy of her coven," he said in a subtle way that only Emara and Artem could hear. "I would choose your battles with her wisely from now on."

"Likewise, brother," Artem replied with a taunting glint in his eye.

Emara didn't dare hide the smile that spread on her face, even though the churning in her stomach didn't cease because being here felt right.

After walking through one of the longest corridors in history, Magin and the guards at the front came to a halt, stopping everyone on their tracks.

One of the palace guards pointed at the door. "This will be the room of the heir."

The guard Magin knew said, "The supreme has asked for everyone to settle in before she calls on them by fireletter." He looked over Torin and back at Emara. "She will let you know how she wants to proceed with the evening in due course."

Torin nodded and a guard handed Magin a set of brass keys that wound around a ring, keeping them all together. "Your rooms are down the hall, to the left." He gestured to a corridor that wound around a bend.

Magin nodded and the guards moved forward in sync with each other as they took their leave. It was evident they had done this a few times already, and she found herself wondering which empresses were already within the palace walls.

House Fire? House Earth? Was Gideon here?

Her heart twitched.

Maybe it was House Spirit.

Or Water.

She wondered if the heirs in waiting felt the same way she did. Of course, they would know more of the ceremonies than she did. They'd probably grown up with a life full of magic and witchcraft, learning the ins and outs of what it took to become an empress of magic.

Dread and fear coursed through her mind, brewing up a storm of doubt. Could she really do this?

Before it could take over her, a brass lock turned, giving way to the key, and the door to her room opened.

She walked in sheepishly, Torin on her heels.

The room was beautiful, but it didn't feel like her one in the Huntswood Tower. Oddly, she missed the view of the city. She missed the bed she had just made familiar, and she longed to sit on her windowsill with a book on witchcraft, or train in the common sparring room.

Was the tower somewhere she could feel at home?

Never in a million moons did she think she would feel like the Blacksteel Tower was home, but compared to this, it was.

The flames were already alight in the fireplace, across from her bed, warming the room as she walked forward. Quickly, she realised the flames were more golden than red or orange, and there was something about the stillness of them that had her questioning her sight. She blinked a few times.

Emara turned towards Torin.

"Magic," was all he said, as if he had anticipated her question.

"It feels real," she said as she placed her hands closer to the flames.

"The heat is real, but the flames are not." He looked at her over his shoulder. "In the early world, only witches used this type of fire to communicate, but now we all do. Witches are basically responsible for our timely letter service due to one crafty little fire spell."

"Your mother told me about these flames." Emara recalled her conversation with Naya, and she was grateful that she'd had it. "I know how to receive a fireletter and send one—I think."

But she had never done it before, never practised, only knew of it.

It was a start.

"We have witchfire in the tower," Torin told her. "So

that we can also send and receive fireletters." He dipped his head. "That's how my clan and Father get their information so swiftly. Can you see now why having an alliance with a witch is powerful and efficient?" He pressed his full lips together. "It would take a carrier days to deliver a message; witchfire can do it in seconds."

"Now I can see why you hunters always want us witches on your side," she joked with a smirk. "I guess I will see how I will make myself useful in House Air."

But the point he made was valid. Witchfire was astounding.

Torin grinned. It was so genuine and bold that it caught her off guard, knocking the air from her lungs.

"What?" she asked, unsure what to make of it.

"That's the first time you have properly referred to yourself as a witch, used your faction and referred to yourself as one of them."

She looked around the room again, taking a break from his striking face. "I suppose it is starting to settle in."

"It suits you."

Her head snapped to him, standing over by the fire, the sweet magic of the room glowing around him. He looked over at her through his thick, dark lashes, and the sharp angles of his face softened.

"Thank you." She dipped her chin, warmth heating in her cheeks in a different way than usual.

"I will let you settle in," he said, and strode to the door, brushing past her. He looked over his shoulder and said, "You know, if you miss me, you can always send me a fireletter." Mischief broke over his face, and it complimented him so well. "Just think of me when you drop it in the fire. I know it will be hard not to." He winked and closed the door with a cheeky grin.

"I know how it works!" Emara shouted towards the door, but nothing came back from beyond it.

Loosening her cloak from around her shoulders, she took everything in. The room was warm and toasty, and she was so thankful for that after her waterfall escapade and the chill that came with her reckless actions. She huffed out a laugh and she shook her head as her feet took her exploring. She walked through an archway that divided up her room, and it reminded her of a crescent moon on its side. The first thing she saw was a high-rise, stand-alone tub beside another lit fireplace.

Emara was certain she let out a little squeal of happiness.

Turning back around, she moved through the archway again, this time running her hands along the polished quartz. It was cool against her fingertips, and so smooth. As she felt a little spark of magic in her fingertips, she wondered who had stayed in this room before her. Could it have been someone in the Air bloodline?

Suddenly, there was a small crackling noise, and her attention snapped towards the fireplace in the main section of her room.

A small, folded square hovered above the flames.

It was a letter.

Her feet moved quickly, her heart fluttering. It was her first ever fireletter. As she neared the bewitched flames, she darted her hand over them quickly and snatched it. The letter was warm in her hand, but not the kind of heat you would have expected. It was comfortable, not burning.

Her nimble fingers unwrapped the folds and she straightened out the letter to read the words.

> *Dear Heir of Air,*
> *Miss me yet?*
> *Yours truly,*
> *Your favourite guard.*

Rolling her eyes, she bit back a smile that tried to spread across her face.

Of course, Torin Blacksteel could be just as obnoxious over fireletter as he could be in person.

She reached for the leather satchel that Torin had placed on her bed when he came in. Rummaging through it, she found a small pot of ink the size of a coin and a blue feather quill, both bound to the journal that she had been taking notes in. She ripped a page from the spine. Dipping her quill in the ink, she scribbled:

> Dearest hunter,
> You have only been gone a few minutes.
> Therefore, the answer is no.
> Yours truly,
> Your favourite witch.

An odd thrill ran up her spine. It was the first time

she had ever written it down, and it felt a little more intimidatingly official as she scribbled it with black ink.

Witch.

Looking down, she realised how much neater Torin's writing was in comparison to hers. Every letter was perfectly spaced to the next, every curve of his calligraphy was delicate and precise.

Of course, he has lovely handwriting too, she sneered inwardly.

The black ink on her paper dried, reminding her of the colour of his hair.

Was everything about him now?

Emara rolled her eyes again as she folded the paper neatly. Walking over to the fireplace, she exhaled and closed her eyes as she muttered his name into the fold before dropping it into the flames. It vanished, leaving behind no embers or no ash.

Gone.

Well, she wasn't sure it had gone to Torin, but what could she do now?

She bit into her lip as she sat down on the edge of the bed. A few minutes went by, and still nothing had been delivered to the witchfire.

Damn, she had messed it up already.

With a sigh, she unpacked some of the items from her satchel before a crackling sound was once again heard, and she snapped her head towards the fireplace.

Another letter.

She hurried over to it and plucked it from where it levitated. She really should be more shocked about receiving a levitating letter through fire, but nothing surprised her anymore.

Dearest witch,
How you do hurt one with such bluntness.
Although, I do believe you are not being very truthful. I would miss me if I were you.
Take note, Artem is guarding your door. Play nice.
Yours truly,
Your favourite guard and handsome sparring partner.

She barked out a laugh, ripping another page from her journal before she dabbed her quill in the ink and wrote:

To my least favourite guard,
Overconfidence is not attractive, Torin Blacksteel.
I do wish you would see a healer for that affliction of the ego, it is becoming rather intolerant to all who have to suffer it, and some say it isn't pleasant when it bursts.
Take note, I always play nice.
Yours truly,
Your favourite witch and eager waterfall explorer.

She bit into the tip of her thumb, indecisive if she should rewrite her letter. She wished Cally was here for a little guidance. She would have probably egged her on to write something even more scandalous, so she quickly folded it and threw it into the fire, his name on her lips as she did.

A moment passed, and she headed back to unpacking, looking through everything that needed washing as a laugh rang from a distant room down the corridor—a hearty laugh that made her smile even if it shook the palace.

Another letter lingered above the flames within minutes.

> *Dearest empress-to-be,*
> *Emara Clearwater and play nice don't tend to fit into the same sentence.*
> *But that's what makes you so intriguing, I suppose.*
> *I look forward to seeing you try to play nice later.*
> *Yours truly,*
> *The most stunningly striking, undeniably talented, beloved hunter.*
>
> *P.S. Be sure to let me know when you are up for another exploration, angel. There are plenty of landmarks made for all of the other Gods, not just Uttara. I would be more than obliged to pick up where we left off in the Waterfall.*

Her heart thudded as she read it over and over. In fact, she read them all again, a few times.

A knock pounded on the door and she gasped.

Dropping her letters, she quickly bent down, gathering them, and flung them onto the bed.

"You are too quiet in there," Artem Stryker's voice broke through the solid oak door.

"Maybe I was sleeping," she shouted back, rearranging the letters into a neat pile.

"Or maybe you were up to no good, planning your next attack against my dear Blacksteel friend."

Her cheeks flushed as she walked over to the door and yanked it open. "And what would you do about it if I were to be planning my next attack?"

Shock hit his face, but he quickly recovered himself.

"Probably join forces with you," he said with a smirk as he sauntered into her room.

"Um, excuse me, but it is impolite to enter a lady's room without an invite."

"Yeah, but we are friends, so it's different." Artem's shoulders danced up a little.

"Uh, I don't think that was ever declared."

"Well, it is now. I have just declared it." He gave her a sharp smile before looking around the room. It wasn't long before he spied the letters on the bed and, like a lightning bolt, he shot across the room and had one in his hand.

Emara flew forwards towards him, heart in her mouth, and tore it from his large, tattooed hand. "Don't!"

His grin was irritatingly large. "Are you sending love letters to Blacksteel?" he shouted, eyes wide.

"Shut up!" she hissed, crumpling the note into a small ball. "If you were smart, you would realise that these letters have been *received,* not sent" She curled her fingers around the note tighter.

"Ooohhh, is Blacksteel sending love letters to you?"

She lowered her voice, but still managed to keep it fierce and unfaltering. "Is there any way I can send a fireletter to the prime to request a change in guard?"

"What's the matter? Did Torin's love letters deeply disturb you?" He leaned an arm against the wall, like he was about to listen to her confessions like a true friend.

"No." She shook her head, eyes bulging. "It's a request for your annoying ass to be shipped back to where it came from."

He tutted playfully. "And I was over here thinking we had built a solid friendship, one that our grandchildren would talk about." He walked over and leaned against the unit of the fireplace. "One that would last for a millennia..."

She tilted her head back and let out an exaggerated sigh. "I honestly don't know what planet you hunters live on sometimes."

Another letter appeared in the fireplace.

Artem stole a glance at Emara before he moved like a cobra and snatched it sooner than she could even blink. But this time, the letter came in a different form, with a seal on it, and was not from *the most stunningly striking, undeniably talented, beloved hunter.*

The seal had a large S imprinted in black wax, with every elemental symbol intertwined.

It was from the supreme.

Her heart almost hit her stomach.

"Here." Artem passed it over to her. "I thought it

might have been Blacksteel declaring his love for you, and I couldn't help myself intercept it."

"I noticed." She glared before grabbing the letter from his hand. He gave her a mocking smile and she gave him one back.

Picking the seal from the folded letter, she opened it and read aloud.

> Dear elemental heir of House Air.
>
> Evening dining will take place in the grand ballroom room after sundown.
>
> I look forward to welcoming you to The Amethyst Palace.
>
> Sincerely sealed.
>
> Deleine Orinmore.
>
> Supreme of the Witching Covens.

CHAPTER TWENTY-NINE
EMARA

"**R**eally?" **Artem huffed.** "After sundown? I could eat a diseased cat, I am so hungry. Who makes a palace full of hungry hunters wait until sundown? That's asking for trouble. Absolutely ludicrous."

Emara let out a laugh and agreed. She hadn't really eaten much today at all.

Another knock on the door startled her. She wondered if she would ever get used to such a busy social life.

She went to move towards the door, but Artem wedged in before her.

She huffed at him.

"You can never be too sure," he reminded her. Artem was a warrior again; no playfulness lingered on his features as he made his way to the doorway, the weapon belt around his waist reminding her of his lethal intent if anyone should present themselves a threat.

Opening it, he stepped aside after a moment and

two women dressed in black entered and bowed before her.

"Looks like they are here to get you ready for tonight," Artem said. He smiled charmingly in their direction, and both beamed back at him, their cheeks red. "I don't need to be present for this. I will leave you ladies to it."

He smiled again, and the dark-haired girl almost swooned as he walked past her.

"I will be outside if you need me," he reminded them.

"I am sure I won't need you." She faked a smile and he closed the door.

Emara turned her gaze to the two girls who stood before her.

"I am Lorta," the dark-haired girl said, bowing her head again. "This is Kaydence."

The girl with bright eyes lowered her gaze and bowed deeply. "We will be your help as long as you stay within the palace walls. We are the empress maids of House Air; we belong to your coven."

Your coven.

Emara's chest nearly heaved.

Naya didn't inform her about empress maids!

"It's lovely to meet you." Emara dipped her head too, out of respect for them. "But I am sure, I can manage okay. I don't want to trouble you."

Kaydence spoke this time, her voice high and angelic. "You are not troubling us. It is an honour for us to be at your service for as long as you are here, for as long as you want us."

She was young, probably a few years younger than Emara, and she could tell by her youthful skin and the eagerness in her eyes that this was probably her first time in the role.

Emara's lips thinned into a line, and she took in a deep breath. "It would be my pleasure to have you help me." She smiled, feeling like she had appeared ungrateful. And to be honest, she needed all the help she could get.

The door opened quickly, and ocean blue eyes met her stare. Torin was back in full, clean, silver-grey guard regalia, and it drove her heart into an unimaginable pace. It looked like he had washed up too, his hair still a little damp, and it instantly reminded her of the waterfall. His face was cleanly shaven, and his swords at his back.

Her throat closed in on itself and she stuttered out, "Did you need anything?"

Her maids gawked at him too, waiting for his response.

Torin shook his head, biting into that full lip of his. "No." He smiled, and it practically shattered her heart into a million tiny pieces. "You just hadn't replied to my letter."

"Oh," she said. "Your friend distracted me with his insufferable crusades to annoy me." How she managed such a casual tone when he looked like that, she would never know. "But you will be happy to hear that I played nice."

A wicked grin cut over his white teeth and his dark brows pulled together. "Good girl."

A moment passed between them with unsaid words that she wished were kisses before she cleared her throat. "Torin Blacksteel"—she turned to the girls, who stood like they had just been hypnotised by his dark magic. Kaydence's mouth was practically hanging open —"meet the empress maids from House Air who will be helping me whilst I am here." She put out her hand towards Torin. "Lorta, Kaydence, meet Torin Blacksteel."

They both bowed low, their eyes still wide. She couldn't quite tell how they were feeling. Astonished? Awed?

"It's a pleasure to meet you both," he said with a smoothness that could have charmed the underwear off a woman of faith. Their faces turned scarlet, and she hoped hers never did that around Torin. It would give him too much satisfaction. "I trust you will take good care of the heir to your coven." He nodded in Emara's direction, and his eyes lingered for a second longer than they should have on her face.

"Of course," Lorta blurted.

"It's an honour," Kaydence repeated.

His presence in the room was so staggering, it held every morsel of power and dominance, and for just one second, she saw what he would be like as commander of the Blacksteel Hunting Clan.

Charming, violent, and desirably wicked.

Her breathing halted.

"Well, since everything seems in hand here, I am off to dress down Stryker for having the balls to even touch one of my letters. I will see you at dinner." His eyes dragged from her face with a smile. "It was lovely to meet you, House Air." He gave a small bow before the three women, and then took his leave with a grin.

When the door shut, a gust of cool air broke through the room and she wondered if it was her or her maids.

Lorta turned to her, mouth wide. "Okay, let me get this straight. You have both Artem Stryker *and* Torin Blacksteel as your guards?"

Kaydence was still silently dazed, her eyes a glittering sign of a youthful crush as they still stared at the door.

She couldn't help but roll her eyes. "Yes," Emara breathed out. "And the third in my cluster is Magin Oxhound, in case you want to fawn over him as well."

Lorta gasped. "We heard that House Air had gotten a fantastic cluster to protect our empress, but we had no idea!"

Emara laughed, feeling her cheeks heat once more. "They are seriously not that big of a deal."

Kaydence let out a laugh of her own that was sweet and quick. "You must be the only female in this kingdom not to think so."

Lorta looked over Emara, admiration filling in her eyes. "I have never wanted to be someone more than I want to be you right now," she admitted.

Emara laughed as her head dizzied at the girl's reaction. "Trust me, there are plenty of other girls you could be right now."

Were her trio *that* infamous across Caledorna?

Lorta gathered herself, smoothing out her dress. "Okay, let's get started."

Lorta had hurled questions towards Emara quicker than a hunter could move, as Kaydence measured her hips, bust, and length.

What is your favourite colour?

What is your preferred fabric?

How much tulle is too much tulle?

Black or grey?

Hair up or hair down?

Diamond or emerald?

Who would she rather kiss, Torin or Artem?

Emara had answered every question she could, but she had pushed her lips together at that question.

Tightly.

Of course she knew that answer. She had *done* that answer.

And as she stood in front of the fire being fussed over, a gentle heat caressed her lips where Torin's mouth had been; a reminder of where his hands had been on her skin, where his body had lay on hers.

"P.S. Be sure to let me know when you are up for another exploration, angel. There are plenty of landmarks made for all of the other Gods, not just Uttara. I would be more than obliged to pick up where we left off in the Waterfall."

She drank down the thought. Did she want to go

exploring again? Maybe the question wasn't regarding the 'if's' but the when?

Emara found relief when both girls scurried away to find the *perfect dress* for this evening's dinner, and she threw herself onto the bed and thought about how tonight would go. What would they talk about? What would they eat? How was she supposed to present herself to people?

There was still so much unknown to her of the night ahead; it made her feel nauseous. Distracting her mind, she propped herself onto her elbow and pulled her journal towards her. Lifting her feather quill, Emara ran the feathers over her face a couple of times before she began writing.

Dearest Naya,

I hope this letter finds you well. I have learned the new skill that you very kindly informed me about. I would like to thank you for all the compassion you have shown me since you entered my life. I wish our paths crossing could have been different, something with less destruction, but as someone once told me, we must trust the path the Gods have set for us.

I would take most comfort in you being here with me, but you reminded me that I have a choice. Instead of being afraid, I can embrace everything this new world has to offer. I have a choice to turn my fear into strength, and I will certainly try.

My words on this paper will never express my gratitude for you and your family.

It is my hope to do you and the witching community proud when I ascend—especially my grandmother.

I look forward to seeing you at the winter solstice ball.

Yours truly,
Emara Clearwater.

As she stood, she folded the paper and kissed it once. She said Naya's name as she dropped it into the fire. Just as it disappeared, Lorta and Kaydence came through the door, opened by Magin. He nodded to her and she gave him a thankful grin. He, too, looked freshly cleaned up. Artem had obviously taken his leave to prepare himself for tonight.

Lorta and Kaydence bowed again, struggling to hold all the fabric that was clutched in their hands.

"You really don't need to do that every time you see me," she assured them as she scurried over, trying to help hold up all the gowns that they had brought in.

"I say this with no disrespect, as I appreciate how humble you are," Lorta said, "but it is witching etiquette to bow before someone of higher status than yourself. It's how we have been raised."

"Oh." Emara winced. "I didn't mean to offend you, it's just so new to me." Emara choked over her words. "I wasn't raised with witch etiquette." She looked to the ground. "Only human values."

"We know." Lorta smiled gently. "But that's why we are here to help. Naya sent word to our elder that you would need some looking after."

Emara smiled. Thank Rhiannon for Naya.

"We will keep you right," Kaydence chirped, like it meant more to her than anything in the world.

"Thank you." Emara looked over them both. "I need all the help I can get." She placed a hand on her navel, steadying the waves of nausea that crashed in her belly.

"It will be our pleasure. You will be the empress of our coven soon enough. And then the full kingdom of magic wielders will know that our empress' bloodline has been restored." Lorta's eyes lit up. "The fact that I can assist you in the moments before your ascension gives my life ultimate fulfilment."

Emara smiled at her, a full smile that she made sure reached her eyes too. For these girls, this was their ultimate achievement... For a sickening moment, a deep-rooted guilt ran over Emara's skin, and something like shame scratched into her heart.

Here she was, standing in front of girls who had been primed their whole life to assist an empress, and she had been thrust straight to the top of the hierarchy.

That disgusting swirl in her stomach made its way for her throat and Emara did all she could to cough it down. She didn't deserve this position. She had done nothing to achieve it but be born into the bloodline of her grandmother. A bloodline she hadn't known existed until recently. Maybe the covens wouldn't find her worthy. Maybe her grandmother's visions hadn't found her worthy and that was why she had kept her from the magic community—to save herself from embarrassment, to stop her ascension.

Maybe, just maybe, that was why her grandmother had stepped down as Supreme.

"Which gown catches your eye?" Kaydence asked, having set all the evening dresses on the bed.

A lost tear tracked down Emara's face.

"Miss Clearwater, have we offended you?" one of them asked, but the buzzing in Emara's mind was too much, her vision starting to blur. A bubbling in her stomach and a watering in her mouth had her running to the bathing chamber. She flung herself over the marble sink and hurled up everything in her stomach. She hurled and she spewed, her guts wrenching, her belly riding the tide of her nausea. Hot and cold flashes breached her skin, and dizziness invaded her senses as she panted for breath.

Emara felt a cool flannel at the back of her neck, and someone braided the long strands of her hair back from her face.

"Breathe," Lorta's voice drifted to her ears. "I am no healer, but I can get you something to settle the nervous. That's what this is, right? You are not unwell?"

Emara inhaled as she deflated to the bathroom floor, which was cool to the touch of her burning skin. "Off," she shouted towards the fire, and to her utter astonishment, the fireplace in the bathroom turned to silver smoke, instantly cooling the room.

Emara hadn't known she could do that, she had just listened to her body, and the fire had bowed to her command.

Interesting.

Lorta fixed her black cotton dress around her as she lowered herself to the floor. Her hand came up and her fingers danced just as a cold breeze reached Emara's face, cooling her.

Air. The element of Air.

Emara took a few deep breaths.

Her hazel eyes found Emara's, and another smallish hand reached out to touch her. "Is it the nerves?"

"Yes." Emara whimpered.

Not to mention the shame, the guilt, and the sudden imposter syndrome that almost swept her legs out from underneath her.

Lorta's features softened. "Don't be scared. The Gods have picked you for a reason, Emara Clearwater, and they don't just give anyone the power to be an empress. Don't for one second doubt that you are not worthy of your title. It is in your blood. The Gods choose their bloodlines wisely."

And somehow, just after mere hours, Emara had found herself a new friend to help navigate this mess of a world. She reached out and placed a shaky hand on

Lorta's arm as her cooling air still drifted over her face and neck. "Thank you so much."

I have a choice to turn my fear into strength, and I will certainly try.

For Lorta, for Kaydence, and for anyone else who would look to her as their empress, she would find the strength.

CHAPTER THIRTY
EMARA

The grey gown that she had picked out hugged her body tightly, pulling at her curves, cinching in her waist. The dresses that the maids had picked out were elegant in a way that was both stunning and proper for someone who bore a title.

They were exactly the opposite of what Cally would have dressed her in, but going into tonight, she didn't exactly have room to feel more self-conscious than she already did.

So safe and simple were good.

Kaydence had fixed her hair atop her head in barrel curls, and she must have poked a thousand pins into her scalp trying to hold the mass of midnight-black hair in place. By the time they were done, Emara looked ready to play the role of *empress*.

Her cheeks glistened and her eyes were a darker shade of coal. Her lips were tinted like cherries, and Lorta had clasped dangling smoky diamonds to her lobes. When she looked at herself in the mirror, Emara could see a small glow shining through her darkness again.

Someone knocked twice, and she could hear deep laughter in the hallway from her guards.

"Enter," she said as her heart missed a beat.

This time, all three of her hunters strolled into her chambers, Torin leading the way. His eyes caught sight of her, and it looked like air had gotten lodged in his throat. For just a moment, it felt like only them in the room with the way his icy glare turned to a warm pool of hot springs. His eyes glittered with sinful magic before he gathered himself and squared off his shoulders.

Artem let out a small whistle from behind him. "You scrub up well, my feisty little friend."

"Thank you."

"I almost didn't recognise you with the leaves out of your hair and dry clothes on." Artem gave her a friendly wink.

Her cheeks beamed bright, and she hoped her rouge would hide it. "I can see you have at least bathed." She threw a whole lot of sass towards the tattooed warrior, who barked out a laugh. "Although, I do take comfort that it is not my bath water that you used this time."

Torin smirked, his eyes not leaving Emara's, and Magin bit into his lip, revealing his subdued amusement.

"What's wrong with a little bath water shared among friends?" Artem chuckled deeply.

She heard her maids have a chuckle too.

"You are truly disgusting," she murmured with a laugh.

Torin stood straight, his hands behind his back, puffing out his strong chest. His favourite weapons lay strapped to his back and the little pin that represented her coven's name glinted on his chest. "Enough laughter. It's time we headed to the great ballroom," he announced. "Before I kill Artem for whining about how hungry he is."

The formalities of Torin's duty had begun.

"That's if I don't die of starvation first."

The girls laughed again, and a smug grin found Artem's face as they stroked his ego.

As Emara reached just in front of Torin, he lowered his lashes, taking in every inch of her. His gaze made her very aware of the most feminine parts of herself and she fought the tingling heat spreading low.

"You look remarkable," he whispered as he held out his arm for her to take. She wasn't even sure if he was supposed to do that.

A little gasping noise from Kaydence confirmed he wasn't.

She ignored everyone's glare and placed a hand atop his arm.

"Are you ready?" he asked, loud enough for everyone to hear this time.

"As much as I will ever be." She swallowed a breath that was meant to exhale from her body.

"I am here. If you need me, just signal." His stunning eyes locked on hers sincerely.

She nodded, not even sure she was breathing as they walked into the hallway.

She pulled her gaze from his and tried focusing on the steps of the men who walked in front of her.

After a while, they came to a large set of doors at the end of the corridor, and she had to tilt her head back to see where they ended. Was everything in this palace gigantic?

Torin lowered his arm, and she slid her curled fingers from where they had been wrapped around his arm to her navel.

"Signal if you need me," he said as they waited to enter into the grand ball of the Amethyst Palace.

"What kind of signal?" Emara looked up at him, her mouth going dry.

"You could blow me a kiss." A dimple appeared in his cheek.

"Not going to happen."

His eyebrows danced up in delight. "How about you say..." He paused for a moment before his eyes flashed with carnal fun. "How about you say *waterfall?*"

She rolled her lips in the effort not to laugh. Something about being with Torin in this moment took a weight off her chest. Maybe it was because he was doing everything in his power to distract her from the nerves that threatened to flatten her.

She appreciated it.

"Waterfall it is, then," she agreed, swallowing any remaining trepidation.

A second later, the ballroom doors opened like a gust of wind had blown them ajar. Light chatter filled the room and a scent of sage and baked meats swirled to her nose. A long table that striped down the middle of the room displayed candles, floral arrangements, wine, and food of every kind. She heard a sweet sigh of relief from Artem, who had already started walking faster to take his seat. Looking around, she saw both men and women, none of which had yet sat down. They lingered around, mingling with each other. Everything seemed rather sophisticated.

Out of the corner of her eye, she spotted Marcus Coldwell in his guard uniform. Knowing that Marcus stood beside the soon-to-be Empress of Earth, she suspected that Gideon wouldn't be far. Marcus caught sight of them arriving and paused his conversation with the almost empress.

"Blacksteel." He grinned from ear to ear. "It's so good to see that the cold journey didn't steal you from us."

"Mother Nature doesn't have the guts to take me, Marcus. No one has." Torin winked and bowed. Under different circumstances, they would have greeted each other with something less formal.

"I think someone has the guts." Marcus smiled in Emara's direction. "Speaking of that someone—Miss Clearwater." He took her hand like he always did, his kind eyes warming, standing out from his professional mask only for a second. She politely bowed her head to him. "It's a pleasure, as always."

"You too, Marcus."

His eyes coasted over her team of hunters. "It's good to see you are keeping all three of these rogues in line."

"Magin is by far the best behaved." She laughed,

looking towards Magin. He smiled back at her. Artem threw her a scowl.

"May I please beg your pardon?" Marcus said abruptly as the witch of House Earth approached. "Emara, please meet Sybil Lockhart."

The girl smiled and bowed her head almost shyly. Her gown was a unique brassy colour that clashed against her pale skin, yet it suited her slender frame. Beautiful green and white flowers weaved through her braided hair, that burned bright red like autumnal leaves and she, too, had a painted lip, hers of soft rose. Her face was plain and sprinkled with freckles, her features neat, other than her vast eyes. She was pretty, with the kind of beauty that normally went unnoticed.

"It's lovely to officially meet you," Sybil said.

When she spoke, her voice reminded Emara of someone older than she looked. "Likewise," Emara said as she took a bow of her own.

After the others were acquainted with the Earth Witch, the hunters struck up a conversation of their own, about how the cold had reminded them of the Selection, where they had camped, and what route they had taken. Sybil had come from a village that neighboured the Solden Coal Mines.

Emara's heart had pinched and scrambled at the mention of that name. And maybe, just maybe, her fingertips had warmed.

"I hope you are not as nervous as I am to be here," Sybil admitted, the corners of her thin lips tilted downwards.

Emara found some sweet relief in what she had said

—shameful, yet sweet. "I didn't think it was possible for anyone to be more nervous than I am," she whispered back to the Earth Witch. "If I am honest, I am unsure as to what I am doing at all."

"If it makes you feel any better, neither do I." She let out a nervous giggle. "No amount of witchcraft or training could have prepared me for this," she admitted. "It was never supposed to be me standing here."

Emara's eyes darted to the girl's face, hopelessness in her eyes. She paused to allow the soon-to-be Empress of Earth time to speak.

"My sister only ascended here three years ago," she finally said. "It should be her standing with you all tonight."

A horrible sinking feeling worked its way from Emara's heart through her body. Her sister had been the Empress of Earth who had been hunted at her home and slaughtered. An overwhelming level of respect washed through Emara for the girl standing before her. Sybil's sister had been murdered just days ago and here she was, standing strong for her coven and stepping in for her House. Emara supposed it was a different kind of bravery than she was used to with the hunters. Instantaneous admiration broke through her heart.

Emara whispered, "I am so terribly sorry for your loss" as her throat clogged in connection to her own grief.

"Thank you," Sybil said as her lips trembled slightly.

Emara added, "For what I know, the witches in your House thought very highly of your sister. She was well respected and loved."

She had heard of how well Naya regarded her. Emara had taken in the devastation on her face when the news of her death had come through.

"I have big shoes to fill." Sybil's voice shook, and the statement allowed a shiver to run through Emara's spine.

So did Emara.

With one look at Sybil's face, Emara knew she wasn't alone.

A clinking sound pulled them from their conversation, and Emara turned her head to see a brown-haired woman standing between the large doors of the great ballroom. She was smaller than she remembered, but she held a regal grace that one could only ever dream of.

It was the Supreme.

Deleine Orinmore, as her letter had stated.

She entered the room, her personal guards flanking behind her, and a low hush silenced everyone as they watched her glide across the polished quartz floor until she reached the top of the table. Enchanted beacons bloomed their flames higher as she stood at the first seat the table offered, where a queen would sit without her king.

"Good evening." Her eyes scanned over her guests, sharp and penetrating. "I do hope I didn't keep you waiting long." Her lips turned slowly into a heart-stopping smile.

Something about that made Emara feel like Deleine enjoyed the thought of everyone waiting on her arrival.

"Please"—she gestured to the seats—"sit."

Her voice drifted out enchantingly, and the crowd

dispersed at her command. Walking over to the chairs that were dressed in braided violet and ornate silks, Emara felt a gentle hand on her shoulder. She turned to face sparkling green eyes.

Her chest seized up as she took in Gideon Blacksteel standing before her.

"Gideon." She smiled, a little breathless.

"I would have caught you sooner," he said, his eyes twinkling. "But I was catching up with Kellen." He gestured over to where Kellen stood. "One of our men was attacked on their journey here from Tolsah Bay." He lowered his head. "He didn't make it, so Kellen was drafted in for the Empress of Water."

"That's awful," she replied, remembering exactly the moment they had been attacked by demons on their journey too. The spraying of blood. The hunger for nothing but death. Her dagger that went through rotting flesh. Magin's shoulder.

It could have been any of them that fell to the Dark Army.

"Did you know him well?" She swallowed.

"He was in my Selection year, but I didn't know him well." Gideon looked over at Kellen again with apprehension on his face. "I don't know if he's ready for this commitment."

"I know the feeling," she said without thinking.

He scanned her face for a long moment as if exploring her mind, reaching out to see if there was anything he could pick up on. Concern flashed in his eyes, like he wanted to say something.

Instead, he nodded. "You are going to be just fine,

Emara." He placed a hand on her shoulder that felt heavier than it was. "I promise you that."

A long minute passed between them before he spoke again, "I better take my seat beside Sybil." He put his hands behind his back, making him look taller than before.

"Yes." She took a breath, looking over at the Earth Witch who had taken her seat at the table.

He smiled at her before slowly turning on his heels.

"Wait!" Emara yelled, a little louder than she anticipated, and his head flew 'round, shifting his messy brown hair. "I am glad it wasn't you," she blurted out as she took a step forward. "I am so shamefully glad it wasn't you who was the guard that didn't make it here." She looked down for a second before meeting his gaze again. "I don't know what I would have done, how I would have felt." She rubbed her hands together nervously. "I feel guilty even saying it, but I am just so thankful it wasn't you."

The reaction on his face allowed her to believe that he was stunned, but thankful for her words.

"Me too," he said, his eyes shining with gratitude before he stepped sideways. "It's good to see you again." He smiled, and then he was gone.

With her heart in her mouth, Emara made her way over to the seat between Magin and Artem. Torin was speaking with another guard, still standing.

As she sat, she realised Artem was already tucking into warm rolls and salty butter.

"I am pretty sure we are supposed to wait." She eyed

him. It didn't take knowing witching traditions to distinguish that.

"Who died and made you the Supreme?" he sparred with her whilst tearing into bread like an animal possessed.

"That would need to be the Supreme," Magin chimed in dryly. Artem grinned at his brother too wildly.

"Gods spare me." Emara sighed.

Just at that, Torin sat across the table from her. Kellen took a seat on his right, and Gideon on his left. For a minute, her heart stopped. The three Blacksteel brothers, so similar, yet uniquely individual.

She smiled courteously at Kellen, and he gave a polite nod in return.

"Are you going to leave any of the food for anyone else, brother?" Torin asked Artem. Everyone around them laughed.

"If you are not fast, you are last," Artem joked, picking up a leg of lamb from a silver tray. "You should know that, Blacksteel." He took a massive chunk out of the meat.

"Animal," Emara murmured.

"Let's not pretend you are faster than me, Stryker," Torin argued. "I am faster and stronger. Even on a bad day." Torin took a chalice of wine and sipped it. His cocky frontage was now fully back in place.

Rolling her eyes, Emara sneered, finding herself a wine too.

She was going to need it.

"I think we should see about that later, Blacksteel."

Artem laughed in a dangerously taunting way. "I have been desperate to spar with your cocky ass since fate brought us back together."

Torin's features angled themselves with primal intent and he relaxed into his chair. "Bring it on, Stryker."

"Must you hunters make everything a competition?" Emara asked after swallowing a rather large mouthful of wine.

"Yes," all of them said at the same time—even Kellen. But his eyes glittered with mockery.

"Bloody hunters" she cursed out loud.

"You love us," Artem declared confidently, ripping yet another piece of meat from the bone.

Emara made a face that suggested otherwise.

"Can I have your attention, please?" The Supreme's voice rang through the room and her bejewelled gown sparkled in the candlelight as she stood. "I would like to welcome you all here, to the Amethyst Palace." She raised her goblet. "My home."

Everyone at the table raised theirs too, uttering *Blessed be,* saluting the Queen of Witches.

"It has been many a moon since all five witching covens ascended together." Her magical eyes scanned the room, piercing each face as they moved. "Our kingdom has not seen a time like this since the ancients walked these very floors."

A shiver ran over Emara's body.

"May this be a monumental occasion for you, Kerrix Bellfield, of House Spirit." The grand witch gestured to a girl with white hair flowing like a river down her back.

"And for you, Lillian Silverholme, of House Water." Her goblet moved in the direction of where the Empress of Water sat, surrounded by her guards, her hair like wavy, soft sand around her chin.

"For Rya Otterburn, of House Fire."

The girl that represented fire raised her chin up high and nodded, her dark hair spiked against the candlelight behind her. She was ready to take on the title, Emara could see it in her eyes.

The Supreme turned. "To Earth, and our Sybil Lockhart."

Sybil's face stained as red as her hair, but she smiled politely and raised her glass.

"And"—the Supreme's eyes rested on Emara—"to our lost bloodline of Air, Emara Clearwater. Welcome home."

Spirit, Water, Fire, Earth, and Air.

"All representations of the Witching Houses are here tonight, and what a fair representation it is that sits before me." The Supreme lifted her chin and her gaze locked the hunters. "Have a drink with them—to them."

Emara forced a smile onto her face to hide her tremble as she raised a glass with the others.

"May your reign as empress of your coven be longer than the last." The Supreme raised her goblet again and took a drink.

Emara swallowed down a bitter taste in her mouth after the toast and wondered if it was the wine or the sentiment of the toast. Her pulse throbbed in her neck. She reached for a decanter that sat close to Magin and poured into her glass. She sunk the wine in one go, pushing down a darkness that urged in her stomach.

"Please, eat, my friends," Deleine invited. She didn't need to tell Artem Stryker twice.

Conversations from all of the covens flowed, and voices pinged from one end of the table to the next. A blue and green gaze caught Emara's attention. She threw a polite smile towards Kellen again, but this time, he didn't return it. Emara knew she had to have a conversation, one that she had been avoiding, and she would need to have it soon. She had to let him know that his secret was safe with her.

CHAPTER
THIRTY-ONE
EMARA

After a few chalices full of that delicious mulberry wine, Emara had finally plucked up enough courage to approach Kellen Blacksteel. He was standing in a quiet corner of the ballroom, away from the core crowd who were mingling after the Supreme had excused herself from the dinner. She had been stopped by both Rya Otterburn and Kerrix Bellfield to engage in a polite conversation about their Houses.

As she managed to slip away without another empress catching her, Kellen spied her walking towards him. The youngest Blacksteel brother swallowed, straightening his spine at her approach, placing his hands behind his back.

"Emara." Kellen's voice was fluffier than his brother's, higher. His unusual eyes bore right through her skin, to her very soul.

"Kellen." She mirrored him.

"You seem to look somewhat at home within the

walls of the Amethyst Palace," he complimented with a small bow.

"Oh, I don't know about that." She came to a stop in front of him. She would have to get used to the lush train that trailed behind her. "I think I am more suited to be under the roof of the tower. I am not used to settings fit for the hierarchy of the magic world."

"You talk like you are not one of them." He lifted one dark eyebrow, making his boyish face look more like the warrior he was.

He was sharp, and she didn't expect it.

She wrinkled her nose. "And I hope for that never to change."

His forehead creased at her response and a corner of his mouth tugged upwards. He released his knotted hands from behind his back, relaxing his shoulders. "I hope that doesn't change either."

She opened her mouth to speak, unsure of how she would approach what she saw at the Uplift. To assure him, regardless of what had happened, that it was none of her business. She wanted to reassure him that she would not breathe a single word of what she had witnessed to anyone, not even to the moon or the Gods.

Kellen's eyes lifted to the sound of footsteps from behind her, but Emara didn't turn to see who it was. She focused on Kellen's face, which was twisting with fear and disdain.

"The guard regalia suits you, little brother." Torin's deep but lyrical voice floated past her.

Kellen's face lit up at the compliment, but a second later, his visage went still, then pale, then flushed.

Emara turned to see that two hunters flanked Torin, Artem and a hunter she had only seen from afar a few times.

Artem turned to Emara. "Mrs Blacksteel." He beamed from ear to ear.

Emara felt her fist twitching at her side and it almost became unbearable not to punch him. But she couldn't, not here.

"You do know she could crush your windpipe with the flick of her wrist, don't you?" Torin taunted.

"Let's hope she never learns that trick," Artem jested, his eyebrows dancing.

"I will make sure that it's the first *trick* on my list," Emara sneered.

Artem ignored her threat. "Emara, please meet my younger, devilishly handsome brother." He gestured to the other male. "Arlo, of Clan Stryker."

"It's a pleasure to meet you, Arlo." She slipped him a smile.

"The pleasure is all mine," the hunter said, his dark eyes dazzling like an intense storm that you could see from the coastline, where lightning met the sea. His reddish-brown hair was long, unlike his brother's, adding more tones of auburn and russet through it. There was no sign of any tattoos that Emara could see, but as he stood there, something clicked into place.

She held in a gasp.

Arlo flicked his eyes over to Kellen for only a second, but that was all it took to confirm what lay between them. It was discreet, but for a moment more than it should have, a fiery desire revealed itself. Emara assumed Kellen knew better than to return his stare, as he kept his enchanting eyes on her. She wished with every part of herself that Kellen knew what thoughts lay in her heart.

If he wanted that night to be lost in the chaos, then it was.

Emara cleared her throat, cutting through the tension the only way she knew how. "I am sure you are the more pleasant Stryker."

Artem placed a hand over his heart, and his silver nose ring caught the candlelight. "Do you actually plan on taking this friendship seriously? It can't be one-sided, you know."

"Oh, that's *exactly* how I intend for it to be." She smirked, letting him know that his teasing wasn't going to best her anymore.

"Okay." Torin held a hand up, patting his best friend on the shoulder. "I think I should take Emara back to her room before there is a full-scale riot on our hands. Stryker, find Magin and let him know where we are. There is no need to follow, I will take up the post for tonight. You guys get some rest."

Emara's heart quickened at the sound of that, the temptation fizzing through her blood.

Torin held out an arm and Emara took it. "It was a pleasure to see you all." She motioned to the line of hunters who were staring at Torin like he had just done something out of character.

Well, maybe he had.

They all bowed, and she returned the gesture gently.

As they started walking, Artem shouted from behind, "Remember our deal, Blacksteel. Me and you, tomorrow. Sunrise."

Without looking back, Torin smirked. "Like I would miss it."

Walking over the threshold of the great ballroom, Emara released a sigh that sent Torin turning to face her.

"Relieved to have made it through your first ever community dinner?"

"I don't think 'relieved' even touches how I am feeling right now."

"They won't all be as daunting as this one."

They only managed to get around ten more steps in before Torin whisked her into an alcove in the passageway, curtained by heavy material used to cover the stained-glass windows during summer.

"What are you doing?" she squealed.

Shock and delight thrummed in her veins as his mouth landed on hers. It was warmth, darkness, light, and savageness all wrapped into one.

"Are you mad?" she breathed against his mouth.

"Absolutely," he answered, his large hands grasping at anything he could. Her hair, her jaw, the material of her dress...

"Someone could see us."

He let out a small laugh against her open mouth that told her he didn't care.

Her stomach fluttered.

Emara returned his fire then, clasping her hands at the nape of his strong neck, and that's all he needed to ensure that she wanted his wild mouth on hers. This time, the kiss was sharp and daring, and it sent a wave of dizziness over her. He wrapped a large hand around the nape of her neck, pinning his body even closer to hers as he enclosed her against the cool stone of the alcove.

He hadn't kissed her since the waterfall, and she hadn't realised how much she had needed it—the taste of him. A sense of earth-shattering desire flooded through every part of who she was, and her lips parted, opening further for him, to take...take everything. The effect of his kiss utterly consumed not only her mouth, but every inch of her body, and the palace around them faded away as his tongue brushed against hers. He had just gifted her a kiss that could never be removed from her lips.

Finally, he broke free, "I have wanted to do that since I saw you in that dress."

"Then why didn't you?" Her heavy breathing affected her efforts to speak, or even think.

"Because we wouldn't have made it to the dinner at all if I had, and the whole palace would talk of the empress who hadn't arrived to dine with the Supreme." He ran his teeth along her jawline, still angling her neck with his hand. A small moan parted her lips. "That sound," he rasped, "has been running through my mind ever since the cavern. Did you know how tortuous it was to be on a horse with you the whole journey here, knowing exactly what my name sounds like on your lips when I make you come?"

Emara's mouth went dry. She inhaled, stomach pulling in. "That sounds like a terrible problem to have."

Her heart banged in her chest, and she cursed to herself at how much he affected her. "However, you are a trained and skilled hunter, I am sure you have endured worse." She swallowed, her toes curling.

His blue eyes dilated in a way that made Emara forget to breathe. "You see, I don't reckon there is a greater torture than sitting behind you, with your body so close to me, and not getting to feel you against me the way I want."

She giggled, trying not to let another moan escape her mouth as he leaned forward and nuzzled into the soft spot in her neck, teasing her skin with his teeth.

"I would have let you," she whispered to him in confession, her hands pressed against the coolness of the alcove to ground her. "Kiss me. Even if that meant we wouldn't have made it to the ballroom."

Suddenly, he stopped and pulled back from her.

A lazy smile appeared. "And I would have savoured every last minute of it."

He spoke with a slow huskiness that made her toes curl again, and she sent up a prayer to the Gods to give her more willpower than she had now.

A cough interrupted their secret moment. "This looks cosy."

Emara's heart leaped, and she turned to see the Supreme's guards standing before her. Torin didn't react the way she thought he would, by pulling back and acting like nothing had happened. Instead, he kissed Emara's temple and turned slowly towards his brethren from another clan. "It was."

A knot of dread tightened in her stomach at his tone,

and as she looked over his tensed back, she could feel the air pull from her own lungs. She couldn't see much of Torin's facial expression, but she knew it would have turned stone-like, masked, a warrior again.

"Are you not supposed to be *guarding* the Supreme's witches instead of kissing them in dark nooks of the palace?" One of the guards' eyes didn't falter from Torin's face; the other's looked over her, his eyes roaming to places she didn't want.

Emara straightened her spine.

Torin placed his hands behind his back and Emara's eyes went straight to his fingers that were straining white, fisted. "With all due respect, she's not *your Supreme's* witch." His sour tone made Emara take a step forward. "She's not anyone's property."

The guard's coldness snuck through even when he spoke, his beady eyes still on her. "She is her coven's witch. She works for our queen."

Torin sucked in a breath before a dangerous smirk revealed itself. "Your queen?" he asked. "Since when did hunters have a queen? You may work for the Supreme, guard her, but she is not your faction leader. It would do you good to remember that." He winked towards the heavily armed guards.

One of the guards growled.

"Let's just go, Torin." Emara reached out and tugged on the arm of her protector.

Torin didn't move. He didn't move his gaze from the two guards standing before him.

Finally, the second guard broke away from the stare

off to glance at Emara. "The Supreme would like to see you at once."

"What for?" Torin questioned.

"It is none of your business, Blacksteel," the cold one jeered. "It would do you good to remember that."

CHAPTER THIRTY-TWO
EMARA

The watchtower had been an age away from the alcove, with flights and flights of steep steps that made Emara's eyes strain in concentration to be careful. Her lungs tight in her chest, she panted for breath as she climbed her way to the top, where the Supreme had requested to see her. Torin stalked up the steps in front, and she could already feel the heat from his rage radiating from him.

That was never a good start.

The Supreme's guards, who had named themselves Easton and Silas, opened the locked door to the watchtower to reveal that people were already congregated there.

All empresses and one guard each.

The Supreme sat against a lilac chaise longue that angled itself so that she could stare out the floor-to-ceiling windows. Emara could see the rocky mountain terrain cuddled around the palace, like protectors of their own, but the darkness of the night was sweeping in, and stealing the scenery.

All of the eyes from Houses Earth, Spirit, Water, and Fire followed Emara as they watched her enter the large room with Torin. He straightened, becoming more statuesque, and she saw the look in the Supreme's eyes as she glanced at Torin the way all women did.

Deleine stood gracefully, looking over the people in front of her. "I can feel the power of you all, even as you stand before me." Her voice had a hint of delight. "I can see it now as I look in all of your eyes, and it is wonderful. We will be strong."

Emara wondered what colour swirled in her irises tonight as she looked upon her Supreme. A darkness would swirl there, she presumed.

"I wish that you all were standing in front of me due to different circumstances, but I am unable to change the past or the trauma that we have suffered."

Emara looked over to her right, where the Empress of Earth stood with Marcus Coldwell, her eyes filling with sadness.

"As you are all going to be coven empresses, I need to trust that all of you will take care of my witches. And not only that, but have faith in me as your leader."

"We have faith," a voice said, strong and dominant. It was the voice of Rya Otterburn. Her impressive demeanour represented how majestic and proud House Fire could be. She stood like a lioness beside her guard, her shoulders back.

The Supreme's glance flickered Rya's way, and then over the others, who hadn't been brave enough to say anything to their leader. Her lips parted, and her chin dipped in a way that showed all angles of her skeletal collarbone. "I need to protect my faction, and that means I can have no more casualties. I need to know that I have the correct witch supporting her elemental house. I need to know that you are willing to let me guide our covens through this treacherous time. We are at war, and we need to stand as one." She took a small breath. "I trust that every witch who stands before me has no other dominant element that should invalidate their crown. It will weaken us. You all know that it is forbidden to take the title of empress in the eyes of Rhiannon if another element should exceed the one that you will bow before. If that is the case, you need to make yourself known to me now."

Emara thought of her mother. And how, although air had been in bloodline, fire was dominant in her magic. But she had seen the desolate spark of fear in her grandmother's eyes as it had turned to rage, and then fear again, as she shut down Sereia's claims of what she bore. Theodora had silenced them.

It was dangerous for a witch to claim another witch's crown unless she was going to take the ultimate crown. Even Torin had confirmed that.

A broken breath stammered through her chest, but she did not move. She didn't dare.

"At the moment, I bare all elements," Rya said, lifting her chin so that every empress in the room watched her in envy. "But nothing is greater than my fire."

She had every element in her arsenal.

The Supreme nodded. "I appreciate your integrity."

A voice floated from the Empress of Water that was

both lulling and vigorous. "I am strong with healing magic, and I dabble in some spirit work, but my waves could destroy an entire city; therefore, I am confident to declare water as my only House."

Emara watched as the water witch spoke casually, as if unaware that wiping out an entire city with a wave of her magic was unnatural. She had no idea how powerful she was.

"I could raise a spirit army on the Otherside," Kerrix Bellfield announced, with a smirk on her purple-painted lips. "I have no interest in exploring any other element. I like living with the dead. I am happy conferring with the wise ancestors of the past; there is no need for me to practise anything else."

A cackle blew through the room like a draft of wind, and Emara could feel it around her. It was Kerrix tapping into her magic and pulling through ancestors from the Otherside. Gusts of energy lifted strands of Emara's hair into the air, and she felt the temperature of the room drop. Chills ran up her spine the same way they had when she had first met Melione—the spirit witch—in the Huntswood markets. Her magic began ringing in her bones. The candles flickered, and there were a few murmurs from the guards, but the Supreme nodded in Kerrix's direction, acknowledging her claims.

Sybil spoke next, a shake in her voice confirming how anxious she was. "I am a healer through and through. I could place my palm into the ground, frozen to death by winter, and in seconds, the gardens around me could be blooming with life as if it were spring. I have a little water magic, and my element for air is strong. But not like my will to empower earth or nurse the broken bones of a warrior."

Emara was stunned at how well Sybil had warmed into her conversation, and she could see that there was a little bit of her who was still with her sorrow to be strong in front of the other covens.

All gazes turned to Emara.

"And you." The Supreme's starlit eyes were upon her face.

Emara tried her hardest to hide her tremor, her fear, but couldn't. She stuttered.

"Miss Clearwater has shown signs of healing, and signs of fire, but I have seen first-hand her power in air magic. Although she is a new witch, that is where her strength lies." Torin's proud chin lifted, and he didn't take his eyes from the Supreme. "Air magic is in her bloodline."

The Supreme's eyebrow lifted, and Emara presumed that it was in shock at Torin stepping in to speak. "She is not a new witch; she has been a witch since she was born." Her eyes ran over Torin, and then to Emara.

Emara noticed the others shifting uncomfortably.

"I hear you have quite the temper when provoked." Deleine Orinmore tapped a foot against the marble floor, and a terrible feeling devoured Emara from the inside out. Torin shifted beside her as if sensing it. But the Supreme continued, "Even though you are set in destiny to ascend as the Empress of Air, a little birdy told me rumours have come from the Uplift that.

Rumours that you have a strength in the gift of fire, and it came to you in your time of need, strong and powerful, like the Gods had willed it themselves." Something serious flashed in her eyes, making Emara's lungs squeeze. "Should I know of any claims that you may have to the House of Fire?"

She could feel the stare from Rya's darkened eyes on her face, all of them looking upon her, awaiting her response.

"I don't," she choked out. "I have no claims to the fire crown. I only used fire magic at the Uplift because I knew it would protect me."

That was a lie. Fire had come to her fingertips as naturally as air had. But the lie hadn't sounded like one as it floated through the room to where the Queen of the Witches nodded in response.

Torin admitted, "She is an untrained witch, and only used fire to protect herself from a threat that had worked with the Dark Army. As you know, it was vital for her to use what she could at that time. A member of the elite faction had provoked her, and, in her temper, fire emerged instead of air. It was a natural reaction to her distress at the time. I have witnessed her talent in air, and I, as well as my mother—Naya Blacksteel, Commanding wife of Viktir Blacksteel, and healer of House Earth—can confirm that her dominant power is air."

So Torin would lie for her too. He knew that when he had provoked her in training, air had whizzed around them like a tornado, but he had seen the flames of her wrath too, and had questioned them on their trip here. As a little murmur found its way through the silence, Emara found Torin's gaze, and she hoped he could see the thankfulness in her eyes.

The Supreme spoke with a smile. "That's quite all right. We know how it feels for our magic to seem untrained, especially in times of fear."

"How can I be sure that she will not come for my crown of fire?" Rya Otterburn's loud voice boomed through the room, and everyone turned to face her. "If what you say of her power in fire magic is true, how can we be sure that she will not exceed my magic for the crown and title?"

Emara swallowed, and as Torin tensed, about to jump to her defence, she got in there first. "Because I have no interest in taking your crown, Rya. I think it's best I should turn my focus to my own, and learn how to handle that before worrying about any other crown."

Rya gave off a look that told Emara that she wasn't sold, but what Emara had said was the truth, and she held her gaze boldly, unwilling to back down. She wasn't interested in two elemental crowns. She was barely getting to grips with one.

"That sounds like a clever plan indeed, Emara Clear-water." Deleine's shoulders relaxed, and it seemed to elongate her neck.

Emara nodded graciously at her acceptance. "I promise to dedicate everything I can to learning how to control whatever Rhiannon has willed me to have. But air is where my focus and heart lies. I am not interested in anything else. My grandmother was Theodora Clearwater of House Air, and my intentions are to make her proud as I serve the House of my bloodline."

Torin finally nodded beside her, and Emara took a breath. She had said the right thing.

"Perhaps if you reach out to the girls of each element, they will help you work on controlling your magic." Deleine glided like a swan, across the glassy backdrop of the night, moving towards where Emara stood. "It is interesting, though; you are not what I had imagined. Your mother was a petite woman, from what I remember. Sereia...very delicate."

Emara's heart stopped at the mention of her mother's name.

"But you..." The Supreme stood like a Goddess clad in gold. "You're not so small, are you?"

Something punched so hard into Emara's gut that she wished it had been her face to receive the blow. It would have been easier to handle. A burning in her blood made her want to lash out, but she tugged on the leash that was hanging onto her self-control by a thread.

"You are larger than I thought you would be." Deleine smiled like she hadn't just cut an insult across Emara's heart. "When I heard of the girl who had risen like a phoenix from the ashes of her mother's death, I certainly didn't picture you."

A treacherous silence came from the other empresses in the room, like they were afraid to even look in the direction of where the Supreme stood, face to face with the heir of Air.

"I didn't know my mother," Emara exclaimed, trying to keep her hands at her sides. But her nails dug a grave in her skin. "But as you've gathered, I am not so delicate."

"That's good." The Supreme nodded, a twinkle in her eyes. "We don't need any more *delicate* witches. They haven't fared too well recently."

A dangerous snarl came from Torin's throat, and it had her gaze lifting to look at him.

A dirty laugh cut from Deleine's throat. "Torin Blacksteel." She smiled, and a flame lit in her eyes, her voice light. "I have heard you can be a very disobedient little hunter. Rumour has it that you like to bite. You are a Warrior of Thorin, and it shows." Her eyes roamed over his body and face as the compliment of his physique settled in the air. "Maybe if you were a little better behaved, we could have gotten to know each other." The beading of her gold gown made a scratching sound as it traced the floor, and she stopped just before him. "That could have been a match made for the Gods. Powerful." She raised her hand and flames in the shapes of two arrows crossed over a sword, danced in her palm, then formed the shape of his crest before snuffing out.

He smiled at her, and it was a smile so dreadful that Emara barely recognised him. "I don't like being obedient."

She giggled. "Neither do I. Maybe we have that in common, you and I." She seemed to enjoy seeing the feral beast that lay underneath his guard exterior. "Maybe I wouldn't want you to behave after all, Torin, of Clan Blacksteel." The tip of her tongue reached the roof of her mouth as a seductive smile tightened the small wrinkles around her lips. "I have heard about the relentless destruction you cause in the wake of a battle, and I am always in need of a new ally. Perhaps I should put my offer in writing to your commander to see us bonded. After all, two strengths can only make a unit stronger."

Emara's heart burned in a way that she didn't understand.

"Thank you for your offer." He paused as he let a wickedness darken in his gaze. "But I am afraid I will have to pass. I am already in ties with someone of a much *younger age* than yourself. I believe she is suited to me in ways that you are not. Like you said before, *she* is not so delicate, and I think that is marvellous."

Emara heard everyone suck in a gasp at Torin taking a jab at the Supreme's age.

Her face turned to acid before Deleine gave one flick of her wrists, and the huge doors opened behind them. Her guards unsheathed their swords, but she put up a hand and let out a low laugh, pretending to brush it off.

In that moment, Emara saw her Supreme toy with the idea of killing Torin Blacksteel where he stood as rejection filled the room with bitterness. It was strange to see two people who she assumed rarely faced rejection stand face to face. The fear that baulked in Emara's heart was unnerving and frantic.

Deleine's lip curled over her teeth before she gathered herself and took a step back, placing a mask over her enraged face. "You really should get my witch back to her room before we are another guard down. That would be unfortunate, a day before she ascended, would you not agree?" The Supreme laughed, but no one joined her.

Not as Torin Blacksteel's glare threatened to shatter the mountains around them.

CHAPTER
THIRTY-THREE
EMARA

"**S**low down," **Emara begged,** her feet tumbling after Torin. The shoes Lorta and Kaydence had placed on her feet for the dinner this evening were not made for running. "I can't keep up with you."

Everyone had fled from the watchtower after the Supreme had dismissed them, hurrying as fast as they could to leave such a hostile environment. Torin had been the last one to leave, Emara drawing him away, and when he had left the room, he had gone scarily silent, walking like a lunatic.

"Torin, will you slow down?" she screamed.

Without saying a word, he spun, grabbing her under the ass with one arm and throwing her over his shoulder, in between his lethal swords. It was a miracle that the air was not knocked from her lungs at the swiftness of his movement. It took Emara a few seconds to realise what had actually happened.

"What are you doing?" She shifted, kicking and

pounding a fist into his back as he took powerful strides down the passageway.

It was useless, of course, and she could feel the blood rushing to her brain, weakening her.

"Hey!" She pounded a fist again. "I am talking to you."

"You were too slow," he stated sharply. "And you were about to snap an ankle."

"Why are you always so concerned about my ankles? Ever think about just slowing down and having patience?"

"Patience." He sneered. "Coming from you."

She punched into his back again, a few times, but he just laughed madly and kept walking.

Emara heard pounding steps along the corridor behind them and she strained to look up.

Her other guards were running, their expressions unreadable as they tried to catch up.

"What in the three-faced Mother God did you do now?" Artem's jaw dropped open.

"I did nothing!" Emara screeched.

"I doubt that." Artem grinned wildly. Magin shot him a glare.

"She's not in trouble," Torin barked as he marched on.

"You're right, I am not in trouble." She pounded her fist again, and this time she got a knee into his stomach too. "So put me the Gods-damned down."

"She sounds really mad, Blacksteel," Artem declared as he began jogging to keep up. "You better put her down."

"Yeah?" He turned to face his brethren. "Well, I am angrier." He seethed, and Emara could feel his heart pounding, his blood racing all over his body.

"What the fuck happened back there, Torin?" Magin demanded, his weapon belt moving as he broke into a jog too.

Torin ignored them, his steps more violent than before as he took the corridor to Emara's room.

"The Supreme offered him an alliance with herself," Emara finally said, going dizzy as she hung upside down. "And when he refused her, clearly insulting her, she threatened him."

"Shit!" Artem groaned.

"Gods above." Magin almost went into prayer.

"No, fuck that." Torin snarled. "She insulted you. I don't give a fuck about her fucking threats."

Emara stilled.

That was a lot of cursing in one sentence, even for Torin.

She heard a hiss from Artem as they arrived outside her room. "What did she say?" he asked.

Torin placed Emara down in a gentler fashion than when he had swooped her up. Her head swished inside, causing her to sway. He steadied her with two hands, ensuring she was okay to stand before he turned to his brethren. "I am not getting into it with you."

The blood finally drained from Emara's head, and she could feel it running down her skull as she steadied herself against the door.

"I've got the first watch," Torin said. Magin and Artem looked at each other as if they had no idea what was happening. At least they seemed to know better than to challenge him in this mood or pry for any more information. It wouldn't be worth the risk to their lives.

They took their leave, not even looking at Torin again and bowing to Emara.

Once the final sounds of boots had gotten lost down the corridor, she turned to him. "What was that? Why are you so angry?"

"Do you even have to ask me that question?" His brows collided on this forehead.

"I get that the Supreme got under your skin, but you went in there ready for a fight and she hadn't even provoked you."

He shook his head, thinning his lips into a taut line. "No, Emara, you don't understand." He looked more like Viktir Blacksteel than ever, and it unnerved her. "She wasn't trying to get under *my* skin. She was trying to get under *yours*. She was trying to make you feel inferior to her, and I won't have it. First with the name calling, and then with the challenge of our treaty. She fucking knows what alliances her covens have. She signed the Gods-damned papers." He clenched his fists, and his arm muscles threatened to burst through his uniform. "She was trying to get in your head and make you look weak in front of the other empresses. She didn't want an alliance with me. Fuck, she has hundreds of alliances. She's the most protected woman in the kingdom."

"Why would she do that?" Emara's voice was gentle against the rage that steamed from Torin. "Why would she want to get under my skin?"

"Because, Emara, one of the empresses in that room

tonight is going to steal her life, her magic, her power." His eyes turned like a roaring storm that threatened to rip out forests from their roots. "And there is a one in five chance that that person is you. She wants you all to know her status as a queen of her own faction."

She stilled at his words.

He turned away, cursing under his breath.

It was a one in five chance that she would take the power from Deleine. The natural life cycle of the witching world. *As one supreme rises, the other fades.*

He braced himself against the wall with one hand, his neck bent. "I knew you would be in the firing line of witching politics soon enough, but I didn't expect her to go in like a vulture." He placed the other hand on his hip, shaking his head. "Not when you are so new to it all. She struck fast and hard tonight, wasting no time at all to make you feel weaker than her."

Emara stood silent, running over the scene in her head again.

From what she could see, Emara knew he was thinking about how he could kill the Supreme. She moved towards him, placing a hand on his arm, smoothing out the fabric of his tunic with her thumb.

"She doesn't intimidate me," she said. It was a half-lie, but one she could keep telling herself in the hopes that it would come true.

"I should have just killed her."

"And start a war against the hunters and the witches?" Emara giggled, and it sounded a little crazed. "You can't just kill everyone in life who insults me."

"Wanna bet?" Torin's eyes met hers. Although they

were finally full of dark amusement, she knew that the rage was still there, lurking in the shadows.

"No, I don't want to bet." She shook her head. "I am tired of you boys and your betting games."

"Boys?" he questioned with a devilish grin.

"Animals." She looked up at him with a grin of her own painted on her lips.

He swallowed before cupping her face with his hand. "It's not just the Dark Army whose blood I want on the end of my swords. It's anyone who is a threat to you."

Her heart hesitated and her stomach dipped at the warmth of his large hands around her jaw. Her throat swelled at his words. "The Supreme is not my enemy. She might be bitter about one day losing all that she has gained, but you need to trust that I can handle myself."

"I do trust you. I know what you are capable of."

Instead of speaking, she stood on her tiptoes and kissed what she could reach on his face. She almost reached his chin, but like a magnetic force, his lips found hers. She ran her hands up into his hair, working through that beautifully silken ink before she broke off. His eyes were still closed and he held still, tilted in the fashion that made her want to kiss him more. But she knew that if she continued the kiss, it wouldn't stop there. She didn't want it to either, but Emara needed time to prepare. She had to focus and prepare for tomorrow.

The Cold Moon had almost reached its full potential, meaning she would ascend.

Reading the space between them, he pulled back too.

"Good night, Clearwater." Torin's voice was low and suggestive, like he wanted to beg her for one more kiss.

It was impressive that he had refrained from kissing her again, especially when Emara was seconds away from pulling that uniform over his head.

"Good night, Blacksteel," was all Emara said before she opened the door and made her way inside.

After taking a few moments to recover from the intensity of the night, she wriggled out of her dress. Torin would have undoubtedly, impatiently, ripped it from her body if he had come inside. Having washed up and taken the pins out her hair, she noticed a familiar folded square hovering over the swaying gold flames.

She found herself moving quickly and grasping the warm letter between two fingers. She opened it, and her heart exploded.

> *Dear Emara,*
> *Please never be intimidated by anyone when I am by your side.*
> *Although tomorrow is the night in which your crown will be fitted, you still have training at dawn.*
> *I like it when I am confident that my empress can wield magic and a sword.*
> *Yours truly,*
> *Torin Blacksteel*

Emara was unsure how many times she read it over. But every time she did, the same overwhelming feeling lay deep in her heart. She told herself she had to shut it down. But somehow, it still swarmed around her chest. Cosying into bed, she folded the letter back to its original square and floated to a world of unplagued dreams, clutching it for dear life.

CHAPTER
THIRTY-FOUR
EMARA

I am a droplet of water.

I am an ember of fire that burns.

I am the gust of air that gives breath.

I am the grounding grains of earth below my feet.

I am the spirit that my soul calls on, like the ancestors before me.

In my magic, I trust.

In my element, I trust.

In my House and Coven of Air, I trust.

In myself, as Empress of House Air, I trust.

EMARA HAD BEEN CHANTING the same spell that bound her to the crown of House Air since this morning. Even when she had been training with Torin, she had chanted in her head. Every punch, every kick, every squat, every sequence, every turn, her mind was focused on the verse.

After training, she had then watched Torin spar with

Artem. Both of them had turned into animals in the height of their combat session. A few of the other hunters had come to see the show out in the harsh conditions, and a show it had been. Both males had been unbelievably quick in their sparring dance and unswervingly brutal, trying to best their opponent with every move they made.

No weapons were involved, only limbs, and in the end, Torin had taken advantage of a split second of weakness in Artem's stance. He had swept his feet before delivering a knockout blow to the face, their bodies crashing down to the plains of the open mountain. The ice-cold wind had battered against their training gear as Torin pinned his brother to the dirt below. As soon as the fight was over, they were both laughing, and Torin helped Artem to stand. In an instant, the fierce fighting had been replaced by friendship and jest.

Torin had won, and she was sure Artem would never live it down—until the next time.

But that felt like days ago as Emara sat in her room, awaiting the sun to fall behind the mountains before the ceremony could begin.

Lorta and Kaydence had been and gone in something that felt like a blur. They had bathed and cleansed her. Lorta had brushed out her flowing curls from the night before, leaving them tumbling loosely down her back, and Kaydence had arranged flowers of vervain, acacia, and aspen in her hair, the flowers of her House.

Her coven.

They had dressed her in nothing but a modest white dress that was flowing and free against her body. It was the complete opposite from what she had worn the night before, but it comforted her. It felt right. They had washed her feet in lavender and lemongrass oils before smudging in an enchanted balm that would protect her soles as she walked barefoot on the rocky terrain. No shoes were to be worn tonight, only her flowing dress and the flowers of her coven in her hair.

Now that she was alone and the preparation finished, it felt like time had slowed. It had felt like hours since the maids had left her, and she didn't know what time of day it was. The sky outside was beginning to take the form of a moody oil painting, confirming she didn't have much longer to wait.

As nerves attacked her stomach, Emara chanted the words that connected her to the element of air again as she looked to the golden flames of the magical fire, grounding herself somewhere in the witchcraft. She recited the same words over and over until they were carved into her mouth and mind—and quite possibly, her heart.

A flicker in the flames sent a few embers into the air, and a sealed, folded letter floated in the pit. Leaping off her bed, she took the letter and peered at the seal. Ripping it open, she read:

My dearest Emara,

You should have trusted that your letter would always find me, as it was sent from a very talented and soon-to-be powerful empress. Compassion is something that you must show to your coven, but do not let them mistake it for weakness, my love. Nor any other House, for that matter.

You will do the full kingdom proud tonight. Do not falter, as this was what the Gods paved for you before you were born. Believe in yourself.

I will look forward to seeing you at the Winter Solstice Ball.

On an additional note, I hope my sons are on their best behaviour. You have my permission to ensure they are, by any means necessary.

With an abundance of love,
Naya Blacksteel.
House of Earth.

Emara beamed as gratitude swarmed in her eyes at Naya's letter. For the first time in what felt like forever, her heart felt more whole. The truth of how much faith Naya had in Emara was humbling yet staggering, and it felt like she could see something more than what Emara could. She supposed it was in Naya's nature to see the best in everyone. It was what made her beautiful and inspiring, along with her strength and determination to make the world a better place.

Emara folded the paper and stuffed it into a hidey hole in her satchel, along with every other fireletter that lay there.

All of which were from Torin Blacksteel.

A horn soared through the evening air, causing Emara to stiffen where she stood. After the horn's sound fell into the depths below the mountain, a distant beating of drums could be heard. Emara felt her magic prickle under her skin, the constant beat singing to the blood that ran through her veins, inviting her to follow the music—the enchantment.

Two knocks on the door had her heart in her mouth. But no one opened it, they waited outside for her. Swallowing down her most vital organ, she walked to the door and met her guards.

It was time for them to escort her to the ascension ritual.

CHAPTER
THIRTY-FIVE
EMARA

The protection balm on Emara's feet had been a Gods-send as she walked barefoot through the mountain range to an open field. It looked down on the entire Kingdom of Caledorna; the view was incredible, even as the darkness of night threatened to swallow it whole. Emara wondered how many witches before her had stood in this exact spot, admiring the kingdom from its breath-taking peaks. As the light of the winter sun slipped away and the sky welcomed the brightness of the Cold Moon, glowing and blue, Emara's mind wandered to every other faction that made up the magic world, from the Shifters to the Faeries.

Had they all stood here too? Had they seen Caledorna through the eyes of the north mountains?

She thought about the ancient Gods standing atop this very pinnacle, moving and creating the world that she knew today, instilling the magic she had in her blood into the streams of the world.

Her blood tingled.

Turning from the view, the drumming bass still sought out her magic, being the only sound in her ears as it still lured her closer. Her heart hitched in her chest as she witnessed the ritual space for the first time. The other empresses were already there, in the same humble attire as she. Lillian, Kerrix, Sybil, and Rya stood alone in a line without their guards. She walked over to them, not looking back at her own guards.

Not finding Torin's eyes.

She hadn't allowed herself to when he had stood outside her door to bring her here. There could be no distractions, not now, not in this moment.

Taking her place beside Sybil, the Earth Witch gave her a nervous smile as transparent fear shimmered in her eyes. Emara took her hand in her own, not caring about any traditions or if etiquette vowed them not to. A sharp exhale from Sybil told her it was the right thing to do, and the healer squeezed her hand to say thank you. Emara squeezed back.

A heart-wrenching pain in her chest drove tears into her eyes.

That is what Cally would have done to reassure her, to prove that the unspoken words were heard through their special bond. Emara pulled back on her sentiment as she looked up to the stars that twinkled in the sky. Was Cally watching her now? Was she here?

I am always with you.

She fought back tears and focused on the white candles that were ablaze in the shape of a circle in front of her. A gust of wind hit her face, allowing her to smell the fresh sea salt that bound the ceremonial ring. To the right of the circle was an altar—too old for this world—draped in golden fabric with black runes weaved through. Atop the altar sat a black witching bowl, and burning inside were sticks of incense in jade, cobalt, white, scarlet, and violet, each symbolising one of empresses. Elemental runes that represented each House were painted in the same colours around the circle. Many witches stood in silence, cloaked in black robes, no colours showing which House they represented, their faces unseen. Not being able to see any of their eyes sent a churning into her stomach so strong that Emara was sure she could vomit any second. She realised members of her own coven would be here to watch her ascend, but she could not see anything that identified them.

Maybe she did need a distraction.

And she found it instantly, finally allowing herself to look in Torin's direction.

He stood in a line of hunters whose faces weren't important, and his sapphire eyes were on her.

His brow pulled into a look of concern, and he mouthed, "Are you okay?"

She nodded.

She would dig deep and find the same courage that every other witch before her had done. Like her grandmother, like Sybil, like the current Supreme.

As if responding to her name in Emara's mind, the Supreme revealed her face in the crowd, as did an elder witch. The Supreme's gaze wandered over all five of them.

One of them would be her end, and she did not hide the deadly undercurrent that lingered in the dark waters of her eyes. She was a lethal being, and she smiled like she knew it. She was their leader, their queen, and she would guide them through the ceremony that strengthened their faction.

Emara flashed her eyes to Torin, who, for once, was hiding his scowl underneath a professional façade. She looked to Artem and Magin, to Gideon and Kellen. She looked to Marcus as they all stood, hands behind their back, faces stony and unreadable, all of their eyes on her. Every one of them looked like they had been born in the glory of the black cauldron that sat before her, enormous and archaic. It bubbled, but no fire boiled it.

The Supreme walked forward, her cloak decorating the earth behind her, and for a moment, Emara wished she could wrap herself in a cloak like it, protecting her from the frigid temperature. The drums came to an abrupt stop, and the silence in the air felt somewhat unnatural as it drifted through the crowd of witches and guards.

"Welcome," the Supreme said. "Tonight, under the Cold Moon that is full in its cycle, five new witches will ascend." She looked over all of them. "You will ascend to become Empress of your Coven." Her features sharpened, but she gave a proud smile. "Leader of your House."

The tartness of the fresh air stole Emara's breath.

"We will begin the ascension ritual with House Air." The Supreme's starlit eyes swept over to Emara. "Emara Clearwater, elemental blood heir of House Air, step forward." She was razor sharp in her delivery, like a queen would be, and Emara did as she was asked.

Her knees wobbled as Sybil let go of her hand, and she stepped forward, making sure her feet did the simple task. A gust of jagged wind ripped at the curled strands of Emara's hair and sent dark silk spilling over her shoulder as she walked towards the altar.

The Supreme's lips parted, and any political intimidation that had taken place last night was gone from her face. Emara could see in her eyes how much this ritual meant to her Supreme, and she was thankful for it.

"In the name of the three-faced God, Our Mother, give forth your left hand."

Emara's hand shook, but she held it out quickly, palm facing the moon. Deleine moved to the altar with grace, the wind tugging at her cloak, and retrieved a small dagger from her pocket. The magic from its blade called her hand towards it, and the Supreme slashed the knife across Emara's palm in one swift movement. They both winced. Emara flinched again as the sting grew stronger from her broken skin. She placed her other hand behind her back to keep it from coming up and holding the pain that now burned in her slit skin, and she understood why the hunters hid their hands so much. There were always tell-tale signs on how someone felt when looking at their hands, how they flexed or strained or relaxed. She didn't want to show anyone that she felt pain, so she scrunched her right hand behind her back until the pain subsided. Dark red blood escaped the slice in her hand and began pouring down her wrist.

"It will heal quickly," the Supreme assured her. "The blade is enchanted with healing magic."

The elder witch brought forth the dark bowl, and the Queen of Witches' fingers curled around Emara's wrist and squeezed hard. The blood flowed from her hand and splashed into the bowl where the burning incense had turned to ash. The purply-black ashes mixed with her blood to make a thick paste, and the Supreme stuck her thumb into it. Bringing her finger to Emara's forehead, she etched a symbol onto her skin that marked who she was, who she would always be from this night until death claimed her.

It was a triangle with a score through the top.

The symbol of House Air.

The flames of the candles, all around, erupted higher, responding to the magic in her blood. The drumming boomed through the night again, this time elevated and harsh. The hairs on Emara's skin rose, covering her in new signs that her magic heard it too. She could feel it, stirring in her bones, calling to her, threatening to reveal itself, but again, she talked it down.

The elder witch, who was now walking around the circle, dragging a broom, chanted in a language that was too ancient for Emara to know, and then stopped.

Torin, Artem, and Magin, stepped forward, and Emara's gaze darted to them.

"Escort her to the circle," the Supreme said, and her guards did their duty with haste.

Making her way to the cauldron, the Supreme began chanting in that same mother tongue of the ancients that once walked this earth. The elder witch, once done with a sweep that cleansed the circle, gestured for Emara to step into it.

Breaking the ancient tongue, both witches said in unison, "Bless the sacred circle." The candle flames flew higher as Emara stepped inside the ritual space.

Other witches from the crowd stepped forward, causing Emara's eyes to dash around. They were witches of House Air. They all held something in their hands, and as they walked over to the Supreme at the cauldron, Emara couldn't make out what they were sacrificing to the cauldron. She thought she saw herbs and stones, maybe even living creatures, but they were sacrificed to the cauldron regardless.

A surge of energy jolted through her body, causing her spine to roll and her lips to part. Her heart accelerated. The cauldron was speaking to her as her blood mixed with the offerings to the Gods—to Rhiannon.

"The words that you must speak under the full moon," the elder said, her voice wry and rough. "Speak them now, child, with meaning to the Gods of Light."

Pulling on her courage, Emara swallowed her fear and looked to the moon that bloomed full against the dark blanket of the night. She always did have an entanglement with the moon that she'd never understood until now. It had been leading her here. That crafty, magical moon had always been guiding her here, to this moment.

She lifted her chin for everyone to see her bravery. With moonlight on her face, she began her chant.

"*I am a droplet of water.*

I am an ember of fire that burns.

I am the gust of air that gives breath.

I am the grounding grains of earth below my feet.

I am the spirit that my soul calls on, like the ancestors before me."

The magic swirled in her veins; it pounded in her heart, sparking and igniting. Its strength could be felt, soaring through her soul. The staining of its power could be felt all over her body, causing her to feel nothing and everything all at once. She felt a rumble in the earth under her bare feet, and she curled her toes into the ground as heat began to swirl up her legs.

"*In my magic, I trust.*

In my element, I trust.

In my House and Coven of Air, I trust.

In myself, as Empress of House Air, I trust."

Everything that was light, blood, water, salt, and dirt moved in her. A phantom wind of stars and moonlight swarmed the circle, aiding her magic, stimulating it. It whirled around her like the violent wind of the wild hunt. The vortex of magic seemed to pull up gravel, and it swirled it into the air. Sparks began lighting in the magic around her, and she was sure she could hear voices of ancient spirits speaking in a tongue lost to her now. Her head tilted back, and the beating of the drums felt like ecstasy in her mind as she let the enchantment pulse through her, beckoning to every spellbinding part of who she was. Her breathing deepened as she felt the push of sorcery build within her. It ripped at her loose dress and lashed at her dark hair.

"Repeat after me," the Supreme's voice could be heard from her place near the cauldron. "I hold the title Empress of Air."

"I hold the title Empress of Air," she repeated, feeling her magic rumble from the deepest parts of her soul.

"And I shall wear the Crown of Air until I take my last breath."

"And I shall wear the Crown of Air until I take my last breath," she breathed, her chest rising and falling to the beat that coursed through her, to the charmed river that coursed through her blood, thriving and alive.

Even on this winter night, sweat began beading on her skin, her panting breaths blowing out frozen smoke. The Supreme spoke in the ancient tongue and Emara copied, knowing that it translated to *My Coven and House come first. I will honour my crown in life and in death.*

To Emara's surprise, her guards unsheathed their swords and knelt outside the circle, holding their blades above their heads as the wind ripped at them too.

"I, Magin Oxhound, of Oath and Blood to the Hunt, vow to protect the Empress of Air until I take my last breath." He slammed his sword down into the ground, and the flames of the candles burned brighter.

"I, Artem Stryker, of Oath and Blood to the Hunt, vow to protect the Empress of Air until I take my last breath."

Emara had never heard Artem speak with so

much raw meaning. She knew how deadly he was just by looking at him, and his playful foolery didn't allow her to forget how skilled he was at killing, but something more shone in his eyes. All that jest was gone. He brought down his sword and it penetrated the earth too. The flames of the circle blazed again, causing her throat to catch as a spirit wind whirled around her, coating her vision in a combination of stars and fire.

"I, Torin Blacksteel, of Oath and Blood to the Hunt, vow to protect the Empress of Air, *Emara Clearwater,* until I breathe my final breath." His eyes found hers and the world stopped. Everything around her faded away, and it was like the magic had cleared a path for him to be seen. His face was extraordinary, the raw emotions passing over his expression sharpening the ruthless angles of his bone structure. "I vow to protect her even after my bones turn to dust and we are nothing more than stars gazing down at the earth."

His scorching gaze didn't falter, and Emara couldn't breathe. She couldn't breathe!

"My soul will protect yours, even in the afterlife." He spoke solely to her, and every hair on her body stood to the profoundness of his words. Her skin prickled, and her lungs shoved every particle of air out from them.

Emara had a feeling that Torin wasn't supposed to vow what he just had. He was supposed to vow the same thing Magin and Artem had, what the other guards would do tonight. But he'd vowed something more sacred than this ritual itself. In front of everyone, in front of every coven, in front of every important guard from their hunting families, Torin Blacksteel had vowed to protect her against anything.

Claiming his soul would find hers on the *Otherside*.

And she believed him. She believed every word. His soul would search for hers.

Her heart left her body.

Without breaking their stare, he brought down his sword, causing the mountain to shudder beneath them as he made his promise final and absolute to the world.

The Supreme, who had been brewing something in the cauldron, dipped her hand into the bubbling blackness and fished out her creation.

It was a crown, a crown of violet crystals and gemstones, twigs and moss, light and dark fractures of the world. It was a mixture of life and Air, and it was a mixture of her. It had been created by the gifts of her coven.

The Supreme sat it atop a silk cushion and delivered it to the elder.

Emara swallowed, taking in the unchained power of the crown's magic as it came towards her.

"Bless the sacred circle," the elder said before entering.

The drumming stopped dead, and all notes of the music rang off the grandness of the northern mountains before disappearing entirely. All Emara could hear now was the drumming of her own heart as the elder witch placed the crown atop her head.

"The ascension is now complete," she said with a dry smile that sent more of her wrinkled skin into deep folds. She looked up to the sky with a glaze in her eyes.

"You have made the Gods happy on this Witching Moon."

Her guards stood, causing Emara to turn, and it was the first time she felt the weight of her crown move with her head as it clutched to her skull like it had tiny little fingers holding onto her hair.

"The kingdom has an Empress of Air once more," the old crone acknowledged.

"Blessed be," the cloaked witches said in unison, and bowed.

Emara looked to the Supreme, who was staring directly at her.

"Blessed be," Deleine said, her eyes lowering in respect.

The elder issued Emara out of the circle, and the power from the ascension crashed. Torin caught her as she swayed, and the world around her blurred. The indisputable supremacy from the circle was no longer with her as she broke through its ring, salt cutting into her feet like small shards of glass. She swayed again.

"It's okay, I've got you," Torin said, taking her to stand with the crowd that were no longer looking at her. They were done with her, thankfully, and now looking to the next witch in the line who would complete the ritual. She took in a huge breath, letting the cold air embed itself in her lungs.

"You did amazing," Torin assured her. Artem bowed his head in her direction, his face a little less professional than it was a few minutes ago. She smiled back at him, and then to Magin. She wondered if he'd looked at the late Empress of Air the same way he was looking at her now.

It was done. Her fate had been sealed at the hands of the Gods.

She had ascended.

She was the Empress of Air.

CHAPTER THIRTY-SIX
EMARA

Torin had carried Emara back to her room in the palace after the ritual, Artem and Magin flanking him. She had tried to walk back, but her legs had failed her, and without asking, he had picked her up and started the hike back up the trail.

She hadn't protested.

The elder had told Torin it was normal for her to be limp; he had requested a healer, but it was denied. The elder had insisted Emara would recover with a solid night's sleep, and right now, she felt like she could sleep until the next new moon reached its cycle.

Torin lay her on the bed, and she managed to wiggle under the blankets as he pulled them up to meet her chin. Her toes tingled under the warmth of the fabric, finally feeling some heat in her bones.

After a few minutes, Lorta and Kaydence, who had also witnessed her ascension from the crowd, filed into the room. She noticed their cheeks blushing at the presence of her guards before Lorta asked, "Is there anything we can do for you, *Empress of Air?*" Her smile lit up the room.

"Even though I have ascended, you don't have to call me that," Emara said. "We are all friends here. Emara will do fine."

"I will remind you that in the morning," Artem Stryker cut in, a boyish grin on his face.

She wished she had the energy to strike up a feud with him, as it had been a few hours since their last, but her mind and soul requested just as much rest as her body did. So she glared at him instead.

"It's all right," Torin said, his face still as unreadable as when he'd carried her up the mountain. He looked over to the two girls, who now fell under Emara in ranking. "I will see to it that she gets a good night's sleep. You girls can get some rest too."

A snorting sound ripped through the room. "Is that what we are calling it now? A few days ago, it was falling into a waterfall, and now it's *sleeping.*"

Torin's jaw tightened, sharpening his features. "She won't be needing you as her guard tonight, either." His tone was more threatening than amused. "You can take your leave."

Artem looked to Emara, as did Magin and the girls. Realising they were all waiting for her instruction, awaiting her command, she nodded.

Before heading towards the door, they all bowed, wishing her well and good rest.

As the door closed, leaving them alone, Torin moved from the archway over to the bed. He took a seat at the end of it. The mattress dipped as his weight settled in, and his lips parted, a thoughtful look on his face.

But it was Emara who spoke. "Are you about to tell me that the fearless and ruthless second-in-command of the Blacksteel Hunting Clan is about to tuck me in to sleep?"

He gave a low laugh, but his eyes were still on the floor. "I am staying a little while, so I know that the magic from the ritual hasn't gone wrong."

Oh.

He leaned forward, placing both elbows on his knees, and Emara could see his strong muscles move under his uniform.

"I want to thank you for tonight," she said, feeling more emotional than expected. She put it down to tiredness, but her voice was wavering with something more. "I couldn't have done it without you."

His gaze in the crowd had steadied her before a nervous vomit crawled up her throat or her knees gave way.

The hardness of his eyes softened as he looked over at her. "Of course, you could have. You don't need me to be strong. You were strong before you met me."

Her stomach flipped at the sound of admiration in his voice, and she lowered her lashes.

"I have to ask—"

"Yes," he breathed quickly, a strain lingering tight on his face.

Her brows dipped closer to her eyes. "You don't even know what I was going to ask you."

"Yes, I do." He lifted his dark, thick lashes, revealing a sincere shimmer in his eyes. "You were going to ask me if I meant what I said tonight at the ascension."

How could he possibly know that? How could Torin Blacksteel somehow know her better than anyone in the world?

"I meant every word," he said.

She gripped the blankets as her lungs squeezed.

For one brief second, just one, she allowed herself to think so subtly about what it could be like if she explored something deeper with Torin. She could have a union of marriage to forge an alliance for her community, for her people, protection and armour, but what if it could be for *love* too?

A rush of heat hit her stomach, and it sank like a boat in a storm.

"Was it not foolish of a guard to declare something to an empress that a man would do to his wife?" she said quickly, her cheeks turning pink.

There was a tick in his jaw before his azure eyes found hers. "I would say it again in front of the whole kingdom." Her heart fluttered. "Because I can protect you, Emara." His nostrils flared as his hand lay down on her sheets, and she stilled where she lay unable to move. "Not only that, but I want to protect you." He paused, and the ocean waves of his eyes crashed together in something so meaningful. "I want to protect all of you—your heart, your body, your soul, all of it." His voice thinned as he swallowed, his powerful throat bobbing. "I want to protect all of you until my last breath on this earth."

Her protector.

Everything that mattered in the world vanished, with the exception of him.

"Somewhere along the line..." He looked down at his hand. "Somewhere along the line, I realised that you are everything that I have ever wanted. Probably from the first time you challenged me or yelled at me." He laughed faintly, his mouth pulling to one side. His jaw hardened. "And when I discovered who you were and then everything that happened, I realised that *you* could be my future." He stared over at her. "I want you to be my future, not because it was forced upon us, but because I would choose you." His voice broke in a way she had never heard before, and a string in her heart plucked like a harp about to break. "I would choose you over everything."

The bluntness of his tone made her realise what he meant. He would choose her over *everything,* including his duty, his oath, and his family. He wouldn't force her hand to the treaty. He would be lashed, exiled, and tortured if he disobeyed his commander, but he would endure that so that she had a choice.

Regardless of all of that, he would still choose her.

She sat upright, reaching out to him. "Torin," she breathed.

"No, you need to hear this." His glittering eyes narrowed. "I would choose you again and again." He lowered his gaze, and it was then that Emara realised that the dark glittering of his irises was fear. *Fear.* The fear that she wouldn't choose him back was pencilled into his face. Her heart both swelled and broke at his truth. He rolled his full lips before he spoke again. "I didn't think I would get to choose who I spent my life with. I didn't think I would get to choose who I bore every inch of my soul to but it's you," he croaked, his face paling. "The Gods know it's you."

Stunned, unable to find words, she moved to him, wrapping herself around his body as burning tears fell from her eyes.

He pulled her onto his lap properly, embracing her as she sat there. "And if it is not you, and you don't choose me back, then no one else will have my heart, Clearwater."

Nothing that passed over his face told Emara that he wasn't being truthful. He was. He would choose her. Rawest pleasure tore at her heart, his words following the pleasure as they rooted themselves deeply in the alcoves of her soul. "I would choose you too, Torin Blacksteel," she said back, her voice shaking at the truth she spoke into the world.

He smiled, and with the way the room had darkened, it made him look even more handsome. Pulling her against his lips, kissing her, the smiles didn't fall from their faces as their mouths intertwined. It was deeper and more meaningful than the other lustful kisses that had passed between them.

This was different.

This was more.

This kiss was hope. It was a promise. It was trust.

The barrier which she had set around herself, around her heart, had been smashed, replaced by her undeniable feelings for Torin Blacksteel.

He pulled back, leaving her leaning in for more of his lips.

"As much as it is killing me to stop kissing your irresistible mouth, you must rest."

"I am okay."

"You need to rest." He kissed her nose. "Healer's orders. I don't think I have ever hated myself more for being sensible right now, but you need your strength, and you will not get that if we keep going, trust me."

Trust me.

A promise of what could happen if they kept kissing, kept devouring.

He was right, but she was never going to say that out loud. She sighed.

So instead, with her heart beating crazily, Emara asked, "Will you stay here with me?"

His eyes warmed, his features relaxing as he leaned back, his hands still on her hips. "Like you have to ask me twice, angel."

She shimmied back with a smile and moved from where she'd straddled his hips. Emara shifted up the bed, cosying into where she had been before she moved to kiss him. Torin stood, removing his weapons and laying them on the floor. There were more of them than she would have guessed by looking at him. He unbuttoned a few buttons that held his tunic in place against his neck and pulled it off. It landed in a place Emara couldn't see as she stared at every divine inch of him.

He really was carved by the Gods. His golden skin was smooth over his core, and the muscle between his hips and lower stomach shaped into a prominent V. His shoulders and his back were broad.

He was a lethal warrior with a body designed to destroy.

Torin walked around the bed to the opposite side and jumped in next to her.

If she hadn't been too tired to keep her eyes open, she would have stared at him all night, lying in her bed, his head on the pillow that she had laid on too. He pulled her against him, the warmth of his chest now caressing her cheek as he took a lock of her hair and twisted it in his fingers. He let out a sigh.

"What are we going to do about how you make me feel?"

She giggled a little. "I have been asking the Gods the same question for a while now."

"A while, huh?"

She could hear the mischief in his voice, but instead of responding, Emara placed a hand to where his heart lay and said a prayer to the Gods for it to never stop beating.

He pecked three little kisses atop her forehead just as sleep claimed her. But as her dreamy, soft slumber began, she realised what he was doing. Torin had kissed the symbol that had been drawn on her forehead. Slipping to a land of the subconscious, she slept against his chest. Safe.

Home. It felt like home.

When her eyes fluttered open due to the light that seeped through the window, she knew instantly that she was alone. Where heat and strength had lay between her sheets last night, only the cold empty space of the bed could be felt under her palms as she rolled over.

A note that had been ripped from the spine of her journal lay in Torin's place. Pushing the hair from her face and flicking the rest of it over her shoulder, she grabbed the note and opened it. His perfectly neat handwriting advised her that he had a "Blacksteel" meeting, and he instructed her to get dressed and ask Artem to bring her for a training session.

Rolling from the bed, her ritual dress still on her body, she made her way to the door. Pulling it open, she flicked her wrist out, handing Artem over the letter.

"An instruction," she said. "From your boyfriend."

His eyebrows danced up and she finally took in his grin. Taking the note from her hand, he unravelled it and read it for himself.

"Did lover boy not seal this letter with a declaration of his love for you?" He held the paper up. "I was hoping for some steamy gossip about what you had gotten up to last night, not an instruction."

She pinched the letter from between his tattooed

fingers. "You don't need to know anything about what happened last night, apart from that I am your empress, and should be treated as such."

He straightened, his face grave. "I am sorry if I crossed the line."

She let a smile worm its way onto her lips. "I am certainly getting better at acting like an empress. Don't you think so?"

He looked up, hearing the mocking tone in her voice, and a smile tugged at his lips too. "Nice work. At least we know now that you have it in you."

She laughed, leaving the door open, and moved into the room. "I hope I won't have to use that voice often."

He followed. "It's not a bad thing. Respect sometimes needs to be commanded. I don't think you are going to have any issues with that, though." His voice was full of bedevilment once again.

"Let's hope not," she said, meaning every word. She stopped short of the fireplace. "I have a meeting soon with my coven."

"You will smash it...in a way that witches smash things."

Emara looked over at Artem with an eyebrow raised, and he gave her a lazy smile. She walked towards where her sparring clothes had been neatly placed over the vanity chair.

"I was wondering," Artem began, but didn't finish the thought. The way he said it, so full of sincerity, had Emara turning around to face him.

His visage changed for a second, something like

vulnerability flashing in his eyes. "I was wondering if you could help me with something?"

"Help you with what?" Emara blinked.

"Well," he said, leaning against the fireplace. "It is the Winter Solstice Ball soon..."

"Yeah?" Emara's eyes widened.

"And it is a hunting tradition to get a gift for a female of choice." He looked up at her. "I met someone, and she's something else entirely." His hazel-gold eyes turned molten as he mentioned her. "And I kind of want to catch her attention."

This is not how she'd thought this conversation was going to go.

He coughed and straightened, puffing out his chest. "And so I would like to get her a gift. I am sure she will arrive with the rest of the Baxgroll pack for the celebrations."

Emara choked. "The girl you want to give a gift to is Breighly Baxgroll?"

He nodded, looking down at his weapon belt and sorting through a few of the knives that didn't need rearranged. Something on his face made Emara's heart feel light. Was Artem Stryker being coy?

Never.

She clamped down on her lips. She couldn't smile, not when he was being so unguarded.

"You're a girl," he said, squinting as he looked up.

"Thanks for stating the obvious, Artem."

He signed a little. "What would you want as a present?"

The question threw her. She wasn't quite sure if she

had ever asked for a present before. Her grandmother used to get herself and Cally matching canes of sugar each year from the village, with their names squiggled in icing. And then when they became older, it was books or something for their rooms. Cally, however, would go all out with presents, and the more coin she earned, the more outrageous they would be. But Emara had never asked for anything specific.

Her heart cracked as she thought of the last gift Callyn had given her before the Uplift. Her crescent moon hair pin, dripping in stunning crystals. It was magical.

She almost whimpered. "Um...I don't know. Something personal?"

He lowered his gaze, and all of a sudden, Artem looked innocent even though he was a large brute covered in ink and weapons.

Emara bit into her cheek. "She's a wolf, right?"

"Yeah, and she has the temper of one too." He laughed like that might be the sole reason for why he was fond of her.

"Why don't you get her something that compliments who she is? To me, I think, deep down, Breighly would like something with little coin value, but high in sentiment."

He took a long breath. "I have a few days to think, I suppose." He turned and walked towards the door. Artem flung a glance over his shoulder. "Thanks for the advice, *empress*."

"Any time, *Stryker*."

His face lit up a little too much. "Get dressed."

"Why are you smiling like that?"

"Because today is going to be a good day. I am joining your training session with Blacksteel." He broke the threshold of the door as he walked backwards. "And I can't wait to see what you've got."

CHAPTER THIRTY-SEVEN
EMARA

The clearing on the mountaintop was busier with hunters than she would have thought. Some of them were already warming up or doing drills to increase their heart rate, and it looked like the Selection. Well, in her mind it did. She had to give it to them, they made training efficient, even at the high elevation and moody clouds threatening bad weather.

Stalking in front of Artem in black training gear, she made it over to Torin, who had been eyeing her coming from the distance. He ran a blade through his fingers and the sincerity that had been in his features last night had been replaced by a diabolically handsome grin.

Her heart skipped a beat.

"I thought you might have slept all day long at this rate," he purred.

Ignoring him, she asked "Why do we have to train outside?" Her teeth chattered as the wind iced her veins, pulling out parts of her braided hair. "Surely, the palace has a big enough room for us to practise in?"

"Of course, it does," Torin said. "But we are not allowed."

"Not allowed?" Her nose scrunched up.

Artem cut in. "The Supreme thinks we are too violent to train in her palace." He smiled like it was a compliment.

"I wish I could show her how violent I can really be," Torin said with casual coolness, which stopped Emara's heart.

"She acts like we are barbaric," Artem scoffed. "Even her guards need to train outside."

Emara just raised one eyebrow as she investigated the space for anyone she knew.

Closer to a rocky path that led up the mountain, she noticed a green cloak and fire-red hair blowing in the wind.

"Sybil's here?" She looked to Torin before glancing back over to where the Earth Witch stood beside Gideon. They were speaking, and it looked intense, but she couldn't quite work out what it was about.

"She heard whisperings of you being trained and decided to come and watch," Torin said as he unsheathed his sword from his back. "Gideon invited her, knowing how much it helped you in the early stages of dealing with your grief."

It still did.

The grit, the adrenaline, the pain everywhere else in her body other than her heart—it felt euphoric.

"Maybe she will get involved. Gideon said something about how she wakes up screaming every night and doesn't want to end up like her sister. Although she has magic, she was never trained to fight."

Torin's words punched into Emara's stomach.

She didn't want to end up like her *dead* sister.

Emara knew how hopelessness felt. She knew what it was like for fear to control her thoughts, telling her that something would attack at any moment, and she wouldn't know how to survive. She looked over at the Earth Witch again as Sybil's face paled from watching Marcus spar with another male.

Sybil caught her eye and Emara gave her a small wave, chased with a smile, encouraging her to be here.

"It's good I will finally be sparring with a woman." She turned back to her guards. "It will be a nice change from you brutes."

A laugh sounded between both Artem and Torin, and they looked at one another like they knew a secret that she didn't.

"What?" Emara's tone was demanding as she dragged her gaze over them both.

"Oh no, angel." Torin's eyes sparkled like polished sapphires and his voice sounded like warm honey. "You are far more trained than she is." He paused. "And much more equipped to handle us. We couldn't pair you two together."

"You spar with the big boys now." Artem's eyebrows danced up and he rolled his shoulders—a grin, of course, on his face.

Emara's hopes of having an easy session went flying into the wind. "Please don't say *'big boys'* ever again." She shot a look at Artem, and the boys chuckled. "I feel disturbed."

"It's true," Torin cut in with a chuckle. "You are not at the beginner level now." He looked her over in a way that made her heart hitch in her chest. "You are better than that. You have gained a few skills. You are stronger, faster, and you know a good amount of combat. If we matched you two against each other in a sparring fight, with you not qualified to actually teach combat, it could be messy. One of you could get hurt."

It was true; she didn't know how to teach. She looked over at Gideon, who was showing Sybil how to warm up, and she knew how much guts it must have taken her to attempt it, especially in front of all these warriors.

"Have there been any sightings?" Emara asked, not sure if it was only hunters that got to know that kind of official information.

"Not on the mountains," was all Torin said.

So there had been sightings or maybe other killings, just not here.

But before she could pry for more information, Artem threw a sparring stick at her, causing her mouth to close. She caught it with ease.

"You better watch that she doesn't charge at you with that." Torin laughed, nodding to the stick.

"That's exactly what I want her to do," Artem revealed with a cunning smile.

"Your wish is my command, hunter," Emara said, straightening herself.

"Stryker versus Clearwater. Are you up for it?"

Emara swallowed. She wouldn't back down, wanting nothing more than to wipe that smug grin off his face. "Absolutely."

Torin rallied around her. "Play into his weakness, Emara," he commanded from the side. "Find his before he finds yours."

"Not everyone has one," Artem shouted, looking cockier than ever as he walked over to an empty space.

Torin moved closer to Emara's ear, her heart fluttering, and whispered. "Trust me, he does. Feel the magic in your blood. Find your inner strength. Trust your instincts. He doesn't know how *trained* you are."

"I heard you don't really train with weapons, you just like to throw elbows," Artem baited her.

But recently she had, and she wondered if Torin had left out that she had been using a training pole for a reason. He liked her to keep her abilities discreet until she needed them.

She took one step forward, feeling the weight and texture of the stick—something that she had spent an entire day's training on—and rolled it over her hand once. Emara eyed up how Artem held his.

He gave her a confident grin, but she didn't return it.

She had a lot to prove. She had respect to gain, especially in her new status. Maybe she could show the hunters, who had been looking at her funny as she walked through the training peak, that they were wrong. Witches could fight without magic—and win.

Once she had centred herself, she kicked off, powering from the grainy surface underneath her boots. She gathered strength in her legs and gripped the pole tight, but not too tight, otherwise she couldn't work it to her advantage.

Torin had also taught her that.

Artem met her in the middle, their sticks clashing. He was much, much, much taller than her, and she struggled against him as he forced weight down on her stick.

"So little," he teased.

She had found his weakness already.

Artem couldn't shut up, especially when he thought he didn't need full concentration.

From the corner of her eye, she saw Torin step back, watching intently, probably so that he could critique her and then make her do it again "the right way."

But all she had to do was keep Artem distracted long enough to strike. He wouldn't expect such a new fighter to play mind games with their opponent. But the Black-steels had taught her that from the first training session.

Emara ducked under his arms, relieving the tension building against the two sticks, and the weight of him stumbled forth. She turned quickly, and it was good that she had, as Artem was attacking. His wooden pole came towards her; this time it was not horizontal, but vertical. It slashed down like a sword, almost skimming her shoulder, but she veered to the side just in time.

This time.

"Faster, Emara!" Torin coached from the side. "Move before he does. Keep him guessing what you will do next. Don't be predictable."

But she had a tactic of her own that she would like to try out.

"I was thinking about that *present,* by the way." She made herself sound distracted, like all she could do was think of helping him as they circled each other.

He looked like he wanted to ask what she had come up with, but didn't.

"I think I know what you can get *her,*" she said all too loudly. "And it's perfect."

His left eye twitched and he blinked, knowing that if she revealed her name in front of all these warriors, he would never live it down.

He swallowed.

This was it. This was her chance.

Leaning on one leg, she spun, kicking out with as much strength as her core could manage. Her foot collided with his hand, jamming his fingers against the wood enough for him to let go of one side. She took advantage of that too as she lurched forward, thrusting her pole under his, flicking it upwards and into the air.

It landed on the ground beside her.

"Yes," a deep hiss could be heard from the side as Torin approved of her move.

A grin formed on her face.

"Oh, it's not over, *Princess of Air.*" Artem bent his legs into position. He was ready to attack, barehanded. He wanted combat. "You played dirty, Emara."

"I am an Empress," she said, lifting her chin as she crouched into a battle stance. "You just underestimated me. I found your weakness when you didn't think you had one." She shot him a glare. He would never have been so relaxed with Torin when sparring. He would never have let his guard down fighting a man.

A string of irritation dangled in her chest.

Cocky hunters!

Artem Stryker's face went bright red, and he was silent for once.

He might spar with men every day, but he didn't spar with women, and they also had their advantages. He was right, it wasn't over. It was time for her to strike again.

She lunged forward, swinging the stick to hit vital parts of Artem's body. She swung right and then left, then right again, like she would if this were a real weapon and him a real foe. But with each swing she took, his foot work and dives were quicker, more precise than they had been before. He had switched modes. He was no longer a guard playing with an empress; he was a hunter, and she was his demon.

He lowered himself to the ground and swung out with his foot. She jumped, his boot missing her ankles. As she landed, her knees bent, and she wobbled slightly. Looking up, Artem was already driving forward. Kicking at her had allowed him time to change from being on the defence to being on the *offence*.

He charged her, swinging those big fists. She blocked each one, backing further and further on the grass. She could hear Torin roaring for her to stand her ground and attack, but Artem was quicker this time. Grabbing the pole, he yanked it. She fell towards him, but instead of dropping the pole or finding herself locked in his hold, she dropped her body to the ground, sliding under his legs. Pulling and yanking as hard as she could, Artem's torso came through his bent-over stance and his legs went over his head as the pole tripped him.

He practically somersaulted. She had used her weakness in height and turned it into a strength. And she had used his advantage in weight to throw him off balance.

She didn't have time to think about what she had done as he rose behind her. She rolled, keeping her poles grip, and sprung to her feet. She had no idea how she'd managed it, but Emara now stood above him, her pole angled towards Artem's throat to deliver the killing blow.

Both shock and respect shot onto Artem's face, but mostly shock. It thrilled her to the core. A few gasps from the watching crowd had Emara's senses tingling.

She had won. *She had won.* She had really done it.

"Did I never tell you I was good with a spear?" A jaw-aching grin arched in Emara's face. "It must have slipped my mind."

Her chest heaving from the effort it had taken to put him on his back, she finally drew in an icy breath of air. He wasn't a small creature by any means, and she certainly didn't have the power that he did. So she had to be craftier, play to his weaknesses, use the element of surprise.

"No." He laughed, raising his hands in the air. A surrender. "I forgot about your abilities with a spear."

A horrible flashback hit her mind of the last time she had held a spear. Blood, screams, and Taymir Solden's face appeared in her mind. She dropped her training weapon instantly and took a few steps back. She took a breath, trying to gather herself.

Artem laughed, unaware of what memories he had just triggered in her mind. "I don't think a witch has ever put me on my back before." He looked thoughtful. "In fact, I take that back, there have been a few that have—"

"I don't need to know." Emara closed her eyes, shaking her head. "I. Do. Not. Need. To. Know."

Artem put his hand out for her to take it, a truce in their sparring, and she took it, hauling his mass up.

"Nice work," he said as he stood. "I am impressed."

"As am I." A rich, sensual tone drove a tingling sensation deep into her core as it arrived from behind her.

She turned to Torin, pride splashed in every part of his face.

"That," he said, with both dimples showing, "was fucking marvellous."

She couldn't help but let a gleaming smile form on her lips too.

He had coached her and pointed out where she needed to work. Where she needed to get better. Always pushing her...

Artem laughed. "She clearly has a great mentor."

"Was that a compliment, Stryker?" Torin hit the shoulder of his best friend.

"Actually, it was a compliment to Emara. It looks like she learns quickly. You have an eye for combat."

Torin turned to face her. "Agreed. That is absolutely your weapon." His eyes darkened, looking at the pole.

"But I don't want it to be wooden next time we practise. Let's keep it steel."

A lethal smile devoured his beautiful face and struck a chord in her heart.

"I would be up for that," she said, feeling the adrenaline from the fight pump in her veins.

By the expression on his face, it was as if she had said something obscenely crude, and he couldn't hide the fact that he loved it. "You, talking about working with weapons...that's just made my morning even better." His wicked dimple appeared deeper.

"Shut up." She laughed, rolling her eyes.

"I think you should fight me with that pole." His eyes blazed like they had just been set alight by witchfire.

"Maybe I will." She smiled back at him, knowing the danger that lurked between them.

"Okay, when you guys start eye fucking," Artem cut through the air, "that, is my cue to leave."

Torin's mouth opened and closed again, but before he could say anything else that could increase the tension swarming around them, Emara's eyes darted to Sybil, who was walking towards her with Gideon by her side.

He looked impressed.

Her stomach flipped.

"That was amazing." Sybil's eyes were wide as she called across the clearing. As they both reached where Emara stood, she said, "You are a natural out there."

"Actually"—Emara's eyes darted between the two Blacksteels, who were both looking at her—"these two taught me. With a little help from Marcus too. I am not a natural." She gave a shy smile.

Admiration polished Sybil's warm eyes. "But you fought today like you have fought your entire life. I didn't know witches even trained."

Something in her voice sounded like hurt and regret, like if she could have fought, she could have saved her sister. And in Emara's experience, that was the worst road for your mind to take.

"Witches don't normally train," Gideon cut in. "We trained Emara because she asked us to. She couldn't stand the idea of not being able to protect herself, and at the time, she thought she was human."

The words from Gideon made her heart cease, but it was true. They had seen how desperate she had been to never be in that position again. "We were only supposed to show her the basics. how to defend herself," Gideon continued.

"That looked like more than the basics to me." Sybil looked him over, her leaf-green eyes wide.

Gideon's gaze lingered on Sybil's face, before he smiled. "Witches can be persuasive when they want something." His gaze met Emara's. "She got sucked into our training, and the rest is history."

"It's our magic," Emara panted, finally feeling the effects of the spar after the adrenaline had died a little. "We pick up the training quickly. It's like if you wanted to be an artist, you could probably learn to paint better than the average mortal, or so Naya told me. But from the minute I began training, I was hooked. I didn't want to be a helpless little girl when any other monster that exists in this world came for me." She found Sybil's large eyes, watching her with understanding. "I practically begged the Blacksteels to start training me so that when the monsters did come, I would be able to handle myself."

Sybil's eyes welled with tears, and Emara had the instant urge to reach out and comfort her.

"I know I have magic now, but I didn't then," Emara said, looking at the Blacksteel brothers, who both nodded. "I still don't know how to harness that properly. So until I do, I don't want to use my...my magic in a situation like that." She shuddered at the thought of air or fire surging from her, unleashed and uncontrollable. "I don't know how to control it," she finished with a whisper.

"Then maybe we can be beneficial to each other," Sybil said, her voice slightly hoarse. "I can teach you everything I know about witchcraft, and you can teach me at least one of those impressive spin and kick things you did." She smiled wholesomely, and Emara now understood how her plainness could turn to beauty in a second. "I would say that could be a deal between us. What do you think, House Air?"

"It sounds like we both have ourselves a very good deal, House Earth."

CHAPTER
THIRTY-EIGHT
EMARA

Sybil had stayed true to her word. After training with the hunters and eating lunch, they found a room to experiment in every day. Their favourite room seemed to be home for unwanted furniture that lay piled on top of each other, but it was quiet and uninterrupted. They practised basic elemental magic, and it was things that Naya had never had the time to touch base with. Torin and Gideon normally stood guard outside, like they were now, and it was nice to see the two of them spend time together in a way that wasn't in the sparring room or at each other's throats. Even if they were on duty in a different way, they could at least talk.

Emara's stomach squeezed inside her body at that thought.

Maybe that wasn't a good idea for them to talk.

Gideon would need to know about them. Her heart dropped at the thought of hurting him. She didn't know if his heart still lay with her, but it would be unfair for him not to understand where hers currently did. Surely, he would have an inclination after what Torin had done at the ascension ceremony. He would have an idea of where his brother's heart lay. But did he understand where hers did? Everyone else in the kingdom seemed to be talking about it, according to Lorta and Kaydence. Is that why he had been avoiding her?

Emara wondered if it should be Torin to tell Gideon about what had happened, about what *was* happening between them. But as she thought about it, she didn't exactly know what Torin would say. That they had kissed? That he had her *feeling* more than just a maddening sexual attraction, more than lust—Gods!— more than any man had ever made her feel before. Should she tell Gideon that it was ridiculous and confusing, yet consuming and spellbinding?

Should she tell him that maybe she did consider having a future with his brother?

I want you to be my future, not because it was forced upon us, but because I would choose you. I would choose you over everything.

Emara knew she should have never let herself *feel* the things she did for Torin. She had picked Gideon first. She had wanted him, and she would have still wanted him had he not betrayed her. With all that swirling around in her mind, a little pang of guilt questioned, *should it just have been Torin from the beginning?* Should she never have felt what she did for Gideon?

All said and done, she had wanted Torin even before the waterfall of Uttara washed away her denial.

She had felt that deep connection when she had looked into Gideon's eyes once. But somewhere in the midst of all her chaos, their connection had weakened. His betrayal had broken anything they'd had left. And Torin had picked up the pieces.

She should have been focusing on gently floating the several feathers that lay on the table in front of her. Why was she so utterly distracted by the turmoil in her heart today?

Sybil's voice became more apparent than the voice that ranted internally.

"How did you seem more focused in a sparring fight with a whole lot of warriors watching you than you do now?"

Emara looked up at the Earth Witch and the truth fell from her lips. "I had more to lose out there."

"Did you?" Sybil's light tone had Emara's head swirling again.

Did she?

She laughed. "I'm sorry. I am normally very focused when it comes to learning about magic. I am just feeling a little distracted."

"Is it because Gideon is outside?" Sybil asked.

Emara choked on the breath she had inhaled.

Sybil's mouth slanted to the side. "He told me about you two."

Maybe Sybil and Gideon were closer than Emara thought.

Not that that was a bad thing. It was great for Gideon to find comfort with someone, to trust someone, but the comment took her by surprise.

Dread crawled up Emara's throat as she asked, "What did he say?"

It would be the first time she would be able to hear the words he had said about her, how he truly felt.

The small witch stood silent against the pane of a large window, dwarfing her in size. The winter glare coming through the glass illuminated the vibrant red in her hair. "Look, if you are feeling distracted, we can continue to practise after dinner." She straightened herself. "You have done a lot of magic in the last couple of days. We can take a break."

"What did he say?" Emara breathed, closing her eyes. "Is it so bad that you can't tell me?"

A long moment passed between them before the Earth Witch spoke again. "He didn't say much more than the facts about what had happened, but I can feel when I look at him that his heart is broken."

Emara's eyes fluttered open as her own heart cracked a little.

His betrayal had been the beginning of the cracking in her heart, and Cally's death had well and truly shattered it. Nothing had been the same after those moments, and her heart never would be the same again.

Sybil spoke once more. "He told me what he did." She hung her head, playing with a stray feather on the floor with her foot. "And I told him that he was wrong for what he did to you, and that you might forgive him one day. You may just need time." She paused. "But I can see that..." She trailed off, looking out the window. "I don't want to offend you."

Emara swallowed down a feeling of trepidation. "You can see that my heart is somewhere else?"

"Yes," Sybil said under her breath, meeting her eyes.

Emara's chest felt extremely heavy, like a lake had frozen on top of her, its weight crushing.

If Sybil, who barely knew her, could see it, then so could Gideon.

"You should not feel guilty of where your heart lies, Emara." The Empress of Earth held her gaze, her features still soft and soulful.

Emara shifted on her feet. "I just wish—"

"That they were not brothers by blood?" Sybil finished her sentence.

Emara nodded, clasping her hands together so tightly that her skin strained, and a sickness climbed in her throat.

"Your heart does not feel guilty of what it desires, only your head." Sybil's voice was smooth and wise, the way Naya's was. It was such an earthy trait, she realised, and one she admired. "Once your head gets around the technicalities of your heart, you will be able to forgive yourself. Don't be so hard on your heart, Emara. It's sometimes the only truthful thing you will find in this life."

Emara looked up at the girl she now considered a friend and let out a sigh. "I thought my whole life that I would fall in love with someone like Gideon." She hesitated. "I had always wanted someone kind and sensible, someone who was reliable and loving. Someone who would give me that...feeling of security. I think losing my parents so young, I had trouble trusting the world, the fate of my path." Her cheeks pulled in. "I always looked for someone stable, but in Mossgrave, stability was the only thing a husband offered. And I couldn't stand the thought of that small village life. I couldn't stand settling for just stability. After a short period of knowing Gideon, I thought it could have been him. You know, he has the stability, but there is also that edge to him, that warmth, that passion. I thought he could have given me that and more. He was kind, tentative, and patient. I believed he could have given me everything I ever wanted in someone."

Sybil's brow smoothed out as she walked towards Emara. "Are you trying to tell me that Torin Blacksteel is none of those things?"

The fact that Sybil said his name out loud sent her heart into her mouth. The question stunned her, even though she had pondered it more than enough for herself.

"I would hardly call Torin Blacksteel sensible," she said.

They both laughed.

"I am not going to lie to you." Sybil snuffed a laugh, but then her face straightened. "I knew who Torin Blacksteel was before I came here, and before Gideon became my guard." She looked over at Emara, "I knew of Gideon too. Anyone who is someone in the Kingdom of Caledorna knows of the infamous Blacksteels. But I do find myself surprised."

"In what way?" Emara couldn't hide the intrigue from her tone.

"Pleasantly." She raised a brow. "With both of them." She loitered near the chair that was close to the table of feathers Emara had been trying to move for an hour. "The way he declared his vows to you at the ceremony of our ascension." She swooned, blowing out a low whistle. "He has it bad for you, Emara Clearwater."

Emara laughed, her heart swelling as much as her throat. "I think he was just trying to take over. He loves attention." Heat rushed into her cheeks, knowing well he didn't do it for any of the reasons she had just stated.

"No, don't play it down. I know what I saw." The slight witch batted her lashes, and the freckles danced along her cheeks as she smiled a little. "What we *all* saw. And it was more than just his vow to protect you as your guard."

Emara knew that.

He had already told her how he felt about her, and it had rattled her soul to the core.

Emara blinked a few times. "Before I was the Air Empress, the commander of the Blacksteel Clan promised his firstborn son to my coven." She stopped speaking, her chest feeling a little tighter. "And the Empress of Air was promised to him in an alliance forged by marriage."

Sybil's fingertips drummed on the wooden chair she hovered over. "And you're scared that an alliance is all you are to him?"

Emara's shoulders slumped as she chewed the inside of her cheek. She hadn't even noticed how much she had been tensing until now. "I don't know, it's more complicated than just admitting feelings for each other and then living happily ever after. I don't want an alliance for just artillery, and I know he doesn't want a *bride* who will raise wards and create portals just because she can."

Not that she could do that either. Yet.

Sybil walked over and placed a hand on Emara's shoulder, and instantly, a sweet wave of calm projected through her. "I am sorry, but you needed that." She smiled. "I could see the tension creeping into your forehead, and my grandmother always told me that my forehead would stay that way if I kept frowning."

Emara laughed, really laughed. "Mine too," she gasped. "She told me I wouldn't fare well if I made such un-ladylike faces."

They both chuckled for a moment more, and then it died on the air.

"What Torin did at the ascension, Emara, declaring that in front of everyone..." she said, her leaf-coloured eyes bright. "That is not a declaration of someone who is settling for something he isn't ready to die for." She placed a hand to her heart. "And it is evidently not just because of his duty to keep you safe or thinking about his clan requirements. It's more than that."

"What if it's not real?" Emara said, when what she really wanted to ask was *what if I am not enough?*

"What if it is real?" Sybil countered. Emara's heart pounded in her chest, her magic thrumming in her veins at the thought of it being real. "It looks real to me. There are so many things in life that you can force or fake, but true love is not one of them."

True love.

"I didn't say I loved him."

"You didn't have to." Sybil smiled gently, her curls bounding around her like a fiery sunset. "I am a healer. I can feel what lies in your heart by just being with you. I think you are scared to get hurt, I think you are terrified of what you feel for him because you know it is bottomless. But you shouldn't be scared."

Emara pulled her lip between her teeth and looked towards the bundle of feathers sitting on a limestone table, ignoring her friend's last statement.

Bottomless.

She wasn't ready to go exploring in *that* cave. Not now.

Call to your magic, Sybil had instructed before this conversation had sneakily distracted them. *Tell it what you want it to do, command it.* Concentrating on the air that gave her breath, she inhaled. When she exhaled, she commanded it forward, asking it to *listen.* The feathers twitched, and as the air reached them, she asked her element to help them *rise.* The air moved unseen, but Emara could feel it and the feathers began to shift and float. One at a time, they moved into the air and hovered above the table.

Sybil let out an excited squawk and clapped. "Yes. That's it. Now place them down."

"Not yet." Emara smiled. She closed her eyes, harnessing the feelings running through her body, the *bottomless* feelings of passion and magic. She spoke to the air again, asking it to help the feathers *drift.* She moved her hand, acting as a guide for her magic to follow, and as a light flurry of coolness bristled her hair, she opened her eyes to see the feathers circling and floating in the air.

Her magic was more controlled for once, and a laugh bubbled in her throat before it burst into pleasured hilarity. Sybil was laughing too as Emara moved her hand, guiding the feathers towards her. They giggled, but she dug in deep to that well of magic as the air carried the white feathers and floated them around the Earth Witches head, circling like a halo.

Like an *angel.*

The feathers fluttered down around her shoulders as Emara flicked her wrist. They flew to the table, levitating for a second before falling onto the surface of the limestone.

"Very good." Sybil beamed. "I can see that when you are focused, you're a quick learner. It's a trait you have picked up through your bloodline."

Emara smiled. "Well, let's see if combat is one of yours."

Sybil snorted as she moved to clean up the feathers. "Not likely. Did you see me out there?"

"I did. And you are doing amazing. You just need to keep working on it." Emara exhaled, feeling the magic compliment her blood. "Thank you for today."

"Don't mention it." Sybil shook her head, her face sincere. "You learn so quickly, I will have you moving mountains in no time."

"No." Emara smiled, her cheeks a little flushed. "Not for that."

Sybil's nose crinkled in confusion.

"For being there for me. For just chatting with me." Emara looked down, not sure she should say what she was about to. "I know what it is like to miss someone, especially when you want to talk to them and tell them everything about your day." Emara's lips pursed and then parted. "I didn't have a sister by blood, but by the Gods, I had a sister by loyalty and friendship, and she was taken from me too."

Emara's nose started to sting as her heart ached so harshly, and Sybil stilled where she stood.

"I would have told her everything from my mess with Gideon, to everything that's happened with Torin, to even just the small things, like learning how to float feathers or sending a fireletter." Emara inhaled, trying to gather herself, but failed.

Tears streamed down Sybil's face too, but she didn't make a sound.

"I know how much you can rely on one person to always have your back or to hold your hand when you are scared. Or even just to talk utter nonsense with until you both fall asleep, and a sister is one of them." Emara let her tears flow, and they fell hard and heavy. "I just wanted to let you know that I had a sister too, and the darkness took her from me. And now I have an empty void of where she used to be. She was my best friend." Emara choked a little on her words. "I will never be able to replace her, and I feel like you know that feeling too."

Sybil nodded, her face wet with emotion and her eyes puffy.

"But we don't have to replace them, I suppose." Emara swallowed, feeling bravery kick in her broken heart. "I haven't known you long, but you have shown me kindness. You earthy witches seem to do that a lot." She laughed through her tears as they leaked onto her lips. She wiped them. "I just wanted to let you know that I...I will be that person for you, Sybil." She paused.

"When you need a friend or even just a chat like today, I will be there."

Sybil's hand found hers and she squeezed, like she had the night standing in the line of ascension.

Emara nodded to Sybil. "I cannot be your sister by blood, but I can be your sister by loyalty." They both smiled through teary eyes. "I can be that person. Even if we are not in the same coven. Witches are allowed to form unions too, right?"

Without speaking, Sybil threw her arms around Emara's neck and wept. She hugged her back, consoling her. It felt so natural to be here with her, and it felt like she had known her a lot longer than she had. Maybe their paths had crossed in another life.

"Thank you," Sybil finally whispered, sniffling. "You have no idea how much that means to me. To my family, my coven." She inhaled. "I needed to hear that more than you know."

"I had a little inkling of how much you needed to hear that." Emara pulled back, smiling at her newest friend. "Maybe your lessons in Earth Magic are paying off already." She picked up two white feathers and handed one to Sybil. "To Sisters of Oath." She raised the feather.

A gleam brightened Sybil's vast green eyes, and she placed her feather against Emara's. "To Sisters of Oath."

CHAPTER THIRTY-NINE
EMARA

T he next few days in the lead up to the Winter Solstice ball were mainly made up of training sessions and learning how to move and create with her magic. Once she finished a combat session, she and Sybil would take lunch to Emara's room, where they practised witchcraft until it was dark outside.

Her maids had joined too. Lorta and Kaydence told her about the legends of her coven and the secrets of others. They had actually spoken a little of her grandmother, and what their mothers had once thought of her abdication as the Supreme. Their families had both seemed to think it was out of character for a woman like Theodora Clearwater, who had reigned proudly for years, to suddenly renounce her crown and disappear. Lorta even admitted that witches from House Air had tried to search for her, but simply couldn't locate her.

It was like she had fallen off the face of the earth, hiding behind some magic veil.

Lorta had darted out the room when the chat had turned to fashion and frocks, squealing that she must show Emara a few ball gowns that had come in from a seamstress in the city. The girls had gone over colour palettes from green all the way through purple as they sat atop Emara's bed. A debate had sparked on if she should wear lilac or silver, and Emara smiled as she clamped her lips shut, not willing to get involved.

"You could always wear black." A deep voice came from the doorway, and she instantly cranked her neck around to see Torin standing in the frame, his body competing with the space to fill it. "Or red." His eyes found her gaze as a lazy smirk developed on his lips. Pleasurable nerves infiltrated her stomach at the sight of it. She hadn't even heard him come in. "Red always suits you." His lips parted slowly, and she watched them open, seeing all the things he wanted to say lingering on them silently. He peeped over his long, dark lashes at the girls, smouldering his gorgeous eyes at them. "Could I have a moment alone with the Empress of Air?" His voice was low and alluring, making her imagination turn to all things delightfully mischievous.

They hadn't been alone in days. She had been busy meeting new witches, witches of her coven, or she had been training her craft. With the Winter Solstice Ball coming up, she had also been arranging with the empresses and Supreme how the palace would be decorated for the festivities. The only time she had seen Torin was at combat training in the mornings.

A taunting pleasure ran through her, landing straight in her centre at the thought of them being alone. It sent a wave of shivers over her skin.

"Of course," Sybil croaked like she had just snapped

out of his invisible charms. Emara dragged her eyes from Torin's and looked at the girls. They were stunned stiff, not moving.

"That would be kind of you." His smile dripped of pure sexual masculinity. "Make sure you look after my brother," he shot at Sybil.

She stood, cheeks as red as her stunning hair, and just about squeaked, nodding her head.

Emara rolled her eyes.

He wasn't *that* good-looking. She glanced at Torin again. He knew exactly what he was doing as he winked at her.

Okay, maybe he was that good-looking.

Folding her arms over her chest, she tutted. He probably used his charm to get his way with women all the time. Her brows lifted and she watched as the girls brushed past him, taking their leave at his request. His jaw tightened to hold a smile, pressing his lips together. After the door closed, she shook her head.

"What?" he asked, dimples already deep on his cheeks.

"Just by flaunting a little charm, smouldering your eyes, and smiling obnoxiously wide, do you think you are always going to get your own way with every woman you come across?"

"I am sorry, was that a question or a dig at my character?" His lips tugged, showing every sign that he was trying not to laugh. "It's getting harder by the day to tell."

"That eye thing that you do"—She pointed one

finger at him, and the other hand rested on her hip.— "it doesn't work on me. So you can cut that out."

"I don't know what you are talking about." He walked slowly to her, taking his sweet time as his gaze trailed over her. "Maybe my eyes don't work on you..." he said as he reached her. He dragged a strand of her hair between his fingers, watching it as it glided through them. "But I know what does work." His stare found hers again.

Her heart punching out of her chest, Emara dared to ask, "And what would that be?"

"My mouth," he said in a way that stole the air from her lungs.

Almost all at once, she pictured his lips on her flesh, travelling with no boundaries.

"Is that so?" She pushed out her chin, trying to hide behind a façade she wasn't even sure *she* thought believable.

"I am sure of it." He looked down at her, his shoulders relaxing, setting out even wider than before.

"And what makes you so sure?" She cursed herself for asking the question, knowing full well that his answer was about to stir unholy feelings in her.

"Because every time my mouth meets yours"—he looked down at her lips like he was stopping himself from claiming them with his own that very second— "your body reacts in a way that tells me you like it." He wrapped one hand around her waist, dragging her to him. "And that pleases me."

"It pleases you?" A strangling sound escaped her throat.

"Mmmm..." His brow pulled down as a deep rumble left his mouth. "It pleases me when I can see you fighting against the pleasure and knowing that I am giving that feeling to you."

"I see." Her voice was two stages huskier than before.

"There are a few things I have noted that you like, actually."

"You are so very observant," she said, breathless.

"I know you like it when I put my mouth here." He brushed her hair back, his eyes on the sensitive spot on her neck which always made her toes curl when his mouth found it. "And you like it when I kiss you here." He trailed a fingertip along her jaw and then to her lips. "And here, actually." His finger dragged down her lip, causing them to part. She fought a moan as the soaring heat from his touch made her want it all the more. Her heart thundered, but she wouldn't let him win his wicked little game of *who would cave first*. She was on a winning streak.

Emara remembered how he had looked, how he had acted, when she finally started fighting back with some teasing of her own. She had loved every minute of that power.

She always had a choice.

Choosing to stir up a little fight of her own, she closed her eyes and kissed into his fingers, giving them one slow embrace with her lips. She fluttered her eyes open to witness sweet, glorified victory as desire arose in his eyes.

He quickly gathered himself and trailed his long fingers over her throat, feeling it bob underneath his touch. Torin circled a finger over her heart and down to the peak of her feminine curves. She fought back a gasp at the pleasure.

He didn't take his eyes from hers as he said, "And you like it when I kiss here."

A spine-tingling ache drove itself into her core. "That's a lot of places you think I like being kissed."

"I can think of one more place that you would like." A tightening in his jaw revealed just how much he wanted to kiss her where he had in mind.

She almost begged him there and then to show her, to kiss the sacred place he had in mind and ease the thick tension that lingered in the room around them, building and building.

"I can show you," he said. "If you would like to go exploring again." There was no banter in his tone. He was deadly serious. "All you need to do is give me the signal."

Him and his damned signals! Before she could agree, before she could say yes and push him down her body, her lips crashed into his. That would silence the wicked taunts that came from them. He pushed back on her, fighting for dominance. Warm lips opened her mouth, opening them only for him. Heat climbed all over her skin as his hands pushed themselves into her hair, his tongue moving against her mouth in easy, fast strokes. A pool of warmth heated between her thighs, and she pulled him closer, not quite getting enough. She needed more.

And he obliged, moving her backwards towards the bed. Instead of reaching the bed, he pivoted, spinning her. A swoosh of air left her lungs and she gasped into his mouth. He pressed her against the wall, one hand against the cold quartz above her and the other pinned below him.

Emara panted in anticipation, in hope that he would bow down and kiss her *anywhere.*

But instead, he caged her between his arms and said, "Unfortunately, we don't have the time I would like to take you to bed tonight." His voice was raspy and full of want. "Not with the things I want to do. With all the things we could explore."

She didn't know if it was the comments or the sounds of promise that broke over his lips, but her hips pushed out from the wall, meeting every inch of hardness that he offered. He looked down at her body grazing his own and then he faced her.

A carnal smile engulfed his lips. "Can you feel what you do to me?"

A rush of searing hotness blushed her cheeks and coasted all the way down her spine. She had done that to him—and it wasn't the first time.

"You should feel what you have done to me." Her voice came out smaller than she had wanted, but at least it had come out at all.

"Angel," he breathed, lifting a hand to her cheek, his eyes dazzling with a soulful danger she was enamoured by. "I fully intend to feel how ready you are for me." He grinned. "Again."

Her breathing hitched at the promise.

"And the next time I do, I want to take my time with you." The tamed embers in his eyes ignited into fully fledged flames. They were two untamed, icy fires, full of delight and sin. "I don't want to be disturbed when I kiss the area I have in mind." His sensual gaze drifted down to her naval and then lower. "Lorta will be back any second. I didn't see her in your little gang tonight, so I assume she didn't get my message for us not to be disturbed," he said. "And I don't want her to see what I so wish I was doing to you right now."

Emara had completely forgotten of Lorta's anticipated return with the gowns.

Gods, she barely knew her own name right now.

Emara tried her best to control the rise and fall of her chest. She brought her hands down, unpinned from the wall, and rested them on his chest. "That would be very indecent of us."

"It would be my favourite kind of indecent." He grinned.

Unable to stop herself, Emara beamed back.

"Anyway, you distracted me," he said, pulling back ever so slightly, relieving her hair from his hands. "I didn't come here to have an *improper* conversation with you, believe it or not." His brows raised. "I came here because I wanted to give you something."

"You wanted to give me something?" she echoed.

"Yes." Gone were his cheeky taunts, replaced with something more genuine and real. "I got you a gift for the winter solstice."

"A gift?" Her voice was small again, and she hated that she couldn't stop it as the sound left her lips.

"You know the tradition, right?"

She almost grinned, remembering Artem and his

efforts on thinking up a gift for Breighly. "But you didn't have to do that."

"Close your eyes," he instructed with a grin that she didn't really trust, not when it caused her chest to ache.

"What?" she squawked. "You have gotten me a gift that involves me receiving it blind?"

He chuckled before backing to the door. He put out a hand, commanding her to stay where he had pinned her only moments ago. "Close your eyes," he said again.

"I am not closing my eyes." She widened them out of sheer defiance.

"Just do it."

"Absolutely not."

He stopped moving. "Do you trust me?" His brow smoothed, causing his sharp features to soften.

Did she?

With protecting her? *Yes.* With her life? *Absolutely.* With her heart? She swallowed, unable to answer that just yet. With a present? *Absolutely not!*

But with blind faith in him, she closed her eyes, fluttering them shut with a sigh. She could hear the footsteps towards the door, its opening, and him coming back in. Whatever he had gotten her must have just been right outside her door. The urge to open her eyes overwhelmed her senses as he could be heard coming closer. The warmth from his presence gave her stomach a dipping sensation.

"Put out your hands," he commanded softly.

She did, not knowing exactly what to expect.

Oh Gods. A present from Torin Blacksteel? It could be *anything.*

Something heavy and cool was placed into her palms. She braced herself for her cheeks to bloom bright red as he said, "Open your eyes."

She did.

In her palms was a silver and gold double-edged dagger. It was short, but the detail on it was captivating. The metals merged together in a design fit for a goddess of war. Embedded in its handle was a beautiful ruby begging her to touch it.

"Be careful," he said. "It's not as it seems. It has an unexpected side." He smirked, flashing his teeth. "Like you."

She looked up at him, his face unreadable as he drew back from her.

"Place your palm over the ruby and grip the weapon tight," he instructed.

Holding the dagger out at arm's length, she squeezed. Two poles shot out, elongating from its centre, stabbing out blades. It was now the size of a spear. It was magnificent.

"A spear." She gaped at Torin.

"Do you like her?"

"Her?"

He closed the space between them and ran hand over the pole, directing her to engraved writing—*The Agnes*.

Callyn's middle name.

A swelling in her heart caused her to choke.

"You did this for me?"

"She's yours. Every woman should have her own weapon, right?"

How did he always find a reason for her breathing to stammer?

"Thank you," Emara mouthed, sounding a little strangled. She shifted the weight of the weapon into her other hand. It fit perfectly in her hand. "Torin, it is so beautiful."

"Just like the empress who will command her." His voice came out strong, but something softer floated in his eyes.

Looking from the weapon that felt so impressively at home in her hands, she looked at him. "Torin, I haven't gotten you a gift." Shame crept into her tone. "I should have gone into the city before we left or—"

"Emara," he stopped her, placing a hand atop her raised weapon to lower it. "Hunters don't expect a gift in return. That is not the tradition." He still held on to her wrist, not telling go. "I am just grateful I could give you something." His blue eyes flickered bright, something momentous lying deep within them.

"I absolutely love it." She gaped down at it again, her breath catching in her throat as she spoke. He worked a hand around the back of her neck, pulling her head forward to his lips. He placed a gentle kiss on her forehead whilst he disarmed the weapon from her grip.

"Thank you so much," she whispered. He must have gripped the band where the ruby lay, because the poles slid back in, disappearing like they were never there.

"And when it's this size, you can strap it around that pretty thigh of yours."

She bit down on her lip to trap a smile. "Maybe I can match it with that little burgundy dress you love so much," a velvet purr left her mouth, and she was stunned that she could sound so in control when her heart certainly was not.

"Now, Clearwater..." He ran the hand that wasn't holding her weapon over her cheekbone and onto her jaw. "Do you know how much of a tragedy it would be if my heart gave out before I got to taste every inch of you?" He lowered the hand that had cupped her jaw down her plain white shirt.

"You always did tell me how important it was to find the weakness in my opponent before he found mine," she breathed as he loosened a button at the top of her blouse and played with it.

"You normally can't hear me over the rolling of your eyes." His glittering gaze narrowed.

Just as a giggle escaped her, she heard two sharp knocks on the door. It was a warning from outside that someone was coming in. Taking the hint, Torin handed Emara her weapon and moved back in time for Lorta to usher everything that she had pulled together into the room, including the other two guards that made up her cluster.

A laugh burst from her mouth as she caught sight of Artem Stryker carrying in a stack of dresses that over-whelmed even his physique. Magin looked at them over boxes that she presumed had shoes in them.

"You owe me for this, Clearwater," Artem grumbled.

Emara looked over at Torin, who was one second away from losing control over his features. His hand went up to his mouth. "You would look good in all of them, Stryker."

"Shut up, asshole." Artem's eyes dragged from Torin's to the bundle of material in every colour in his hands. "I look good in anything, I will have you know."

Emara giggled again, biting into the side of her cheek.

Lorta's face was bright red as she glanced at the guards standing in the room. "It's girls only, I am afraid."

The cheeky expression on Artem's face dropped. "You promised I could watch if I helped you carry them."

"Like I would allow that." Torin's jaw hardened as he shot his friend, a look that forced him to reconsider his words.

"I lied." Lorta bopped her shoulders up. "Sorry."

After tugging his eyes from Artem's face, Torin looked to Emara. "I will see you tomorrow." He hesitated a moment before closing the space between them. Taking her face in his hands, he kissed her passionately. His lips hovered over hers for a precious moment that she wished was longer and then he was gone. Feeling like her knees could buckle at any given second, she looked at who was still left in the room.

Artem stood with his mouth open, even though a grin pulled it to one side. Magin's face was still unreadable, but his eyebrows were higher on his forehead than normal. Lorta just stared at her, in wide-eyed silence.

"Well," Emara said, trying to pretend like nothing had just happened, like Torin Blacksteel hadn't claimed her mouth in front of them. "Let's look at these dresses for the Winter Solstice Ball, shall we?"

CHAPTER FORTY
EMARA

The night must have been fading into the early morning as the wind battered little shards of ice into the window. Not sure if the outside conditions were responsible for keeping her awake or having never ending thoughts of Torin Blacksteel, Emara rolled on to her side. Her eyes caught a glimpse of the stunningly fatal weapon on the pillow next to her. It glowed from the embers of the eternally burning witchfire in the fireplace. Her new weapon was strong and unyielding, and it was a promise of who she could be when she held it.

Pulling her hand from underneath the heavy blanket, she stroked her fingertips along her gift. She had never owned such a deadly item. It was hers to train with and to use. It would be used to prevent someone or *something* from taking her life like she had done before, driving a similar spear through Taymir Solden.

Her body stiffened, trying to purge the memory from her mind.

But it lingered. The smell, the screams, the death...

Muffled voices came from outside her door, causing her to raise from her pillow. She knew at least one guard stood outside her door, but she didn't know who it was. Torin hadn't returned after taking his leave that evening, so the possibility of it being Artem or Magin was high.

The muffled voices grew louder.

Was someone arguing? The blankets fell around her waist as she sat up fully.

"The Empress of Air will be sleeping," she heard Magin hiss.

"I must see her," a familiar voice said. "It is urgent."

Before Emara could rack her brains thinking whom the voice belonged to, her door opened. She heard boots along her floor and a sigh from Magin before seeing another hunter stand before her fireplace.

It was Kellen Blacksteel.

Magin shuffled in after him.

"I tried to stop him." Magin looked towards Emara apologetically. "But it seems he has something of importance to tell you."

"I am deeply sorry to have awoken you, Emara," Kellen said.

He was panting. Something was wrong.

Shoving the covers from her legs, she stood, every hair on her body standing with her.

"You didn't wake me," she said, searching his face for anything that would give the reason for his urgent visit, some clarity. "Is there something wrong, Kellen?" She looked from him to Magin.

Whatever it was, Magin seemed to look as lost as she was.

"I must speak with you," he said, his normally olive skin pale against the darkness of his hair. Broken moon beams glared through her window, casting shadows onto his face. "Alone."

Magin stood forward to object, but Emara nodded. "It's okay," she said to Magin. "I am safe with a Blacksteel. You know that."

His eyes narrowed, but his lips pulled into a line at her silent instruction to leave them alone.

As the door closed, silence filled the space.

Kellen stood in what looked like nightwear for hunters, in grey breeches and a long-sleeved tunic. His hair lay limp against his head, his features dragging.

"Is everything okay?" she asked again, knowing it couldn't be if Kellen Blacksteel had requested to see her in the premature hours of the morning.

His eyes were dark pits as he glared at her, his features dripping with troublesome thoughts. He parted his lips, then looked away.

Oh Gods, this was it. The conversation she knew they needed to have was about to happen.

"Kellen, it's okay," she began to say. Her tone was so soft and gentle, it reminded her of Huntswood cotton. "I won't tell anyone about what I saw."

His eyes suddenly flew to hers and he swallowed. "That's not why I am here."

Confusion fell over her. She opened her mouth to speak, but Kellen was quicker.

"I need to tell you something about myself," he said. Distress almost drowned his youthful appearance.

Emara's heart started beating at twice the pace it

should. "Kellen, I do not judge you. Love is love, regardless of the person your heart chooses."

He spoke with a cold frustration this time. "I cannot echo again that I am not here for that reason."

She blinked. "Then why?"

His jaw tightened, and in that moment, he looked more like Torin than Gideon. "I am different from my brothers." He coughed. "And not in the way you think." His heterochronic gaze found hers again. He continued, "I know you are new to this world, but there are complexities to magical blood that even the ancients didn't understand."

He must have realised that she was not following, because he continued.

"I see things." His voice shook as he explained. "I dream of-of *things*. I have since I was a child." He paused. Emara stood quiet, not wanting to interrupt him even though she had no idea what he meant or where he was going with this conversation. "I dream of things and then they come true. They happen." The hairs on Emara's body stood again as a shiver snaked through her.

"My dreams—well I wouldn't call them *dreams,* they would qualify more as night terrors—but I *dream* and then they become a warped reality. I dreamt of the battle of the Blood Moon and what happened with the demon blade in Gideon's arm. I saw how outnumbered we would be. That's why I was so terrified to fight that night; not because it was my first big hunt, but because of what I had seen in my dream the night before." He looked up to the ceiling with a sigh. "I thought my brother was going to die. If I had told someone, then—then maybe we could have prevented that from happening." He looked at her. "I could have stopped it. Lucky for me, we have the best healers in the city."

"You're a seer," she breathed, heart pounding.

"My mother refers to them—*me*—as a True Dreamer." He rubbed his hand over the back of his neck. "Only my mother and one other person knows about what I am."

He meant Arlo Stryker.

It had to be. Artem had said on the trip here that his brother, Arlo, and Kellen were in the Selection together. It looked like Arlo Stryker was the only person in the world Kellen Blacksteel let in.

"But the hunters don't like having a True Dreamer in their clans, one that bears mixed traits of both a witch and a hunter," Kellen stated, his eyes hardening. "Males of the hunter bloodline are only supposed to take the warrior gene. They are afraid that we spook the brethren before a hunt. In the ancient times, we have been branded as bad luck. The old clans used to blame the deaths of clan members on True Dreamers. They believed that people like me brought what they had envisioned from their dreams into reality, like we wanted to cause harm. So when my mother worked out what I was as a child, she swore that she and I had to keep it a secret." His gaze intensified as he looked at her.

A sickening flush crept over her skin. "Kellen, why are you telling me this?" Fear, more than anything, lined her tone. If he was sworn to secrecy about his abilities, then why was he telling *her*?

And then she saw it too. Fear glowed from him like it had in the sparring room that one time she had trained with him. She hadn't been seeing things.

"You're glowing again," she stated as she stumbled back slightly. It was subtle, but she could see it in the darkness of her room. It was like a golden veil around him. "I can see that glow on your skin," she exclaimed. "I am not making it up, I can see it. Like I did before."

"I know you can. That is what happens after I dream." His voice was coarse, and he took in a large breath. "I couldn't tell you that before. My mother used to be able to give me a tonic that hid it from hunters or *seeing* eyes. But it can't be disguised as easily from witches. They can see through the tonic's magic." He paused. "Well, a powerful witch can."

If he was glowing, then that meant...

"What did you dream about?" It was a wonder that Kellen even heard her voice at all. A terrible, terrible darkness swept across his face, and he looked down at her floor. "Kellen," his name was more like a plea on Emara's lips, "what did you dream?"

He moved towards her, running a hand through his hair and over his face. "It was confusing." He shook his head, and the blood seemed to drain even further from his face. "But it didn't feel good. It didn't feel good at all. You were taken." He looked at the fireplace quickly and then to her again. "And it was definitely you, because I heard the roars of my brother. But I couldn't see the person or what took you. It was like it had a dark cloak over it, unwilling to show itself. It moved in ways that I couldn't work out. And an ancient language was being chanted and drummed in my mind, not one that I have been trained in. It felt wrong."

Her stomach churned violently.

Emara could see the sweat from his night terrors still damp in his brow and hairline. He must have just had this nightmare for it to still be lingering on his skin. And with what he had endured in that nightmare, he had come to warn her.

"What else did you see?" she asked in the unbearable silence, her head dizzying.

He swallowed. "There was darkness and blood-curdling screams. I thought I heard steel, but the vision wasn't clear enough to know if it was a weapon or something else. But the dream felt like you were being sacrificed, the magic dark enough to snuff out the light, and you were screaming for it to stop. And there was fire and air...and death," he finished, cringing as he told the last detail.

A hideously cold tremor ran through Emara, causing her whole body to shake.

"How accurate are these dreams? It could just be a nightmare, right?" She let hope into her heart when she knew she shouldn't.

He looked over at her. "That is unknown. I haven't explored this side of me enough to know. It's not like it's openly allowed." He bore a terrible sadness, and Emara found it insufferable. She just wanted to *heal* him. Her magic urged her to go to him, but she rooted herself to the floor. "I normally shut them down, but I couldn't with this one." He shifted on his feet. "All I know is that the feeling—the dream—was strong enough to shake me from my sleep. I had to tell you. I can't unhear the cries of death."

Cries of death.

"I am sorry," he continued as he ran a shaky hand through his hair, "for coming here at this hour." His complex stare burned into her face and shadows darkened his eyes. "But I had to tell you to be careful. You must always be looking over your shoulder in case whatever is coming creeps up on you. I would have felt endless guilt if I didn't tell you and you weren't aware of the danger you are in. I know it's not easy for me to spring this on you in the dead of night, but I just needed to tell you. I have seen you training, and you are good. I just want you to be prepared." His throat bobbed again. "Be ready."

She cursed.

The problem that now lay in all of this was that she now had another secret with a Blacksteel brother. She couldn't even hint to her guards about this danger because when questioned, Kellen's secret would be revealed, and Gods only knew what would happen to him if anyone found out that Viktir Blacksteel's son was a True Dreamer.

She didn't know if she should curse again or throw up, but it felt like both were coming up her throat. "And there is no way to tell what the danger is?" she asked, beginning to tremble. "Who the danger is or when it's coming?"

Shaking his head, he said, "Whatever it is, it feels...close."

A rough breath left her. The shaking took over her

body and Emara held on to the bed frame to keep herself upright.

"Surely, not here. The Winter Solstice Ball?" she asked. "This place is so heavily guarded."

"I wouldn't think so, with the palace swarming with hunters and the strength of the wards around us, but I can't know for certain. Look what happened at the Uplift. Every faction will be invited to the festivities here. The elite have let the demons in before, but I am not sure it is them behind the danger, my father said so himself." He took a moment to breathe, and the embers of the fire glistened behind him. "I am sick with myself that I cannot provide you with any more details, Emara." Kellen's eyes watered. "Truly, I am ill with the knowledge of this. I wish I could tell you more. But I felt like letting you know what I could was better than watching something unfold in front of my eyes without opening my mouth at all."

"Thank you," Emara said after a long moment, "for trusting me enough to tell me of this, even though it reveals a secret of yours."

Even if it caused a crushing anxiety to spread through her, she was grateful.

Kellen looked over at her for a long moment before his lips parted. "You probably know more of my reality than most, empress." His voice was lower than she had ever heard it before, the truth pulling at every word and weighing it down. Emara could tell he was extremely uneasy with the information he had disclosed about himself but, in the same breath, she realised he'd had to warn her. If she was unsafe, the likelihood was that her guards were too, regardless of their training. It was a threat to everyone.

"I will not betray your trust, Kellen." Emara's hands shook as she tried to gather herself.

"I know," he said, "or I would never have come tonight." His blunt honesty was something she respected. He cleared his throat. "You seem to be closer to my brothers than I will ever be. And yet, I can only assume you haven't told them what you saw of me at the Uplift, since I have not been exiled from the clan with gaping wounds."

She flinched at the visual that took place in her mind.

"I have not spoken of it," she finally managed to whisper, "to a single soul."

It was strange to see his youthful features take on a more mature look as he spoke. "You could have exposed a part of me that night." He shook his head, his forehead creasing. "Not even my own mother knows *that* about me. But instead, you bought me time to get out of there." His eyes fluttered. "Why?"

She thought over his question before answering, "I did not have to question my actions that night. And I would make the same decision again." Her chin raised. "Because to me, there are no issues with who your heart wants, be that female, male, or anything in between. If you are choosing love, it shouldn't matter who your heart gravitates towards." She looked him in the eye as she spoke her own truths. "I heard what you said about what the clan would do to you, if they found out." A little disgust crept in at the thought of them hurting him, but she tried her best to hide it. "I would never have forgiven myself if that had happened to you on my behalf. Your heart is not mine to expose, nor is your truth. I may be naive to the world of hunters and witches, or even all things magical, but I am not naive to know what is right and what is wrong in the world." She stopped as Kellen straightened his spine. "And what they would have done to you is wrong. You should not be made to feel like you cannot show who you really are."

"That's the catch, though, Emara," he said quickly. "I will never be able to show who I really am. Two massive parts of who I am are locked away in the deepest, darkest pits of my soul, where they need to remain." His hands shook. "And I have to be okay with never unlocking them. I have to pretend they are not there, clawing and scratching to get out." A tear fell from his blue eye, sliding down his cheek. "Because if I reveal who I am, what I am, my fate is worse than all the pretending and suffering in the shadows alone. I would never put that shame on my family name."

In that moment, between her and Kellen, Emara realised that not all hunters wore a mask of confidence and bravery, but one that was made up of oppression and secrecy. Kellen was made to feel like he should be ashamed of who he was, but he would wear the mask of a proud hunter even if it destroyed who he was on the inside, even if his duty didn't like the colours of what painted his soul bright and beautiful.

Emara's heart broke into several different pieces.

He should not be ashamed or made to feel wrong

because his heart fell a certain way. He should not have to hide a side of him that he had adopted from his mother's genes just because it did not fall under his *hunting* qualities. Who he was did not compromise or take away his abilities as a warrior of Thorin. It didn't change him as a person. It shouldn't. It should be a part of him that was accepted without question.

But it wasn't.

Anger burned up Emara's throat, eating away at every part of her that was sad for him. It turned into something else entirely.

"You should never be ashamed of who you are," she said, fiery passion fighting its way onto her tongue. "For what it is worth, I think who you are is beautiful and brave."

He looked up at her incredulously. "How...how can you say that?"

"I am not just *saying* it, I mean it." A steely tone slid into place, the tone of an empress. "I do not look at you like you are something immoral, and you shouldn't either. You are just the same as Torin and Gideon regardless of what preference they have. As a matter of fact, I see you as more courageous and valiant than they will ever be." Tears poured into his beautiful eyes. "You square up to a darkness and prejudice that they will never understand. It makes me so incredibly angry at the world that you even have to hide yourself." She closed the space between them. "But I want you to know that"—she took his hand—"you are not alone. You are not wrong for having feelings for someone who isn't who you ever thought you would love." A chord struck in her own heart. "You should never feel dishonour." His chin trembled as the tears escaped his eyes, but he made no sound. He even cried like a true hunter. "You should feel proud of your bravery and resilience in a world full of hate and outdated values."

He intertwined his fingers around hers and bowed deeply. He didn't kiss her hand, but he held her tight.

"You have a pure heart, Emara," Kellen said. "And maybe one day you will be part of my family. I would be honoured."

An overwhelming rush hit her at what he said, and her throat closed shut.

Part of my family.

"You don't deserve the darkness that is headed your way." He shook his head.

Emara's guts dipped and twisted at his words, and it was her turn to grip his hand.

"But just so you know, when that time comes, you are not alone either." He nodded officially and his fingers left hers. "I will fight with you in any way I can. I am certainly not as skilled as my brothers in combat, but I know how to fight. I know how to guard something with my life."

Her hand fell heavily against her side, and she uncurled the curve in her spine, finally finding the strength to stand without shaking. "It seems that we both have a world of uncertainty in front of us, Kellen Blacksteel."

They both stared at one another for a moment before Kellen spoke, finally looking more like himself. "That we may. But one thing I know for certain: after seeing your heart in this light, the Blacksteel Hunting Clan needs someone as forward-thinking as you to stand beside their commander."

In matrimony, in an alliance, in oath.

Emara knew what Kellen had left out in the unsaid words between them. When the time came for Torin to be appointed commander, when Viktir was gone and the new age was brought in, he wanted someone like her to be behind him, backing him, keeping him level-headed. But what was more, the clan needed someone who would bring forth change and open-mindedness, someone who could challenge and crack ancient views of how the clans were run, shattering them entirely. He longed for someone to bring in a new way for hunters to be raised, someone who would create a safer world for people like himself.

Something connected within her, deep and unchanging. It was like the mountains moved under her and her soul rattled. Could she be the one to make the world a safer place, not just to the humans of the world, but for the hunters and the witches of the world who were viewed differently?

For the women of the world who wanted to wield a sword and not a knitting needle without being challenged? For girls to wear fashion for themselves, and not for men? For the oppressed to feel liberated? For power to rise and for a woman to be behind that energy?

Only the Gods knew the answers that were swelling in her heart, and only time would tell if their plan for her was to take on that duty. But until then, she would embody an empress that she aimed to be proud of.

"I will protect your secrets and who you are." Emara finally looked up at the youngest Blacksteel brother that stood in her room. "But you do not have to hide these parts of yourself from me. With me, you have a safe place to be what you want, who you want."

"Thank you." Kellen's voice was now strong and held together, like he had never shown a strain of weakness. He looked at her, his eyes storming with promise. "And from this moment, I vow to protect you from whatever darkness is coming your way."

CHAPTER
FORTY-ONE
EMARA

Kellen Blacksteel's visit to her room had haunted Emara for days now. And she even found herself training with the clans with the vivid memory of his fear-struck eyes still lingering in her mind. The truth of what he had said about himself, niggling against the possibility that she wasn't safe at the Amethyst Palace, had shook her. But duties of being the leader of House Air had taken over, and she was already swarmed by paperwork regarding alliances, territory, food supplies, and trade deals with merchants or seamstresses for her witches. It all went to her for approval, and if there was anything of concern, she passed it on to Deleine to have the final say. The days on the lead up to the winter solstice had been a blur of training and signing her signature, so it had been a welcome distraction to think about the ball.

Emara had just come from a private dinner with the Supreme and the other empresses—to talk through a possible alliance for a clan in the east and House Water

—to find three fireletters hovering above the golden flames in her room, all from Torin.

She wondered if he had noticed she had been so distant. If she didn't see Torin, she didn't need to keep her new secret to herself.

Wasting no time, Emara hid herself in her bathing chamber, trying to complete a calming ritual. But the thoughts of Kellen's words crawled into the bath with her like a water serpent ready to drown her. When she wasn't tied down to her covenal duties, it's where her mind spiralled.

She couldn't tell anyone about it. Even after training this morning, watching Torin spar with Gideon, the words wanted to scream from her mouth that something was coming, something was wrong. But Emara knew she couldn't tell a soul that she wasn't safe here, not without outing Kellen.

Somehow, in the foolish caves of her mind, she had tried to pacify her thoughts by telling herself that the vision Kellen had seen through sleep might not come true.

I still cannot unhear the cries of death.

She was screwed.

She was screwed regardless of how many times she tried to convince herself that the vision had no weight. It wasn't a coincidence that her grandmother had left a note to warn her of the dangers of this world. It wasn't a coincidence when Callyn had skimmed over the darkness of their conversation and focused on the good, on the light. It wasn't a coincidence that the Solden heir of a fortune wanted her to be his wife. He had been toying with darkness, immorality, and things that crawled out of the underworld to devour. And she had wondered, more often than not, why that had led to her, why an elite man found a path to darkness through her.

She ran a bar of sweet fig soap over her skin and took a breath.

She had to breathe.

The Winter Solstice Ball was tomorrow, and she had to focus on one thing at a time. She had to take her mind off the darkness that lurked at her heels and focus on the light of the Gods. That's what her whole existence meant, right?

The light. Her witches. Her duty.

Brushing a wide-toothed comb through her damp hair, adding some jojoba oil to the ends of it, she worked through her mind to find something positive.

Sybil. Sybil had been continuing to train her in magic, helping her form small wards around glasses. They kept the glasses safe from whatever Sybil threw at them, physical or elemental. They had been working on control and execution of the elements, and it had been liberating to see her magic finally take a shape and form in a controlled way. Working with Sybil was beneficial. It was going just as well as training with the hunters. It felt purposeful.

Sybil had joined yet another training session in combat, and after Emara had sparred with Artem and Torin, Sybil had found some time to have a girly chat.

"When you look at him..." Sybil said, stretching from her training session. She nodded to Torin, who was stacking up

weapons. *"It's like you have just seen a new world materialise in front of you."*

Emara snapped her head in Sybil's direction; the witch's face was pure and genuine.

"And when he looks at you...it's like, for him, you are the world."

Emara had stood in silence as she let the words soak into her very being, sliding in and warming around her heart.

"He got me a gift for the winter solstice. I want to get him a gift too," she finally managed, her voice tickling her throat. *"But what in the world of Rhiannon would you get Torin Blacksteel?"* She looked at Sybil.

"There are many things that he would like. A new weapon, a present that involves liquor, even a book of war, perhaps." Sybil circled round so that she was facing Emara directly. She fought to keep her auburn hair out of her face. *"But something in my gut tells me he would appreciate something more personal than that."* Her eyebrow danced up again.

"What?"

Emara had been two octaves away from squawking, and she laughed now as she remembered her friend's expression.

"You." Sybil's leaf-green eyes were two shades more meaningful than they were before. There was no hint of sarcasm in her voice, nor was there any quip.

Emara coughed out a broken laugh. *"And how do you gift someone yourself? Surely, that would be an inadequate let down of a present."* Emara scoffed, cheeks burning.

"I can't believe how much you are underestimating your-

self right now," Sybil said with a hint of a smile. "You clearly have no idea how much you mean to him." She paused to push her fiery hair from her face. "Or what it would mean to him if you showed him how you truly felt." Sybil lunged into a stretch, leaving Emara to stare over at Torin once more. When she straightened from her stretch, Sybil said, "Maybe there is no better gift than giving your heart and soul to someone this solstice."

Sybil's words consumed Emara as she pulled the plug in the tub, letting the water flow down the drain. She had known from the moment Torin had given her the spear that she had wanted to give him something back. But never for one second had she thought about it being the knowledge of where her heart lay. Telling him fully, letting him in fully.

It was absurd, wasn't it, to even consider her heart an adequate gift?

It was haughty, and surely not enough.

As she jumped from the tub, she pulled a warmed towel from the rail and wrapped it around her, scanning the room. Just as she tucked the soft towel into a fold that held it on her body, a hand touched her shoulder, and her heart leapt into her mouth. She spun, eyes darting around the room, but not a soul could be seen.

"Hello?"

No one had come in the door. And it was still firmly locked.

But maybe they didn't need to.

"Callyn?" she dared to ask out into the room, but silence was her only answer.

Calming herself, she listened to her magic, but it was

also silent. A shiver swept through her, then she noticed a gleaming light under the arch that split her bathing chamber and bedroom. It was a tiny orb of light, like the one that had led her to the waterfall, only smaller.

It was spirit.

It was Callyn, she was certain.

Emara let out a gasp as she waited for something to happen, but nothing did. She didn't appear or even flicker in and out. Emara could only hear the echo from her voice in the woods at the back of her mind before the orb flashed and disappeared. A wave of sadness struck her, causing her to sit down on the edge of the tub. Cally didn't have the energy to come through and show herself again, she realised.

It is time for you to give in to your heart.

Cally's words at the waterfall almost mirrored what Sybil had said today. Had Callyn been standing there on that mountain top too?

Sybil's words turned over in her mind again for the millionth time.

I don't believe how much you are underestimating your-self right now. You clearly have no idea how much you mean to him. Or what it would mean to him if you showed him how you felt.

Showed.

It was true.

He had shown his cards time and time again. Not only had he declared how he felt about her, but he had shown her too. He had walked in his actions instead of just talking about them. Torin had shown her a side to him she would have never known was there, a softer, caring, and considerate side—a side that could wipe her tears and hold her hand. He had shown a side that was fiercely protective, yet he never doubted that she could handle herself. He trusted her. Gods, he had given her his own sword at the tower, and he had given her a personalised weapon of her own. He had shown her a side of wild unpredictability, and yet he had also shown that he was stable. He kissed her like he was ready to give her everything, every breath, every beat of his heart. He was ready for her, and she for him. And that didn't involve the alliance between their factions.

She had been ready for him to sweep her up into his arms the minute he had broken her down in the forest when he had provoked her into using her magic, even if she didn't like to admit it. She was ready for their bodies to be closer in a way that wasn't just dancing, like when he had whispered into her ear at the Uplift. She had been more than ready for his lips on hers as she had finally spoken the words he had longed to hear.

Kiss me.

And, when his lips had found hers, something had consumed her. Something had well and truly overcome who she had been before and who she no longer was. Her blood sang for him, for his touch, for his smile, for his kiss. And she knew it sang for more, much more, but she had silenced it for so long, unwilling to admit when would be the right time to release herself to it.

The magic in her blood tingled.

This was her choice. She was in control of her choice.

Now was the time to show him how much he meant

to her. Now, before the darkness, or whatever was coming for her, did.

Getting up from her bed, she found her journal and feather quill.

It was time for her to orchestrate a gift that she had never given to anyone before. Something that she was in control of. Something that she had thought about for a long time.

Her heart slammed against her chest as she put ink to paper in a request that would send her cheeks into a pink flush if she had to ask for it in person.

She only knew of one place in which you could retrieve such things as she required, and it was far from where she was now, much too far to travel. There was only one person in the kingdom she would write to for such a request.

After the ink dried, she folded the paper with a wish that the recipient would retrieve it with no one else's peeking eye. However, that was a risk she took as she dropped the paper into the enchanted flames and whispered Breighly Baxgroll's name out loud.

After all, the wolf did say she owed her one.

CHAPTER
FORTY-TWO
GIDEON

I t was the night of the annual Winter Solstice Ball, and that meant the hunters were on high alert. And it also meant that Gideon Blacksteel had to be more vigilant than ever. He was guard to the Empress of House Earth, and it was an honour to be in the position of protecting her life. Big events like this weren't faring well for witches these days, and he wouldn't be the one to falter if anything did go wrong. Although it was a formal ball that the majority of the magic community would be attending, Gideon was in full guard regalia.

He was off duty, but it didn't feel right to be.

So he had insisted on wearing his guard uniform. It would keep him focused and remind him why he was here. Unlike the last major event where he was upstairs kissing instead of helping his clan slaughter the beasts that had murdered so many innocent people. It was a hard potion to swallow that he had let his focus stray that night; it had haunted him every single night since.

He didn't blame Emara for it—he couldn't. He

blamed himself. If he had been in the Uplift Hall instead of courting a girl that was never really his to begin with, maybe he could have saved more people. The Uplift wasn't just a reminder of the witches' slaughtering, but a stark reminder that Emara was promised to Torin.

It was a reminder that the girl he had so quickly fallen in love with was promised to his brother. That familiar, dull ache in his chest reared its ugly head again. He had seen them recently, the exchanges of their glances and how close he stood to her. Emara's laugh when she spoke to Torin, the whispers, the jokes, the touches...

His brother's words at the ascension as he drove his sword into the earth, promising to protect her soul after his bones turned to dust.

It was his own version of the Underworld, without the demons.

A knock came from the inside of the door he stood outside. His brow furrowed. That was strange.

A small voice spoke through the dark oak door. "Um, is one of my guards out there?"

Sybil's voice shook in a strange way that made Gideon stand to attention.

He took a few strides over. "Is everything okay in there?" He pressed his head against the wood of the door, listening to see if he should be worried or act on instinct. His hand went to the small hunting knife he carried on his weapon belt. "It's Gideon. Are you all right?"

"Everything is okay." Her pleasant voice rang

through him. "But I have made a very silly mistake. It's quite embarrassing, actually."

"What have you done?" He laughed, one hand pressed against the door.

"You see"—Gideon heard Sybil's head fall against the door.—"I have allowed my maids to go and prepare themselves for the ball, underestimating the weight of the gown I must dress in. I picked one with intricate fastenings on its back, and I will never get it on alone. I fear I have overestimated myself after all that training you've had me do."

Gideon's trained heartbeat skipped a little, and a smile broached his lips. "I cannot leave my post to fetch your maids, Sybil." He spoke in true hunter fashion, firm and assertive. Or so he thought. "It would require me to leave you alone, and none of the other guards are around to relieve me yet."

A moment passed. "I wasn't going to ask you to go and get the girls." Her small voice floated through the door and touched his chest. He pictured the look in her large eyes as she stood against the door, mirroring him.

He swallowed.

"And then what would you have me do?" He leaned against the door.

All too quickly, the lock clicked, and the wooden door fell away. He stumbled a little, humiliation flushing on his face.

He straightened, pulling down his tunic.

Gods of the world unite! Solid oak doors were going to be the death of him.

Sybil appeared around the door in what seemed like

a loose robe. Her hair still sat wildly untamed on her shoulders, the vibrant red curls spiralling out in all directions.

"I am sorry to ask you to do this, Gideon, but you did take an oath to protect me, and right now, I need to be protected from myself. Trying to get those fastenings at the back of my dress without any help has snapped every imaginable string of patience I had left." She huffed, her brow creasing, and Gideon found himself chuckling.

She opened the door wider, inviting him to come in.

Helping her into her dress wasn't exactly on a guard's list of duties, but he had grown to like Sybil. She had such a gentleness about her. Even when she would awake in the woods on the journey here, with screams in her throat from the memories of her sister's death, she would apologise to him or the other guards.

Stepping into the room and shutting the door behind himself, he said, "I don't know how much help I will be, but I am happy to aid an empress in need." He let a smile warm his face.

"Thank the souls on the Otherside it was you and not Marcus on the door." Sybil laughed, all too alluringly. "His face would have been a picture worth painting." Gideon agreed and Sybil turned, walking over to the gown that lay on the floor. Her head snapped up. "Okay. This is the tricky part."

Gideon placed his hands behind his back, a reminder that everything that was happening in this room was just a professional aid. "I am listening. I will take your lead on whatever you need me to do."

She hesitated. "So I am sort of naked under this robe." Her face beamed red, and her large eyes found the floor. "But I also need to come out of the robe without you seeing me...naked. And get into the dress."

Gideon's throat bobbed like hers. "I see the quandary you are having over sending away your female help."

Something flashed in her eyes, but it was gone as fast as a travelling star. Her petite throat bobbed. "What I need you to do is take the robe from me as I pull the dress up." She blinked. "Got it?"

Her voice was higher than normal, and it made him want to chuckle.

Hiding the amusement on his face at her predicament, he nodded and said, "Got it."

He threw her a smile too.

"Good," she replied with a small smile of her own. "I wouldn't want any awkward moments between an empress and her guard."

Gideon felt his lips twitch again, and his gaze followed her as she moved to a place where her back faced him, stepping into the dress that was sprawled out on the floor. He shifted and stood just behind her, not too close.

"Where would you like me to take the robe from?" he asked.

She threw a look over her shoulder at him like he had grown a third eye. "My body."

Gideon bit into his lip, subduing his smile. "No, what I meant was," he said softly, "where is an appropriate place for me to take the robe from first?"

"Oh!" She turned away from him, but he could see the redness of her cheeks now that he was closer to her. "Just anywhere, really."

He placed one hand on the small of her back. "Is here okay?"

She loosened the belt for him, her voice low. "Yes. There is fine."

"Okay," he said, gripping the material on her warmed skin. "On three."

"One, two..." Her voice wavered slightly.

He got ready to pull.

"Wait," she yelled, causing Gideon's heart to almost combust.

"Close your eyes," she sputtered out.

He did as he was told.

"Three."

He pulled the loose robe from her body and stood with his eyes closed until instructed otherwise.

Gideon heard a few scuffles and then one curse that had him trying not to show his teeth in a smile.

"Okay," she said a few moments later. "You can open your eyes now."

He did, casting the robe onto her bed. The majority of her navy-blue gown covered the front of her body, but her back was open completely, baring her creamy skin. Gideon squinted as he took in a scar that dragged down her spine a few inches. It wasn't completely healed, but it was in the process of it, and it looked like a claw had tried to dig out her heart from behind.

Her head spun round to see him gawking at her wound.

"It's disgusting, isn't it?"

Her words punched him. He didn't like how small her voice was.

"I didn't know you had a scar like this," he said, unable to stop himself. "But no, it's not disgusting at all. Believe it or not, I have seen much worse."

Her face paled, but she kept her chin raised, her hair swept around to one side, clutched in her hand. "The demon who had been sent to kill my sister...it wasn't a high demon, but it was clever enough to know who its prey was. It had its target marked. And I got in the way of it. The healers of my coven tried their best to mend my skin, but after the death of my sister, their empress... it's hard to mend something when you are broken inside." She cleared her throat. "Plus the demon magic had rooted itself deep. Too deep."

"You tried to protect her."

"Of course, I did." Her voice trembled a little and the corner of her eyes started to reveal a dampness that he had seen in her eyes a few times when she thought he wasn't looking at her. She pressed the gown closer to her skin. "Just like you would have for your brothers."

He nodded his head, in complete agreement. He had taken many scars for his brothers, and he would do it again in an instant.

Sybil inhaled a sharp breath. "I need you to do the fastenings," she said, pulling him back from his thoughts.

"Course," Gideon said, his voice a little throatier than expected. He coughed it down whilst he moved closer to her.

He shifted a loose, untamed curl of fire from her left shoulder blade and placed it around her neck. She lifted a hand to grab it, and their fingers brushed ever so softly. She quickly pulled her hair tighter around the nape of her neck, gathering any other loose strands.

Gideon had seen Sybil's hands grow flowers from a seed in a matter of minutes, and it had been beautiful to watch her use the element she bore to create life. Her presence had a calmness that he had always appreciated in an Earth Witch. They were normally serene and balanced, and he worked well with them. After all, he descended from a great line of them. His mother was an Earth Witch, his late grandmother, and even the females beyond them, had all been members of House Earth. So it was natural for him to feel comfortable around their energy.

Sybil remained still and silent as he worked all the buttons into their tiny fastenings, which he counted thirty-three of, all the way down her spine. His knuckles occasionally made slight contact with her skin. The final button was at the very base of her spine, and it clasped together like the rest, closing her in.

"That's all of the fastenings closed, I hope."

She turned, pressing her palms into the fabric. "Thank you," she said, turning another shade of red. "I am honestly too mortified to have even asked you to do this."

"Don't be." He smiled and ran a nervous hand through his own untamed hair. "I actually wanted to catch you before we went down into the grand ball-room, anyway."

"Really?" Confusion set in her features as she pierced a diamond earring through her ear.

He had wanted to catch her alone at training, but she had run off with Emara, eager to teach witchcraft. So that is why he had opted to escort her to the celebrations instead of Marcus or Arlo.

"Yes." He swallowed and reached into the lining of his tunic. He pulled out a little leather grimoire. "It's not much, but I wanted to give it to you for the winter solstice."

Her face changed in a way he had never really witnessed before, and her hand dropped from her lobe.

"It was my great-grandmother's grimoire," he said, extending a hand to give it to her. Eyes wide, she took it, her lips parted. "It has been rumoured to have been an Empress of Earth's grimoire as the covens of this kingdom started to emerge. It's that old." Her gaze found him again, and for a moment, he felt a little twinge in his heart. Ignoring it, he continued, "But you know what old tales are like." He laughed. "They always run away with themselves, so it really could have just been my grandmother's."

She ran her small hand over the face of the leather, and then opened the first page. "Gideon, this...this is...*ancient*," she finally said, a smile forming on her lips.

He laughed at the unexpected truth.

"Well, you told me the other day that you believe you have an old soul." He titled his head to the side, remembering what she had said at their training session. "And I knew my mother had it. She doesn't use it, having read it over and over. So I thought I could pass it from one old soul to another."

Sybil looked back down at the grimoire, which now lay in the palms of her hands like it was the most expensive diamond in the kingdom, though he was sure this was more impressive to her than a rock.

"It's amazing," she breathed as she turned a new page. "I can feel how old the magic is on the leather and paper. Gideon, this is incredible." Her leafy-green gaze touched his.

For whatever reason, his heart skipped a beat. "I hear a lot of powerful witches have healed and protected these lands and our warriors with the help of this grimoire. Maybe now that it is in your hands, you will too."

"Maybe I will," she said, placing the old grimoire to her chest before setting it on her vanity with care.

"It's been through the wars, that thing." Gideon nodded in its direction. "I don't think you need to be so delicate with it."

She turned to him, a small smile passing over her lips. "As a healer, I tend to hear that a lot." She looked him over, her large green eyes wise and bright. "But you can't change the nature of a *true* Earth Witch. Not until you get them a drink of Winter Solstice wine." A smile broke across her face, her little freckles moving on her nose and her cheeks.

"I guess I will need to make that happen as soon as possible, then," Gideon said, his grin wide.

She beamed as she walked towards the door with a twinkle in her eye. "Come on, then." She turned her head as she passed him, her navy gown drifting over his feet like the calm waves of a night's sea. "Since I need your assistance to go everywhere, you may as well assist me in getting inebriated too." She laughed and opened the door.

And it was almost impossible for Gideon not to smile back.

CHAPTER
FORTY-THREE
BREIGHLY

Breighly Baxgroll and the pack had arrived at the Amethyst Palace a few hours ago, giving her enough time to bathe in one of the most sickeningly wealthy tubs she had ever laid her Shifter ass in. It wasn't like the one she had back home.

She didn't have her own room for the trip, she was sharing it with Roman, which was the usual set up at the annual winter solstice event. She didn't expect anything less, the palace would be housing a shitload of Shifters and Fae, and it was already home to witches and their guards.

It was the winter solstice, after all, a tradition that should bring every magical faction under one roof—or so the old books say.

Roman had gone to catch up with some old friends who had travelled here with them from Ashdale. The Baxgroll tradition of racing to the palace had made conversation impossible.

Of course, it had been Waylen, the pack's beta, to reach the palace first. It was him every year. She had almost clipped his paw with her fang just so it wouldn't have been him to finish first. Wolves were happy to fight dirty, and she had thought about it for a *long* moment, but she had opted against it, knowing how much of a sore loser Waylen was. The win wouldn't have been worth the whining for days on end.

The male ego really does go back to the most animalistic parts of existence, Breighly thought as she pulled on her dress for tonight.

Her attire was nothing like what the females here were going to be wearing. It was not lined in elegant lace, nor was it deemed classical. It did not have ruffles or tulle, or any signs of sleeves or a train.

It was black and it was tight. And maybe a little too short for an event like this, but screw them. Elegant balls were not her thing. The only reason she was here was to please her father.

Messing up her hair that sat a little too perfectly on her shoulders, her eyes narrowed in on her body in the mirror. She looked like she was going for a night in La Luna, maybe even a night's work in the forbidden lanes of the Huntswood Markets. Everyone else at the ball would be too concerned with looking respectable to have painted their lips dark crimson or covered their eyelids in glitter.

She absolutely did not look like she was going to a *grand ball* hosted by the *Supreme*.

It was perfect.

Smiling, she picked up a little white box that had been strapped inside a satchel. She had to admit it, not in the eternal life of Vanadey did she expect a fireletter from Emara Clearwater yesterday. And she especially hadn't expected a fireletter to request such items. But then again, the newly ascended Empress of Air seemed to be full of surprises. And Breighly liked that about her. So she had gone into the Huntswood Markets before her travels and picked out the garments she thought best complimented the empress.

Closing her door and walking along the corridor swishing her hips, Breighly made her way to where Emara had said her room was. It hadn't taken her long to make her way to that side of the grounds, passing a few magical factions on the way. Some had smiled, knowing how lethal she could be if they so much as sneered at her. But some had been brave enough to draw their eyes off her like she was dirt on the floor.

All for what she was wearing.

Didn't these assholes know that fashion was changing? Women and men should make it their objective to visit Huntswood every so often and educate their little backwards minds on the new trends.

Breighly sighed. "The life of a woman," she muttered under her breath as she noted the faces that were screwing up in distaste at her fashion statement. If she ever saw them outside of the palace, they would pay for the way they had snubbed at her.

And she looked forward to it.

Rounding the curve of the corridor, knowing that Emara's room was directly in front of her, she stilled. A familiar scent drifted to her nostrils. The scent was masculine, but it was also like toasted orange and summer rain. She cursed under her breath, knowing exactly who she was about to come face to face with. His scent still covered her blankets at home.

Breighly swished a little more sass into her hips as she walked, raising her chin, taking the final few steps before he would be able to see her with his golden eyes.

And he was waiting for her, almost like he had caught her scent too.

That was impossible, of course, since he wasn't a wolf. He didn't have her instincts.

She rolled her eyes as she stood before him. His brute mass spread across the door like he was the solid oak frame himself. He was probably less likely to break.

"Hello, wolf." His rich, deep voice sprung from his ever-growing smile.

She hated it.

"Hunter," she addressed him, giving out an over dramatic sigh and looking over every inch of him. "Step aside and I won't hurt you."

He took a moment, his gaze raking all over her, before he huffed a laugh. "You must have been thinking about me, because I can see you are all worked up already." His broad shoulders squared out even further.

"Don't piss me off, hunter," she warned, popping out a fancy shoe. "I am here on business. Tell the Empress of Air I am here."

His eyes stroked from her toes to her face again, and she swallowed down that inner wolf who always responded to such glances.

She was a traitor.

"Are you not here to see me? I am a little disappointed." His eyes danced with delight, telling her he felt no such things as disappointment.

"If you don't want my claws slicing into your neck in the next few seconds"—She drew her eyes from him and looked down at her nails. They were sharp and polished.—"I suggest you let me through that door without any more hassle."

He let out a wolf whistle. "You do like playing at Alpha, don't you?"

That struck a chord.

It struck a chord deep in Breighly's soul, because regardless how she felt about the role, she would never be Alpha.

She inhaled a breath. "The only thing we are about to *play* is *me* smacking my fist into *your* nose." She smiled innocently. "Step aside, dickwad, and I won't make you cry."

He chuckled, a deep rumbling coming from his chest. "Why do you have so much fire in your belly?"

Ignoring how intrigued he sounded, irritation grew in her veins. "Are you going to be stupid enough to continue talking, or are you going to let me inside like a *good little guard?*"

His warm brown eyes roamed her face again, moving down her bare arms and over the dress that clung to her body. She straightened her spine, knowing what he saw.

"Get a good enough look?" she cut out sharply. "Emara knows I am coming." Breighly held up the present, feeling the air thin in her lungs at his obnoxious grin. "I don't need to be kept at the door for you to check out how stunning I look tonight. I have things to do."

His nostrils flared, reminding her of that enticing, silver nose ring. "Is that a present for me?" His jaw hardened into a maddening smile and she was torn between kissing him or punching his mouth.

As they stood, gazes locked in on one another, Breighly noticed that the hunter's intricate ink-work travelled all the way up his neck and into his short, russet-brown hair. It was clear he had tried to cover it, but Breighly could see it peeking out from under the rim of his grey guard regalia.

She had a momentary lapse of weakness as a forgotten memory leaked through her barriers. She'd flicked her way across his tattooed neck with her tongue, drawing primal, guttural moans from him.

She swallowed all the feelings of desire down.

"Get a good enough look?" He looked like danger; his features were strong and prominent when he was not laughing. His tunic was tight and fitted to his colossal physique. A band of weapons around his hips and the badge of his clan gleamed in the light of the hallway. She didn't want her eyes to hover too long on what crest lay on his chest, because she simply didn't care. Shouldn't care.

He was a cocky prick.

She strolled over to him, pushing out her chest and relaxing her shoulders. His eyes followed every movement her body made as she walked. Breighly knew what she was doing, and she would never be ashamed to use her body to her advantage. It gave her great pleasure to see a warrior of his size and strength bend a little, all because she had a pair of breasts.

"As much as I would *love* to see you in deep red lingerie..." She clicked her tongue, dangling the box in front of him. His face went the same colour of the lacey garments inside. "I don't think they are your size, sweetie." She winked at him. "If you don't let me in, I will make you try them on for me instead, and we can see how Torin Blacksteel reacts to you wearing them."

"Emara!" The warrior called out, not fully returning to his natural colour yet. He knocked on her door twice, warning her that he was about to enter, and then opened it. "You have a very promiscuous and persistent little wolf to see you."

He shot her a grin.

She growled back.

"Breighly," Emara said, coming from somewhere in her room in a champagne-coloured robe, her hair in loose waves around her shoulders. "Let her in, Artem, I told you she was coming."

Artem. That was his name. *Artem.*

I told you she was coming.

Breighly's head snapped towards Artem. He raised one eyebrow and winked. He'd known she was coming, that's why he had known it was her strutting around the corner.

Asshole.

"I come bearing gifts," Breighly said, ignoring Artem and presenting the box to Emara. The Empress' face turned three different shades of pink.

"Can I ask—" Artem started to say.

"No," both Breighly and Emara cut him off.

But he continued anyway, sparking a little more annoyance into the fire that was already burning in Breighly's stomach.

"Why are you getting special presents of lingerie delivered by a wolf? Maybe, as your guard, I should be vetting these boxes. Just in case, I should—"

"You told him what was in the box?" Emara's eyes triggered wide. Her face had now skipped the pink on the colour chart and was basking in a deep sea of red.

"He wanted to wear them himself," Breighly said. "Couldn't wait to get them on."

"I said nothing of the sort." Artem looked over at Emara, his mouth open, and then over to Breighly. She gave him a wink of her own. He clamped his lips into a tight smile. "However, *wolf,* maybe if we ever get the chance to give round five a go, you might be able to change my mind." His eyes were steady and warm on her face, like he had no shame to admit he would do anything with her. A charge of energy rushed over Breighly. "I always say you should try everything once." A smirk appeared on his face.

"I honestly have no idea what is happening right now." Emara's voice was shaky but loud, pulling Breighly from the metallic pools of Artem's eyes. "You," she commanded, pointing over at Artem, "I have no idea why you just agreed to wear undergarments made for me, but you need to go further down the hall."

"I think I should vet—"

"Absolutely not," she raged. "Do you think Torin would allow you to see what is in this box?"

He fought with a smile but obeyed her, taking his leave. As he moved down the hall, he threw a look over his broad shoulder at Breighly.

She gave him a smile that showed every fang.

It was great to see a six-foot-plus slab of tattooed muscle take orders from a smallish witch.

"You," Emara snapped towards Breighly, as she closed the door. "I need all the help I can get right now, so you need to be focused."

Breighly wasn't sure if the witch had put her under a spell or not, but she also straightened to her command.

Emara looked a little frantic. Breighly didn't know her well, but she was normally quite poised when she had been in her company. Right now, she looked a little pale.

"What can I help you with?" Breighly offered, walking further into her room.

Emara's eyes looked over at the box. Her hair was all done in gentle waves, and her face had been painted to make her eyes look shimmery with her cheeks more defined. Her lips were a lovely shade of red, plump and shapely. Classy. And in that moment, just by looking at her, Breighly knew how unaware of her beauty Emara really was.

"I have never done this before," Emara finally breathed. "I feel a little overwhelmed."

"Do you mean go to the Winter Solstice Ball? Or wear underwear like this?"

"I have worn underwear like that before." Emara's voice was small as she paced in front of the fire. "But it was for me, not for anyone else."

Ah!

Breighly felt a twinge for Emara.

She understood. "You haven't done *that* before."

Emara halted and then nodded, her silken champagne nightcoat swaying slightly. "Never."

"And you thought I was the right one to call on for a little *sexual education?*" Breighly snorted.

"I am not looking for you to give me advice on that." Her cheeks blushed a little. "You had to pass through Huntswood to get here. And I don't know of anywhere else in the kingdom that made what I required." She lowered her head, but her gaze still held Breighly's. "I didn't have anyone I could trust. I would have saved myself some embarrassment if I did."

There was something in that steely gaze of hers, with the cosmic magic that swirled in her irises that allowed Breighly to immediately understand why the Blacksteels had been so intent on fighting for her, why they were both so smitten.

She was clearly stunning and obviously intelligent, but something enchantingly ancient stirred within her, something otherworldly.

Fuck, if the Blacksteels didn't want her, Breighly would have her.

But she better not admit that just yet.

The Empress of Air looked over at Breighly. "I know I have only really been properly introduced to you once, and I know that what I asked for was a little unconventional since we are only acquaintances, but I feel like we can look out for each other. I truly enjoyed your company that night in La Luna. You took my mind to a place where it needed to be for the night. I had fun for once."

Emara had lived such a sheltered life, or so the whispers in the market had said, only finding out who she was mere moons ago.

Breighly's lips pulled together.

However, Emara had a point. Breighly had only been in her company once, but it hadn't felt that way. They'd partied like best friends. Emara had absolutely been in tow with her, drinking shots, dancing like there was no one watching, like she didn't have a care in the world.

But Emara was more than a fun convenience. She had healed her brother. She had taken his pain before he passed on. She had saved herself from being taken at the Uplift, and she had shown signs of pure power. Emara Clearwater was a force to be reckoned with.

Maybe Breighly could use a friend like her; a friend who wasn't a wolf, who didn't see things the same way the pack did. Breighly had also caught wind of how trained Emara now was in combat. And if anyone could fight with the hunters, it would be her. And that lured Breighly in.

"I think we could make our little nights in La Luna a recurring event if you really wanted." Breighly let her mouth fall open slightly into a grin. "And maybe this time I won't be a hot mess." She laughed, and then mummed her lips shut. "I would have always helped you tonight, Emara. I told you I owed you one for what you did for Eli."

There it was.

The hideous pain in her chest that she would normally numb with liquor, men, and music.

"Thank you." Emara dipped her chin gracefully. "And now I owe you one back."

She smiled at her gently.

A handful of seconds passed over as Breighly's eyes searched Emara's room, noting how much bigger and fancier it was than hers. "So, you have really never..." Breighly shook her head, the unfinished question pushing from her lips.

"No," Emara said quickly, her unusual eyes pinning her to where she stood.

"How have you survived?" Breighly blurted out. "How have you not boiled over and cracked right up the middle?"

Emara's laugh broke through the air. "It's not easy."

All awkwardness between them had gone, and the foundations of an organic conversation finally began.

"No, girl." Breighly stuck out her neck. "I know it's not easy. That's why I am in awe right now." She flung a hand up to flick her hair. "I need to stop having sex. I need to stop having meaningless, great sex with..." She tried to find the words. "Well, with just anyone."

Because that's what it was, *meaningless.*

Emara gestured to the bed as she laughed a little. "Please make yourself comfortable."

Breighly sat on Emara's bed. "Maybe I should take a leaf out of your book and just not have sex with anyone."

Emara gave a hearty laugh. "You don't need to take a

leaf from my book." She sat on the other side of her mattress. "I need to take a leaf from yours."

"Oh, Emara," Breighly warned, "you do not want a leaf from my book. It will give you a sharp tongue and a bad attitude."

"Well, I already have the sharp tongue thing down," Emara said, sagging against the bed frame. "But the leaf I seem to be missing when it comes to all of this is *confidence.*"

Breighly sat for a moment, pondering over what to say. She thought about how she could be constructive or gentle. But Breighly didn't know how to do that.

"Emara"—The witch's name on Breighly's lips pulled her attention away from her fiddling hands.— "you are the fucking Empress of Air. You don't need a leaf from anyone's book. You have all the leaves you will ever need. You have a degree of composure and talent that every witch in this kingdom desperately wants, even without being trained. Not only that, but you have also gone and melted the icy heart of the most eligible and unattached bachelor in Huntswood, forging an alliance with him. One that he cares about. You shouldn't worry about being enough. You are his equal, if not better. You're both basically magical royalty now."

Oh, how the gossip travelled, even from the secluded north.

Emara flinched a little, going red again. "The magic world really is a vicious rumour mill."

Breighly smoothed her hands down her legs before leaning forward. "The rumour mill will spin regardless of what you do, so you may as well do what you want.

The Gods aren't going to condemn you for living your life freely. That's what I tell myself, anyway."

"I like that theory," Emara admitted, the curve of her mouth lifting upwards.

Breighly grinned a little. "I am the gift that just keeps on giving this winter solstice. First the gift from Huntswood, and now a cracking piece of advice. Shit, I am good." She winked and then looked for the goodies that she had brought. "Okay, empress," she said with momentum that could shake a small house, "let's see what you got." Her eyes darted to the unopened box on the bed. "Get your underwear on and I will show you a thing or two to send your *lover* wild."

A laugh burst from Emara's mouth, so hearty and genuine that Breighly could have sworn she felt a draft of warm air caress her skin.

"What?" Breighly asked. "You asked for my help and my proficiencies. So that is what you are going to get."

"It's not that." Emara dipped her chin. "Although I am a little nervous about what you are about to show me. It's just...you reminded me of someone, that's all." Her dark hair fell around her shoulders as she played with the lining of the bed.

It didn't take a Spirit Witch to know who Emara Clearwater was talking about. Waylen, her brother, had said the same thing about her. *Callyn Greymore.* He had said that it was like the two of them, Callyn and Breighly, had been cut from the same cloth.

Whatever that meant.

It was a shame she never got to meet her. She sounded like unchecked fun.

Breighly offered Emara a kinder smile than the usual sarcastic and cutting one. "Get that robe off and that underwear on. We are all friends here." She laughed, looking down. "It's not like I am wearing much more, anyway."

When her gaze resurfaced, the witch's unusual eyes were on her again, bright and bold. "I have a feeling you are going to be a good friend to have, Breighly Baxgroll." Emara smiled as she grabbed the box and disappeared through the arch that led to another part of her chamber.

An unusual feeling snaked up Breighly's organs and into her stone-cold heart. It was warm and...dare she say, it felt nice. She had never really had a friend that was a girl before. She had always been stuck around hunters and men. The human girls that lived in the Ashdale forest never did like to hang out with a wolf.

But Breighly had a feeling that the Empress of Air was different.

Very different, indeed.

CHAPTER FORTY-FOUR
TORIN

Torin stood in his guard regalia with his weapon belt around his hips. He was not required to be on guard duty tonight, but he would be, just like his brethren. To restore the magic community's faith in the Gods, it was crucial that tonight went well. The factions needed it. Already in the grand ballroom, all sorts of species were wishing him well, as the winter solstice moon drew her powerful glow in the night's sky. She wasn't full, but she was beautifully curved in her waning phase. The soft enchanting music lingered through the crowd, and everyone seemed to be forgetting that the magic community was under attack, which was what this ball was about.

But Torin wasn't able to forget that easily.

Canapes of skewered beef and winter vegetables floated through the room by enchantment and expensive champagne bottles could be heard popping every few minutes. Hanging wreaths dangled from above, and shining glass baubles of gold, red and green were heavy on a giant tree that took centre stage in the middle of the room. A scent of baked cranberry and mulled wine lingered everywhere in the space, and a litter of candles warmed it, creating a glowing ambiance.

It was the longest day of the year. And it felt like it.

Maybe it had a lot to do with not being able to see Emara much today. Or the day before that.

And maybe it had something to do with the fact that he had been carrying around his mother's precious ring in his tunic pocket.

A tiny flutter began to take flight in his stomach.

He shut it down.

He was a warrior; he didn't get nervous. He took those nerves and turned them into steel. He straightened out his tunic and rolled his neck, shoulders back. The sound of the ballroom door opening caught his attention for the fortieth time. His neck craned forward to see past the gathering guests, but it wasn't her.

Where in the underworld was she? Why was she taking so damn long to come down and greet everyone? Was something wrong? Did something happen?

If Artem Stryker had let anything happen to her, the God of Sun and War himself would need to awake from his ancient slumber on the Otherside and restrain him. It would be the only thing that could stop Torin from killing him.

He looked to Magin and Marcus, idly chatting with Gideon and Sybil, who seemed to be fitting into her empress role nicely. Regrettably, that thought reminded him of his aim to catch his brother at some point tonight and chat through his *intentions* with Emara Clearwater, however uncomfortable that would be.

He had never had intentions for a woman before. Well, none of which had involved that little box burning a hole in his tunic pocket. However, the conversation between them both was a long time coming, and they hadn't exactly sorted things out between them since the night in his mother's cottage.

Could you lie next to her for the rest of your life, and give her your whole heart? Because I can.

Gideon's question had gone unanswered then, but now it wasn't, not in his mind or his heart. He had to let his brother know.

But was Gideon still enamoured by her? Were *his* intentions still to fight for her? Had he been fighting for her and it had gone under Torin's radar? Is that why Emara had been distant? Conflicted?

The door opened again.

Not her. The Empress of Water and her guard.

His patience was *really* wearing thin. He was about to go to her room himself to check on her. He would know if something wasn't right, he always did. She was with Artem, and probably just taking her sweet time getting ready. Or she could be threatening to beat Artem within an inch of his life, for winding her up the wrong way. He smiled before taking a sip of his spiced rum on ice.

He liked the idea of that way more than the first.

He watched the room, searching for who he could see that had been at the Uplift. That threat was still out there, unsolved, and Torin still couldn't accept that Taymir had been working on his own, not just a puppet.

He caught the eye of his youngest brother and gave a

nod. He stood with Arlo Stryker, his comrade in the Selection. Torin saw the Empress of Spirit looking cosy with her guard. Nice. He saw Fae, none of them the king or queen, of course. They liked a private occasion on a night like this. He took in a few important Shifters, the Alpha of the wolves being one of them, in the corner of the room, lounging on large, cushioned chairs. Which meant Breighly Baxgroll and her brothers were also here somewhere. He looked over the room, scanning it thoroughly for her.

Mmmm.

Nowhere to be seen. She would normally be at the bar. A wave of anxious energy rolled low in his gut, making him move from the bar. Torin wasn't the type to just sit around and wait. He was the type of person to take action. If Artem Stryker had left his post to pursue the wolf he had recently taken a liking to, his head would roll tonight.

Clan ally or not.

Son of the chief commander or not.

Torin's strides across the ballroom floor were cut short as the doors swung open, revealing her face.

Emara's face.

His muscles tensed and then relaxed. Artem was at her side, and flanking her other was Breighly. He'd had a feeling that they had somehow ended up crossing paths, and he was not wrong.

But how did Emara fit into that?

He let out a breath and his lungs thanked him.

Emara's gaze found him instantly, like they were two magnets being pulled across the room to one another.

She smiled and her face lit up, causing her magnificent eyes to change, swirling full of charming stars. He tightened his jaw, so that he wasn't standing in the middle of a room smiling like some sort of lost fool.

So he winked.

He saw that hitch in her breathing, the one he liked to take responsibility for.

"Blacksteel," Artem's voice reached him over the stringed instruments that he couldn't really hear anymore. Not when she was in the room. Not when she was dressed in the tight-fitting mermaid cut dress that hugged every one of her delicious curves. It was a rich violet, and the colour was glorious on her. Her lips were a deep red, so plump and full, her skin glowing and shimmering.

She was so fucking beautiful that it hurt his heart.

"When did you get here?" He didn't take his eyes from Emara's.

Breighly answered, "A few hours ago." He finally looked at her. Her voice sounded suggestive. "You're welcome." She patted his shoulder and went to take her leave with a smile full of sin.

"For what?" Torin's brow pulled down so much that it almost obscured his eyesight.

"You'll see." She glanced back over her shoulder before strutting in the direction of the bar.

Odd.

Torin turned back to Emara. "Do you know what she's talking about?"

"I do," Artem piped up with an annoying grin.

It was fast, but he caught it. Emara's foot came out

quickly from under her dress and her heel landed in Artem's boot, right at the front of his big toe.

He hissed.

"Have I missed something?" Torin asked, looking between them. It wasn't like him to not be able to read between the lines. Had something happened in the hours that he was not on guard? Perhaps the weight of tonight was lying too heavily on his chest for him to get a true feel of what was going on. But he would get to the bottom of it.

"You haven't missed anything," Emara said in a way that wasn't very convincing.

Artem huffed out a sigh after rubbing his foot. "Now that she is with you," he declared, "I can finally take my leave."

A nervous laugh escaped Emara's mouth and Artem moved through the crowd.

"I need a stiff drink," she declared, her long dark hair waving beautifully at her shoulders as she tried to take her leave.

"And where do you think you are off to?" Torin followed.

She looked flushed as she said, "The bar."

"Are you stressed?" he asked. "You seem a little stressed."

Being between Artem and Breighly must have rattled her nerves. But why?

"I am fine." Her voice was higher than normal.

It wasn't like her at all.

He grabbed her hand and stopped her walking. She turned to face him. "Did something happen whilst I wasn't there? Is there something I should know? You have been a little distant."

She gazed up at him, her beautiful eyes that were, tonight, a grey-blue, a mist of pure magic, set on his face. "I promise, there is nothing wrong."

"Okay, good." He relaxed a little. A floating tray of polished silver came by and she swiped a glass of what looked like brandy on ice and a glass of fizzy wine from it. Before he could thank her for getting *him* a drink, she necked it, throwing back every drop. She then moved on to the wine, taking large sips.

Something had happened, and he was going to work it out.

"Is it hot in here?" she asked. "Like it's warmer than normal?" She fanned herself. "Isn't it?"

Stunned at the alcohol she had just put away, he said, "You have been friends with Breighly Baxgroll for five minutes and you are already firing alcohol down your throat at an impressive, worrying rate."

"Don't blame her," she said, placing the glasses into a passing tray. "I can hold my own with liquor."

"Ah, that's right. You still owe me an expensive bottle of rum."

That night, on the rooftop of the tower, she had saved him. She had drunk his favourite bottle of rum that cost more than he made in two months, but she had saved him that night in a way she would never understand.

From that moment, he'd known that Emara was going to be more to him than just some stranger he had saved from the Dark Army. She was going to be more to him than just some girl who he wanted to fuck. She was going to be more than the hunt, more than his oath, more than just an alliance. She had seen right through to his soul that night.

He swallowed as he watched her take in the room. The long column of her neck exposed the flesh she liked to be kissed. The curves of her breasts in the gown, full and shapely, led down to her small waist, and then her hips expanded out beautifully.

Maybe it was warm here. He pulled at the neck of his tunic. Very fucking warm.

"It is a little warm," he admitted. "Shall we go outside to the veranda?"

"Actually," she said, her eyelashes fluttering a little. "I was hoping we could go somewhere private."

Torin's eyes flicked to her throat as it bobbed and then back to her face. The alcohol seemed to be working quickly in her bloodstream. Was that flushing in her cheeks?

"You want to go somewhere more private than the veranda?" His eyes narrowed.

"It's freezing outside," she said so fast that her lips barely moved.

"It is only wildlings like us that would go out there in such temperatures, exploring," he purred, testing to see how she would react. "You said it yourself, it's warm in here. The veranda would cure that."

She didn't laugh. "I don't really want to stay around here and have meaningless conversations with people I don't even know. I've done that all week. Since it is the winter solstice, I need a break from all of that." Her voice trembled a little, causing him to worry. "I have something for you." She looked up at him through the most perfectly fanned lashes he had ever seen.

His heart picked up its pace.

"You got me something?" he said slowly, feeling like the ring in his pocket was now a heavy boulder.

"Yes," she whispered. "But you must come with me now whilst I have the chance to show it to you." She grabbed on his wrist and began pulling him along.

"Angel..." He wrapped an arm around her waist and pulled her into him so closely that their bodies were pressed together. It didn't matter to him that he was being affectionate in front of so many people. He didn't care if anyone was watching. They could look. "As much as I like the sound of going somewhere private with you for this very *intriguing little* gift"—She stilled in his arms —"I need to know that you are all right." He heard the worry in his own voice this time. There was no time for him to mask that. "You are acting strange."

She had been for a few days.

Emara relaxed in his embrace, which took him by surprise, and he ran a thumb across her spine as she said, "You asked me to trust you. I closed my eyes and trusted you." She looked over at his face. "And now I need to ask you to do the same thing." Her voice was a little husky, but he found that irrefutably attractive. Anything she did, he found attractive. "Do you trust me?" she asked.

"That depends." He smiled, a smile that he knew made her heart rate increase. He had felt it. "Do you have your favourite new weapon strapped to that gorgeous thigh under your dress?" He moved a strand of her silken hair from her face to stop him reaching down to feel it under her gown. Now *that* would be inappropriate. "Because if you do, maybe I should be worried."

"Maybe if you shut up long enough and just followed me"—She screwed up her face, and her nose wrinkled.—"You would find out."

Why did his cock always harden when she was angry?

She turned, tugging him with her out of the grand ballroom, leaving one question on his mind.

What in the underworlds had she gotten him?

BREIGHLY

THE STRING BAND WAS ANNOYING. And the food came in parcels small enough to feed a forest mouse. She was hungry and bored.

That never boded well.

She swiped another drink from a passing waiter carrying his tray atop his shoulder. It was a fizzy wine and not a straight shot of hard liquor, but that didn't matter. It would do the trick.

Breighly scanned the room for any signs of trouble that she could get herself involved in, anything that would at least give her a *little* thrill. Her brothers were mingling with a pack of wolves from Tolsah Bay, and her father was probably somewhere bored too, listening to a stuffy elite shithead talk about his wealth and power.

"You look like you need some company." The scent of baked orange and summer rain hit her instantly.

She rolled her eyes. "Don't you have an empress to be guarding?" She sipped her drink, not taking her eyes from the mingling crowd.

"I am off duty," he said, his arm now brushing her shoulder. He stood beside her, much taller than she was, his gaze burning into the side of her cheek.

She didn't remember him being that tall. "I am ecstatic for you." She flipped her hair over her shoulder. Breighly didn't meet his gaze, making sure she maintained a bored expression on her face. "You should be on your way now. Have fun."

He chuckled. "I must admit, I have never met anyone quite like you."

"What can I say?" She smiled, showing all of her wolfy teeth. "I am a treat."

He laughed out loud, and a few seconds later, a small smile pulled his lips together. "Yes, you are."

Finally, she turned to face him.

That was a mistake. She knew it the minute his big brown eyes met hers. They were like pools of liquid chocolate. Why were they so fucking powerful?

She had to look away.

His voice was low and seductive, and she sipped her drink again, pushing away any lust that lingered in her core. "Are you really going to pretend that we didn't spend seven glorious hours making love?"

She whirled to him again.

Seven hours? Had it really been seven hours?

"First of all..." She pushed out her glass towards his chest, so far it almost touched him. He was already smiling so infuriatingly. She could have cracked the stem of her glass. "We did not make love. We fucked! Once."

"It was four times, but continue." He drew his tongue over his lips. His enormous weight shifted, and he leaned his head to one side.

"It was once. All the different times in the same night don't count, Adam."

"It's Artem, and, well, I am counting them."

Breighly actually had to stop her hand from ramming her glass into his chest. It was incredibly worrying how many violent thoughts she had in one day. Maybe when she got back to Ashdale, she could summon a healer. She would put that one on the long list of all the other things she needed to see her about.

"If that makes you feel better about yourself"—she raised her voice a little higher in tone—"then be my guest. But I absolutely will not be. The night was average at best." She sipped her wine again, not really able to appreciate the bubbles on her tongue.

The sex hadn't been average, it had been very good. Very fucking good. It had been the only thing to make her feel anything in a long time.

He let out a shockingly loud laugh, and then his eyes found hers again. "That's a real shame." He shook his head. "I even brought that knife you like to roleplay with in case you were up for round five. Or two. Whatever makes *you* feel better about yourself."

She dragged her eyes from his face. It was a handsome face, probably one of the most handsome here, but she didn't want to look at it for too long.

"Poor Emara. I would hate to have you as my guard." She turned to the crowd again. "You are so incredibly annoying."

"I have a feeling, wolfy"—he pressed his rock-hard torso against her arm—"you wouldn't need a guard at all."

"I also have a feeling that I could tear that chest of yours apart if you press it any further against my arm." She looked him up and down once and then looked away. "In case you have forgotten, I have very sharp claws and even sharper fangs."

A rough laugh passed his lips. "I haven't forgotten." He leaned into her ear and her stupid heart stammered for a moment, reminding her it was there at all. "I still have the scrapes on my back to remind me of it." He pulled back instantly as if expecting her to lash out at him.

Instead, she handed him her empty glass and kicked into step.

"Wait!" he called from behind her.

She spun, ready to give him a series of sharp and explicit curses. But she realised he was holding out a small flower.

"What is that?" she asked him.

There it was again. That stammer in her Gods-damn heart!

"It's mistletoe." He grinned sheepishly. "I want to give it to you as a gesture of goodwill." His face turned a little more serious and she didn't like it, not one bit. She swallowed. "The flower dates to before humans even walked the earth. It can still blossom even in the coldest winter." He stepped towards her, twirling it between two inked fingers. "In the most frozen of all places, it grows." He took her hand and put the flower in her palm. Stunned by the gesture, she let him. "It is a symbol of hope, and the Gods admired its vivacity. And it is tradition that when given the flower, you must kiss the person who you received it from." His grin widened on his face.

The stone that was her heart almost shattered.

That smug bastard!

She laughed, the sound escaping her before she could stop it. "Well, the night is still young, I suppose." She raised her eyebrows. "I will see if I receive any more gifts, and then I will kiss the person who gave me my favourite one, Arkus."

"Artem." He corrected. He looked over his lashes at her, causing a tingling sensation to move in her lower region. "Artem. Artem of Clan Stryker."

Finally, she looked down at the crest pinned to his chest. Before it could overwhelm her and cloud her better judgement, she turned and lost herself in the crowd with the only gift that a man had ever given her that she appreciated.

CHAPTER FORTY-FIVE
EMARA

Her hands had shaken as she had tied a strip of fabric from her robe around Torin Blacksteel's eyes. It was an utter travesty to cover them, but she didn't trust him not to peek.

"Now I am very intrigued," Torin informed her as he leaned back against the blankets of her bed. She straightened to move away from him, but he struck, grabbing her waist.

Even when he was blind, he could find her.

"I hope you weren't about to leave me lying here without giving me a kiss first."

Emara's heart wavered, causing her chest to take a heavy inhale at his words. She held it.

"I don't mind the fact that you have blindfolded me —in fact, I am rather enjoying it—but you can't leave me on this bed without at least a little kiss. That is *tortuous.*"

Torin's lips pulled into a seductive smile as his sultry tones vanished into the night, and Emara considered if her heart would ever not crash in her chest at the sight of his dimples.

Leaning forward, she pressed a gentle kiss against his lips. He moved to deepen it, but she pulled back, leaving him with only the air around him. Torin bit into his lip, sweet frustration lingering on what she could see of his face. The room was dark besides the witch flames that burned in the fireplace, and its crackling was the only sound that could be heard apart from the pulse in her ears.

She swallowed, taking a step back, and he let go of her.

Walking over to the arch, creating space between herself and Torin, she reached up for the newest addition to her dress. Instead of fumbling with buttons or ribbon, it just slid open as she pulled down. Apparently, the *zipper* was sweeping through the female fashion society, and Lorta couldn't wait for her to try it. Parting the fabric from behind, she moved out of the dress and it fell to the floor at her feet, revealing what she had on underneath.

The deep red bralette hugged the curves of her breasts in a fashion that was clearly made for nothing but seduction. The sheer lace that covered her rear was the same matching pattern and it was embroidered beautifully, hand stitched and so very delicate over her hips.

It really was a masterpiece.

Breighly had outdone herself. She had even added to the box two lacey garters, designed for fantasies.

Emara walked over to where a matching sheer robe

hung over her towel railing. Draping it over her shoulders, leaving it hanging open, like Breighly had instructed, she took a breath.

The buzz inside her head increased, either from her magic or the rate her heart was beating, but she knew she wanted this.

She wanted him.

She wanted him over everything else that she felt right now. The darkest parts of herself had probably wanted him well before she was ready to admit it to herself. But this was her choice, she was in control of this moment.

"You can remove the blindfold." Her voice broke from her lips, not sounding like her own at all.

Torin removed his mask with a calm confidence and dropped it onto his stomach casually. His azure eyes caught her standing in the middle of the archway, and she straightened her spine. Emara lifted her chin, and a gentle wave of goosebumps spread over her skin, causing her to shiver a little. Every morsel of that calm confidence fell from his face as he took her in. What composure had been set in his eyes before was now replaced by utter shock.

He hadn't been expecting this.

His eyes filled up with a lustful smoke, so thick that it consumed every part of them. His mouth fell open, and Emara could see the quickening in his breath with the rise and fall of his chest.

He sat forward slowly, the muscles in his stomach rippling underneath his tight tunic and his elbows found his knees, the veins in his arms straining under his weight. The blindfold fell to the ground.

A pooling of warmth gathered low in her stomach. And then lower, as she watched him take in every single inch of her body. His icy gaze lingered on all of the filigree detail on the garments that her curves bore, not leaving much to the imagination.

"Tell me," he finally managed to say, his voice so low and raspy she had to draw her knees together, "is it just the lingerie that is my present?" The ice-blue flames of his eyes flicked to her face, turning darker. "Or do I get to keep the angel that's wearing them too?"

Every part of her soul sang at his words, tingling all over her skin.

"You get to have all of it." Her lashes fluttered as she spoke. "If you want it."

Unadulterated desire flashed through his eyes, like a hunger she had never experienced. A muscle coiled in his jaw, and she could tell it was taking *all* of him, every part of him, not to stride over to where she stood and take her against the marble archway.

A heat balled through her, making its way from her stomach into her core.

"If I want it?" he repeated, eyebrows raised. "If *I* want it?" He finally powered strength into his strong legs to stand. "It goes without saying that *I* want it." He hovered close to the bed. Something in his features changed. "Do you truly want this?" His gaze did not move from her face the whole time, searching for any scrap of doubt or ingenuity.

He wouldn't find it.

"I have wanted this for longer than you are probably aware of," Emara admitted to him.

She was finally exploring her darkest desire. And that was him.

A wicked corner of his lips turned up at the one side, revealing a small dimple in his cheek.

Her heart thrashed against her ribcage.

"I want you to know that I want all of you." Torin's low, scorching voice stroked her exposed flesh even as he stood across the room. "I want every. Single. Part. Of. You."

But he didn't move. Instead of saying something, she let the covering fall off her shoulders, the whole thing falling to the floor.

There was no hiding from his gaze now.

A pulse exposed itself in his neck and he swallowed, his eyes darting to her thigh. "You wore your spear?" He swallowed again, like the weapon sheathed in her garter might be the reason his heart imploded right this very second.

How he kept his voice so steady was a true skill, one that she had yet to learn.

"Yes," she breathed. "A great trainer once told me never to go anywhere without it."

He chuckled, amusement in his features. "If you had told me of this earlier, I wouldn't have put in so much protest to head to the veranda. Can you imagine if I found that out there? I would have caused an awful scene in the great ballroom. We would have been the talk of the winter solstice."

Emara's throat bobbed as she pictured how wild that

might have been, how free she would have felt in the frenzy of his lust. "I feel like people were already talking when your hands found my waist in front of every faction there tonight."

"Let them talk. I like letting people know how much I want you. I will never be sorry for that." He chuckled a little before his face stilled, his jaw setting in hard. "You really want this?"

A vulnerability flashed in his eyes, and he left it there for her to see.

Finally.

"Yes, Torin." His name was thick in her throat. "I want this. I want you. I meant it when I said I would choose you."

He looked her over again, emotion riding in the ocean waves of his eyes. "You are so fucking out of my league, it's unreal. You know that, right?"

Her chest constricted at the weakness in his voice, but as quick as it had been there, it was gone. He moved towards her. She braced herself as his lips crashed against hers in a ravishing and unrelenting kiss, and his body collided with hers, hard muscle against soft flesh. Her hands flew up, wrapping around his neck, and his strong hands found her face, pulling her deeper into the kiss. It was burning and savage. It was soul-changing.

"What have you done to me?" he asked as he stole a quick breath from their embrace. But before she could speak, his mouth claimed hers again, melting her bones enough that she wobbled in his hold. He pulled back and she gasped at the sudden loss of him on her mouth.

One of her hands found the cold rock of the archway to steady her.

Gradually, he unbuttoned and lifted his tunic over his head, uncovering layers of solid muscle that could only be earned by years of training. He cast the tunic to the ground and his eyes met hers again.

Her heart clicked. It was locked. And Torin Blacksteel had the key.

His eyes moving from her gaze, his hand went to the button at the top of his trousers. He dug his thumbs into the rim of his leathers, taking everything off with one clean sweep, and the leather and weapon belt hit the ground at the same time. The dim lighting cast shadows into every space that his muscles rose from, defining them even more as it lingered in the shade of his golden flesh. His hair was an inky black and it shined against the light, just like the scars on his bare skin.

A warmth worked its way up from Emara's core right through her stomach as she took in the size of him. She knew she was blushing when the heat hit her cheeks. She had never really seen a man fully naked before. Even in the cavern, Torin had kept his leathers on.

But he was glorious. Every inch of him. A God.

"Emara." His voice was deep but soft. "You don't need to be ashamed or embarrassed to look at me."

And she let her gaze linger a few more seconds before she drove her eyes to his.

The briefing with Breighly had been quick, and she had to admit that she hadn't really been listening after the wolf had instructed her what to do with the robe as the nerves had begun sinking into her stomach.

Another part of her tension eased as Torin moved towards her, making the first move. He removed her long hair from her neck and placed it over her shoulder, making sure it tumbled down her back.

His hand went to her chin. "If there is anything—and I mean anything—you don't like, just tell me and I will stop."

She nodded, short of breath. "Just kiss me."

Because when he kissed her, she would know what to do. Her body always knew what to do when he kissed her.

And he did, soft and slow. Torin moved, pivoting her like he was a ballroom dancer, and the backs of her legs caught the edge of the bed.

How did he move so fast and gracefully?

Distracted by the fact that his hands were now on her back, unfastening the hook that held the bralette in place, she forgot to breathe. His mouth didn't stop from kissing hers, and in one swift movement, the bralette unclipped at the back. Knowing her well, knowing her body, his mouth went straight for the soft and sensitive part of her neck, dissolving any nerves that had materialised in her stomach.

He kissed down and down, his mouth warm along her shoulder, and her body relaxed against his as she held on to his arms, embracing all of him. He sent a scorching hot kiss into her mouth again before he pushed forward, lowering her back to the mattress.

There was a moment of kisses before he stopped.

Torin curled his fingers around the thin straps of the bralette and pulled it to one side, revealing the flesh that lay under the lace. For a second, she had forgotten that his talented fingers had unhinged the clasp at the back and Torin lowered himself slowly—at a teasing rate— towards her lips.

"I told you before that I wanted to take my time with you and savour every moment."

A tantalising sensation ran through her spine at his words, causing her hips to move from the mattress. Emara did all she could to press them back against it. One hand pressed into the bed above her, and one caressed her hip.

Torin knew exactly what he was doing to her, and she couldn't hate him for it, not one bit.

Not when it thrilled every part of her.

He moved downwards, his tongue leaving a wicked trail between her breasts, and she locked her knees into his sides as a gasp left her mouth. The hardness of him grazed the very centre of her just as his mouth found the bare flesh of her nipple.

Her head kicked back in silent delight and Torin rolled his hips into the pooling at her core.

"You have no idea how many times I have thought about this moment. Every day, every time we trained, every time your lips curved up into a smile or you rolled your eyes at me. Every time you challenged me. When I saw you with my sword in your hands, and you swung it at me, I knew it would lead to this. And I am going to get you so unbelievably ready for me before I fuck you." He breathed into the peaks of her skin which had now hardened against his tongue. "I am going to lick every part of you, kiss every part of you." Torin's voice came out in deep, sharp rasps. A moan escaped her mouth at his promise. He moved down, lower and lower, worshipping her body with his mouth. "I am going to finally taste you, and hear your moans as you come for me again and again. " He nipped her hip with his teeth, and a whimper left her throat.

Quickly, Torin sat up, moving from the bed to kneel on the floor. Looking at her with feral desire, he suddenly changed the pace. He scooped underneath her legs and pulled her closer to him, tilting her hips upwards. Her ass came to the end of the bed and he spread her legs. Torin glanced to where she lay beneath him, and with a sinful grin, he ran one finger down the centre of her lace underwear. She bucked, flinging her hands into her own hair.

Torture. This was agonisingly brilliant torture.

"These need to come off." He breathed deeply. "And since I want to see them again, I won't rip them this time."

He flicked a finger under the lace and pulled.

This was it.

That was the last part of clothing that separated them fully, that separated Emara from her darkest desires. It was the last part of what he could take off before he took her into his mouth. The tips of his fingers pulled the lingerie down her thighs, brushing past her knees as Torin Blacksteel removed her underwear completely.

CHAPTER FORTY-SIX
EMARA

Emara had no idea where he dropped the underwear, but by that point, she didn't really care. He lowered his head between her thighs. A deep breath left her as he kissed the top of her pubic bone, an area that she had never really thought of until Torin's lips grazed over it, making it tingle all over.

The centre of her swelled and she knew before he even touched her, she was drowning. Drowning in his touch, his kiss, his intensity. Her core tightened as he kissed down further until he reached her centre. The buzzing in her head had not dulled, it had magnified, and all she could hear were the desperate pants of her breath. His large hand sailed up her navel, holding her stomach, pinning her down. And he was right to do so as he took his wicked tongue and drove it into the middle of her heat.

Her hips bucked against him as unspeakable pleasure rippled through her body with just one stroke. One stroke that turned into two and three—possibly four, but Emara was too dizzied by the pleasure to count. His tongue caressed her intimate flesh again, this time circling and looping around the bundles of nerves that threatened to implode any minute. The sweet ache in her core craved more, much more. She wanted to feel him inside of her.

"I want you." She panted. "Now."

He denied her of it as he licked through the nerves of her flesh.

She cried out, her head twisting to one side, a moan on her lips. The muscles around her spine were tingling and throbbing and so was her core as he worked his tongue on her, picking up the pace, her hips writhing along with it. Anticipating what her body would do, he kept one hand pinned on her belly as he slid a finger inside her. Emara's spine curled against the bed and she had to grip the sheets to hold on to something, anything.

She found his silky hair with her hand and as she gripped it, that only seemed to spur him on more. Nothing about the pace of his kissing and sucking was delicate against her, it was hasty and animalistic, like he couldn't get enough.

And that's when she realised it would never really be anything else between them. It would always be this intense. It would always be this melting inferno of desire.

He introduced a finger again, sliding it in with ease as he nipped at her centre gently.

Emara cried out.

Oh Gods, she knew this feeling. She had felt it only once before and it was because of Torin that time too.

Adding in a second finger, stretching her, she felt a sting that lasted for only a second before it was wiped away by the pulsing pleasure of both of his fingers inside of her. He sucked again as he thrust two fingers in and out of her, and she called out his name, begging for this delightful torment to become something more.

She wanted more. She needed more.

He pumped his fingers, picking up the pace, and in one final, deep stroke with his wicked tongue, he flicked the bundle of nerves at the apex of her centre.

A burst of tension shattered in her core and around his fingers. Emara had no idea what she cried out this time, it could have been for the Gods or him, she couldn't hear it. Her body arched, feeling the tension coil, break, and then scatter around every part of her. Her eyes squeezed shut to cope with the explicit tremor that ran up her core and her head craned back against the mattress. The floodgates of release broke over her body, turning her bones to liquid once again.

She had no time to recover as Torin's mouth claimed hers and he repositioned her up the bed, lifting and moving her with ease. "You tasted better than I could have ever imagined in my wildest dreams, angel." He kissed her cheek and down to her ear lobe. "I could have tasted you all night. But I need to know what it's like to be inside you."

Taking a deep, much-needed breath, she pulled him against her again. The weight of his body coming down on her was a pleasure that she hadn't known existed.

He kissed her and then dragged her swollen lip

between his teeth. "I want you to be mine," he said as her lip finally fell free of his grip. "Say you're mine."

There was something so pure in his eyes, something so much more than hunger and sexual desire. It caused her heart to throb for him. It was something deep that connected them to the stars and the moon and every galaxy beyond theirs. It was something infinite.

"I am yours." The words drifted through the kingdom.

He kissed her again, his fiery mouth still smiling as his tongue stroked hers. When he pulled back, he smoothed her hair away from her face. "If I hurt you," he whispered, "tell me to stop."

"You won't," she whispered back against the cracking of the fire. "I trust you."

It was then he moved between her legs. His arms came over, pinning her underneath him.

She was safe here.

She was always safe with Torin.

Her heart fluttered as he looked down at her.

"Promise me you will tell me?" he asked her.

She nodded once and he kissed her, so gently that she almost couldn't feel him. It felt like a mellow summer breeze and velvet against her lips. His scent of frozen berries and fresh pine swirled around her, imprinting on her skin.

He positioned himself so that she could feel his hard length find its way to her entrance. Torin moved, rolling his hips tenderly, and angled himself. She felt a sharp ache and he moved inside her, stretching her.

She couldn't help a gasp escape her lips, and Torin stilled.

"I'm sorry." He kissed her mouth as he rolled his hips again softly, edging into her. The sting of how big he was made her eyes open wide. Another gasp hitched in her throat at the friction, but she tried to choke it down.

Emara focused on the magic thrumming through her body, fighting the uncomfortable feeling. She knew it wouldn't last long, Breighly had told her that. And Cally had too. So she clutched his back, digging her nails into his skin, taking a deep breath as he rolled again. This time, as he went a little deeper, the tension began easing off, and she could feel her muscles relax. She was still so slick from what he had done before, preparing her to take him fully inside of her, that she hoped the sting wouldn't last much longer.

He sent his hips forward again and she relaxed against the bed, each vertebra of her spine also loosening as his muscled body moved against hers.

"You are incredible," he whispered into her cheek as he rolled forward, now offering every inch of himself. He kissed her over and over as he moved inside her slowly. "Fuck, Emara." He groaned hoarsely, like he was holding on to a tiny thread of restraint that frayed more with every thrust.

Where the sharp friction had been before was now replaced with a delightful stretching, and it was a sensation. Both pain and pleasure combined. She gave a small roll of her hips underneath him, bringing them to meet his. His eyes greeted hers and the dark strands from his untamed hair tickled against her nose. She had never seen his hair so unruly. It was beautifully wild, evidence of her hands having been there. She knew how much he had to be holding back with what he was giving her now, and she didn't want him to.

Not with her. She wanted to see every side of him. Everything.

She could handle his darkness.

Emara grabbed on to his strong neck and her lips smashed against his. "Don't hold back," she breathed as her fingers trailed through his hair. "I trust you."

He moved quicker against her, listening to her command. The movements of his hips were stronger and harder, and she rolled her body to meet his thrusts. Her breathing started to labour again as that tingling sensation worked its way back up her spine, scattering goosebumps all over her skin. Unable to form words, she kissed him frantically, his tongue cutting through her mouth as his pace got quicker and deeper, the rolling of the colossal frame on top of her, the sounds of their skin against each other. Her hands ran all over his back, clutching and clawing as the pleasure of their joining intensified.

"I am not worthy of you." His head bowed down towards her, and his breathing started to labour too.

Oh, but he was. He was so worthy of her. "You are more than worthy of me," she said, staggered between broken breaths. "I promise to show you that...you... are...worthy."

The maddeningly wonderful tension crept back into the muscles of her core as he began pounding inside of her, chasing that sweet release for both of them. The strokes of him being inside her now were so fervorous, a moan escaped her lips as she drove her hips into him, hard, and a spike of rapture coursed through her as she rolled again.

A sensual hiss escaped his lips at her action, deepening his plunge into her, and a wicked smile pulled his mouth up. "You are going to send me over the edge if you keep doing that," he breathed, and he propped himself up, slightly slowing his pace again, watching himself move inside her. "I don't want it to be over just yet." He thrust inside her again, and it took Emara everything she had not to turn her head into the sheets and scream. "I want to explore every limit your body has. In time, I want to explore all of it."

He rolled his hips so hard against hers, she could hear the smacking of their skin meeting again.

"I will always want this, to explore all of it. Only for you," Emara managed to get out before another moan developed in her throat. A guttural sound left Torin's throat at her words, and she could feel how much he was tensing. "Don't hold back." She panted. "I want all of you. All of it."

With one delicious thrust of his hardness inside her, he broke through that tension-filled wall as he found the flesh of her nipple with his mouth and sucked. The world around her shattered again, glittering like broken pieces of a puzzle, bringing with it her second climax.

"Wrap your legs around me," he demanded, and she obeyed, unable to see straight for all of the sparkling stars.

As she did, he moved inside her hard and rapidly. Much more rapid than before, and his hands were over her, running over every part of quivering skin.

Torin ravished every part of Emara that she offered.

A thunder began building in his chest and she could feel it as he kissed her. It was thunder and it was lightning, it was oceans swelling and it was heavy rain that soaked her to the core. It was a storm that broke and unleashed itself around her.

Air raged at them and fire burned in her fingertips, waves of desire crashing against the shore.

He came, a raucous sound breaking from his lips, and every muscle in his body strained. Torin stilled, and after a few seconds, he finally worked into a gentle roll, his breathing more uneven than she had ever heard it before even after a battle or fight. He sagged a little, his golden skin flushed, before cradling her underneath him, moving her to a position that meant no one else in the world could see her. Not even the flames of the fire could catch a glimpse of her as he kissed her shoulder, burying his nose in her neck. Not even the snow on the mountain peaks could glimpse her as his body protected her from their view.

For a moment, there was nothing else in this world. Not darkness, no light—just them.

Fire and steel.

CHAPTER
FORTY-SEVEN
BREIGHLY

A fake laugh left Breighly's throat as she took a side glance at the hunter who had been catching her eye all night. He was still staring from across the grand ballroom, sipping on a drink of his own.

Artem fucking Stryker.

The chief commander's son.

That's who she had let into her bed. She should have checked his crest, because then her heart wouldn't have thundered the way it did now. She would have been prepared.

He winked, catching her glance that had lasted a little too long, and she turned her attention back to the conversation she had been ignoring with the boring twat standing before her.

That's all she needed, to be mixed up with the chief commander's son. She'd known that his incredible build and cocky grin had to mean something. Her father would certainly kill her now. Murk Baxgroll needed the respect of his fellow prime members. There had always been rules about that. No relationships with any other faction member, only wolves.

And if her brothers found out...

Oh, sweet, fucking Vanadey of Life and Beauty.

She was always told never to mix business with pleasure.

She couldn't go there. She wouldn't go there again. Not now that she knew she had taken a lover that could quite possibly be the chief commander of this kingdom one day.

However, it was sure as shit that the Gods were testing her tonight. One question found itself rolling around in her mind: Why was everyone else so boring?

She took another sip of her drink.

"The structure of your face is simply stunning." the man said. He'd been talking *at* her non-stop for the last ten minutes, and was too stupid or arrogant to notice it was clearly falling on deaf ears.

Scraping her gaze from an inky warrior, she smiled at the man. "I know."

Surprise flickered in his too-close-together eyes. "It's not ladylike for a woman to be aware of her beauty," the man said as he tipped a glass to his lips. His pinky finger stuck out in a manner that revealed his privileged upbringing, and as he took a sip of his champagne, a diamond ring winked under the lights. "Did your mother never inform you of such things? A man does not find it attractive."

Bringing her full attention back to the conceited son of a bitch, she flicked her hand under the bottom of his glass and the crystal flute fell an inch from his lips, spilling tinted liquor onto his pretentiously white dress jacket.

"Did your mother never tell you not to miss your mouth when sipping champagne? That could stain your expensive dress jacket, you know," she said, only just managing to keep the rage that burned in her veins at bay. "My mother was a wolf. She didn't teach me anything. But what my father—the Alpha of Caledorna—taught me was to eat the hearts of wealthy men that can't keep their ancient opinions to themselves." She paused, looking at him from head to toe, then threw him a heart-stopping smile, every tooth bared.

A mix of mortification and rage burned in his face. "You distasteful bitch." He pulled on her arm, dragging her a little closer. She didn't flinch; she snarled into her smile. "If I had realised you were a wolf, I would have just offered you a coin to start with instead of buttering you up with small talk. Afterall, wolves do tend to take a cheap rate."

"Coin?" A broken scoff turned into blistering anger on her mouth. "You think I am a whore?"

"You are not exactly dressed to convince me otherwise." His beady little eyes roamed her body, sending hot, deadly rage around her veins. She could feel the sharpness of her claws elongating in her fingertips. "I thought the Supreme had sent us gifts this winter. I would have paid a lot of money to see your pretty mouth—"

"I would rather choke and die," she cut him off, her voice fierce and sharp.

He clearly didn't believe that her father was the Alpha. Either that or his arrogance dumbed his brain.

"That's a shame." He laughed. The revolting sound made every wolf instinct in her body prickle to attention. The wolf was ready to pounce. "You could have been a smart girl and used your head to earn some money. But instead, you opened your uneducated mouth too soon. You wolves are always the same. However, you do have an unbelievable rear for someone of low class, though." He sniggered; his nose high in the air.

"You ought to be careful to go around insulting *low-class* women like me." She offered him a feral look. "Do you know how deep we bite? And as for my ass, I didn't get that by sitting on it like your foolish *highbred mother* or *naive wife*. I work for everything I have. I don't need your coin."

The elite male finished off his glass of champagne before sliding a hand into his silk-lined pocket, his dark hair shining with ointment. "You see, I don't mind a little biting. But what I would prefer is silence and restraint. That's what makes a woman bearable. It's something you should practise, even if you do have an unbelievable *ass.*"

Before she could swipe her long claws across his throat, a gruff voice came from behind her. "That is where you are mistaken."

Breighly turned to see Artem Stryker standing behind them. One of the fastenings on this tunic had opened to reveal his thick, inked throat.

"Do you want to know what I think is a deadly

combination in a woman?" His perfect eyebrow lifted before she saw a little danger burn in his eyes. He stopped short of the elite man, whom he towered above, his broad shoulders squared and strong. "Intelligence, which she clearly has, since she isn't entertaining the likes of you." He paused. "Humour, which she also clearly has, since that expensive champagne has made its way down your stupid jacket," he continued as he pulled a blade from his belt and twirled it in his skilled fingers. The act made Breighly's heart work at a rate she had never felt before, pounding against her chest. The glittering of his golden-brown eyes were a little warmer as he looked over her face and then back to the elite male. "But what I appreciate most of all in a woman is when she can throw a better punch than my own."

She tried to hide the hitch in her breathing. She had never had a male compliment her abilities before, only her body. Even if he was complimenting violence, a tremor ran through her body.

That was another thing she was going to add to the healer's list—to stop being aroused by men who were primal in their approach to life and appreciated violence just as much as she did. It would never end well.

"Artem," she tried to stop him, but he ignored her and continued to palm the knife in his large, inked hand.

"In case all of that exorbitant education has failed you, *she* is the one with the hard-as-granite punch that will knock you on your back. Not to mention those sharp little claws." He paused, pinging a quick look in her direction, and it didn't take much to know what he was insinu-ating. "So I am going to suggest you apologise to her now for the way you have spoken to her." He bowed his head slightly. "And I won't allow her to knock you out."

Breighly flicked her eyes to Artem. "Won't allow her? You can't tell me I am not allowed to punch him." Her head angled. "If I wanna punch him, I will."

His eyes pulled from her face and a grin formed as he looked back towards the male, whose pompous atti-tude had now diminished slightly. "You clearly have no idea who she is, or you wouldn't be manhandling her like that." His dark gaze turned vicious as he looked down at the mark on Breighly's arm where his hand had been. "You better start that apology now," Artem seemed to growl.

The elite male straightened. His gaze dragged from Artem to Breighly as his nose hitched into the air in a way that only the wealthy could. He wiped down his suit and raised his chin. Looking down his nose, he said, "I am sorry that you gave me the impression you were interested."

Another growl left Artem's throat, this time a little louder than before. "That doesn't sound like an apology to me."

Breighly put her hand up to stop the warrior. "I don't need an apology from a weak man," she said, looking the elite square in the face. "Just don't ever look in my general direction again, or I will claw out your throat."

The man's face paled, and he hastily took his leave, saying something about *barbarians*. She watched the back of his head disappear into the crowd, wishing she could have sliced into it with her claws.

Asshole.

Breighly spun on Artem. "What was that?" she asked. Confusion lingered on his face. "You do not get to do that for me." Her mouth pulled together.

"I wasn't trying to jump in."

"That's exactly what you did. I can handle myself."

A muscle in his jaw tightened. "Oh, I know you can," he said. "There are no doubts about that. I just wanted an opportunity to punch an elite prick without getting reprimanded for it. It always looks better if I am defending someone else."

A harsh laugh left her throat. "So you were using me?"

"Just like you did with me the other night." His dark eyebrows lifted momentarily, and she saw something genuine in his features before a pridefulness settled back on his face.

She bit down on her lip. Okay, that was true. He had a point. She had sort of used him as a distraction to forget about how she truly felt inside. That's all she had been doing lately.

"Don't take it personally," she said, allowing her eyes to roam the room again as she crossed her arms over her chest.

"No, but you see..." He stepped a little closer, causing her attention to snap back to him. "I have taken it personally. I have never been kicked out of bed before." A dangerous twinkle glittered in his eyes.

"Well, now you have, and you need to get over it," Breighly snapped. "And fast."

"I have tried," he admitted, and a small laugh graced his lips, tugging up the corners. "Thorin knows I have tried to get over it. But I have failed miserably. And somehow, I just find myself back to where I was, thinking about you." He placed the knife that he had been holding back into his belt. She watched as the white strain of his knuckles returned to their normal colour.

"Then maybe you need to try harder, hunter."

"Maybe the best way to help me to get over it is for it to happen one last time...wolfy."

His smooth-as-silk words provoked every part of the wolf that she had in her. Every part of wolf blood that pumped through her veins called to his suggestion.

Fuck.

She stepped in closer so that her chest was flush with his abs. "I don't think you could handle round five —or however many times you falsely counted to feel *man enough*." Breighly smiled, knowing his eyes were on her lips, his breathing laboured as she pushed her breasts against him. "I don't think you have it in your locker to satisfy the *wolf* in me. So maybe you should quit while you're ahead."

A spine-tingling grin slashed across his face, causing her heart to dive into her stomach.

"Then maybe you should give me one more chance to prove you wrong." He raised his hand and coasted the back of his knuckles down her arm. There was a skull tattooed on the back of his hand. She had to coil every muscle in her body to command herself not to push her hips towards him.

She had to command herself not to feel...*stimulated.*

But she was.

What in the Mother of all Gods was he doing that was so weirdly working for her? She couldn't pin-point it. She looked at the tiny silver nose ring that curved out from his nostril. He was so gallantly handsome that she couldn't deny it. He knew he was too. He was as strong as any warrior should be, and she would put all of her coin on it that he had made it to the top of the Hunter Selection.

The best of the best.

Breighly debated if she loved or hated the fact that he was a little cocky. Already knowing the answer, just not wanting to admit it, she looked around the room. Her father was occupied in conversations that looked formal, and beside him stood Waylen and Roman. Something ticked in her jaw at the vision of her standing there beside her brothers as a woman who could lead her faction just the same way a man could.

But that would never happen so long as the Alpha gene never rose to power in the female wolf.

A little fire kick started in her stomach, and she looked back to the hunter who she was pressed against, his stare still on her face.

She needed a distraction again. This ball was expectedly monotonous and he...was not.

Burning underworlds.

"Okay, firstly," she said, before she could talk herself out of it. "It will need to be your room. I am sharing a room with my brother, and unless you want to die tonight, round five needs to be in your room." A light sparkled into his eyes. "Secondly, if you think that this is anything more than just sex, you are going to be very mistaken."

He nodded, his white teeth biting into his bottom lip. "Just sex, nothing more," he agreed.

The act of his teeth dragging along his full lip distracted her for a second, and she explored his mouth with her eyes. She shook off her moment of unfocused weakness. "Thirdly, if you say anything— and I mean anything—that leads to feelings or some sort of romantic gesture... In fact, if you say anything to make me cringe, I will cut your throat with your own knife." She flung her glass to her mouth, the rest of the liquid to the back of her throat, and swallowed. "Got it?"

He glanced at where she had pinned the flower— the mistletoe—he had given her earlier this evening to the strap of her dress. "Do you have any more demands?" His cheeks drew in playfully as he trailed his gaze back up to hers.

"Yes." She spun and began walking. Artem followed. "You need to stop asking questions. In fact, just stop talking altogether." She flung up a hand. "It will be better for both of us. We don't need these...polite conversations or silly compliments."

She swallowed as she thought over what he had called her just moments before.

Intelligent, funny, and capable.

"So you are telling me that I can't even make a single

noise?" he asked as his strong core pressed so close to her back as he guided her through the crowd.

"Nothing," she replied sharply before she could feel the effects of that warmth. "Not a peep."

"Not even to tell you how pretty you are?"

She spun, her body slamming against his. "You are ruining it already. Shut up and lead the way to your room."

He tipped his head back and laughed out loud. "You are something else entirely."

"And you are one more comment away from getting that round five you *desire* so much knocked out of your cards. So I suggest"—she leaned into him, so close that her stomach brushed the hardness of his leathers— "that you stop talking and start walking before I change my mind."

Breighly's back crashed into the unit that held a few of Artem's possessions. Weapons fell, crashing to the ground, books and trinkets tumbling with them. Artem swept one arm out and the remaining objects flew from the unit and onto the floor.

That's the kind of attitude she liked.

Gripping his strong tattooed neck, her lips met his again, twisting against each other like they had been lovers for years. Her lips already felt swollen with how hard he had kissed her, how thirsty he had been to drink her. And he kissed her like she was the only water source in his drought.

She had to give the hunter some credit, he could kiss like fuck.

In one quick action, he lifted her onto the unit, sitting her atop it. As she parted her legs for him, he filled the space, and her dress came up to her waist in a flash. Her hands greedily ripped at the buttons on his silver uniform, unable to part him from the material quick enough. Frustrated at how long it was taking her to undo them, she sliced a sharp nail through the tunic and pulled it apart. The tunic of his regalia split in half and revealed every intricate detail of his tattooed chest and stomach.

They were beautifully shaded, and she took in some notes of colour. But there wasn't time to explore the meaning of his tattoos, not when this wasn't meaningful. Not when this was just sex.

Not when she'd sworn to herself never to get attached to anything ever again. Not since her mother had left them, and then when Eli died.

She punched at those dark thoughts with every kiss she gave to Artem until they were gone, nothing left but heat and sweat from their desperate passions. His hand wove into her hair again and he pulled her head forward into an embrace that involved her lips.

"I like kissing you," he said into her mouth.

"Stop talking!" she ordered as she fumbled to find the button on his leather trousers.

His lips made their way down her neck and onto her shoulder, kissing spots on her skin that were truly tantalising. It was hard for her to focus on anything when he did that, and she relaxed, finally feeling nothing but his mouth on her. Numb pleasure.

Artem knew how to work his tongue too.

Good.

The trousers were about to get the same treatment as the tunic if she didn't find the fastener, but Artem reached down with one hand and loosened it for her.

He wasn't exactly slow in getting her underwear off either; in one swift movement, they were removed, and he hadn't even lifted his lips from her shoulder.

She was impressed.

Showing her appreciation, she reached for him, pushing her hand into his waistband. He let out a throaty moan before his lips found hers again, and she gripped his cock.

She was impressed again. She didn't remember him being that—

The door swung open, causing the both of them to halt every movement. Her hand whipped out from the band of his pants, and he whirled towards the door.

"Stryker!" she heard someone say, urgent and desperate, but his body blocked every view.

"Magin, my brother, I—"

"I don't need an explanation. Get dressed."

Although the man sounded collected, something panicked him. Something had his blood pumping.

"There has been a sighting."

"A sighting?" Artem echoed.

A small shiver of danger waved through Breighly's spine.

She knew what that meant. Having been so close to the Blacksteels all her life, she knew the terminologies.

"They are here," the man confirmed. "An army of demons swallowed up the footpaths below the mountains. Brother, it's hunting time."

CHAPTER
FORTY-EIGHT
TORIN

Sex had never meant anything to him before,
not really. It was just another way to get lost in
something that wasn't fighting, politics, or pressure from his father. But as Torin Blacksteel lay with
Emara in his arms in the blissful silence of the room, he
knew something had changed.

Something had changed forever.

He didn't know how long they had been intertwined
like this, but he sure as shit wasn't going to change it for
the world. What they had just done, what she had just
given him was...it meant more to him than he would
ever be able to express. Before her, he had never lay with
a woman afterwards and just let the moments they had
shared together soak into their skin. He had never
grown an attachment to a female before, not like this,
and when he had seen her standing before him in the
archway, offering herself, it had shattered him. Shattered his self-control and shattered the ice around his
heart.

She had given herself to him, and what that meant

to him was also beyond words, because he knew she had never lain with another man before. He couldn't express how he felt for her in words. He couldn't express what lay in his heart. He never could.

The nerves in his stomach reminded him that there was one way to express how he felt about her, and it lay in the lining of his tunic.

It had been there all night.

The mere thought of a proposal used to make his skin burn and sweat, his heart ache in a way that he never understood. But now, he realised, it was because he had never felt *hope* in this way before. He was so optimistic about Emara, and it felt strange in his heart. He had never *hoped* that a proposal would be anything other than alliance for his clan, an obligation to his duty, because he knew the chances of actually falling in love with the other party in the alliance was slim. As bad as it sounded internally, he wasn't sure if he would have even found his betrothed attractive, let alone be *emotionally* connected to her.

But *this,* what he felt for Emara, was different altogether.

It was burning, and it was unmatched.

He could be his true self with her.

Torin didn't have to separate his marriage and his alliance, should it be with her. He could be with her and *be* with her, not for what she could do for his clan, but for what his heart desired.

A thought stuck him hard, rattling his every foundation.

He swallowed as he played with a silk strand of her

beautiful hair, her breathing sleepy against his upper body. Torin looked down at her as she hugged his chest, their naked skin resting on each other.

If he had to, he would give up his clan for her, dissolving his oath as a hunter to the Gods' duty. And he knew at that moment it meant there would be no other woman or female in his life who would make him want to do that. No one else in this world would, but if he had to for her, he would do it. He would do it in a heartbeat, because what he held in his arms was so very real and legitimate, and he was prepared to do it.

However...

Here he was, his future laying in his arms, and he didn't have to break an oath or be exiled from his clan. Because the woman that fate would have him wed was right here. She was the Empress of Air, and she was promised to him.

His heart pumped quickly and hard in his chest, and he knew it was all for her.

It would always be for her.

He kissed her temple. She had no idea how much freedom she had just given him, how much weight had been lifted from his chest.

"Are you okay?" he asked. "You have gone awfully silent."

Laughing a little, she turned so that her naked flesh pressed into his chest even more. She looked up. "I am just enjoying this."

In the heat of their intimacy, he had asked her to be his, be only his, and she had agreed. She had said those two beautiful words, more satisfying than when she had said *kiss me.*

I'm yours.

The soft skin of her cheek lay against his chest. "It's just...I have never ever felt *this* in my heart before, and it scares me terribly."

He pushed her hair back from her face, brushing against her warm cheeks. "You have nothing to fear when you are with me. You know that."

She looked up to him again, eyes wide, and Torin had trouble keeping his hands from cupping her face. "I fear what I feel for you," she confessed.

He pulled her closer so that every part of her lay against him. "I know what you mean," he said as he stroked a hand through her hair. "A Spirit Witch once told me that I would fall in love...and that she would be taken from me. I feared her visions were true for a while. And then I would go through phases where I used to feel that I would be forced to spend the rest of my life with someone, and I wouldn't feel anything at all, and that scared me even more than the fortune teller's vision." He played with a loose strand of hair, turning it in his fingers. "Because seeing my mother try to love someone she would have never chosen for herself was unbearable at times." He paused, the heaviness back in his chest. "There were times when I couldn't stand it, because my mother would try so hard with Viktir"—he coughed a little—"my father, and all he could do was dismiss her. He was so focused on the clan or himself." He stilled, dropping the strand of her hair. "And I wouldn't wish that on the person I was going to marry. If I could choose..." He looked down at her. "I would have made sure I was marrying for something more than just an alliance, or I wouldn't have married at all. And I sure as Thorin wouldn't have taken that choice from you either."

Emara Clearwater looked up at him, and her galaxy-filled eyes turned violet.

And then her lips parted, still plump from his hungry kisses. "When I see you, my heart beats so quick that it feels like it could take off like a bird and fly. And when you smile, my lungs tighten to a point where I can barely breathe at all." Her cheeks flushed a beautiful shade of pink. He gave her a smug grin, but underneath that, underneath it all, he was scared of what she would say next. He was scared of where she was going with this or where she might conclude it. "And when you kiss me," she said with a wobble, and Torin sat up to meet her, concern creeping into his gut. "I could have never in my wildest dreams imagined how it would make me feel." She looked at him, her eyes ablaze once more. "Every part of my soul sings for you to kiss me again and again, like it was the first time in that damned waterfall."

He gave a gruff laugh at her attempt at profanity.

"It is like something you hear about in the stories where the deities would fall in love with humans. Like them, it utterly and doubtlessly consumes every part of me. And if that's not falling in love, then I don't know what it is."

He moved, unable to stop himself, rolling atop her. His lips were on hers in that frantic and needing way. She kissed him back, her soft lips against his, and they didn't back down, they claimed his mouth just as much as he claimed hers. It was feverish and it was asserting. It was pure thirst, delightful, drenching thirst. Even though they had just taken everything from each other, he wanted it, her, again. He burned for her, and she for him. He could feel it as they kissed, he could see it in her eyes when she looked at him, and he could hear it in her unspoken words.

He hardened for her again.

He paused, taking a breath.

His heart stilled.

Even though he knew in his soul that the Gods had sent her to him, he had to ask her a question that shook him to his core. Even though fear nudged at his heart, threatening to burst it, he moved from the bed before they got lost in each other once more.

"Where are you going?" she asked, her voice sounding low and alluring. It took him every fibre of strength not to leave the ring in his pocket on the floor and jump straight back into bed.

His lungs squeezed together.

Was she ready to take this plunge with him? It was diabolical, but it was fate. And he was ready.

Retrieving his tunic from the floor, not really wanting to walk too far away from where she lay, he wrestled out his final gift of winter solstice from his neatly lined pocket.

He turned to her and kneeled before the bed, his hand gripping the box so tightly—

"Torin!" Someone banged on the door from outside, causing both of them to jump.

Bleeding hearts of the kingdom, spare him!

"Torin." The banging on the door and the voice was assertive and imperious. "If you are there, open this door."

"Kinda in the middle of something, Magin." He looked over to Emara, who was entirely frozen, an expression embedded in her face that he didn't quite understand.

"Torin! There has been a sighting. You must come at once," Artem Stryker's voice shouted through the door with a little less patience than Magin's had.

Torin stood.

He was going to rip their fucking heads off for ruining every moment he had with her. Especially this one.

He jumped into his leathers and was flying towards the door in a heartbeat.

He threw the door open. "This better be good." He couldn't even hide the sheer rage in his tone.

It was Magin to speak first. "Blacksteel, we are truly sorry for interrupting." He swallowed, his hands behind his back. "But there has been a small army of demons sighted in the footpaths of the mountains."

Torin stilled.

A small army of demons.

"Who spotted them?" He looked between the two hunters. "When and where? Speak!"

"The news broke from the Supremes' personal guards in the watchtower," Artem confirmed.

"It's been ten minutes or so since the call went out.

All of the empresses have to stay in their rooms, all guards have to gather in the ballroom," Magin said.

Torin had forgotten that not everywhere had a loud siren that blasted when a demon was spotted. That meant time had been wasted in trying to locate everyone, precious time that they didn't always have when it came to the Dark Army.

Fuck.

Just when he thought the winter solstice had escaped the inevitability of vile demons ruining everything... He drew a hand over his face and looked at his brethren. They had no idea what he had been just about to do. The ring box was still firmly in his hand; he hadn't had enough time to bury it again. He looked over his shoulder and Emara sat up in the bed, the sheets pulled over her chest. Her dark hair sat wildly around her like midnight satin, and her full mouth was parted. There was only fear in her eyes now, which made him want to wipe out every single demon on this earth just to protect her from that terror.

He pushed his lips together and said, "One moment, angel."

Looking to his brethren, he stepped outside and shut the door, not caring that he was half-naked. He was the commanding guard in this cluster, and he had to make the decisions. "I am not leaving her alone," he stated. But he couldn't *not* fight. "I don't care if we have been commanded to do so. It's my call. I will take the reprimand."

"We figured you would say that," Artem agreed.

Torin looked down at his hand and opened his

palm.

Magin shifted as he took in what lay in Torin's hand. Artem's eyes darted from the ring box clutched in his fingers and then to his face.

"Brother, did you just—"

"Not yet." He pushed the ring towards Magin, who now looked rather pale. "I didn't get the chance to."

"But you were about to?" A breathless sound came from the inked warrior.

Torin gave one single nod, hoping that it was enough to silence them.

It did.

"Listen, I would be expected to be out there in this fight..." Torin looked over at his fellow hunters. "And so I will be."

"We also figured you would say that too," Artem commented. "Are we pulling short swords for myself and Magin to stay or what?"

"No," Torin said. "There is no need. Magin will stay and protect her." He looked at Artem. "We will hunt. We worked fast in the selection together."

Magin nodded in acknowledgement. Torin placed the ring box into Magin's hand. "Do not let a single person through this door until I am back," Torin barked a little more harshly than he had intended. He did everything he could to smooth out his face before saying, "If I don't come back, I still want her to have this." He could feel Artem's glare burn into the side of his face, but he didn't turn. "Give the ring to her should I fall tonight. Tell her there is no one else."

Magin nodded and a strange expression glazed his

face. Artem's chest expanded with breath, but there was no sarcasm or quip. He simply nodded.

"Give me a moment," he asked them, knowing they would go to ready the weapons.

Emara hadn't moved, but she stood as she saw him, dragging the sheets with her. "What is happening, Torin?"

"Don't worry, angel," he said, looking for the rest of his uniform. "I will take care of it, and I will be back before you know it." He flung the tunic over his head. "A few demons, that's all."

She came towards him quickly, and before she even spoke the words, he could hear what she was going to say. "Let me come with you."

He stilled after his weapon belt was secured. His jaw tightened. "Normally, I would never say no to you." He looked up at her. "But this time, I can't have you with me."

"But I have been getting better. Stronger, quicker," she pleaded, her voice shaking. "You said so yourself. I can actually fight now."

"Emara, you are just going to have to trust me on this one. You are under the Supreme's roof, and I might be able to hide what we do in Huntswood, but this is the north, her territory. I won't risk that for you. She could see it as a rejection of your title."

Hurt flashed across her face at first, but then an understanding set in. Her brow pulled together, and she looked away from him.

"Besides, you have never fought in the conditions of a mountain like this either. Especially in the dead of winter. In the dark. One wrong move, and you are off the edge of it." She nodded and a sharp pain struck through his heart. He didn't want to deny her anything, but he couldn't be distracted on the mountain top. And he would be with her by his side, untrained in the terrain of these landscapes. It was always the harshest to fight in, deadly and unforgiving; it had cost a lot of men their lives in the selection. He walked towards her after he had fastened the last button on his tunic. His hand cupped her chin and she leaned into it. "I won't be long, I promise," he breathed. "And then we will pick right back up where we left off, okay?"

Her eyes flashed to him and he wondered if she knew what question he had been about to ask. "You promise?"

"I promise you."

She leaned in and kissed him before her hands gripped onto his neck like she was trying to silently persuade him not to go. If he had any sense, he would send Magin and stay here with her, but he wanted to end the lives of the scum that had already stolen too many moments from him.

And he would. Many of them. All of them.

"Stay in this room," Torin asked her in a soft command. "Please. The wards are up around the palace, so it's safe here. Do not step outside these walls. Promise me."

"I will, that's my promise to you." Her throat bobbed.

She would be waiting for him when he came back. And then he would ask her to be his in a way that promised forever.

CHAPTER
FORTY-NINE
EMARA

Pacing up and down the room was doing absolutely nothing for her sanity. The deep breathing and relaxation techniques weren't helping either. The pulse in her neck drove the sounds of her racing heartbeat into her head, causing dizziness.

She was internally screaming.

Oh Gods. The churning in her stomach increased.

Heading to the window, she tried looking out, but the night was still a murky black blanket. The moon seemed like it was trying to fight her way through to aid the hunt.

It had to be approaching midnight or just past the hour, and Torin had been gone an age already.

Or so it seemed.

She remembered what it had been like when she had been awaiting Gideon's return from the Blood Moon battle, how she had felt in those moments. So much had changed since then. She could fight, for a start, and wield magic. She was an empress of a coven, and she had just given herself to Torin Blacksteel. Her heart had chosen him, and he had chosen her.

It wasn't that she didn't worry about Gideon anymore, she absolutely did, because he would be out there if he wasn't guarding Sybil.

She needed them to all be okay, Kellen included.

Maybe this was what he had envisioned, an army of demons at the palace. And maybe they weren't solely for her, but to destroy them all. However, Torin didn't know any of that, and a pang of guilt slashed across her heart. She had kept Kellen's vision from him. And she would continue to keep his secret, even if that meant she was at risk.

I won't be long, I promise. And then we will pick right back up where we left off, okay?

Tonight had been beautiful and remarkable. She and Torin had pushed away their impending problems, and finally broken the walls down to let each other in. She had seen his want and need for her in his eyes; it was more than lust; it was deeper than that.

Before he had been interrupted, Torin had kneeled beside the bed, like he was going to say something to her—something with meaning, judging by the look on his face and the flush of his cheeks. A feeling in her gut told her it would be monumental when he returned.

Anticipation for his hasty return swelled inside her as she looked up to the moon fighting through the clouds.

The door opened to her room abruptly and Magin stumbled through the threshold. If she hadn't been so startled by his entrance, she might have thought it odd that he had just walked in. She knew that wasn't protocol. He knocked every time.

"Magin?" she asked, concern in her voice.

His face paled like white flour and he choked. Blood spewed from his mouth until it was running down his neck, staining his grey tunic.

"Magin!" Emara screamed, her feet taking off quickly to reach him.

She skidded to a halt as two guards stepped through the door. Two guards that were not Torin Blacksteel or Artem Stryker.

"Run," Magin's blood-filled throat croaked out, like her grandmothers once had. A horrible flashback consumed her. "Fight."

Run? Run? Why was she to run? She was safe here.

A bitter taste crept back into her mouth, coating her tongue, and she tried to swallow it down.

Something was so horrifically wrong.

One of the guards withdrew a dagger from Magin's back and he fell to his knees.

"No!" she screamed. She could have screamed a few times after that, but she couldn't hear anything for the dizzying rush of terror that had engulfed her mind.

Magin, paralysed and unable to defend her, pleaded, "Forgive me." A single tear ran down his cheek before his body slammed into the ground, blood gushing from his back that she hadn't seen before now.

He had been stabbed multiple times, Emara realised.

Pure, staggering fear froze her.

The guards had done this. The guards who had just walked through her door.

Hunters. His brethren.

Confusion and betrayal burned in the back of her throat, causing an uproar of heat to pass over her. Her magic was tingling. They were not just any guards, she realised; they were the Supreme's guards. The ones who had baited Torin in the alcoves of the passageway, and the ones who had escorted her to the watchtower—Easton and Silas.

Why would the Supreme guards have done something so horrific to Magin?

A sweeping chill ran through her.

They were not here for Magin. He had been the only one standing between the door and her. They were here for her.

This was it.

This was Kellen's vision. It had to be.

You were taken.

She stumbled to the side, her heart unable to beat any quicker without bursting in her chest. Every part of her magic ran cold and tense in her body. She tried to gather it, to channel it into something of use, but she was still training. It took time to build it into something controllable.

"It's okay, little empress," Silas said with a smile so acidic that it burned her. "We are not going to hurt you."

"If that's the case," she spat, "then why did you have to stab my guard?" She looked to where Magin lay on the floor, still gurgling on his own blood.

A slow death.

A man who had dedicated his life to protecting the Air Coven had been betrayed by his own kind. If she could just reach him, maybe she could heal him, take his pain.

But the Supreme's guards were not going to allow that.

"Are you not going to answer my question about stabbing my guard in the back?" Emara tried to have the same cruel calmness that Torin did. She tried to scan the room for an escape. She had to keep them busy to buy herself time.

"The Supreme would like some time with you," Easton said, his eyes dark, just like his skin.

The Supreme? The Supreme was behind this?

Emara's heart sank to her stomach.

"Alone." Silas let a vile snigger fall from his mouth, his white-blond hair falling around his shoulders. "No guards allowed."

"You bastards." She ground her teeth, dragging her eyes between the two of them, wishing it was a hunting knife. "You can tell *your* Supreme to come and get me herself."

"The Supreme doesn't take commands from anyone," Easton said with a deadpan expression, a vacancy in his eyes. "That's why we are here."

The vile one sneered at her.

He would be the first one she attacked when she had the opportunity.

She pushed out her palm as the magic burned in her veins, showing them a glow of fire. "You have no idea what I can do."

"You won't get the chance to show us." Silas fired out a thin, silvery chain so fast that Emara couldn't even blink at it. The chain flew towards her, past her burning palm, and wrapped itself around her neck. Emara's hands flew to where it strangled her, but she was too late. The enchanted metal locked itself around her skin. The further she dug her nails in, the more the collar squeezed against her windpipe, denying her breath.

Something dissolved inside her, and it took her a moment to realise that the thrumming of magic that she normally felt in her blood and under her skin had vanished.

"What have you done?" Emara gagged, wheezing for air.

"The Supreme warned us that you could be a little dangerous," Silas said. "So she gave us this pretty little collar for you as a precaution." His eyes crawled all over her, and his tongue slashed out over his lips. Thank the Gods she had gotten back into her night slip, so that she wasn't naked, but oh, how she wished she was in her training gear. "You do look good on a lead." He cackled dreadfully. "You would make a cute pet for our witch queen."

A frightful anger burned and crashed within her, but it wasn't her magic this time. Not air, not fire, just stark, violent anger.

Magic wasn't going to save her tonight. It couldn't.

A moment like this was why she had made the decision to learn how to fight with her fists and weapons. Tonight, she would have to fight with everything else that she had.

Ignoring the squeezing ache across her neck, she dove, flinging her body across the bed. The guards looked stunned.

Had she not felt such gut-wrenching fear, she may have laughed at them.

Hitting the mattress, she rammed her hand under her pillow, the chain now yanking against her skin, stopping the air from entering her lungs. She had already retrieved what she was after as one of the guards pulled her back like a dog on a leash. She let out a strangled scream as the pain of the metal clamped into her windpipe, cutting her flesh.

She managed to stay on her feet. Holding her weapon out, Emara gripped the middle section, igniting the ruby activation on the spear. The double-edged spear elongated, and she heard a curse come from one of the guards.

They hadn't been expecting that either.

To them, she was just a witch, a helpless woman whose magic was now void.

But Emara had a different kind of magic in her veins, and it burned a fire in her belly to fight, to wield a weapon.

She ducked under the chain to face the guards. Easton was already drawing his sword, but she had time to make another move. Emara swung the spear, knocking the hard metal against Silas' head.

She had promised him the first strike, and she had delivered it.

The chain loosened in his grip, and she pivoted before she stabbed to the right, where Easton stood. But

Easton was faster, and he spun on his back leg, his sword now fully drawn.

She was going to give this fight everything she had.

Recovering from the blow to his head, Silas came at her from the side, but she turned again, swinging her magnificent spear. *The Agnes.* She hadn't thought she would have to use the weapon properly so soon, but she wasn't about to become their pet—or worse.

Her spear cracked against his head again, drawing blood down the silver of his hair, but this time, the guard swung up his arm as she tried to stab him. He caught hold of the pole, yanking it towards him, and she followed. Instead of falling into him, she swung a fist, smashing it against the opposite side of his face. It was what she needed; she was able to step back and create space between them.

Just enough, like Torin had always taught her.

Create enough space to work in, to fight in, to defend in.

"Where did you learn to punch like that, you little bitch?" Silas hissed, wiping his bloody mouth.

"I have an excellent instructor." She gripped the spear firmly in her hands as she thought of how Torin would have smiled if she had actually admitted that in front of him. With a grin, she looked from one guard to the other and said, "And when he finds out what you have tried to do here tonight"—she spun the metal pole from one hand to the next, displaying her skill as she bent her knees—"he will kill both of you."

"That's assuming we don't kill him first." The guard on her left—Easton—pounced, and she moved quickly out of the way. It was easier to duck when she was so much smaller than them. Spinning quickly, he was back on her, but she delivered a strong knee to his manhood. Bending over, she then delivered a forceful bash on his nose with the middle of her pole. Emara heard a bone crunch and then a splatter of blood hit the ground. Easton fell and let out a groan, one hand on his nose and the other cradling his bruised balls.

The chain around her neck whipped back and she flew in the opposite direction of the guard on the floor, the collar choking her. She stumbled back and slammed into a hard torso.

Silas.

Large hands swung up around her throat and she tried to kick back, to gain release, but the guard's legs were widely spread behind her. She tried to throw an elbow backwards, but he had her in a position of submission. Yanking forward, seeing it was her only choice, her neck strained, and he followed her.

She tugged again, the metal piercing into her skin, and she could feel a warm wetness starting to drip down her neck. Struggling, she bucked like an animal trying to flee a trap, and they both crashed into the vanity. His body weight was so crushing on top of her that she couldn't even think straight. Her face flattened against the marble as he pushed his weight on top of her, her cheek shattering as it crushed against the cold surface. She opened her mouth to scream, but she made no noise.

She had just made the wrong move. There was no way she would be able to get his brute mass of muscle off her now, not without her magic.

"This was an interesting little wrestle. Who knew a witch could fight with a spear?" He gripped her hair, yanking her neck back. Emara clenched her teeth to stop the scream from building in her throat; she wouldn't give them that satisfaction. "I just wish Blacksteel was here to see his empress forced into submission."

She still didn't let out a cry of fear. "I hope he takes his time killing you."

Silas fisted her hair tighter.

The pain was sickening. Silas smiled into the mirror as he watched himself tug on her hair.

She closed her eyes to cope.

"Finish it," Easton growled from across the room, trying to force his nose back into place. "We don't have time to play around with her."

Silas gripped her hair, yanked her head back, and then slammed her head into the mirror.

CHAPTER FIFTY
TORIN

"Nothing," Artem spat, his arms folded. "Not a single demon." He huffed. "No wings, no red eyes, no claws, no rotten flesh. Not even a trace of sulphur." He let out an even bigger breath. "You have no idea what I left behind for this."

Torin shook his head and ran his tongue over his lips.

It had been two hours since he had left to hunt, and they had seen nothing. It was like they had just vanished.

How could a small army of demons just vanish from a mountain?

There were no footsteps in the fresh ice, no animals slaughtered in the woods below.

Not a trace.

Torin heard a crunch of gravel, and both hunters went to their weapon belts. His youngest brother came around the side of the rock which blocked his view of the pathway.

"Nothing?" Kellen's brow creased as he placed his sword back in its sheath. His face was pale, very pale.

"Nope." Artem looked around himself like he couldn't fathom where this small army of demons had gone.

"The wolves can't even pick up a scent," Kellen said. "They are at the base of the mountain now. Murk is baffled, utterly baffled."

Just at that, Gideon and Marcus appeared, faces grave and mystified like Kellen's.

"Not a single trace?" Gideon questioned all who stood there.

Torin shook his head. "There doesn't seem to be."

Torin cast his eyes further down the mountain as he watched his brethren spread out, taking watch points to keep a lookout on the valley below.

"It's strange," Artem admitted, "they normally leave something."

"The packs that are patrolling are going to keep going further into the forest below to see if there is something they can find for us to work with, a dead body or wildlife or something. Maybe we should send Kellen back to the palace with word of our findings to the other guards."

Torin considered it. "It's impossible for them to have been here and not to have left a scent for the wolves to trace," he theorised.

And it was.

The pack could sniff out a scent even if it had passed through these parts days ago.

Something wasn't right.

"The wards wouldn't take away their scent, would they?" Kellen asked.

Torin turned after scanning the trees below. They looked like small weeds in the ground. "Not normally. And even if they portalled out of the north, they would leave their smell behind," he answered his younger brother as a gust of icy wind stabbed at him. He looked at Artem. "Who told you there was a small army of demons? Who did the order come from to go out and hunt them?"

"Well, Magin found me...eh...in my room." He ran a hand over his short hair that almost looked brown under the light. "And then we immediately came for you."

Gideon added, as his breath swirled like smoke into the night, "We were still in the ballroom when it was announced, and I instantly took Sybil back to her protected chamber."

"Announced by whom?" Torin could feel the niggling sensation increase in his heart as the heat of suspicion fought out the cold.

"The Supreme guards," Marcus answered.

Torin placed his hands on his hips and looked out into the darkness. The moon had finally pushed her way through the snow clouds and was shining like an oil lamp in the sky, sending beams of moonlight onto the faces of his brothers.

"And where did she tell the elite to go?" Torin asked.

"Back to their rooms, and she would call them once we had given her the all clear," Marcus responded.

Something wasn't right, and Torin knew it. "And the fae?"

"There were only a few fae court officiants present. She asked them to guard her vault in case the demons entered the palace. She also scattered some of them outside the doors of the elite." Artem confirmed.

Torin inhaled.

It was strange, the Supreme's presence hadn't really been seen at the ball. She had made no glamorous, extravagant entry at the beginning of the night. She normally loved to indulge in such extravaganzas and being the focal point of the attention and admiration of all. She loved being the centre of the magic energy, showing off tricks and spells to anyone who would watch. But all of a sudden, after a scarce presence, she could be there to make an important announcement to control every other faction?

Come to think of it, she has been extremely quiet for days, not even attending dinners, and she had never made an appearance at the Uplift either.

Maybe she was preserving her energy—

"Fuck," the word hissed out like hot smoke, his mind charged with a new revelation.

His chest began to rise and fall like he had been in a battle for hours.

"What is it, brother?" Gideon asked.

"Fuck!" Torin roared again out into the kingdom below. Birds stirred from their slumber in the trees as his profanity reached them. All the men flinched. Marcus unsheathed his small sword.

Torin turned frantically to face his small cluster. "I

can't believe I didn't see it. I can't believe I didn't put it together! It was sitting under my fucking feet this entire time. I was always considering a different faction, when—"

He began running, hurling his body up the mountain at a pace that would match a fierce mountain lion.

He could hear his clan on the back of his heels, but it was Artem who spoke first. "Blacksteel," he yelled. "What the fuck? You need to tell us what is going on, you're not making any sense. You can't curse a few times and expect us to follow your train of thought."

He halted, his feet slipping on the rocky terrain. He grabbed a rock above him to steady himself. Torin had always thought the monsters that lay on the outside of the palace, waiting for its wards to break, would be Emara's threat. In reality, it was the monster who owned the fucking palace instead.

He caught his balance and centred himself, looking down at his brethren. "It's the Supreme."

"What?" Gideon's face pulled into a contorted version of itself.

"It's the Supreme," he repeated. "The one who has been behind the killings." Torin felt the anger build in his blood. "She's the one who was behind the Uplift attacks."

"How can that be?" Marcus asked through ragged breaths, his face paling. "They were her people, her girls—"

"Because she orchestrated the whole thing." Torin turned again after hoisting himself up a large rock and scaling another. "I am sure of it." He gripped another rock, pulling himself up. "She might be working for the Dark God. She is the one behind the attacks. Taymir spoke of immorality, and who better to want immorality than a wilting Supreme?"

The clan followed behind him, spitting curses.

A gasp left Kellen's mouth. "She was the one who brought down the wards at the Uplift. They didn't die with the empresses, they were already down for the Dark Army to walk right in."

"Exactly," Torin confirmed with venom. "She was the only one who could really have that sort of power. She knows her time is up. And one of those empresses that we have left helpless in the palace with her will be the one to take her crown. She isn't going to have that."

"Shit!" cursed Artem. He was finally climbing at the rate that Torin was, always matching him.

"She has been the puppet master behind it all." Torin fumed. "And it was right under me this entire time."

"It's funny how you never look at the ones at the top," Marcus hissed, making his way across the jagged terrain.

"There are no fucking demons here, this is a diversion. Deleine needed the guards out of her palace, and everyone else was sent to their rooms." Torin wanted to punch something. "She's had us all on strings."

"But why?" Gideon's rugged voice broke from a few feet behind him as he climbed too. "What is she planning?"

"I have a feeling it has something to do with how Deleine feels her power depleting. I was told many moons ago by a trusted Spirit Witch that there were rumours of her powers fading," Torin suggested, looking over his shoulder. "Surely, you all have heard the rumours too. She will be able to sense it in her blood, in her magic."

"That's why the kills were made at the Uplift," Artem called out as his boots made a racket on the sturdy rocks. "She's hunting her successor. She made it look like that elite prick and some demons had formed an alliance, when really it was all for her," he spat. "All the important witches were in the same spot at the same time."

Gideon raged this time. "She was trying to take out whoever her replacement could have been to buy herself more time."

"Exactly," Torin agreed. "The problem is, after killing all of the other witches, she clearly feels no different. She probably thought that the witches that she killed would have been strong enough to take her crown, but it was never going to be one of them. The Gods must have gifted the supremacy of witchcraft onto a current empress, one that we all guard now."

Gideon panted. "Shit! Shit! Shit! Every empress of their House is in the palace with one guard each. Alone."

"The Supreme couldn't have acted alone," Kellen cut in, managing to keep up. "She must have people helping her. People who are willing to betray others. She is only one woman, she can't do it alone."

"That is why we need to get back to them." Torin

growled in anger and frustration with himself. He had left. He had left Emara in a place where she wasn't safe.

How had he not worked this out before? Why had he been so focused on the elite?

The evidence was there.

The Supreme was vain and conceited. Her vanity had always been known. So why would she let someone take her power? Why would she let someone best her?

She wasn't going to.

Torin punched the air and roared as he moved.

"Halt!" Marcus hollered, stopping everyone in their tracks. "Someone must inform the others."

Torin turned and nodded. "Inform the hunters and find Murk Baxgroll, then make your way to the palace as fast as you can."

This could end in so many ways, ones that he dreaded to think of.

Marcus nodded and was gone in a flash, making his way back down to the other clusters of guards scattered across the mountain. Torin whirled and continued his run to the palace, where he would raise the underworld himself if anything had happened to Emara Clearwater.

CHAPTER FIFTY-ONE
TORIN

Running through the corridor to her room, Torin almost hit the wall as he turned the corner, the speed too fast for him to control, his boots wet. He had ordered for Gideon and the others to check on their empresses, and he would head for the Empress of Air with Artem.

His empress.

His mind and heart racing, he powered on. It had been a while since he had run at his full potential, and it pumped pure adrenaline into his body. He noted that Artem probably hadn't run like this since the selection either, where they had both pushed their bodies to their utmost limit, testing boundaries that normal humans would never be able to achieve. He tightened his muscles so that his body would slow, every muscular tissue coiling and shuddering as he did.

Artem almost hit him as they stopped.

He had never felt panic like he did when he noticed Magin did not stand outside her door. His jaw hardened, and he could feel a muscle pulse in his neck. The door was open, ajar an inch or two, and before he moved his boots, he looked down to the ground. Different patterns of blood trickled along the floor, moving in dissimilar ways. His heart leapt into his mouth. His skin pricked, all hairs standing up.

"Check the other rooms, Stryker, all along this corridor."

Artem took his command immediately and moved.

His heart sank to his churning stomach. He prayed for the sake of everyone in the kingdom that the blood on the floor was not hers.

He knew he had to send Artem away, because if this was Emara's blood, he wasn't sure how much he would lose control.

For the first time in Torin's life, he felt genuine fear. Instantly, rage overtook fear as he propped the door open a little. Before stepping in, he could see a body lying on the floor, face down, in full guard regalia. Torin hissed a curse as he took in the amount of blood pooled on the floor. It was too much blood for the guard to be alive.

It was Magin.

But he had no time to feel any emotion. That is not how he had been trained.

He titled his head, even though he couldn't see the sky, and said, "May all the stars in the Gods' sky guide you back home, brother."

He pulled the two swords that were strapped to his back out of their cases. The sound of the metal being unleashed was so satisfyingly beautiful, his heart almost slowed. He couldn't wait to use them, driving his steel through whoever had done this. He would find them, and when he did, the Gods would have no mercy for them.

Stepping slowly through the threshold, he called her name lowly. "Emara?"

No response.

The silence that lingered in the room gave a maddening edge to his violent thoughts.

"Emara," he called again despite knowing that she wouldn't be there.

The sliver of hope that he had withered and died, and a coldness spread across his chest in its place. He looked over Magin's body quickly, not taking his eyes off his surroundings for too long in case there was anything in this room that he could blame for his death.

Magin had been stabbed in the back.

Fucking bastards.

Whoever had done this knew exactly how to incapacitate and kill a man.

But lucky enough for Torin, he did too. And he would, demon or not.

He scanned the room, looking for anything at all that would give him an indication of what had happened, where they had taken her.

He looked to the archway. Nothing.

He glanced over the floor, noting a mixture of bloods, not just Magin's.

Torin pulled in a breath through his teeth.

If the intruder had touched one hair on her head, so help him Thorin, he would murder whoever had taken her, whoever had helped them, whoever even knew about this.

Focus, he shouted inwardly.

Torin followed the droplets of blood over to where things that normally sat on her dresser were lying on the floor. There had most definitely been a struggle. As he took in the details of the fight, his heart split right down the middle as he saw her spear.

She had fought whoever was in here. Pride swelled in his heart before an overwhelming dread took over.

The fact that she'd had to fight for her life stirred the most vicious part of him to the surface.

His eyes worked up the vanity table, where broken items lay messy amongst the blood. Torin moved in a flash, taking in the details of the struggle that seemed to have smashed the mirror.

Whatever had smashed it, had been done at a great force, like a fist or maybe a boot.

His eyes squinted and his heart burst into shards of fury as he took in what he saw. Moving one sword over into the other hand, he leaned forward.

A dark strand of her beautiful midnight hair was caught in the fractured mirror.

Disgust, rage, and revulsion surged through him, causing vomit to rise from his stomach.

It had been her head that was used to smash the mirror.

Her fucking head!

An enraged and feral roar broke from his chest. His breath caught in his throat, and he had to fight with his mind to stay in control. He had to stay in control of his terrible temper in order to find Emara, save her. His mind whirled and rumbled as he tried to still the inner chaos, the wrath that threatened so much more than just violence. But it was too late.

The savage beast that lay under his skin erupted and let loose.

CHAPTER
FIFTY-TWO
EMARA

A strange, relentless rattling could be heard through a buzzing sound. A sharp ache crossed her skull, causing her to flinch. Something warm trickled down her eyes and nose. Emara tried to lift her hand up to inspect it, but she couldn't move.

A horrible, bitter taste like ash coated around her tongue, and even when she tried to swallow, it didn't disappear. Her head rolled to the side and her cheek was met with cool limestone. She forced her eyes open.

The world swayed and rocked, flashed and sparkled.

Trying again, she pulled her hand up to her face. She winced as she touched a sensitive spot on her head. Pulling her hand back, she watched through blurry vision as the crimson blood dripped down her fingers. A throbbing in her skull made Emara's eyes close momentarily and then reopen. Her head was bleeding.

Oh Gods.

Where was she?

Shaking, she rolled onto her stomach and tried to

look around her, the metallic taste of blood filling her mouth. She could see a circle of black salt around her, and as she tried to follow it with her eyes, her brain punched into her skull. Taking a breath that burned all the way down to her lungs, she looked up at the gleaming candelabras that stood tall from the floor, dripping with black wax. A dark fire burned in them, waving like thick smoke. Looking past the warrior-tall candelabras, Emara noticed that she was in a room that had familiar ceiling-to-floor windows. It was still dark outside, indicating that she hadn't been knocked out for long, and she could still see the rocky backdrop of the mountainside, the moonlight licking the dusty white peaks.

She was still in the Amethyst Palace.

She was in the watchtower.

Her gaze caught an altar dressed in dark taffeta, and Emara shifted slowly on the floor to take a better look. Her hands flew up to her throat where she still wore that disgusting chain, forced around her neck to suppress the magic in her blood.

A flood of fear and rage shivered over her skin as she fully remembered what had happened.

She had been taken, just like Kellen's vision. And if anything else of what he said was about to transpire, there was no hope for her.

"It's about time you were awake," an unsettling voice startled Emara. "It would have been unfair to begin with you unconscious."

She turned to see the Supreme standing in a dark grey robe that looked like it was covered in a glittering black web of spider silk, and a gown underneath to match. A crown of the deepest rubies, darkest opals, and black pearls rested on top of her brown hair that was pinned in one simple twist at the back of her head. Her eyes were dark, darker than the obsidian salt, and they were piercing right through Emara's face. Guards in grey tunics stood all around the room, static and stone-like. Some were placed by the door and some were posted close to the walls. Their gazes were not on Emara, but ahead, focused.

Emara gritted her teeth as she gathered enough strength to pull herself up from the ground.

Not all of these men were the Supreme's guards, that much she knew, but why were they here? There must be around fifteen in the room. Why were they not protecting the people of the palace? As she glanced around, Emara noted a House Water guard, then one who protected House Fire. Spirit's guard was there too. Had they all betrayed their empresses? Where were the other witches?

"Aren't you going to ask why you are here?" Her voice cut through the silence of the room, bringing Emara's attention back to her cruel face. Where a look of intimidating power had rested before, nothing but pure hatred seethed from her glare now.

Anger of her own sparked in her blood. "Maybe you should tell me, since you so keenly requested me to be here." Her voice was rough, and it hurt to speak.

Emara wiped a little blood that had run into her eye and her legs wobbled. She dug in deep to find the strength to straighten her spine.

What in the underworld is going on?

The Supreme moved, gliding over to the altar, taking her time; her cape dragged dramatically over the cold floor.

Emara got the feeling Deleine didn't care how big her audience was, she would play to the crowd regardless. How quaint. She picked up a ceremonial knife and looked Emara's way as an ominous glint shone in her eye.

"You see," she said, coming over to the circle that Emara now realised she was the centre of.

Runes in an ancient tongue were plastered in red all around the outside of the circle. Emara tried her best to tell herself it wasn't blood. This wasn't the same kind of circle that she had stepped into when she had ascended. It felt darker, more like a cage.

"I have not been myself recently." The Supreme played with the tip of the knife, running her long, bone-like finger along it. "And I have a feeling that that is because you exist." She pointed the knife directly at Emara's heart. Even though it was from a distance, the fear of it entering her flesh made her throat swell.

Heart thundering, Emara asked through her teeth, "And why would you feel like that is the case?"

"Because, my uneducated witchling, that is the cruel reality of the natural witch cycle."

The Maiden, the Mother, the Crone.

The Witch, the Empress, the Supreme.

"When one great witch rises, one must fade and fall." Deleine sneered, her face looking more like something that belonged in a pack of wolves than a coven.

"You can't for one second think that I am causing your weakness," Emara spat, an acidic rage burning at the back of her throat. "I am so new to this world." She shook her head. "I am barely trained. My magic is untutored, and I am not strong enough." She looked to her leader, intensity blazing in her eyes. "You are mistaken."

Emara understood the cycle of the Supreme, and it was clear that Deleine did not accept her fate. There were four other witches that were probably stronger than Emara. But they didn't seem to be here. Rya was not here, even after she'd declared that she bore every element.

"It has everything to do with you, you stupid girl." The Supreme's eyes darkened as simmering loathing seeped through.

"It can't be." Emara's voice cracked a little. "I have just ascended."

"It has nothing to do with your ascension," the Supreme spat. "Although that might cause the cycle to quicken. Some witches reign for longer than they should. Some have short reigns. And some," she said, venom spewing through her teeth, "abdicate, unfit for their purpose."

She ignored the slander of her grandmother.

Emara swallowed, unsure if she even wanted the next question that was about to fall from her mouth to be answered. "If you truly believe my presence on this earth is your downfall, then why haven't you just killed me? Wouldn't that have been easier than going through the hassle of abducting me? You had your chance tonight to strike me down. I was unguarded, unpro-tected. Why haven't you taken it yet?"

The Supreme grinned like she had no heart or soul left in her body, only a bitter darkness that consumed her features, turning what was once a beautiful face ugly.

Emara's body shuddered at the very sight of it.

"Because where is the fun in that?"

If the Supreme had wanted Emara dead, she could have ordered her guards to kill her in her room.

A single quiver ran up Emara's spine.

But she had kept her alive for a purpose.

"So your plan was to bring me here?" She looked around, still not understanding why the guards were betraying their oath. "And then what? *Ritual* me to death?" Emara let out a sharp, mad laugh as she gestured to the circle. She wasn't sure if it was the concussion she surely had or the blood loss from her wounds, but she decided she wasn't going to back down, and maybe that made her crazy.

She wasn't going to back down now, not when she had come so far within herself.

"As a matter of fact, I do plan on a ritual, yes." Deleine's smile relaxed, showing where her face had aged slightly. "But the plan was never for you to die." Her cold eyes dragged down Emara's face as she twisted the knife in the air like she was writing a letter. "Not when you are so valuable, the perfect bargaining chip."

Taymir had said something similar. Emara's blood ran cold.

"Why is it everyone just talks in bloody riddles

around here?" Emara barked. "Are you going to enlighten me as to why you have your guards bashing me unconscious? There really was no need for the dramatics. I could have walked here."

Deleine's eyebrow shot up. "I thought you would have worked it out by now, no? You were investigating your bloodline before the Uplift. Did my darling Taymir not give you any other clues?"

Taymir had been working with her.

Emara tried not to panic or lose control. Torin had always taught her to keep focus, keep someone talking in a situation like this. He'd taught her to buy herself more time, but she was terrified of where this was about to go.

The Supreme laughed, her cackle travelling through the room, her eyes narrowing. "You really have no idea who you are, do you?"

Deleine's lips pressed together, amused, and a shiver ran down Emara's neck.

"Yes, I know who I am." Her voice shook. "It took me a while," Emara admitted. "But I do. I am the grand-daughter of Theodora Clearwater, and I come from a great line of witches. Ones who looked better wearing the crown of Supremacy than you."

"Oh, so naive." The Supreme's brows raised, creasing her forehead, and then she lowered them quickly. "You take one *lover,* and you think you have found yourself." She clicked her tongue, and a dreadful sound of laughter spilled out. "You think you know who you are inside."

Heat burned in Emara's cheeks at the Supreme's

knowledge of her relationship and the mockery of her tone when she spoke of it.

"You don't know anything about me," she jeered back.

"*You* are the one who doesn't seem to know a thing about who you are." The coldness of her voice sent shivers down Emara's spine. The room vibrated with the echo of her words, and a thunderous clap sounded, like the mountains were shifting. "I thought you might have been smart enough to put two and two together by now." She started walking around the circle, and Emara followed her every step. "But maybe I am giving you more credit than you are worth. Your mother never was smart enough to make decent choices, either."

"What do you know of my mother?" Emara's voice was low.

The Grand High Witch continued to circle her prey, walking slowly. She said, "Everyone knew your mother in the witching world. She was a very talented and beautiful witch, and was well-liked in the House of Air. But, you see, witches tend to be competitive and jealous little creatures. Others were utterly envious of her abilities and rather furious when they noticed that she had no interest or intentions in ascending even though she bore the Clearwater bloodline."

"I know exactly who my mother was and what coven she belonged to." Emara's brow sunk low, her hands trembling. She prayed to the Gods that the Supreme wouldn't notice. "You don't need to run over history."

"You are always so quick to jump ahead, aren't you?" Deleine stopped and squared her shoulders.

"I am only giving you a warning that if you don't speed up your little story," Emara said, toying with a smile full of blood, "my guards will notice that I am missing when they return from the hunt." A stabbing pain jabbed into her heart, and she could feel the rage and guilt rise within her again. Poor Magin. He'd died protecting her. She, too, squared her shoulders, and said, "And that won't be good for you. So get to the point."

"Such foolish youth causes so much impatience." Deleine disregarded her. "Besides, your precious hunters will spend hours scouring those woods."

A horrible smile broke from her mouth. A few of the other guards smiled too, and a few sniggered.

That's when she saw Silas, his white hair now stained with blood, his beady eyes watching her.

She threw him a dangerous grin.

He snarled back.

"Anyway, let's get back to my charming little story, shall we?"

"There is nothing charming about you." Emara tore her gaze away from Silas.

The Supreme's hand flew out, and a surge of air hit the back of Emara's throat. Emara stumbled back, unable to take a breath, her lungs collapsing inside her chest. Eyes wide, she clutched at her collar of steel, scratching and clawing at it like that would help her breathe.

But it didn't.

The Supreme's hand dropped. "That, you insolent little brat, is a very small reminder of what power I have." Her eyes darkened as Emara gasped in any air she could. "I can collapse your lungs in seconds, I can boil the blood inside of your body until it is begging to be released; I can choke you, drown you, and I won't hesitate to use my magic on you. The deal was to keep you alive, but I can think of many ways to make you suffer."

Emara's lip curled, her fury sizzling in her veins. "What deal?"

Again, Taymir had said the same thing. Emara had thought he was the only one stupid enough to make deals with the underworld. Had it been Deleine this whole time?

A long second passed between them before the Supreme ignored her question, lifted her head, and continued. "Where was I? Oh, that's right. Your mother." She smiled horrendously.

Emara wanted to break out of the circle, run over, and smack Deleine on her mouth.

The horrifying part of it all was that there was absolutely no way of getting out of this circle. It was enchanted, and unless someone broke it from the outside, she was stuck. And she sure as Rhiannon wasn't going to look foolish in front of the Supreme for making an effort to try.

A bony finger went into the air. "One thing I do know is that your mother and grandmother had a turbulent relationship."

Emara felt her teeth bare. "How could you possibly know that?"

"Because I knew your mother well, actually" she

answered sharply. "We helped each other learn magic before our ascension. Her air, and I, fire. Your mother even confided in me a number of things, and it seemed that your grandmother didn't appreciate your mother's *morals.*"

Emara slammed her lips together and let her rage burn as she tried not to fall into the Supreme's trap. The Supreme knew information that Emara had always wanted about her mother, especially when it was too difficult for Theodora to talk about it. She knew little about her, and Deleine must know that. The Supreme had found Emara's weakness.

"Your mother had a few secrets of her own, quite like you."

"I don't have any secrets any ordinary woman wouldn't have," Emara shot back.

The fire of the candelabra flared, the black flames growing twice their size. Emara could feel the magic thicken in the room, and for once, she knew it wasn't hers.

Her stomach flipped in trepidation.

"That is where you are lying to yourself." Her cold eyes widened. "Your mother hid too many secrets, one of them being that she didn't truly belong to the House of Air." The Supreme looked over Emara, and she tensed. "But you knew that already, didn't you?"

Emara clamped down on her lips even further, so much so that it became uncomfortable.

"You knew that you had *fire* in your veins like your mother, didn't you?" The venom of threat darkened Deleine's eyes until they were almost entirely black.

"You lied in front of us all. I could see it on your face, especially when your hunter came to defend you."

Tears stung in Emara's eyes, but she choked them back. She opened her mouth to speak, but nothing formed.

"I wonder what the Empress of Fire would have to say about that. Or the whole of House Air, if they knew that a dominant fire-bearer was an empress to their coven. Would Rya Otterburn let you live?"

"I am not dominant in fire," Emara denied, her voice low. She hoped her lie sounded like truth on her lips. To be honest, she wasn't sure if it *was* a lie; she wasn't confident which one she was more dominant in.

Air or fire?

It seemed she was able to heal and connect with souls from the Otherside, too, but that didn't mean she was dominant in earth or spirit magic.

"At least your mother had the decency to bow out and not ascend like an imposturous little bitch." The Supreme's true fury shone for a second before she collected herself. "I wonder what everyone would say if I informed them about you and your duplicitous mother. Would they still want you to wear their crown? Would they exile you? Would you be stoned to death for the treason you have committed against the witches?"

"Stop talking." Emara's nails dug into her palms, her head buzzing.

"Oh, certainly not; I am not done." The Supreme's hand flew out again, and it was like a punch to Emara's abdomen. "I am just getting started."

Winded by Deleine's magic, Emara wrenched

forward, clutching her belly. Just at that, the queen of the five covens turned her wrist, and Emara's legs were swept out from under her. Her back and head hit the hard floor in one swift smack.

Sick crawled up her throat and dizziness almost stole her sight.

"I wonder what your little love match, your *betrothed,* would say if he found out who you really are. A lying *fire* witch who took any opportunity to get her claws into the social ladder of the covens."

The words of the Supreme circled the room in one vicious swirl, reverberating off the walls.

Emara tried to roll onto her side again, but she was whipped back, her spine slamming into the marble by an unseen power. The air around the circle was beginning to build into something fierce and threatening, and Emara's hands flew up unwillingly, taken by the power and pinned against the floor above her. A frustrated scream finally left her lips as she struggled against it. She tried to break her hands free, but the magic was too strong.

"When Torin finds you, he is going to kill you," Emara said to the high ceiling, hoping that the words drifted from her mouth shaped like a sword and stabbed Deleine in the heart.

"Maybe he will be on my side when I tell him who your father is." The Supreme's words cut through Emara's body like an arrow.

Her father.

"Maybe he will want to slit your throat himself when he finds out who, or should I say what, he has been lying in bed with." Pleasure ran through her words, and it sickened Emara.

"Shut your mouth." Emara grappled against the unseen power of the restraints. "My father was...my father was—"

"Your father is the reason you are still alive in *all* of this," the Supreme admitted as the phantom wind pulled around them, swirling the black smoke into a beast of death. "If he hadn't promised me my wishes, I would have snuffed you out at the Uplift."

Emara stilled against the cold floor. A sudden flush of burning rage engulfed her body. "You," she breathed. "It was *you*..."

The Supreme let out a snarling laugh that broke from the back of her throat. "It really is concerning how long it has taken you to work it out. Sometimes the answers are right in front of your face."

It was her the entire time. She had been behind all the deaths.

"Why?" Emara screamed, unable to understand. Cally had been amongst the dead that night, and it was Deleine's fault. "Why would you kill all of those other witches? You know what happens in the fate of the Supreme. Your crown and powers will eventually be passed to someone else. You are a fucking monster."

Tears crawled into her eyes.

"I didn't kill them with my own hands, dear; I just sent in my minions to do my dirty work. After all, you can never be too careful. I had to make sure I ended all the power that threatened to take mine. However, I do admit, it was my mistake to underestimate what you meant to the Blacksteels. It took me by surprise to learn that both of them had grown an attachment to you. Especially the second-in-command. But I won't be making that mistake again."

"Why?" Emara cried again, wishing she could break free from the invisible shackles and dive for her. She had been the one to order the deaths that night, order the killings.

Callyn.

Her Cally.

A sob broke from her throat, but it wasn't one of sorrow or grief, it was one of cold, hard fury.

The Supreme ignored her and continued. "Enough about dead witches. Your mother made a mistake in telling me her deepest, darkest secret. She told me a tale of your father that I didn't think was true until she sacrificed her name and coven to keep you alive and away from him. She had managed to keep you a secret for a while, until he found you. Your mother really picked the worst of the worst to open her legs for."

Emara could hear the horrible smile on the Supreme's face.

Tears streamed from her eyes as she tried to breathe, her gut churning so much that she might actually vomit. The Supreme had caught her hook, line, and sinker. No one had offered answers to her father, not even the library in Huntswood.

No one until now.

And even if she could feel the darkness set in around her heart, she knew she was about to explore her deepest fears.

"Why did she want me away from my father?" Emara asked, unable to help herself.

"Because he didn't belong to this world."

Oh Gods.

Emara's skin turned inside out as the Supreme spoke. "He is of the underworld."

And there it was. The darkest piece of her family puzzle.

Her father.

"Don't lie to me," Emara screeched, dragging a pain down her throat.

"Oh, darling, I am not lying to you," the Supreme goaded as the wind battered against Emara's face, the flames from the candles growing darker and taller. "Your father is Balan, the newest King of the Underworld."

CHAPTER
FIFTY-THREE
EMARA

Emara's cries stole away her breath as darkness gripped at her heart. Her restrained magic dying, scratching, and clawing to get out.

"No, no, no..." Tears blurred her vision.

Balan. The newest King of the Underworld. Where had she heard that before?

Maybe if her heart wasn't breaking, she could focus and reclaim the information of how she knew it.

Newest King of the Underworld.

"There is no truth in that." Emara pleaded with the Gods to give her a sign that it was not true.

Anything. *Please. Rhiannon, please.*

"And now that you are awake, we are about to create a portal to the underworld so that I can fulfil my end of the little trade deal we have with *our* king. I hand you over to him, in the nine realms of hell, and I receive immortality. It should have been simpler than it was, really, but that's what happens when you get a man to do a woman's job. Nevertheless, we got there in the end.

I really should be thanking you for killing Taymir and tying up my loose ends."

"No!" A heavy strain pulled in Emara's chest. "It's not true."

"It is very true." The Supreme started circling around as a rattling began. Emara looked over at her, fighting the force of the wind in her lungs and face, and saw that the Supreme had a cylinder full of crushed bones and stones. Only dark magic knew what that awful concoction it was. As the rattling commenced and the unnatural power in the room started to build, Deleine asked, "Are you ready to meet your father?"

Uncontrollable fear and confusion immobilised Emara.

She was going to be taken to the underworld. To Balan or to Veles. She couldn't comprehend it.

The magic suppressed in Emara's body was responding to the sounds of the rattle as the kingdom's most powerful witch meddled with the darkness, its vibrations stirring and writhing, but it was unable to break free from the chain around her neck.

"Demons of high birth walk through this kingdom every day, undetected, all in the efforts to be the eyes in this world for Veles, our Dark God. Your mother fell for the charms of the most infamous knight of the under-world there has ever been." Deleine's voice turned acidic again. "Forget about what the hunters think or what they have told you; demons are not always blood-thirsty creatures who want to devour everything they see. Some are extremely powerful and restrained, like a warrior of the darkness should be. Your father is one of them." She paused, taking a breath, and the thickness of the air magnified. "Balan seduced your mother. And like a lamb to the slaughter, she fell for it. She fell hard and fast. Poor Sereia, clearly so desperate for love that she would have taken anyone..." The Supreme shook her enchanted rattle.

Deleine was summoning something. Unchecked fear tightened Emara's spine.

"Sereia knew who Balan was, of course. He didn't hide that from her. Part of me wondered for some time if he actually cherished her. But that was never possible." The Supreme stopped dead. Not even the rattling could be heard. "He was the God of Darkness' favourite subject. Born in the dusk of the underworld, Balan was his most treasured creation. Veles favoured him over all. He could come and go between worlds as he pleased, and he did what Veles asked of him in the meantime, no matter what that was." Her voice took an ominous dip. "But your mother, being a foolish, idiotic romantic, believed that Balan had *good* in him. She believed there was good in all living things if you showed them enough love, if you tried hard enough to show them a different path, even things born in unthinkable darkness. But we both know that is not the case when it comes to a demon. Darkness is darkness."

A suffocated whimper left Emara's mouth as she tried to bite down a scream and swallow the vomit that crawled up her throat. The Grand Witch continued, shaking the rattle of bones and darkness again. "She pleaded with him, begged him to leave the underworld for her, for a future, for you. But he was a commander of the Dark Army; he would never choose her over his station. You see, she hadn't yet told him of her situation, of you, and once he learned of the babe that grew in her stomach, he wanted to take her to the underworld, but Sereia refused. Never in her wildest dreams would she have wanted that for her child, to grow up in such darkness and desolation that is the nine realms of hell. So she fled, not ascending as the Empress of Air, not even telling your grandmother. She came to me to aid her in her escape, but you see, I was loyal to my coven. I would not hide the mess she had made for herself, bringing that very darkness that grew in her stomach into this world. I had also seen how powerful your mother was in fire magic, and I was the Empress of Fire."

Emara stopped breathing altogether.

"I was happy for your mother to disappear, taking with her the chances of her coming for my crown, my legacy."

Emara let the tears flow down her face.

"When Balan learned of her betrayal, he pillaged towns, cities, and villages just to find her. And he did."

"Please stop," Emara begged, her sobs coming out in raspy, uneven breaths. "Please stop talking. I've heard enough."

The rattle stopped again, and the tension that had been creeping into the air of the room levelled out once more. "He found her three years after you were born, in fact, in a little cottage in the Fairlands. But your mother had known that he would come for her; she knew he wouldn't stop until he found her, and so she was prepared. Sereia was a clever little witch, and set him a trap. She used the time apart from him to find a powerful set of stones that she had read about in ancient grimoires. They had already bound Veles to the underworld, and so she mirrored the same spell that the ancient ancestors before her had used to ensnare him. Sereia only found two of the stones in her time of searching, but it was all she had, and it was enough. When he came through the door of that cottage in the Fairlands, Sereia began the ritual that would send Balan back to the underworld and keep him trapped there. She used every part of magic that she could pull from, forfeiting herself to trap him. And that, my dear empress, was the fate of your late mother. She died in the fires of her own enchantment," confirmed the Supreme, "unable to stop the dark magic she had tapped into to create it. It was too much for her. Unspoken magic that had existed long before the Gods gave us human life." She paused. "That's when your grandmother abdicated and was never seen by the magic world again, and I assume now it was to hide you. No one knew if you'd lived or died until you showed up a few moons ago with that untamed power of yours, just like your mother's."

Emara scrunched her eyes, hoping for darkness to find her, hoping she would feel nothing soon.

But her mouth betrayed her. "And what of my fath— Balan, what of him? Did the spell work?"

"He is still stuck in the underworld, like Veles. He cannot walk in these worlds until he finds the keys to his cage, which his armies have been on the hunt for."

"And he thinks I will know where they are?" Emara

couldn't help but allow the disgust in her voice to come through.

"The Dark King has no other reason not to believe that you would be the key to finding them. You are your mother's daughter, after all, sly and crafty. If he applies enough pressure, you will figure it out."

The key.

Emara let a snicker burn up her throat as the restraints of the magic still pinned her to the floor. "That's ridiculous. I didn't even know my grandmother was a witch, never mind being entrusted with powerful stones that she kept hidden from your king."

"Are you forgetting I know about how you held the key of resurrection in your very hands?" Deleine's teeth bared.

"It is no longer in my possession, and if you want to fight Viktir Blacksteel for it, then be my guest," Emara hissed.

The Supreme looked unfazed as she said, "The king will have it in due course." She began to rattle the bones again and a darkness formed, circling around her.

A smoky screen like a mirror began forming, and swirling blackness festered in the void.

A portal to the underworld.

Emara let out a curse as she tugged at the unseen magic that bound her body to the floor.

"You took it upon yourself to tell my mother's story." A coarse laugh barked from Emara. "No guilt parted your darkened heart as you divulged the details of her sorrows, did it?"

Deleine chuckled coldly. "That is something not

even I could wrap a lie around. I couldn't help but take just a little bit of pleasure in telling you who you really are, especially now that you have fallen in love with the very thing that hunts the blood that runs in your veins." She cackled, and another thunderous crack bellowed, the portal to the underworld growing larger. "Now tell me again, which one of the Blacksteel brothers do you love, Gideon or Torin? I can't possibly keep up. I wonder which one will be the first hunter to try and slit your throat when they find out you have demon blood running in your veins."

Emara wasn't going to think of that. This was all mind games to distract her from the fact that the Supreme was dying and someone was taking her power into their own. And that someone could be her.

And if it was Emara who was to enter the path of supremacy, it was because the Gods of Light wanted her to. That would be her purpose. And if she were to die here, in this moment, or to be delivered to the underworld, she would fight to show the Gods of Light that she stood with them.

She would show them what lay in her heart.

Emara realised that there was nothing to be afraid of anymore. If this was her fate, then so be it, but one thing was clear: the Supreme was afraid. Deleine was afraid of dying, of fading, so much so that she had turned her back on the Light Gods for a way out of her fate. And as she lay on the ice-cold floor, Emara realised something else.

Deleine was afraid of following through with her deal to the underworld, because she could have completed the ritual by now. She could have had this over with as Emara lay unconscious, unknowing.

But she hadn't carried it out.

Deleine was terrified.

Emara found that last thread of fear that lay in her soul and forged it into steel as she said, "I really wish you would stop running your mouth and just get this over with. If my father really is who you say he is, do you think he would be pleased that you have failed in your attempts to deliver me twice? For the highest regarded witch in the kingdom, you don't seem to be good at keeping up your end of the bargain."

The Supreme's hands flew out again, but instead of stopping Emara's air supply, she allowed a spout of flames to soar from her palms, mixing with the darkness of the festering portal. The fire circled around Emara before forming into the shape of a snake. The fiery face of the serpent weaved towards Emara, but she was still stuck against the limestone, unable to move away from the serpent's path. Emara let out a scream that broke through the room as the snake hissed out its terrible tongue, the flames licking her bare thigh. Another scream shattered from her throat as the fire creature did it again.

The pain was so overpowering that her breathing stopped. She held in another scream, trying to manage her agony. Tears burned like fire drops in her eyes, blinding her.

The serpent went to strike again, and she screamed before it hit her.

Something broke against the doors from the outside like a body or something strong, maybe a weapon.

It must have been concerning enough to have caught the Supreme's attention; her head snapped towards the commotion outside, and the fiery snake vanished, dissolving into ash that dropped like snowflakes over Emara. The heat from the phantom beast disappeared, and a cool rush swept over her clammy face.

Emara took a breath in and looked down at her leg where the beast had burned her skin.

Nothing. No mark or wound.

It had been a trick, Deleine toying with her mind.

Suddenly, a man and his death scream could be heard from outside the doors, and then a snapping sound. Emara fought down the sickness that stirred in her stomach to turn and see the doors burst apart like a battering ram had pummelled them open.

She let out a small cry as Torin Blacksteel stood in the doorway, both swords dripping with crimson blood. The gore from whoever he had just killed lay at his feet as he stepped over the body and into the room. His eyes found hers and the burning rage simmered for a second before igniting fully.

He knew she was alive, Emara realised, and that's all he had needed. She let out a little whimper as her hope died when she remembered how many guards stood in this room. Warrior of Thorin or not, he was only one person.

A curse left her lips as well as a sob.

He was going to die.

CHAPTER
FIFTY-FOUR
EMARA

"**A**h, the hunter named after the God** of the Sun and War," the Supreme taunted. "I thought you might show up."

Torin stepped into the dim light of the room, looking like war itself. Blood streaked his face, and tunic, and his dark hair looked dishevelled from battle. He held a sword in each hand.

He snarled, "Let her go, and I won't carve that wrinkled skin from your face and make myself a new case for my swords."

Deleine sniggered, her features contorting into something truly wicked. "You won't get close to my face, hunter," she spat. "I have lined myself with lethal reinforcements." Her eyes drifted casually to the guards around the room. "Should you try and attack me, they are under my command to kill you. All I need to do is raise a finger, and they will destroy you. You might know a few of them." Her dark eyes winked. "They are your brethren."

He let out a laugh that sounded like an insult. "Who

the fuck do you think you are?" Torin growled. "Hunters are not your personal play toys. They do not answer to you. Stand down, men, I am not here to take you down. Only her."

When the other hunters didn't move, the Supreme smiled. "No, but I've made deals to grant them immortality when the underworld rises. Their loyalties lie elsewhere now."

"Fucking cowards." Torin growled at his brethren with splattered blood down his face, the blood of the brothers he had cut down to get here. He was menacing and wild.

Deleine walked over towards the guards. "You see, magic has two sides. One, which is full of good intent and used for pure reasons. The cost of it is fatal. You will lay down your life to protect a God's magic, and in return, you get restrictions and rules." She slid her eyes back to Torin. "Or you could form a dark alliance and be promised magic that can never die. It knows no bounds, no limits. You could be immortal."

"If you think that doing deals with Veles—"

"Veles?" The Supreme laughed as she repeated the name. "Veles is not the King of the Underworld, my blue-eyed boy, Balan is. Your father really should update you more in those inefficient briefings of yours. Whilst Veles rests, Balan will reign." Another cruel smile tugged her lips over her teeth. "In fact, speaking of fathers, did our beautiful Empress of Air ever tell you who her father is?"

The Supreme's laugh filled the air again, and the flames from the black candles hit an all-time high.

"Please, don't do this. I beg you to stop," Emara cried out.

Not yet. Not here. Not like this. Her body shook against the floor. She was unable to even meet Torin's gaze. She wanted to beg the Supreme to stop talking, but she knew she wasn't going to be given that luxury.

The Supreme was going to take great pride in telling Torin who her father was.

What if Torin couldn't look at her? What if he was disgusted by her blood? What if he tried to kill her?

Her heart cracked open, old wounds now raw flesh once again.

Deep down, in the darkest parts of who she was, Emara knew what the Supreme had said about her father was true. It had to be. It explained why her grandmother had been hiding her from him for all of these years. It explained why her mother had died to protect her. And it explained why she was always surrounded by darkness.

"Why don't you go to the underworld with Emara? You can meet your new father-in-law." The amusement in the Supreme's voice sparked even more unimaginable anger inside Emara. She was ready to explode.

A cry escaped her.

When Torin didn't speak, she wondered if he had worked it out or was just in the process of piecing it all together. Had he worked out that he was promised to a girl with demon blood in her veins? He had lain with a girl who had the very thing in her blood which he despised above all else.

That crack in her heart that had slowly started to heal because of him split open again.

It would be over between them. Demon's blood ran in her veins. *Demon's blood.*

"I don't give a fuck who Emara's father is." Torin's voice was so low and vicious, it forced Emara to look at him. His striking face raged with brutality, yet his rapid breathing was calming. Emara blinked. She had trained with him and watched him enough in the sparring room to know what he was doing. She had studied him in combat sessions so thoroughly to know that he was readying himself to strike.

"I'm sure if you just asked her"—the Supreme gestured to where Emara lay panting in agony and rage on the ground—"she will tell you herself who he is."

"Please, stop," Emara begged again, unashamed to plead, rage building in her heart. "You have taken enough from me. Stop!"

Something snapped inside Torin, she could see it in his eyes. The muscles in his body tensed and he scowled. "No one, and I mean no one, makes her beg." His jaw angled like a predator as he looked from his brethren to Emara, then to the Supreme. His eyes turned to black ice. "What the *fuck* is that around her neck?"

"A chain for a badly behaved witch cunt," Silas spat, and a few of the guards chuckled.

Torin nodded once. "I see."

He moved like lightning. Leaping into the air in two swift steps, he brought down his swords and ended the life of one of the guards who had laughed. He spun, moving on to the next one, and sliced into the area which housed most of his vital organs.

Two guards fell in perfect synchronisation.

"Are you really going to kill the brothers you took an oath to protect over a witch with demon blood running through her veins?" Deleine seethed.

Torin's eyes narrowed in on her face. "Thanks to you, they are no longer my brothers." His face turned to iron. "A traitor is a traitor, no matter what faction they fall under. But I bet you know a thing or two about that."

She raised an eyebrow, and then she glanced at the guards around the room. She gave Silas a small nod.

Boots hammered into the floor as guards ran to swarm Torin. Flashes of black and grey started moving so fast that Emara's eyes couldn't keep up. Steel could be heard clanging through the room, and the guards, some determined and some dying, began shouting.

I still cannot unhear the cries of death.

Three more went down in the blink of an eye.

Torin Blacksteel was a dark wind of sheer violence. He was destruction and fury and unbelievable talent as he swung again, bringing down his sword and cutting clean through a guard's neck. The man's head rolled. He pivoted and dropped to his knees, swinging out his foot and taking down another hunter. As he sprung to his feet, he drove his sword down through the man on the floor. As another charged him from behind, Torin threw out his other sword and the guard ran into it, skewering himself. He pulled out his weapon, and blood sprayed.

Heart almost combusting, Emara's eyes scrunched shut as blood splattered against the limestone. She took a breath and then reopened them, unable to take her eyes from him. Torin was magnified brutality as he assessed who to take down next, but he was outnumbered, even with the eight men that he had just killed. There were still seven left, and six of them were working together to cage him in. Emara noticed the last one had gone to the Supreme and ushered her back.

Silas.

Traitorous bastard.

Emara shook with anger.

They had taken an oath to protect the magic community, not a kidnapping bitch with a personal vendetta against anyone who posed a threat to her magic. Emara had to find a way out of this circle. She could fight. She knew she could. She only had to get out.

Another man's pained scream screeched through the air, and she knew Torin had taken down another one.

"Are you hurt?" Torin shouted at Emara as he fought, his eyes darting from the battle to her.

"Stay focused," Emara screamed. She moved, realising that she could now free her hands.

She could move her hands.

She glanced over to the Supreme and was greatly surprised to see a fear in the depths of her eyes as she watched her men go down one by one. She wasn't focused on keeping Emara in place anymore, she was focused on Torin. Emara could see that the probability of Torin's death was dwindling with every man he took down. And so could the Supreme.

The dark portal that was spitting out blackness and

whirling catastrophe closed shut. The door to the underworld was locked.

Emara noticed her uttering something under her breath. After a moment, she realised it was chanting.

Was the Supreme gathering her strength to take down Torin?

She needed out of this Gods-damned circle—now.

"You have to break the circle," Emara shouted to Torin, taking advantage of the stillness of the head witch.

"Angel, I am busy breaking necks, not circles," he shouted at her from across the room, his swaggering confidence returning.

"No, for once in your life, Torin Blacksteel, listen to me. Break the circle."

The Supreme was in disbelief, frozen by shock at the unrelenting power of Torin Blacksteel as he brought down yet another who had betrayed his clan. She clearly thought he would have fallen by now, or she wouldn't have gone into shock as she watched him defy the odds. Emara knew she had to get out of this circle before that shock wore off.

"Torin!" The scream left her mouth as the tension of time ticked on.

He heard her.

He spun, crossing his swords and slamming them into a guard. The man flew through the air and skidded into the circle. The black salt crunched under the man's body, the metal from his belt scraping a line in the shape that held her captive.

She heard another clash of steel to see two of the

guards now cornering Torin, doing everything they could to stab him. He blocked the blows, but how long could he keep it up?

Shit!

The guard who had broken the circle began to stir on the ground.

Emara scrambled across to where he lay and removed his sword from his hand before he could fully wake. It wasn't exactly her weapon of choice, it was much too heavy, but it could cut through flesh in a way that she knew was necessary to survive this. The guard's eyes flew open, but before he could speak, she straddled him and drove the weapon right through his heart. He choked, gaping up at her. She looked away, unable to digest what she had just done. He didn't have the same red eyes as demons did, but if she hadn't stabbed him, he would have stabbed her—or worse, Torin.

The Supreme glared at her. As she took in the Supreme's dismay, Emara finally let a smile cross her face.

"You may have put a chain around my neck to suppress my magic," Emara said as she rose from the ground. "You may think you know who I am." Crimson blood now soaked her nightgown. "But you made another mistake here tonight."

Doubt set in around Deleine's features as she watched Emara rise instead of the battle behind her. Emara was about to take advantage of that doubt as she realised the Supreme wasn't cordial to violence. She wouldn't let the hunters train in her palace. She hadn't been at the Uplift to witness the destruction she caused, choosing instead to pull the strings from the background.

Violence was Deleine's weakness.

"What you failed to realise is that I have another power, a trained power that you don't have." Emara gripped the sword in her hand. Fright and indignation crept into the dark pools of the Supreme's eyes. It was the most human emotion Emara had witnessed cross her face. "I can wield a weapon. And not of fire, air, water, spirit, or earth, but of *steel*. And I am going to drive this weapon right through your soulless, dark heart."

The Supreme flinched, actually flinched. But then she gathered herself with a dark snarl on her mouth. "Try your best."

"Oh, I will."

"Angel, you can't distract me like that," Torin panted as he fought with the other guards. He turned, kicking back. His foot connected with a guard's face and he went down, unconscious. Torin's sapphire eyes found hers, and that beautifully wicked smile warmed his lips. "You can't say things about wielding a sword, wearing that nightgown, and expect me not to get excited and utterly distracted."

"What did I say? Stay focused," she barked back before bringing her eyes back to the Supreme. "If you think immortality is more important than integrity and honour, then maybe you don't deserve life at all."

The Queen of the Witches' temper shattered. "And you think you do? You don't deserve to rise in any form of power, you're an imposturous little worm." Her jaw shook and she clamped it shut. "You don't deserve the crown of air or of fire, and you absolutely don't deserve *my* crown. Just like your demon-loving whore of a mother didn't deserve it either. That's why I told your father where she was the night he found her, to make sure he would smite you both." Her eye twitched.

The most indescribable fury rushed over Emara, shaking every part of who she was. "You told Balan where my mother was?"

She'd thought she could never hate anyone as much as she hated Taymir Solden, but the Supreme…

"Of course I did," Deleine shouted. Emara flinched. "Even though she wasn't practising magic for the ascension, her power was still untouchable, unmatched." Abhorrence engulfed her eyes as her gaze bore through Emara. "It was only a matter of time before she took it all. And I was supposed to be Supreme. Me, not her. She didn't even want it. That ungrateful bitch didn't want any of it." She paused, shaking now too. "I wanted it. I wanted it all, and she was going to take it from me. She was predicted to take every crown I wanted."

In that moment, something so stark and disturbing snapped in Emara, something that should never have been touched in the depths of her soul stirred.

One woman, full of envy, greed, and jealousy had caused all of this death and pain, fear and chaos.

The Supreme would stop at nothing until Emara and everyone she cared about no longer existed.

Emara felt something unhinge.

A dark smoke started to mist out from her fingers, passing the blade in her hand and making its way out into the open air. Emara shook violently, the magic in her blood thrumming and banging against every door to get out. As the dark mist filtered from her, she could smell sulphur as it came up and wrapped around her neck. The ancient mist gathered, swirling around her throat like a necklace of death.

The Supreme scrambled back, Silas stepping in front of her.

A carnal smile slashed across Emara's face as the chains around her neck snapped and broke, the sound stopping everything in the room as the metal hit the floor.

She let out a gasp, feeling the darkness curl around her heart as the black smoke gave her air again.

She looked up, eyes catching Deleine. "My mother was never going to take anything from you because it was not yours to have in the first place. You stand there because of my grandmother's abdication to protect her family. A family which you"—she pointed the blade at her—"ruined. That crown never belonged to you." The fighting behind her had stopped, and the dark wind that swirled like air and fire combined, built around her like a personal bodyguard. "My mother died because of you. My grandmother died because you didn't protect your own. And my sister, the only family I had left, my best friend, was murdered in cold blood because you used her as a pawn to get revenge on a dead woman."

The curl of the Supreme's lip returned as she wiped the blood from her now-bleeding nose.

She was bleeding? But no one had even touched her.

A split second later, Emara realised that the blood

running from the Supreme's nose wasn't because she had been struck, but because she was weakening. Her power was failing.

"It appears I still have one bitch to kill in that family, then." The Supreme flung out her hands, severing her deal to keep Emara alive, and a gust of power surged forward.

Emara's side hit the ground with a crack, but she tucked and rolled like she had practised so many times with the Blacksteels. Her knees connected with the floor and then she found her feet again quickly. The magic flew past her, narrowly missing her, and slammed against the window on the other side of the room.

The window cracked, but she didn't have time to study it as Emara moved to dodge a ball of crackling fire.

Heavy footsteps could be heard running along the corridor, and as Emara turned her head, the Supreme struck again, sending out a wave of fire. Emara spun, grabbing a guard who had been travelling to attack her from behind and shielded herself to the flames. She let out a scream as the fire burned the body in front of her, heat coursing through every part of her, singing her hair.

The guard's soul left his body as he turned to dust. The ashes fell over her bare feet. Vomit travelled up Emara's throat, but she didn't have time to hurl it up, so she swallowed.

Steel clashed again, signalling that Torin had commenced his death dance with anyone who was left.

Gideon, Kellen, Artem, and Marcus entered the room, and she was grateful that the running boots hadn't belonged to more of the Supreme's guards. They drove straight into combat, no questions asked.

She wondered how they all knew about the Supreme's betrayal, but that was a question for another day.

"Keep one alive," Torin commanded. "I don't care what one."

Within seconds, they finished off the remainder of the guards, leaving one. They restrained him, and Marcus Coldwell hit a spot on his neck that sent him to sleep.

Emara turned and gathered all the power she could to send a surge of uncontrolled fire the Supreme's way, but she ducked it.

With a scream of frustration, the Supreme batted her hand, and a whirlwind of air found Emara. She couldn't duck or dive to miss it. It went straight for her throat.

The weapon she held, fell from her hands and clattered to the floor.

She couldn't breathe.

Torin was beside her instantly. He looked from the Supreme back to Emara as she clawed at her throat, choking, suffocating.

Her own element had lodged itself in her windpipe, and no breaths could get through.

"No, no," Torin muttered as he touched her face with one hand. Blood imprinted on her cheek. "Stop. Fucking stop!" he roared at the Supreme. When she gave him a vile smile, he quickly set into action towards her.

Deleine's bony hand flew up, her normally sleek

brown hair all dishevelled, drips of crimson blood falling from her nose. "Don't move, or I will draw out every particle of oxygen from her lungs."

He skidded to a halt as Emara dropped to her knees, her face turning a horrible shade of reddish-purple. The burning in her lungs was unbearable, the pressure in her eyes about to break through her skull.

This was it.

She could hear Torin shout, but she couldn't listen, not when he had fought so hard to keep her alive. Emara knew she had seconds left, seconds left of breath, and she couldn't tell him what she wanted to. She closed her eyes as dizziness took her down.

Her shoulders hit the marble.

Another desperate gasp clutched in her lungs and her heart slowed.

Blackness was folding in around the glittering dust.

I love you, and I promise that when you are finding it hard to breathe, I will be there, keeping the air in your lungs. I will be there, holding your hand. And I will have your back. Always. We all will. Your ancestors have waited a long time to see you wear your moonlight. The road you are about to take will not be easy, but when you walk it, just know that you are not alone.

A single tear fell from Emara's eyes as a soft voice coasted through her.

She was not alone.

Not now and not ever.

She could breathe because Cally would be there helping her. Emara put out her hand for someone to grip it, squeeze her hand like Cally would. Everything around her started to move. The pain in her chest was unbearable as the element that she had become empress of killed her.

She thought of her best friend's golden hair and her wonderful face.

I love you, and I promise that when you are finding it hard to breathe, I will be there, keeping the air in your lungs.

Something squeezed her hand.

Someone squeezed her hand.

Suddenly, a surge of water vomited from Emara's throat, wiping out the air that had rooted itself in her windpipe. She spluttered out more water, coughing up everything as it cleared her airway. As Emara inhaled, finally catching her breath, she smelled the coastal air of Tolsah Bay.

The salt and the sand and the sea.

Like her dream where she and Cally had visited the beach.

I will be there, keeping the air in your lungs.

Cally.

Cally had somehow helped her to breathe. Emara clutched her throat as she dragged breath back into her lungs. *Cally.* She was a witch of House Water.

She had helped her to breathe. Callyn was here. Even though Emara couldn't see her, she was here. Emara rolled onto her stomach as tears threatened to blind her, and the sounds of the room finally came back to her as she gasped another breath.

Cally had just helped her live. Her only jolt of power had been to give Emara life again. Water had fought the air and won.

Emara let out a sob.

"Kill me instead," a deep voice begged, rugged and feral. "Kill me."

She looked up and realised the words had come from Torin. She scrambled to get onto all fours.

Torin's face was strained for breath, and Emara realised instantly that the Supreme was now suffocating him.

He choked, and she could hear his brethren shouting at Deleine to release him.

No, no, no, no.

Emara didn't know if it was fear, adrenaline, or even if it was Cally helping her, but somehow, she rose, clutching the sword she had dropped.

She couldn't lose anyone else, especially not Torin. Her heart almost folded in on itself.

It was time to end this.

She powered forward, fighting a scream on her lips.

The Supreme wasn't even looking at her anymore, underestimating her again.

But Emara wouldn't let Deleine take another person from her, not when she and Torin were meant to face this world together.

She ran faster than ever before, the steel in her hands feeling heavy and indestructible. Just then, four hunting knives whizzed past her head from behind her. She ducked, still running, rapidly realising that they were not meant for her, but the only remaining guard left protecting the Supreme.

Silas.

Each blade stabbed into the guard, and he fell to his

knees. She turned, and a second later, it clicked that one knife had come from each hunter—Kellen, Artem, Marcus, and Gideon.

And they were clearing a pathway for her that led straight to the Supreme.

CHAPTER
FIFTY-FIVE
TORIN

Torin couldn't breathe.

And it wasn't because the Supreme threatened to smother him with more air than his lungs could endure. No, her power had stopped choking him the minute his brethren landed four knives into her guard's body.

He had crashed to the ground, a poisoned scream in his throat.

Torin didn't care. He was too busy watching Emara.

The whole world had stilled, and it was like time had slowed to the brink of stopping altogether. Torin watched her take off, knowing this was her window of opportunity. Her muscles powered her legs, and she swung her arms back and forth like he had shown her, a sword in her hand—both hands, actually. He could see strain in her muscles, but she was still slick in her movement, carrying it well. Her lack of training was irrelevant as she ran towards Deleine Orinmore, ready to strike. He couldn't move or even breathe as he watched her take her chance. The Supreme, too, looked like she was in disbelief.

From what Torin could make out, Deleine was bleeding from her nose and ears.

That was never good.

She had used too much power.

The all-mighty witch stumbled back, flinging out any sort of magic she could muster in her desperate state of shock. Fire, water, and air made efforts to take Emara out, but nothing stopped the empress.

His breathing hitched again.

Torin had never seen someone so elegant, someone with such exquisite beauty, holding a sword with the full intent of using it. She was breath-taking. His lips parted, as he realised it was something that his heart had needed to see—her stunning face so intensely focused on what she was about to do. Her hair was like a flag of vibrant, dark silk behind her. Her delicate nightdress was covered in blood, both hers and of others, and her eyebrows were down in determination.

She was remarkable.

His heart skipped several beats as Emara bounded up the steps towards the Supreme, bringing the sword across her body with decent accuracy and precision. He scrambled forwards on his knees, trying to stand, anticipating a fatal blow. He felt sick. He wished he could take this death blow from her innocent hands, hands that weren't made to bear something so heavy, but she stopped.

He almost choked.

"Maybe my mother was never going to take anything

from you," she said, her voice full of promise. "But I will."

She plunged upwards, pushing the sword right through the abdomen of the Grand High Witch, who still looked like she had never seen a woman with a sword before. The dark flames of the candelabras died on the wick instantly and a thick, grey smoke swirled into the air as the Supreme screamed in agony. She fell to the ground, but Emara didn't move, her back still facing Torin.

He wanted to go to her, he wanted to pull her away from the witch, dying on the floor like her traitorous guards.

But he was so stunned and in awe of her that he couldn't move.

She had been unyielding and fearless.

She had been an Empress of Steel.

His heart burst with pride as he looked at her. So many pieces of his heart knitted together. It was wrong of him to be in such awe of someone who had just rammed a sword through a living person, but he felt a sordid relief and satisfaction at what she had done. He would have done the same, and would continue to do the same. He would kill for her, anyone that ever tried to harm a hair on her head. A tightness in his chest eased a little to know she would do the same. She would protect herself. She would fight.

He had feared coming into this room, knowing he might have to take down his own men, his own brethren. He wasn't worried or apprehensive about removing men from this earth who had once fought beside him in the hunt; no, he was worried about how Emara would look at him after it. After he had slaughtered every single one of them for assisting in this, he was worried about what she would see him as.

A killer. A slayer.

He could never deny that part of himself—violent, uncompromising, and brutal—and he never would need to if she were his. What shook him to his very core was that she had not looked away as he had taken each life. She had wanted him to win. She had been there to make sure he survived, and because of that, he found her so much more extraordinarily brilliant. She was beautiful, powerful, and lethal, and she accepted him for who he was. Not just for one night, not just for passion or lust. She accepted the darkest, most ferocious parts of him.

And she was his.

An overpowering wave of something so unfamiliar to him rocked Torin where he stood, threatening to take him to his knees more than any man or beast ever had.

But a gurgling noise sounded through the room, drawing his attention to the other witch.

The Supreme's mouth snagged open in the effort to say something, but instead of words, she let out a terrifying scream that sent a blast of magic out from her body. The explosion hit Emara first, and before he could run to help her or stop it, he, too, was flung back. His shoulder connected with the hard, cold floor, and with a little momentum, he was able to roll backwards to try and reduce injury. The magic buzzed in his ears, but he managed to get to his feet, crouching. Looking down at the ground, he steadied himself. He glanced behind him to his brethren; they had also been blasted back from the impact of Deleine's magic. Kellen was down, but as Artem steadied himself, Marcus and Gideon were already on their feet, moving in the direction of the Empress of Air.

Torin found himself running towards Emara's lifeless body.

"Emara..." A strangled sound escaped his mouth as his boots pounded the floor. He got there first, sliding to his knees beside her body and flinging his swords to the ground. He looked over her, checking her body for any fatal injuries.

Head, heart, torso, neck...

Torin didn't know what injuries she'd had before, but she was bleeding, and it looked like she was covered in dried blood too. Her poor neck bruised where that chain had been.

Her head. He could see the blood pouring out of her skull already.

"Fuck!" he screamed as Marcus and Gideon arrived by his side.

Gideon dropped to his knees beside her and put his ear to her mouth. "It's okay, brother," Gideon said. "She's still breathing."

He blinked, looking for a pulse or a rise in her chest, but an unbearable feeling froze him solid.

"She needs a healer," Marcus barked at Artem, who was already running from the room. "Now. Get Sybil —anyone."

Undiluted rage soared through Torin, burning away

the fear.

He should have known the Supreme was sinful enough to take Emara with her to the Otherside as she passed over.

A long, rage-filled breath poured from him.

He turned back to Emara and kissed her forehead. "It's going to be okay. You are going to be okay, angel." He cupped her face, and even though she wasn't looking at him, he could feel the air charge around them. "I am going to make sure of it," he promised her.

Torin turned, looking over his shoulder to see that the Supreme's body was lying lifeless, surrounded by her own blood.

But then her wretched body twitched.

He ran, reaching her body in no time.

Deleine was still alive—barely, but breath still entered her lungs as his boots met her blood on the ground. Torin leaned down, withdrawing the sword that Emara had shoved into her torso. Her body jolted, but no remorse crossed his heart. He knew that by removing the weapon, the blood from the wounds would spill faster into every part of her, swarming her ruptured organs.

Death would come quicker now.

"Immortality?" He laughed. He leaned down lower, holding the weapon in his hands. "All the efforts you have put into becoming immortal have been in vain. Every betrayal, every time you sold a little part of you, every effort, every plan, every deal you have struck," he said, grinding his teeth, "have not been worth it. You have not won. Good always prevails."

It wasn't that he was good—he certainly wasn't—but Emara and everyone else who had been slaughtered at the Supreme's hands were. And he was more than ready to deliver justice. Her eyes glazed a little more as a deceitful tear ran down her pale cheek, making its way through the splattered blood on her face.

"There is nothing *immortal* about you now. The darkness is coming for you as you lay dying on the cold ground like the rest of the treacherous monsters in this room. No dark magic is here to save you. The Dark God seems to have left you unprotected, after all." He gripped the back of her head and yanked her towards him. "This is what happens when someone tries to take the thing I love most in this world," he whispered into her ear so that no one else could hear him. She made a whimpering sound. "This is what happens when you cross a Blacksteel. I only wish I could tell your *king* the same fucking thing. But I guess that will have to wait for now." He smiled down at her with everything that was dark and uncompromising. "You will die an dishonourable death, and when the insects feed on your corpse in the shallow ground, no one will whisper your name. No one will want to remember a witch who picked the darkness over the light of her own Gods. No one."

The Supreme let out one last pitiful cry before he stepped back, swinging the sword. Her head came off before her body had the chance to hit the ground.

Her crown of deceit and ruin flew across the space, tumbling to the floor, and Torin watched it roll down the granite stairs all the way to Emara's feet.

CHAPTER
FIFTY-SIX
TORIN

The sun had gone into the earth twice since Emara's eyes had closed. They still hadn't reopened.

Torin had not left her side, not even to eat or drink. He had even slept in the chair he sat in now, no matter how uncomfortable it was. But he was back on home soil, and that was something to be thankful for. The tower, despite being a training facility, was still one of the best infirmaries in the kingdom.

Sybil and his mother had been the healers assigned to her. They had created a portal to bring her back here to heal properly. She would be safe here.

He stifled a laugh of rage that crawled up his throat. She wasn't safe anywhere. He had thought she would have been safe in a palace filled with witches, but he had been wrong. He'd thought she would be safe, protected by hunters, but he had been wrong again.

By now, rumours had spread to every part of the kingdom. The prime had found out about the deception and dishonour that had taken place under the roof of the amethyst palace. Torin's jaw ticked, and he straightened his spine against the back of the infirmary chair.

He wondered when the prime would congregate to battle this one out. He knew his father was leading investigations into the hunters who had betrayed their oath, and the chief commander would need to address it soon.

Their world was no longer as straightforward as the Light Gods against the Dark One. Cracks were starting to form in units that had been so polished and controlled for years. Factions were unsafe from the inside, never mind the lurking darkness of the underworld. There was evidence of hunters, witches *and* the elite now having dabbled with the dark side. Were the Fae involved and just missed exposure, or was their faction as clean as it looked?

One thing Torin couldn't wrap his mind around was the clans. How could his brethren have turned to Veles —or Balan, or whoever the fuck ruled the pits of the underworld these days? How could they have turned their backs on their oath, their blood?

Torin looked over to where Emara lay on the bed, so still and so silent, her bold and beautiful face drained of colour. Her head was still wrapped in a white bandage in the efforts to stop the bleeding from her injuries, poultices and white ash gelling into her wounds. Something strained in his heart. Her skull had been bleeding from two areas, one from the impact of being smashed into a mirror, and the other wound from when she had landed against the watchtower floor from the Supreme's final effort to kill her.

She had been so courageous and heroic in her efforts to save herself, to save him. Every part of his heart hurt with how fortunate he was that she was alive, but in the other part of his heart—the dark half—craved to be so unbelievably violent to whoever had hurt her. He knew they were dead. He had killed the majority of them, but that didn't really take away the urge to lash out again.

Thorin knew how many hunters had *really* betrayed the oath to their Light God, Thorin's wrath on them all.

A huff of breath left his chest.

He should have been there to protect Emara. He shouldn't have left. He had made that call, and she could have died because he was hungry for violence.

He should have been there to stop any of this from happening to her.

A bottomless pool of guilt swarmed his heart, threatening to drown it entirely. If he had just—

Movement came from her wrist, and she squeezed his hand, causing his chest to stop rising.

His eyes darted to her face. "Emara?" he said, his voice so desperate that he didn't recognise it.

Her head tilted to the side, her knee pulling up, ever so slightly ruffling the blanket which had been draped over her.

He was out of the chair in an instant, cutting through the space between them. He ran a hand over her forehead gently, and she responded.

"Mother," he called. "Mother!"

The full kingdom must have heard him roar.

Emara hadn't opened her eyes yet, but he could tell

that she was fighting something in a dream as she roused, not fully in reality yet.

"It's okay, I am here. Emara? Can you hear me? I am here."

She stirred again, the white pillow showcasing all the knots and dried blood still in her hair. Her eyes drifted open, blinking once and then again. Her lips parted before she flinched, like the acute pain of her wounds found her instantly.

"Clearwater, it's me. Can you hear me?"

An acknowledgement came in the form of a groan. He let out a short, raspy laugh. Torin dropped to his knees beside the bed, putting his hand on hers. "Can you see okay?"

She nodded, shifting to her side to see him.

"Don't move too much," he advised, putting a protesting hand out.

"Stop bossing me around," she groaned out. A taut smile graced her lips, and he could have lunged over the bed and kissed them.

Torin found himself smiling for the first time. "You know I like to be the boss."

"Well, you're not," she croaked.

To feel her spirit—that vibrant, addictive, spirit—stir back to life wedged air in his throat.

"I thought I had lost you for a moment," Torin whispered as he ran a gentle hand over her bruised cheek.

She waited before responding, but a flood of tears filled her eyes. "I thought I was going to lose you when you came through the doors to the observatory."

"You were never going to lose me." He squeezed her hand and contemplated kissing her again.

"I...I...have so much to say—"

"Shh." He let a thumb run over her cheek again. He knew she was going to start a discussion about the blood that ran through her veins. That didn't need to be a discussion today. "It's okay," he reassured her. "We can talk later, when you are feeling better."

She gave him a sorrow-filled smile, one that broke his heart. "Why are you still here? Why don't you hate me?" A small tremor started wobbling in her chin.

"I could never hate you," he breathed.

Even if her father was Balan.

He swallowed.

"Hello, my love," his mother said as she entered the infirmary, dressed in her healing attire. Gideon followed at her heels, his face grave. His mother's hair was tied back in a bun, but a few of her curls had come loose, like always. No matter how hard she tried, she was never able to tame them.

"She woke around a minute ago," he informed his mother, still holding Emara's hand. Naya looked down to where their fingers met. A sparkle flared in her eye as she looked back to Torin. He glanced at Gideon, whose face was unreadable, but he refused to let go of her hand. "And she has already told me off, so that seems like a good sign to me."

His mother smiled at him and then Emara. "Well, it seems like she is in fighting spirits for a steady recovery."

"It's good to have you back, Emara," Gideon said, a strain in his voice.

She nodded at him, her eyes lowering.

"I feel fine," Emara said through gritted teeth. She began to rise, pushing against the bed.

His mother moved. "Oh no, my love, just stay put with your head against that pillow. You have suffered a bad concussion and head wounds. You can't move around just yet. We brought you back to the Blacksteel Tower so that you could rest in your old room until you are ready to go back to normal life. All the empresses send their love for what you did for them." Naya's hand reached Emara, and Torin saw Emara take in all the flowers in the room that had been sent. "They will be eternally grateful. Every witch in the kingdom will be. What you endured, what you—" Naya placed a hand to her mouth.

"Honestly, I feel okay," Emara said. She winced again as her head touched the soft fabric. "I should get up. I will have so much paperwork to catch up on."

Torin laughed. "Stay put, please. Lorta and Kaydence have organised everything for when you have made a full recovery."

She always had something to prove.

"No, my darling, your duties will have to wait for a little while," Naya said, moving the blankets back around her. "Rest up. Healer's orders." She raised an eyebrow and ushered Torin to step back.

Placing a small kiss on the back of Emara's hand, he pulled himself away reluctantly, then took himself over to the fireplace to stand beside Gideon.

His heartbeat quickened as he watched his mother tend to her. Devotion and affection swirled in his heart, and it caught in his throat as he watched the two women that meant the most to him interacting.

What was wrong with him?

He needed to train or spar or something.

Fuck.

Emara's eyes caught his, her beautiful irises the colour of swords now. As their gazes locked, the whole room spun for a second.

How he felt was indescribable. It was something he had felt only for her.

He was ready to admit that to her.

He had been ready for a while. He was going to ask her to be his wife and join him in the merging of their souls, combining two into one; not just because it was an ancient tradition or because he needed power from the witches, but because he wanted her and he would never stop wanting her.

He would always want her. It would always be her, no one else.

Emara Clearwater.

He was just so glad to have retrieved the ring he had given Magin before the hunter's body had been cleared. After arriving back home, he had placed his mother's ring back into a drawer in his room so that he could collect it when Emara was better. Maybe he would even take her somewhere nice, somewhere in the city.

The door flew open, causing him to stand to attention, and Viktir Blacksteel hurried over the threshold. The coldness of his eyes made Torin's spine straighten.

"I thought you might be here," his commander said in a way that sounded both annoyed and dismissive.

He hadn't seen his father in a while. Viktir hadn't even bothered to attend the winter solstice festivities, the miserable bastard. But Torin had tried to keep his distance where possible. He couldn't stand to be around his father.

Torin sent a look Gideon's way, a look that both brothers knew well.

What's going on?

The glance Gideon threw back was one that he knew well too.

I have no idea.

"Commander Blacksteel," Torin said, taking the plunge to break the ice.

"Torin." Viktir looked around the room and not at him.

Naya finished what she had been doing with Emara and rose from the bed.

"Do you have something to say?" Torin glared. "Or did you just come for a visit?"

The commander's smile was the same as it had always been, without any warmth, the complete opposite of Naya's.

"I don't have time for visits that don't mean something," he announced, walking a little further into the room. "I have been extremely busy informing the prime of why my *son* would cut off the head of the highest-ranking witch to grace this fine kingdom." He stood, his feet shoulder-width apart, his hand always hovering close to his weapon belt.

Too close.

Torin's eyes narrowed. "Then I hope you didn't leave out any detail on how she was trying to summon the *Dark One,* using *dark magic,* and turning our own faction members against us." Torin sneered. "I also hope you informed the prime that you knew of the change in hierarchy in the nine realms of the underworld." He tilted his head. "Pray tell me, *father,* did you tell them that? Because you seemed to have forgotten to inform your second-in-command."

Viktir should have told him that Balan had been named keeper of the underworld. Rumours had been circling years ago, but nothing had ever come of it. If there had been truth to it, they should have been informed.

Veles is not the King of the Underworld, my blue-eyed boy, Balan is. Your father really should update you more in those inefficient briefings of yours. Whilst Veles rests, Balan will reign.

Viktir let out a cruel hissing sound.

Gideon flinched.

Viktir's teeth ground together, his features sharpening. "You have no idea what you are talking about, boy."

"Thanks to you." Torin lifted his chin. "You have left us blind, time and time again. First with the wards, and now this. What's next? Did you know our men were looking for immortality? Have you switched sides to the dark?"

Viktir growled, squaring his shoulders.

"Enough." Naya took a step away from Emara's bedside. "I will not have this in here. Need I remind all

of you"—she looked from her husband to her boys—
"that the Empress of Air is recovering from horrific
injuries and needs her rest? Her recovery doesn't need
to be plagued with hunter politics."

Viktir turned, facing his wife, and Torin's fist
twitched at the way his father scowled at her.

"The message I have come to deliver is for the
benefit of all of you." Viktir looked from Emara to
Gideon, and then to Torin. His stare lingered a little
longer before he dragged it from Torin's face. "So why
not kill three birds with one stone?"

"Viktir, what possible matters must concern an
empress in recovery?" his mother asked, her facial
features changing.

She could sense something.

Torin's stomach dipped.

"Don't question my authority, *wife*. Not now." He
threw her a dismissive look. "I have come here to advise
on matters regarding our agreement," Viktir informed
brazenly, looking at Emara. "As commander of the
Blacksteel name, I have reviewed our clan's current situation and made some changes. Times have evolved so
unstably that I find myself looking for loyalty more than
ever."

Torin scoffed at the word loyalty.

"Made some changes?" Naya repeated. "To what?"

Gideon walked in a little further, closing the
distance between the three Blacksteel males. He folded
his arms around his chest and listened.

Viktir walked into the middle of the room, stopping
just before Emara's bed. "I have been doing a lot of

thinking, especially now that the magic community is in tatters, and I need to look at where my priorities lie."

"Get to your point," Torin spat out.

Viktir turned slowly, looking over his shoulder at him. A strange likeness drifted between them, reminding Torin of how cold both could be and how alike they could be.

Turning around, facing Emara again, Viktir placed his hands on the bed frame. Torin instantly wanted to remove them. "I have been thinking of your marital treaty to the clan."

Emara sat up on the bed, her face as white as a spirit. "What about it?" she asked, her voice a little less hoarse than before and a note higher than normal.

Torin stiffened.

He looked over to Emara, her eyes wide as she looked at the commander.

"I have made amendments to it."

Torin shifted. "You've amended what, exactly?"

A sinking began nudging his heart.

Viktir dismissed Torin, continuing to stare at Emara. Naya stiffened beside her.

"I have changed which son I present in offering my alliance to House Air."

"What could you possibly mean?" Naya gasped. Gideon stepped forward—well, it was more like a stumble.

Viktir dragged his eyes from his wife. "What I mean is that I no longer present my eldest son to your coven, Miss Clearwater." Viktir's tone changed in a way that rose the hairs on Torin's arms. "I am no longer wishing to present Torin for a marriage alliance in the name of the Blacksteel Clan and of House Air."

"What are you talking about?" Torin couldn't hide the brash tones of his voice.

Viktir placed one finger into the air. "I feel like I moved hastily with that decision, and now that times have changed and we are all in a vulnerable position, I believe that my second son is a better suitor for you. He is more reliable and disciplined." The control with which his father said those words was like how he used to control the whips of punishment. "And he should provide a steady alliance now, when your coven so desperately needs it."

"Your second son?" Emara's words flew off her tongue as she gripped the blanket.

"Father—" Gideon tried to interject.

"We don't need to be blindsided by instability," Viktir added. "Wouldn't you agree, Miss Clearwater?"

A vicious, burning roar took over in Torin's mind.

When Emara never answered him, Viktir raised a hand. "I can replace the name on the treaty between our clan and your coven in order to instate an agreement between you and Gideon."

"But you said before that couldn't happen." Emara gawked, wide-eyed. "You said—"

"What I said no longer matters when your head witch was a traitor and she is no longer here to interject with the terms of the treaty. It is in my hands."

Torin moved, and this time Naya flung herself between the commander and her eldest son before he could reach him. Torin's body was rigid as he found the words. "You can't do that!" The words ripped from his mouth.

Viktir turned and glowered at him. "I think you will find, *son,* that I can. You didn't sign the marriage contract when I asked you to therefore, it can be disregarded. No real ink was put to paper in your name, only the coven's."

"I will sign it now," Torin spluttered, finding his mouth didn't move as quickly as he wanted it to. The air in his lungs thinned.

Viktir put out a hand and pointed to Emara on the bed. "And I don't see a ring on her finger, the ring I gave to you to give to her as a sign of commitment. Do you see it?" He glanced over at his eldest son in a mocking glare that made Torin want to obliterate him where he stood. "Or is it still locked behind a door, just like your loyalty?"

Torin pushed forward, but Naya's hand shoved against his chest in warning. "Stop!"

"You gave that ring to me before the Uplift." Torin's arm flew out in rage. "Before the late Empress of Air was murdered, before I even knew Emara would ascend or needed to ascend," he barked.

"Yet moons have passed and I still see no ring on her finger, no real commitment to your cause. You have had long enough. I cannot trust you."

"I—" Torin stopped before he told everyone of his intentions the night of the winter solstice. "Give me more time," he pleaded. "Do not break the alliance between us. I don't need long."

The fact that he almost begged made him so unbelievably livid, and it seemed that his father liked it.

"You are too late, Torin." His father's piercing eyes drove a dagger through his heart just as much as his words did.

Torin knew that this was his punishment for not giving him every part of information he had on Emara or the stupid Resurrection Stone. It was his punishment for choosing himself over his commander, for choosing to protect Emara's secrets over his own.

He always knew it was coming.

Torin thought his father would have whipped him, possibly tasked him with some hard labour, maybe some training that pushed his every limit. But never in a million lifetimes did he believe that his *father* would be this cruel, this vindictive, this outrageously manipulative.

Torin's head dizzied, and his pulse hammered, slamming his heart into a frenzy.

"Don't do this," Torin begged his father through his teeth.

"Father," Gideon choked out again, lost for words. "I can't—"

Emara pushed off the blanket and stood. Torin looked at the floor in disbelief and then looked over to her. It hurt to even look at her as she looked from him to Gideon. Then her gaze set on Viktir, stony and fuelled with anger.

He begged shamefully as he turned to his father again and said, "Whip me, put me through anything mental or physical, anything. Just not this."

"Don't I get a say in this?" Emara's voice was short, but Torin could hear the emotion crawling along her throat. He couldn't look at her; if he did, he would crack and he would crumble.

Or he would wreck this entire fucking room.

"Viktir," his mother said, "this is not something that needs to be done. The treaty was—"

"I think you will find, woman, that it does need to be done. *Someone* must teach him a lesson." He threw Torin a look of sheer destruction. "He can't disobey simple commands and not suffer the consequences."

So it was about his punishment, not about what would benefit his clan.

"And what exactly do you think you are going to teach me by doing this?" The insatiable anger burned under Torin's skin. "To be as cold-hearted and unreasonable as you?"

Viktir spun, coming nose to nose with him, and it was too late for Naya to work her way between them. "What you are about to learn is that when you cross your commander, you will live miserably until he says otherwise. I own you," he ground out. "Until my dying breath, I own you, and then when you become the commander of this clan, I hope you will see what it is like to have a disrespectful, disobedient hunter under your lines."

Hunter. Not son. Not family. *Hunter.*

"You can't do this." Emara's voice cracked, and emotion flooded through, revealing how she truly felt. "I didn't sign the contract just as much as Torin didn't. If it is so easy to remove a signature, couldn't we draw up another one? One that I could have a say in?"

Even in recovery, she was courageous and valiant. She wasn't rejecting the alliance. She was trying to make it stronger.

Viktir looked her over. "I will find a way to force your hand, Emara Clearwater. I can be quite the diplomat when it comes to finding out where my opponent's weak spot is. I have spoken with the prime, and they are in favour of Gideon taking you in marriage. Given your *fiery* nature, they see it as a more *balanced* fit."

Emara began to shake, and anger spilled into Torin's heart, replacing the hurt, washing it down. "If you do this, I will never forgive you."

"I don't need your forgiveness, Torin." His father's eyes narrowed. "I am your commander; therefore, the only thing I need from you are your skills, your obedience, and your loyalty. If I don't have that, then you will quickly find yourself exiled."

"Exiled? Viktir—"

"Silence from you, witch," he shot at Naya. "It's your fault he has disobedience in his blood."

Naya flinched, her hands coming up to her heart, tears in her eyes.

Torin's teeth almost shattered under the pressure of his jaw. "If you continue to address my mother by anything other than her name, I will end your miserable excuse for a life right here." Torin stepped even further into his father, his commander. He would defend his mother even if it meant exile.

Fuck him, he would take the exile right now just to punch Viktir once.

"Do not get yourself hurt defending me, Torin." His mother placed a hand on his arm, and it was the only thing stopping him from smashing his fist into Viktir's face. "It is not worth the sore hand."

He begged to differ.

It was Gideon who spoke next. "Commander, can we please talk about this treaty and my involvement? It is not right for me—"

Viktir flew across the room and pinned Gideon to the wall. "Are you going to defy me too, like your insolent brother? Are you going to defy my command?"

The fear on Gideon's face snapped the last thread of tolerance Torin had. He dove through the space, grabbing his father by the neck and twisting him into a headlock.

He heard his mother and Emara shouting in the background, but the rage was too great to hear what they were saying as he punched his father in three, sharp uppercuts. Viktir tucked in and broke loose, swinging a punch that struck Torin's ribs. It crunched. His father's left hand came up and then connected with his cheek.

Fuck! Viktir could punch.

Torin blinked off the punch and swallowed the tang of blood in his mouth, regaining his balance. Moving his feet to the stance he always did, he swung, connecting his fist to Viktir's chin. Viktir flew into the fireplace, candles toppling, a vase that held water and flowers smashing. He gripped the ridge of the wood before catapulting himself back up.

Torin felt something pulling at him, unaware of who or what it was. He swung again and landed another punch to his father's jaw, and then he introduced a knee to his ribs.

There was enough time for Gideon to get between them, and then his mother had too.

"Torin, please." Emara's voice reached him over the buzzing of fury. "Please."

She pulled him back, and he let her as he wiped his bloodied lip.

"If you do this," he seethed towards his father, ignoring anyone holding him back, "it will be declaring a civil war amongst the Blacksteels. Me against you." He snarled. "And I don't fancy your odds in this war against me, *Father*."

A commander against his second...

Viktir straightened, wiping blood from the corner of his own mouth. "You don't decide the odds. I do." A cold smirk twisted in his lips. "My second son will marry the Empress of Air." He looked towards Emara, tears flooding her cheeks. "If you want an alliance in a time where your coven needs it most, you will marry Gideon and fulfil your duty as a woman." Viktir's cruel gaze finally landed on Torin again. "And that is my final command."

Torin straightened, taking a deep breath. He felt that icy fire in his blood return, numbing him of everything he had ever felt.

"Then it is war."

THANK YOU FOR READING BOOK 2!

As an indie author, reviews are crucial to our careers, and I would be forever grateful if you left a review on any platform you have. Social media is a powerful tool, and the reading community is so fierce. Let's make it count.

Remember to follow me on Instagram, Facebook & Tiktok @authornoellerayne for updates on my writing journey.

Sign up for my newsletter to get exclusive information on the books & much more at...

www.noellerayne.com

ACKNOWLEDGMENTS

An Empress of Fire & Steel, wow. What a ride. I can't believe I am still in this crazy journey and already planning books three, four and five.

Yes, you heard it. FIVE.

And I will be forever grateful to the community who absolutely loved An Empress of Air & Chaos and want to continue this journey with myself, Emara, the Blacksteels and everyone in-between.

Firstly, I would like to thank my Alpha Reader, who is my sister in oath, Chanley. Even though you are not a fantasy geek like me, you have never doubted me. You have loved every magical twist and turn, even when you were reading my first or second draft and it looked a little crazy. Love you, always.

I want to say a massive thank you to my beta-readers, Heidi (My cheerleader), Kaylee (My encourager) Charlie (My doodling angel), Alexa (My Scottish word checker & incredible smut critique) and Shell, (my heart of gold). I couldn't have done the edits without you. You made me laugh, you made me cry (in a good way of course) and you took time out of your own lives to help improve An Empress of Fire & Steel. Forever thankful to you guys. Much love!

To Melissa Hawkes—had I not found you—I probably wouldn't be writing my acknowledgements (again), still stuck in a formatting rage somewhere. Our paths were meant to cross, I am sure of it. You have helped me more than you know. Your friendship is so valued.

To my editor—RaeAnne—Please forgive me for my terrible grammar and punctuation. You are the best, and I am so glad to have found you. You make my work so much better. My editing life would suck without you.

TO HOUSE RAYNE—You are the most fantastic, funny, wonderfully supportive, and full of filth team of people I have ever met. You support me endlessly and I can not express in words how much you do for me. Never forget your power. You are my coven. The people I was meant to meet.

And to my soulmate—Scott—without my heart finding yours, I would have never been able to write about intensity, sacrifice or real love.

"So I told myself I wouldn't settle. I wouldn't settle for anything mediocre. I would settle for nothing short of breathtakingly powerful love that awakes your soul and stimulates your mind. I want a purposeful love" - *Emara*

And I didn't settle.

I found everything in you. Here's to more adventures and more love.

ABOUT THE AUTHOR

Noelle Rayne is the debut author of An Empress of Air and Chaos. An Empress of Fire & Steel is book two in her debut fantasy series. She has an Honours Degree in Drama and lives in Ayrshire, Scotland. When she is not writing, she is binge watching supernatural TV shows, cuddling her fur baby or curling up with a good fantasy book under fairy-lights. *Or possibly doing all three at once.* She is obsessed with storms, glitter and all things witchy. If you like any of these things, I have a feeling you might like her books...

AN EMPRESS
SERIES
BOOK 3
COMING 2023

9 781919 610931